# THE AMBASSADOR OF BOSSES

KEVIN KASHMIR

PUBLISHER'S NOTE

# IN LOVING MEMORY OF K.J.

# *Rest in Peace*

*To my Grandmothers who both passed away during the editing process of this novel - Rosie Lee Hagans and Gloria Dean Bailey-Smiles, Aunt Delores Singleton, Aunt Sharon Lewis, my Grandfathers - Louis Hagans and Norwood Williams, Aunt Dorothy Miles, Uncle Renard Jones, Uncle Earl Jones, My second mother Judy " Juju" Green, Delinda Henry, Uncle Terry "Chump" Bailey, cousin Earl Jones, Donnel " Uncle Duck" Bailey, Ida Mae and Big Joe Robinson, Gesilar "Gee" Joseph, Gloria Brown, Sabrina DeSilva, Margie Shorty, Trenice "PeeWee" Sam, Derrick Lucas Jr., Nancy Henry, Aunt Gloria Scott, Rene Scott, Lenny Garnett, Gabriel "Mikey" Angelety, Debra and Scottie Dorsey, Yolanda Moore, Jermott " Dadimont" Briggs, Soulja Slim, Mo3, Pop Smoke, George Floyd, Breonna Taylor, Alton Sterling, Michael Brown, Rayshar Brooks, Trayvon Martin and countless others who've lost their lives...*

*"Any harm you do to a man should be done in such a way that you need not fear his revenge."*

*–Niccolò Machiavelli (1469–1527)*

# THE AMBASSADOR OF BOSSES

# PROLOGUE

**South Beach, Florida**
**12:21 a.m., Sunday, June 23, 2013**

*"RUUUUNNNN!!!"* and screams were all that was heard as a flurry of gunfire erupted throughout the Million Dollar Spot nightclub. The shooters were five unmasked Columbian henchmen aiming for their intended target, the ingenious - Santana Bailey. But Santana, the owner of the club, was vigilant and prepared for gunplay at every interval. Without hesitation, he took cover and returned fire with assistance from his compadre, Levi Savage, and also from both of his personal assassins who were also brothers - Korey Metz who was known as Korey Witha K and Marlo Metz who everyone knew as Get'em.

Levi was the first to drop one of the Columbians by sending his lifeless body sliding pass his fellow goons with three gunshot wounds to his upper torso. The second kill shot came from Get'em by catching the enemy from the blindside and pumped a hot hollow tip into his temple causing brain fragments to splatter in the faces of two of the Colombians.

Then Korey Witha K took advantage of their obscured vision with his marksmen precision and flatlined the two simultaneously by shredding their midsection with the baby missiles from his trusty twin Mini Dracos. Santana had the ups on the lone hooligan but opted against taking him out to postpone his demise until after a torturous interrogation. So he shot the gun from out of the guy's grasp to strip him of his weaponry.

"Korey, you and Get'em show our intruder to the penalty box in the kitchen area and tie his ass up until I get there," Santana instructed. "Levi, go to my office to see if Xiomara's safe while I go out front to see where in the hell are my two cops that's supposed to be working detail preventing shit like this from happening," Santana stated in a heated tone.

Miami Beach police officers Randy Parker and Jose Estrada were stuffed into the trunk of their cruiser beating frantically. When Santana approached the car, it was confirmed there was no stopping the misfired hit that was designated for him. Without any keys in sight and the car doors locked Santana shattered the doors window and opened the glove compartment to pop the trunk.

He was grateful to find both of his officers unharmed, only handcuffed with their mouths taped shut. They were twice as thankful to see Santana's face when the trunk opened. From out of the club came Levi running with his smoking gun in hand along with Xiomara with her little pink and chrome derringer to assure Santana's safety.

When Xiomara realized the drama had passed, she dropped her gun then ran to Santana and gave him a hug. "Aye, papi, are you okay?" asked Xiomara. "Yeah, baby, I'm straight," Santana said as he kissed her. "Xiomara, I want you to go upstairs to the poker room and shut it down for the remainder of the night. Also, express my sincere apologies to our guests for the abrupt inconvenience and inform them that they will each receive a $25,000 allotment on their next visit - compliments of Santana Bailey."

"Okay, papi. Is there anything else?" "Oh, I almost forgot. Tell Lebron and D. Wade I said congrats on the repeat, and I'll call them later." "I'll take care of that for you, papi. I love you, Santana." "I love you too, Xiomara." As she headed back towards the club Santana yelled out, "*Xiomara*," "Yes, papi?" "Aren't you forgetting something?" Santana reached her the gun he had made specifically to her likings. Then continued, "Did you forget our golden rule?" "No, papi, I remember. Stay strapped at all times." "Now *that's* my girl."

Santana went to give aid to Levi by removing the handcuffs and duct tape from the officers. "Señor Santana, thank *God* you're alive. We heard all of the shooting and stampeding and I feared those renegades had taken you out," said officer Parker. "Please don't hold us accountable for this incident. As officer Parker and I separated to do our routine sweep of the perimeter we were ambushed and forced into the trunk," pleaded officer Estrada.

"I won't hold either of you in contempt for that close call but you both know firsthand that I have zero tolerance for slip ups. Just make sure to always keep in mind that my clientele is amongst the most elite celebrities, athletes, entertainers, and prominent figures in the world today. And their safety and privacy is my top priority.

So I'm beefing up security around this place as of this minute," Santana barked. "Sí Señor, I understand," officer Estrada muffled.

"Levi, how many casualties were in there?" asked Santana. "Only four of those guys who came here looking for a death wish. Besides that, there's six females who are still inside that suffered minor injuries like cuts on their legs from falling on broken glass or sprained ankles from trying to run in their stilettos."

"That's the greatest news I've heard all night, Levi. Since the incident is contained, I can keep it under wraps and out of the hands of the media. Those vultures would make a spectacle of the club at my expense." "That's a feasible perception, but it's gonna take one helluva gag order to keep this from leaking," said Levi. "I can downplay any rumors because the injured are still here and I'm sure I'll keep them all tight lipped with a little hush money. Speaking of which, notify the ladies that I want them to come back here tomorrow around noon so they can be compensated for any medical fees they might acquire and also for pain and suffering. Oh yeah and tell the cleanup crew to spruce up the place." "I'm on top of it, fam."

"Only four guys? But it was five of them that sacked us," said officer Parker. "Indeed, it was, Randy. The last desperado is awaiting my arrival as we speak," Santana responded. "Are you ready for us to call it in, Boss?" asked officer Estrada. "Since no one was gravely injured besides those Columbian motherfuckers, there's no need to involve the Miami Beach P.D. or any other unwanted law enforcement agencies so they can have their noses sniffing around."

"Whatever you say, Boss." "And guys, don't worry yourselves about protocol. I have a superb in-house staff, which I will personally supervise to make it seem as if this situation never occurred," Santana stated firmly.

"Do you need us to stick around?" asked officer Parker. "Yeah, Randy. Just long enough for my men to get rid of those bodies because if more cops showed up, you and Jose can run them off by letting them know that everything's copacetic."

"Who sent you, motherfucker?" Get'em demanded as he continued his vicious assault by pistol whipping the Columbian. "So he's playing the *Iron Chest Charlie* role, huh?" asked Santana as he walked in. "Yeah, that's how it appears for the moment," said Korey Witha K.

Santana kneeled to stare into the battered man's eyes then said, "I already have a good idea of who sent you. All I want from you is confirmation. So If you would rather a much quicker and painless death, then it would be in your best interest to start talking. But if you choose to maintain your little tough guy act, well, how can I put this in layman's terms? You'll go through so much pain that you'll wish your mother was never born."

The Columbian smirked then hog spit a mixture of blood and saliva in Santana's face. Santana didn't flinch. He just pulled out the handkerchief from his *Armani* suit to wipe his face, and said, "Well, my friend, that was definitely not a wise decision and extremely hazardous to your health. Nevertheless, you've made it clear that you're either immune to pain or feeling rather lucky tonight. Either way, it's time for you to cash out."

Santana pulled out his Desert Eagle then pointed at the Columbian's leg and let off a round. *"BWAOW!" "ARRGGHH!"* screamed the Columbian. In the midst of him wailing, Santana punched him so hard in his mouth that he knocked out three of the Columbian's front teeth. "Korey, get the van ready and pull it around the back to load up what's left of the four dead guys up front." "Done deal, big homie." "By the time you're through with them I'll be done with this piece of shit and then you can drop them all off at the mortuary to have those fuck boys cremated. And Get'em, give your brother a hand." "We got you, Santana," said Get'em.

"Levi, you ready to have a little fun with this asshole?" asked Santana. "You already know I'm *tweakin'* to make his ass go *pop*." "Okay then, do what you do," Santana said as he removed his suit coat and loosened his tie then went on, "First we'll start off with the razor cuts and alcohol treatment. Since there were five of them, Levi, give his ass five deep slashes wherever you wish and I'll pour the alcohol." *"ARRGGHH*!" the Columbian screamed as Levi went to work on him.

Santana ridiculed the Columbian by saying, "Those cuts look pretty severe. I'm no expert but I'd bet my bottom dollar that you could use a doctor right now. Let's see if this will alleviate you of some of your pain." Then Santana poured alcohol in the Columbian's open wounds and his body shook violently as he proceeded with loud cries.

Santana sighed at the sight of his heavy breathing then asked, "So, you're still not ready to lay all of your cards on the table, huh?" The Columbian had no response. "All right, tough guy. Suit yourself. Levi, since he still won't cooperate grab the needle-nose pliers and remove all of his fingernails. "Levi willingly obliged and peeled off every one of his fingernails despite his constant screams of protest. "All right, Levi, that's enough. It looks like you're trying to have all the fun. It's *my* turn *now*," Santana said with a sinister grin.

He then grabbed a butcher knife and hammer then cut and hacked until one of the Columbian's kneecaps gave way. "***ARRGGHH!***" cried the Columbian. "Aww, quit all of that bitchin'," said Santana, mockingly. "Oh, damn! I *know* you didn't just shit on yourself. We were just getting started," shouted Levi as he covered his nose to deflect the foul odor.

Santana walked over to one of the kitchen drawers to get his tiny jigsaw then said, "My patience has run its course with you, what*ever* your name is. And I've lost interest in attaining any info you have since my request seems to have fallen on deaf ears." Santana circled the Columbian then stopped behind his back to pat him on his shoulders and said, "I have some good news for you, my friend. This will all be over soon since you've lost a great deal of blood already. But the bad news is, this little toy right here is gonna carve you into a thousand pieces by the time I'm finished with you."

"Where do you wanna start, Santana?" asked Levi. "Since he don't want to point out the guilty party, hold that motherfucker's hand out so I can start with his fingers." '***VRRMMM***,' sounded the jigsaw, causing a freshly cut finger to hit the floor. "***ARRGGHH!***" Then Santana grabbed another finger. '***VRRMMM***'. "***ARRGGHH, FUCK!***" cried the Columbian. As Santana reached for the third finger, the Columbian caved in. "Okay, okay. Please stop, ***please***! I'll tell you anything you wanna know!"

"You see that? All of this was unnecessary if you would've just come clean from the beginning. Now tell me who's responsible for sending the hit." "It was Javier. Javier Ochoa who's the leader of the Nariño cartel." "Why is he trying to kill me?" "Señor Javier says that you are the one who's responsible for murdering his workers for 3,000 kilos in Columbia five years ago."

"And who told him this information?" "It was An..." Before he could reveal the source, his body went limp. He had spoken his last words.

"*FUCK!!!*" yelled Santana as he slammed his fist on the table. "He knows now," Santana said referring to Javier Ochoa. "I just wish I could've found out where the leak came from before that motherfucker croaked," said Santana as he pointed to the deceased. "So, what's the next move now that Javier exposed his hand?" Levi asked.

"I really have to think this one through since the guy's about to be my father-in-law. I know he'd never bring any harm to Xiomara. He's crazy about his only child. And she's a daddy's girl who loves her father to death. And it would eat me alive to see her grieving over him if I were to kill him. And she'd never forgive me if she'd ever found out that her father's blood was on my hands."

But he's never gonna stop coming after you so something's gotta shake, and I mean pronto," said Levi. "True enough. Since I know now that he was behind the hit, I can't send the guys we just killed to be cremated. They must be found for them to have a proper burial for good measure in case an agreement is ever reached."

"That's understandable. But I can't deny it, I really wanted to give all five of them the Columbian necktie. That's always been a dream of mine." Santana smirked at Levi's comment.

"I always told you how that shit was crazy how you met Xiomara. I mean, the odds of you meeting the daughter of the man we jacked must be a trillion-to-one," Levi teased as he sprinkled a little humor on the situation. "You're right about that Levi. I guess I might be the luckiest man on the planet, huh?' "Yeah, my nigga, you just might be. And if we come out from under this shit still standing, then you *are* the luckiest man alive."

Santana sat and paced around lost in his thoughts. He thought of Xiomara and how she wouldn't rest well until she knew that retaliation had been rendered on those who were held liable for seeking to steal the love of her life away. She was completely innocent of the ordeal and unaware of Santana's past. He was torn between love and war. Pandora's box was finally unsealed, and revenge's ugly face was none other than the same as the man that would've greeted him as son-in-law in the upcoming months. Santana would never implicate a woman in his street affairs but deep down he knew that Xiomara was the key to preventing further bloodshed between the only two men that has ever consumed her heart.

Santana didn't know when nor where it would happen, but he did know that the Nariño cartel wouldn't sleep until that one special day came when they'd find those accountable for robbing them in their own country of Columbia for 3,000 kilos of cocaine. He couldn't let another day pass without confessing the secret to his future wife that he vowed to take to his grave. And now was the time to confess his darkest secret to Xiomara Ochoa.

# CHAPTER 1



"I'LL BURY EVERY LAST one of them motherfuckers from the head honcho all the way down to his chihuahua!" Donavan Mercadel yelled angrily. "Yeah, my nigga, they got us fucked up if they think we're paying for this shit," Meatball responded.

"We've been copping hundreds of kilos for a minute from them niggas. And now they're trying to play the game raw?" barked Donavan. "They stepped on that coke so much to where one brick is cooking all the way down to a half," Meatball retorted.

"Santana, so there's nothing else that you can do with this shit, huh?" asked Donavan. "Yeah, Donavan, I can *still* get you thirty-six ounces out of each of the one hundred kilos if that's what you want. But you'll get more complaints than President Bush got from the way he handled Katrina," Santana warned.

"What do you suggest I do before I start warring with them niggas, Santana?" "Just call him and tell him the shit ain't right. He *is* your connect. You've been dealing with him for a few years and this is the first time something like this happened."

"That shit *sounds* good, Santana, but those Columbian motherfuckers won't be trying to hear that shit. The only four words they know in the English language is *FUCK YOU, PAY ME!*" Meatball said vehemently.

Santana responded by ignoring Meatball's sarcasm. "You'll never know unless you call him, Donavan. And he can't say that the package was straight." "You sound really sure of yourself, Santana," said Meatball. "Nigga, I vouch for *my* work, because ain't *no*body fucking with me when it comes to cooking cocaine…nobody."

Donavan elected to call Columbia to speak with the man himself, Señor Javier Ochoa - leader of the Nariño cartel. He was only scheduled to call once a month and Javier always knew exactly when that call would come through. And Donavan was aware that his unexpected contact would catch Javier off guard but he had a significant dilemma which needed to be addressed. Tonight.

"Good evening, Javier," said Donavan. "Donavan, my friend, I hadn't anticipated hearing from you for at least a few more weeks from now. Not to mention it's late," Javier spat.

"Yeah, Javier, I know but I have an urgent situation up here which places me in a compromising position." "And what might that be?" "Something isn't right with the batch you sent me."

"There must be some sort of mistake, my friend. I've always sent you my best to ensure your satisfaction and a lengthy relationship." Donavan was losing his composure by the nanosecond. "You *are* correct about one thing, Javier. There *is* a mistake if you think I'm paying for this bullshit you sent me."

"I'll only excuse your heated temper *this* time Donavan because I can understand your concerns. But the world has not yet ended, you see. This is a rather small matter, my friend, a mere grain of sand on a beach. And it is certainly not a contingency that is insurmountable."

"My apologies, Javier, but I have mucho dinero on the line and I'm losing it by the minute." "So, who is it that brought this matter to your attention?" "The legendary Santana. He's the best go-to guy on American soil that hooks up packages." "Oh really? You speak extremely high of him."

"He's very prolific, highly sought after all over the country, and I consider him to be the *Iron-Chef* of our time." "Is that so?" "Yeah, Javier, and I put that on *every*thang."

"Then I would really like to meet Señor Santana to witness his expertise. So, I'm sending my personal Gulfstream-Five jet to New Orleans tonight to pick up the both of you. And I'll see you and the legendary Santana upon your arrival."

# CHAPTER 2

Medellin, Columbia
8:31 a.m., February 3, 2008

"TOP OF THE MORNING to you, Donavan. I am honored for you to join me in such short notice," said Javier. "How could I have refused you when the stakes are so high?" asked Donavan. "Aah…and this young fellow must be the prestigious Santana. Welcome to Columbia," Javier said as he extended his hand.

"Thanks for inviting me to your beautiful country, Señor Ochoa," Santana responded as he accepted Javier's handshake. "The homage you've paid is welcoming, young Santana, but please…call me Javier. Donavan here speaks of you with high regards, claiming that you are amongst the best in your profession in your country."

"Is that the impression he gave you concerning me?" Santana asked as he glanced at Donavan. Then he continued, "I'm sorry, Javier, but you've been misinformed about me. I'm the *toughest* Don

Dada when it comes to my work…the best on the planet," Santana boasted.

"I must admit, Santana, when I appraised your demeanor, I concluded that you were very reserved. But now I see that you are highly assertive, much like myself." "It's good to know I have something in common with a man of your stature."

As the limousine driver pulled into the massive estate, Javier said, "Welcome to mí casa." Santana marveled at the sight of what lay before him. The land mass of Javier's property was twenty-five hundred acres with his house alone claiming twenty acres.

Santana now understood why the man in which he was in the presence of was known as the *Cocaine Commander-in-Chief of Columbia.* The place that Javier called home, was for the lack of a better word, a monstrous mega-mansion which seemed more fitting. Even the Buckingham Palace in England would have to give his place a nod.

The interior of the three-level edifice consisted of fifty bedrooms, sixty bathrooms, five dens, five living rooms, six kitchens, one game room, two movie theaters, one pool hall, one strip club, two indoor pools, two barrooms, one bowling alley, a state of the art aquarium which expanded thought all three levels, and of course - two elevators.

The outside of the estate seemed to be just as expensive as the inside. The area in which Javier called his driveway looked more like a foreign car dealership. There were four Bugatti's, six Lamborghini's, five Rolls Royce Phantoms - which two of them were convertibles, three Ferrari's, three four-door Bentley's, one two-door Bentley, two Aston Martin's, two Audi's, Five Cadillac Escalades, four Humvees, two Porsche's, one Maserati, twenty motorcycles, and almost twenty more miscellaneous cars and trucks. There was also a ten-car garage that shielded its components from public view. And lastly, a helicopter. Santana had expected to see an arsenal of expensive cars in Javier's possession. But two of the cars, which were Santana's favorite, was an El Camino with hydraulics and a 1996 Chevy SS Impala.

Then Javier showed Santana and Donavan his golf course. "That's an immaculate scenery you have there, Javier," said Santana. "Aah, yes. You know Tiger's a good friend of mine and he absolutely loves the place. He's the one who suggested I do something with all the space, so I let him personally design the golf course." "That's pretty high-powered, Javier." "Yes it is, Santana. It costed a pretty penny but all credit goes to him. He seldom comes here just to beat my ass," Javier chuckled.

"And over there, guys, is my water world." It was his outdoor pool. Javier's pool area made Hugh Heffner's pool at the *Playboy* Mansion look like something that was purchased in a box from Wal-Mart. There were more bikini-clad women out there than all of the beaches in Miami put together. Santana was blown away by all of the beautiful women he saw. And he imagined that if anyone were looking for *America's Next Top Model*, they could easily have chosen any of the women out there and gave them U.S. citizenship.

# CHAPTER 3

JAVIER INSTRUCTED SANTANA AND DONAVAN to accompany him for a ride on his golf cart. They drove to the furthermost point of the northeast end of the golf course. After abandoning the cart Javier led the way to a wooded area. They continued their trek for about fifty yards until arriving at a large warehouse. That building was the site of the Nariño cartel's headquarters.

There were twenty-five armed soldiers guarding the exterior. Inside, Javier had fifty topless women workers packaging his product on assembly lines. After Javier did a walk-through of his entire operation for Santana and Donavan, he ushered them into the sampling sector.

"We are here. This section of the building is where I do all of my testing. The shipment I sent to you, Donavan, is of the same batch that I have before you. And since *you*, Santana, claim that there is something wrong with my product, then I am eager for you to reveal that it is not one-hundred percent," Javier stated seriously.

With a wide variety of tools in the area, Santana elected his weapons for the job then snapped into *Iron-Chef* mode. Javier and Donavan moved aside as Santana went to work. This process was normal for Donavan because he had seen Santana in action hundreds of times. But Javier, on the other hand, was electrified as he observed Santana manifesting poetry in motion.

After the test run was completed, Javier applauded. "Astonishing, young Santana. Your techniques are the works of a masterpiece." Thanks for the compliment, Javier." "I am willing to offer you a hefty penny, if you would enlighten me with the procedure."

"Once again, I appreciate your kind gesture so I *will* tell you this much: I acquired my skills from the *School of Hard Knocks*. And I was taught that once I've discovered that uniqueness that abides in me, to keep it close to my heart and never part with it under any circumstances. So in other words, Javier, my skills are not for sale. And I believe that you know, yourself, that there are just some things that money can't buy."

"Yes, yes, Santana…you are very much correct. And for the second time today you've proven that we share the same traits."

As Santana surveyed the finished product, something aroused his intuition. Javier sensed it then asked, Santana, "so how *is* the quality of my product?"

"Javier, are you positive that this is the same product that you sent to Donavan?" "Yes, of course it is. Like I've told Donavan, I've always sent my best."

Javier had three of his soldiers in the room the entire time and Santana had noticed them whispering to each other. "Javier, I believe the two of us need to speak in private." Javier shot Santana a cold glare and Santana shot it right back at him.

"Everybody out of the room…Now!" Javier ordered. Javier looked at Donavan but Donavan wasn't budging. Santana said, "Donavan is cool, Javier. He also needs to hear what I have to say." "What is this about, Santana? What is wrong with my product?" asked Javier. "*Nothing* is wrong with it. *That's* the problem." "But I don't understand." "Okay, Javier, first I'm going to lay out all of the facts and then I'll tell you what I believe." "Go on."

"The cocaine I cooked here today is one-hundred percent pure. But the cocaine that you sent to Donavan was fifty percent cocaine mixed with fifty percent of cutting agents. With Donavan's batch, I did a test run on the mixed cocaine, and then, after the cutting agents dissolved, I tested what was left. And the finished product of what was left came out exactly how the finished product did here today.

"What I believe is something had to have happened with the package in the time frame of shipping and receiving." Javier was flabbergasted. "Are you insinuating that someone from my organization is stealing from me?" "Yes, Javier, that's *precisely* what I'm saying."

# CHAPTER 4

JAVIER REMAINED SILENT as he brainstormed. He knew Santana was being truthful. The last shipment he'd sent out was delayed much longer than normal before it reached Donavan. And in that window of opportunity is where he believed the treachery took place.

One of his lieutenants, Hector, delivered the package. And Javier had noticed how he'd been acting suspicious ever since his return from the U.S. two days prior. Like Santana, he *too* noticed the whispering that Hector was doing amongst the soldiers during Santana's test run.

It *had* to be Hector. Hector had been engaging in shady dealings in the states right underneath Javier's nose. If it weren't for Santana's mastership, he would have never known. He questioned himself, '*How long had Hector been skimming from him? Who else is involved?*' Javier had a serious internal problem within his organization in which he didn't know how far it extended. Javier Ochoa was about to revise his tactics and most definitely about to make an example out of Hector.

"I believe you, Santana," Javier professed. "Thank you for bringing this matter to my attention." "It was nothing, Javier. I was just doing my job." "If there is one thing, I despise more than anything else in this world, it's a snake." "I feel the same way. They have a saying in my country, that goes like this: *Keep your friends close, but keep your enemies closer.* But I see things like this: *if you keep your grass cut, the snakes will show and with the ability to see them coming for you, you can implement whatever transitions necessary to prevent them from getting close enough to ever have the chance to bite you.*"

"I'm an avid listener and that was exceptionally deep coming from you, Santana. I see that you are very intelligent for your age. I think I might write down that quote." Santana smiled.

"Your visit here has been very fruitful, Santana. And to show my gratitude, I would like for you to keep half of the package that I sent to Donavan. And Donavan, you keep the other half for your troubles and I will send out an emergency shipment for you expeditiously."

After leaving the sampling sector Javier led Santana and Donavan into his office. After taking a seat at his desk he reached for the receiver to give his secretary a buzz.

"Maria, page Domingo and have him come to my office please." "Okay, Señor Ochoa." A minute later Domingo entered.

"Domingo, I would like for you to meet the Americanos, Donavan and Santana. From this point forward, you will be in charge of shipping." "Sí, Señor Javier." "Donavan is the connection you will be making in the states so you'll no longer see Santana after today because Donavan is the one who I conduct business with." "Okay, Señor Javier. When do you need me to leave?"

"At sunset. But things are going to be done much differently now. I have recently discovered that Hector has been stealing. And the repercussions for such actions constitutes death. So, I am replacing Hector as well as the other transporters. Since I have yet to learn of who helped him deceive me - if there's anyone at alI - I will hold back the army I normally send to guard the shipment as it prepares to leave the transportation point. So, I will be sending you, the new driver, and only a handful of helpers to make the trip. I want you to go now to apprehend Hector then chop off his sticky hands and tie him to a tree. And I'll be out shortly to set his ass on fire." "Sí, Señor Javier."

After Domingo left the office Javier pressed a button underneath his desk. Then the wall behind him slid open. It was a secret corridor. "Come now, follow me," Javier stated. After walking through the dimly lit passageway for a few yards, they came to a room which was a colossal-sized workshop. There were eight men in there who'd been working around the clock building submarines. Santana and Donavan had just been introduced to Javier's transportation division of the Nariño cartel.

"Very few people have seen this room," said Javier then continued "and since you guys are my guests that's visiting from America, I am merely doing something that an individual from your city known as, *Baby*, once did so well. *Stuntin'* - I believe he calls it." Santana and Donavan laughed heartily.

Then Javier led them to an object that was covered with tarp. He removed the tarp to reveal a black submarine that was ready to go.

"This is the vessel that will meet you in Miami, Donavan. I paint all of my vessels black to elude the U.S. Coast Guards, so I only ship out at night. They are very expensive to make, but once the shipments arrive on U.S. soil the vessels are discarded."

"Why don't you ever bring them back to Columbia to reuse them since they're so costly?" asked Santana. "Because the risk of the Coast Guards ever seizing one coming back is not worth the risk of them getting hot on my trail. This is why I constantly build them." '*Damn, this nigga really on his shit*,' Santana thought.

"Donavan since you will be getting a fresh shipment delivered some time tonight, we will resume business as usual. So, your next shipment will be on this same day, one month from now. I thank you guys for coming down here today. I've already taken up much of your time, so I will prepare the jet to take you to Miami so that you can get back to your business. But if you would like to delay the flight and extend your stay for a few more hours, I am sure you will enjoy yourselves with the women by the pool area." In unison, Santana and Donavan chose the latter.

# CHAPTER 5

Miami, Florida
Miami International Airport
11:35 p.m., February 3, 2008

"IF I'VE EVER HAD even the slightest doubt about your talent or your heart, Santana, today that shit went clean out the window. Only a Boss nigga could've flown to Columbia to tell a cartel Boss that his own people is fucking him blind. That took a lot of balls," said Donavan.

"You already know how niggas be rockin' that's built with no cut: we do it like Soulja Slim and give it to 'em raw," Santana said. "It's a good thing you're thorough with your craft because we could've flown straight into a death trap since I went off of your word and told Javier that his coke was bullshit. You saw how they did poor Hector."

"I can't say that I blame Hector for trying to make a come up. He *was* the one who took all of the risk. Who knows, he probably was making pennies compared to what Javier was making but decided to go about making extra money the wrong way so Hector got what he deserved."

"I wanted to thank you for getting us both blessed with that free package. Nigga, your mouthpiece is *official*." "It's only natural to bless a nigga whose whip game's proper." "And I thought *I* was that nigga. I tilt my hat to you, Santana, because as much hustlin' as I had to do to get to the level I'm on, you be coming up on kilos without even paying for the shit. And thinking about it, after I pay you the ten percent that you charge for preparing my package, I'll owe you five kilos. Damn, I'm in the wrong business. I need that formula, Santana," Donavan said jokingly.

"That's how I eat, Donavan." "I can't complain because you always make sure my shit's done right. Besides, if I had a rookie doing the job that you do for me, I'd probably get into more shootouts than a motherfucker." They both laughed. "Speaking of those free kilos, Donavan, as soon as we both touch down back in New Orleans, I'll be swinging through to scoop up my half."

"I don't know how much longer we might have to wait for that damn submarine," said Donavan. "*We*? No nigga, *you* have to wait. Our business picks back up in New Orleans. None of that shit's for me anyway so I don't want any part of it."

"You're right, Santana. I was only wishfully thinking you'd hang around to keep me company until Domingo made it." "You remember Javier put five hundred kilos on that vessel. You're only getting one hundred of them so others must be waiting as well. So, it appears you *will* be having company after all."

"You're right about that. And on that note, I'm about to go check on my runner to make sure everything's on point." "Sounds like a plan. I'll tell you what I *am* about to do, Donavan. I'm about to maneuver through these streets in Miami to see what it's *really* hittin' for in this city. And if I feel like it would be a good look for me, I may decide to relocate out here one day."

"Be safe out there, Santana. And I'll link back up with you in New Orleans." "No doubt."

After shaking hands with Donavan, Santana walked away then turned around and yelled, "Aye, Donavan! Have you ever heard how that old saying goes?" "Which one are you referring to?" "The one that says '*Gangsters gain weight then move to Miami*'."

As Santana went on his excursion throughout Miami, he could see himself doing big things in that city. Miami had sold herself upon him and the move there would be inevitable.

He also reflected on how he'd encountered the opportunity of a lifetime. Javier Ochoa had unknowingly laid out a blueprint that Santana could use to outwit him. Javier had given up a bit too much information on how he'd run his drugs to the states now, after Hector's unauthorized dealings.

Santana didn't alert Donavan of his intentions because he was only a customer. But once Santana made it back to New Orleans, he'd have just the right people in place who could execute his scheme to the decimal. Javier Ochoa had a tiny crevice in his organization in which the cunning Santana Bailey spotted. And with an audacious effort he would soon contest the odds of robbing the Nariño cartel.

# CHAPTER 6

**New Orleans, Louisiana**
**9:27 p.m., February 4, 2008**

IN A DISCLOSED LOCATION, Santana had called a meeting with five of the most relentless men who had the heart of hearts and could perform in the theater of war and victoriously deliver a death blow. All in attendance were Levi Savage, Derrick Payne, Byron *Ham* Hamilton, *Korey Witha K* and Get'em.

Santana began, "Good evening, gentlemen. I specifically petitioned each of you here tonight because of your skills and cohesive personalities. There is a covert mission in which your assistance is needed. I will fully fund every entity of the assignment and it will only require a few days of your time.

"You each have a choice on how you wish to receive your payout. It will either be a half-million dollars each or you can choose to accept fifty kilos of cocaine. So, whichever option you'd prefer its fine with me.

"Now, before I go into any further details, I need to know who's in and who's out. So, all of those in favor, say *I*." Everyone's hands went up as they all screamed, "I!"

Korey Witha K threw up both of his hands. Santana laughed then said, "Nigga, is there *anything* you don't use both of your hands for?" The entire room broke out in laughter.

As Santana stared into the faces of his meek soldiers, he knew he'd chosen well. Levi was his closest friend. They'd graduated together from John McDonogh Sr. High School in New Orleans where they befriended one another after Santana was involved in a fight at school against three guys.

Santana had gotten the better of two of them until the third guy came into the picture. Then out of nowhere came Levi, jumping in to side with Santana by stabbing one of the guys then helped Santana finish off the other two, without even knowing Santana at the time. Since then they've been running mates and inseparable from drug dealing to shootouts.

Derrick and Byron were cousins who also were ex-U.S. Navy SEALs. They grew up with Santana in the lower ninth ward section of New Orleans. After graduation they went on to enlist as Navy SEALs. And even though both of the cousins were deadly, Byron earned the nickname Ham because that's precisely what he does - goes *Hard As a Motherfucker*.

And the last two were brothers, Korey Witha K and Get'em. They were Santana's young protégés, collectively having over twenty bodies under their belt. Korey Witha K got his alias from being whispered about in the streets on how he slaughtered his victims with AK-47's or any guns that uses those type of bullets.

And Santana gave the younger brother Get'em his nickname because all Santana ever had to do was point, and Get'em *got'em*.

Feeling gratified with his selection, Santana started pacing the floor as he began to explain. "All right, fellas, here's an overview of the logistics. Yesterday a rather delicate situation which needed to be addressed called for me to be flown in to Columbia. My skills were requested by one - Javier Ochoa."

"Javier Ochoa? You mean, Javier Ochoa - leader of the Nariño cartel?" asked Derrick. "Yeah, that's the guy," Santana responded. "Santana, is that *the* Javier Ochoa who's known as the *Cocaine Commander-in- Chief of Columbia*?" asked Levi.

"The one and the same. During my visit to Columbia I was privileged to see Javier Ochoa's home and most importantly, his entire operation. Javier transports his drugs into the United States by way of submarines. And I have a strategic plot in place that would intercept the submarine in Columbia."

"Wait a minute. You're talking about the six of us going into Columbia to pull off a heist from the fucking cartel? That sounds more like a *suicide* mission," Ham declared. "Man, fuck all'*at*. For fifty bricks I'm silencing any and everything moving," yelled Get'em.

"Hey, fellas…fellas, just listen for a sec. You all know me well enough to know that I'm a thinker. A *cave*man can do this shit. As of this moment a golden opportunity is ours for the taking because the Nariño cartel's conventional way of conducting business is in disarray. We won't have to shoot it out with an entire army, only be a handful since Javier's pulling back the soldiers who usually escort the submarine to it's drop off point. And the reason being is because of the newly discovered foul play within his inner circle.

"The advantage we'll have is, I know the exact location of the drop as well as the exact day the shipment will be sent out which means the element of surprise is on our side. So are there any more questions or concerns?"

"The only question I have, Santana, is when will this rendezvous go down so I can touch them fifty kilos? My damn palms is itching, big homie. Yeah, *DatWay*," said Korey Witha K.

"The freight ships out at nightfall March 3rd. We'll arrive in Columbia a day beforehand so we can set up and inspect the scenery. Levi, I'll need you to tag along with me to Miami towards the end of this month so we can scout for a secluded location along the oceanfront where we'll receive the submarine.

"Korey and Get'em, you guys will drive the transportation vehicle to Miami around the same time Levi and I will be out there. Ham and Derrick, you guys just stay put and gather all of the intelligence which may be useful to us such as compasses, maps of Columbia and Miami and whatever else you can think of. Since four of us will be in Miami when the day approaches, we'll charter a jet to Columbia. And Derrick and Ham can bypass Miami and fly there directly from New Orleans.

"And gentlemen, if any of you have any other concerns or helpful ideas from now until the time we leave the states, I'm open to suggestions. And just to be sure we all have a clear understanding, let me know how you wish to receive your compensation."

"Derrick and I will be content with the half million dollars since we're not into the drug business," said Ham.

"Korey Witha K already stated his claim. So what about you, Get'em?" "You already know how I coming. *Drop and give me fifty, big brudda*," Get'em said as he rubbed his hands together. "And last but not least, how you want it, Levi?" "My nigga, what's understood don't even need to be explained."

# CHAPTER 7

THE MEETING WAS ADJOURNED in a timely fashion. Shortly afterwards, Santana received a call from Donavan to inform him about his portion of the free package from Javier was available for pick up. Levi tagged along with Santana to make the run by Donavan then Santana extradited the product to his safe haven.

They then headed to the sports bar where Korey Witha K and Get'em were already awaiting their arrival to watch the Floyd Mayweather fight. As Santana and Levi invaded the building they were instantly in the limelight. The groupies in the bar were finally able to put faces to the two guys who'd created a ruckus before ever stepping a foot inside by shutting down the parking lot with Santana's Maybach-Benz with the translucent roof.

Santana had a flawless golden brown skin tone with light brown eyes. And ever since he cut off his dreadlocks two years prior he's maintained a low haircut to display his tapered fade which was complimented with deep waves. Although Santana was considered to be small in size, standing only 5 foot 9 inches and weighing roughly 160 pounds, the respect surrounding his name spoke in volumes.

For the occasion Santana dressed in his *dough boy* swagger. He wore *a pair of Masion Martin Margiela* sneakers, some *True Religion* jeans, *Gucci* belt, crisp white t-shirt, *New Era* New York Yankees fitted cap - even though he's not a fan of baseball - and his chrome .40 Cal on his waistline to make his outfit complete.

But his impeccable jewelry is what reflected radiance and demanded attention. He had five carat studs in each ear, a twenty carat diamond studded chain with the matching bracelet and a diamond encrusted rose gold Presidential Rolex. Levi wasn't too shabby himself with his ensemble consisting of a pair of Prada boots, *Red Monkey* jeans, *Prada* belt, white V-neck t-shirt and some Prada sunshades along with his *Richard Muller* wristband and jewelry selection.

The bar had an overflow of women so Santana and Levi had to bob and weave their way through the crowd to find Get'em and Korey Witha K. In the process, someone who was behind them reached out and tapped Santana's shoulder.

"Hey stranger. Looks like the only time I see or hear from you is when you're out chasing pussy," said Gabrielle. "What's up, Gabby? Now you see, baby girl, *that's* where you're wrong. I chase the money and all the pussy chases me."

"Whatever." "Oh, so you don't believe me?" I can prove to you that I know I'm right." "How?" "Just look at what's in my face right now," Santana said as he smiled while squeezing her ass.

"Boy, don't get yourself in trouble up in this place," said Gabrielle as she instantly became aroused by Santana's touch. "That was just to make you wet yourself and give you something to think about until we get to where we're going in after we leave here tonight." "And what makes you so sure I'm leaving with you?", Gabrielle asked sarcastically. "Because you and I both know that you can't get enough of this dick," he responded assuredly.

Santana and Gabrielle located his friends and joined them in the V.I.P. section. Levi hadn't taken any time at all before he'd been handcuffed by some female. Korey Witha K looked like he was being suffocated by the two Puerto Rican females that were all over him. And Get'em was hugged up with his newly found female friend.

That's just the way it was for the four of them. They were the hottest topic in the nail shops and beauty salons, and the women always flocked to them.

"What's poppin', big homie? I see Gabrielle finally caught up with you. She's been asking about you ever since we hit the door. You see, Gabrielle, I *told* you he would swing through," said Get'em. "Yeah, Get'em, you already know how she be stalking a nigga and shit," Santana joked. "Boy, don't nobody be stalking your ass," Gabrielle said as she elbowed Santana in his side.

Santana and his entourage wound up at the pool tables playing against the girls. And for some odd reason, all of the guys lost. The women were actually high fiving each other as if they were some type of pool sharks or something. All of the couples were enjoying themselves, having laughs with one another as the guys drank rounds of *Balboa* tequila and all of the ladies sipped on *Cîroc* with cranberry juice.

The fight had made it to the end of the twelfth round and Floyd Mayweather had beaten the Australian boxer by decision.

It was getting late and Santana's leisure time was approaching its cut off point. Tiffany - the woman who Levi met at the bar - had her convertible 2-door 650i BMW outside and she refused to let Santana take him home.

"All right now, Tiffany, you make sure to take care of my brother because you wouldn't like it if I had to come looking for you," Santana said in a serious but joking manner. "Don't you worry yourself about Levi, Santana. He's safe with me," she replied with confidence.

"Get'em, you and Michelle better not make an uncle out of me tonight," Santana teased. "Shiiit, I'mma try my *best* to make that happen, ya *heard* meh?!" said Get'em while he was planted on Michelle's ass, hugging her tightly from behind.

Since Korey Witha K did everything by the two's, the ménage-a-trios he'd be participating in in the near future was a part of his normal routine. "And Korey, I see you, lil homie. Try not to hurt yourself." "Santana, you know how it goes, baby. A double dose brings out the most in a nigga. Yeah, *Dat Way*," said Korey Witha K as he walked towards his car with a female under each arm.

# CHAPTER 8

THE GROUP DISPERSED from the Sports Bar by leaving in their vehicles in different directions. Gabrielle trailed Santana to his house in her Range Rover which was his gift to her for graduating from Xavier University to become a pharmacist.

While following, she played sexting games back and forth with Santana. At one point they were halted by a signal light which gave her a moment to take a quick snapshot of her precious jewels since she had easy access by pulling up her *Louis Vuitton* mini dress. She sent the picture to his cell along with a text that read:

*"Here's a lil sumthn 2 get u rocked up and look forward 2 shortly when I'm taking advantage of yo sexy azz! L.O.L. p.s. love Gabby ;-)"*

The message worked as she envisioned for Santana to instantly grow with anticipation inside his jeans. Then he sped to his residence to physically answer those enchanting texts he received.

Santana and Gabrielle had been on a roller coaster ride type of relationship for the past six years. They were the couple to envy up until Hurricane Katrina ripped through New Orleans. They evacuated to different cities until it was clear for residents to re-enter the city. Santana went to Houston but Gabrielle chose to be in Atlanta with her loved ones.

After they reunited, the connection they once shared somehow diminished. But he still took care of her by paying her tuition, taking her shopping, and sexing her from time to time. Nevertheless, he still loved her. But despite their dwindling flame she insisted on wanting a more solidified commitment from him and also for him to leave his lifestyle in the past. But Santana was in his prime on the street level. And the road to marriage was just too rugged of a terrain for him to travel down at that point in his life.

He knew he would only be adding insult to injury due to the lust which was still lurking in his blood. And being truthful just as he'd always been with her, he told her about all of his imperfections which would have been a recipe for disaster for any married couple. Although she was crushed by his denial, Gabrielle still loved him for always being honest. And he loved her enough to let her go in hopes of her finding the right man to give her what she deserved and wanted in a marriage. But that still didn't deter their sexual attraction to one another.

As they entered his home, which was located in a gated community, Gabrielle let her mini dress hit the marble floor as she darted upstairs to take a hot shower. There was no need to give her a tour of the house because she was the only woman whoever had the honor of crossing the doorsill. Besides, she knew her way around the house better than he did.

"Santana, are you coming to join me in the shower or what, baby?" yelled Gabrielle from upstairs. "Yeah, in a minute. I'm checking the answering machine."

Santana only had two messages and they both were from the same person. It was his older cousin, Kevin Kash, reminding him about the trip the two of them were scheduled to go on to Las Vegas for the Magic Show. He thought to himself, *'Damn, how in the hell did I forget about Vegas?'* Returning the call would have to wait until after addressing a more pressing matter…exclusive sex at the highest level.

Gabrielle was exiting the shower as Santana came waltzing through the bathroom door. "Hold your horses, girl. Didn't I tell your ass I was coming?" "Yeah, but you were taking too long."

Santana was mesmerized by the sight of her naked body as it glistened. And like a flash of lightening, he bolted out of his clothes. "So couldn't wait for me, huh?" "Boy, I was telling you to …"

Her words were cut short as Santana grabbed her and started kissing her with heated passion. Then picked her up in midair as she assisted in guiding all nine inches of his manhood into her warm honey pot. She clung onto Santana's neck for dear life then wrapped her legs around his waist as he cuffed her luscious thighs to thrust in and out of her in calculated motions.

Next, he squatted over while they were in the same position and palmed her exquisite backside with a firm grip as he continued his onslaught. Within minutes her love cream melted all over his chocolate tower forcing his release to come sooner than expected but since he wasn't quite ready to release his load, he pulled out of her to place her on her feet then dragged her back into the walk-in shower. After washing each other moderately Gabrielle dropped to her knees to whip a spell on his magic stick.

As Santana's body began to quiver she accepted his full load as he ignited in her mouth. Feeling vindicated, Santana took her by the hand then led her out of the shower. He paused to look at her tentatively. And as always her appearance was earthshaking.

Gabrielle stood 5 foot 6 inches with a body that was sculptured by the works of the hands from heaven - identical to Keyshia Ka'Oir's. Her facial features and skin hue resembled Zoe Kravitz with a set of lips similar to Angelina Jolie's. The way her eyes changed colors were so seductive they could make the sun shed tears. And to top it off, she had that mean strut like Meagan Good.

While laying in bed preparing for another round, all Santana could say was "Damn, baby, you *sure* know how to make a nigga feel like a king." "If you haven't realized by now that we were meant for each other, Santana, then I guess you never will," Gabrielle said sincerely.

# CHAPTER 9

AS THE HORIZON BEAMED through the bedroom windows, Santana parted his curtains to adore the handsome view. He glanced over at Gabrielle and smiled at the sight of her attributes of an angel as she lay asleep in his bed. She was a good woman. And he molded her to be everything he'd ever desire in someone he would one day call his queen.

He could see the silent tears dripping from her heart that were longing for him to say, '*I do.*' But yet, the life he led hindered him from pledging his all to her because he reckoned that either jail or death would somehow enter the equation. And he wouldn't want to force her to have to deal with either scenario on her own. To his credit, Santana truly loved her and he decided then that he wouldn't take her through this any longer and that he would make love to her for the last time.

Gabrielle awoke from her rest moaning sounds of pleasure. He poured on the charm as he indulged in her lap of luxury. "Oh, Santana...*ahhh*, baby, yes...don't stop...ooh...yes. Right there, Santana. That's my spot, daddy...ooh...*yes!*"

Santana shifted into a higher gear when he went from gently licking her pleasure button and marking impressions of passion on her near her inner thighs to sucking her lower set of lips by french kissing her love canal and nibbling on her pearly prize. Gabrielle was in a state of euphoria as she spread her legs eagle winged for the only man she ever loved. And Santana continued to woo her until she finally reached her zenith.

As 'One in a lifetime' - a song by *Monica* - serenaded the room through his *Beats* surround speakers, he carried on with his love session by giving her small wet kisses over her entire body. Then turned her over onto her stomach to run his hot tongue up her spine. He sucked her on the nape of her neck then spiraled downward to plant juicy wet kisses all over her apple bottoms.

Santana's foreplay was chart-topping. He went as far as lifting her assets to lick her goodies from behind. He had Gabrielle wetter than Mother Earth during a tropical storm. And after her resistance level shattered for the need to feel him inside her, she pleaded, "Make love to me, Santana. Please, baby, put it in me *now*."

He turned her back over to give her what she craved for. As he penetrated her warm zone, he rotated in circular motions, teasing her by only letting her feel the tip of his masterpiece. Her reaction caused her to breathe heavily and beg for more. "Oh, baby, it feels *sooooo* good. Put it all in me, daddy."

After Santana had felt she'd suffered long enough, he went all in. Flipping both of her legs over his shoulders, he pushed every centimeter of himself inside of her until reaching the very bottom of her jewelry box - a spot he imprinted himself. He continuously hit that spot for the duration of the song and halfway into the next.

Once Gabrielle figured he'd had enough fun she took control by pushing him onto his back then got on top of him backwards. When the music switched to a more up-tempo beat she started bucking like a raging bull by gyrating her hip muscles and watching Santana's toes curl at the same time.

"Ooh *shit*! Damn, you're working that fire ass pussy on me, mama!" Gabrielle loved it when he called her that. And once he unleashed that magical pet-name, it triggered her to start acting as wild as the *Magnolia Projects*..

While Gabrielle appeared to be winning in the field of action, Santana was rejuvenating himself and caught a surge of energy. He flipped their bodies over while still inside of her. Now he had her on all fours as he legally assaulted her in their favorite position- from the back. He began smacking her on the behind and the harder he did it, the harder she threw that ass back at him.

"Ooh… *fuck* this pussy, daddy! Ooh shit, this dick is so fucking *good*. Oh, Santana, this pussy's all for you, baby." Santana responded to her comments by pumping faster and faster until finally they reached their climax in a synchronized fashion.

Snuggled closely behind her in bed, he heard sniffles. He knew she was crying, but asked to be sure. "What's wrong with you, Gabby?"

"Santana… I can't do this anymore." "Can't do *what* anymore?" "*This…us…*Santana, you know my heart belongs to you and I want nothing more than becoming your wife. I really appreciate you telling me how you felt about that and I understand. But I've tried to get a friend to take you off my mind and the shit didn't work. Just the thought of another man touching me makes my skin crawl. I can't even imagine myself having sex with anyone other than you.

"And every time I see you, all of my feelings for you resurface and I can't handle it. So I'm leaving you with this, Santana… I thank you for all you've ever done for me and will always love you. But once I'm gone from here today, in order to protect my heart, I will be avoiding you at all cost for the rest of my life."

Santana responded, "I apologize for things unfolding this way between us. It was never my intentions on leading you to this point. I felt it in my heart that you were hurting inside. And that's why I made love to you this morning the way I did because I knew it would be our last time.

"And even though I truly love you, the things that I'm into in the streets would crush you a lot more if something were to happen to me while we were married than it would if we weren't.

"Only God knows what our future holds, Gabrielle. And regardless of the outcome just know that I'll always love you no matter what. And as I stand here today, I love you enough to the point where I'm prepared to let go of you."

After sharing his feelings, Santana kissed and embraced her then watched as Gabrielle Celestine walked out of his life forever.

# CHAPTER 10

ALTHOUGH HE WAS SADDENED by losing Gabrielle, he still knew that life goes on. He recalled the message that he'd retrieved from the answering machine. He knew that whenever Kevin Kash called, he'd have to set aside everything on his agenda. So, he called him back off of his cell as he turned a few corners.

"Whoa nah, big cuz. What the *bizness* is?" "It's exactly that - business as usual. You must've gotten my messages." "Yeah, I got'em. So, when are we leaving for Vegas?"

"First thing tomorrow morning. I have prior engagements I need to attend to while I'm in the city, so you have all night to handle anything there is you need to take care of." "Sounds like a winner to me. So, how long will we be out there?"

"Four days tops. I have a shitload of shopping to do for my chain of hip-hop clothing stores called *Mo' Sicka Fashions.* Plus we're gonna touch every casino on the strip if possible."

"I'm wit' it. But don't get mad if I tap-out at them tables because you know I only have baby money compared to *you.*" Kevin Kash laughed.

"You already know your money's no-good with me. I invited you to join me so I have everything covered. My private jet is already fueled up and ready to fly so the only thing *you* need to do, Santana, is make sure your little ass is at the *Million Air* private airport in New Orleans East by 7 o'clock in the morning. And don't be late."

"I'll be there, cuz."

Despite Kevin Kash being the older cousin, he was more like Santana's father figure who taught him everything he knew. And Santana soaked it all in because he knew Kevin Kash was a brilliant business tycoon with money just as long as Javier Ochoa.

When Santana was younger Kevin Kash would make it his business for Santana to roll with him almost everywhere he went. He kept Santana under his wing because he recognized that hunger in his eyes and saw a younger version of himself.

He kept the drug game concealed from Santana because he knew in those gruesome streets of New Orleans it was survival of the fittest and even the most feared gangsters have gotten their issue from some young gunner looking for stripes.

Santana never actually knew the trueness of Kevin Kash's previous reign as a drug Boss and dared not to ask. But rumor had it that Kevin Kash had moved more kilos of cocaine in America than Ricky Ross and Boston George combined. And he was smart because he'd gotten out of the loop of the drug business unscathed by opening nearly twenty different businesses all across the country and abroad.

Santana had never met a more solid figure as Kevin Kash. He felt grateful to have him as his mentor and proud to have the same blood running through his veins. And Santana's unmatched ambition that would be the driving force behind his vision, could one day surpass the many accomplishments of Kevin Kash.

Santana had a boatload of tasks on his itinerary with less than a day to muster all he could. He'd already had the fifty kilos from Javier along with the five kilos from doing the job for Donavan. After he'd finished cooking all of the trash off of the bad batch, he'd came out with thirty kilos of quality cocaine.

He decided to give his men who were in on the *Columbian Job* a little something in advance. He gave Levi, Korey Witha K and Get'em five kilos each. Santana flushed out the remainder of the product taking in $450,000. Then he gave Derrick and Ham $200,000 each, then he put a cashier's check for $50,000 in Gabrielle's bank account.

Donavan needed fifty more kilos prepared for retail that were a part of the emergency shipment he'd gotten from Javier which netted Santana another five kilos. Donavan never had a problem with Santana's flat-rate of ten percent because Santana would put ten percent worth of cut back into it and the finished product still came out good. So the way Donavan perceived it, he really wasn't paying him anything at all.

By the time Santana ran all of his errands it was three o'clock in the morning with only four more hours remaining until his departure to Vegas. So he got with Levi, who'd moved the five kilos he'd gotten earlier, and blessed his friend with a love deal by giving Levi the five kilos -he received as payment from the job he did for Donavan- for $75,000 so he'd have some play money on deck for the Vegas trip.

Since Santana had a few hours to spare so he cooked Levi's package and gave him an extra half-kilo of cut to boost his profit margin. And once Levi sold it all he'd be ninety-thousand more to the good. With only twenty minutes before takeoff Santana let Levi drop him off at the airport and floss in his Porsche jeep until he returned.

# CHAPTER 11



INSIDE THE LAS VEGAS CONVENTION CENTER, the Magic Show consisted of hundreds of vendors who were selling their latest fashions of clothing. Kevin Kash had three separate booths set up displaying his clothing lines: *Torrey Tirrell, SoccaBallin,* and *Vittorio Kashmir.*

There were tens of thousands of clothing store owners from all across America and abroad shopping in there spending tons of money on the latest fashions for the upcoming season. And since Kevin Kash had his chain of *Mo' Sicka Fashions* stores in shopping malls across America, he also was spending money with other vendors as well.

Santana followed as Kevin Kash checked with his employees from all three booths to see how the sales were progressing and they all were raking in the dough. He told Santana that he'd projected to make at least ten million dollars by the closing of the four-day event.

Santana thought, '*I see why he went legit, because if he could make that type of money in just a few days, then why would he put himself in a predicament where he'd have to face legal problems? My big cuz is certified with his game because this event is only a small fraction of all of the other things he had his hands into.*'

They continued on navigating through the convention center meeting celebrities throughout the entire building. To Santana's surprise, they all treated Kevin Kash with the upmost respect.

"Damn, big cuz, it looks like you're a superstar in your own right." "I'm no superstar, Santana. I'm just an individual with a lot of money and people with money mingle with other people with money because we speak the same language. It's the way of the world, son. It wasn't easy amassing my fortune, but the wise decisions I made years ago is what got me to this level. Not to mention that those same smiling faces have been seeing me at least twice a year since I've been coming to the Magic Show and have always spent big money with them to support their product like I did today."

While traveling from vendor to vendor, Santana bought a few items for Levi, Korey Witha K, and Get'em. But the bulk of his spendings were on himself, and of course, Gabrielle. Noticing Santana's selection of his purchases Kevin Kash said, "I see you're buying all of those female clothes. You must be hooking up my girl, Gabrielle, huh?" "Yeah, cuz, but it's a habit that I have to break." "Break it for what? There's nothing wrong with showering the baby with gifts."

Kevin Kash wasn't aware of what had transpired between the two, only twenty some odd hours prior. Santana knew Kevin Kash would come down hard on him for the reason he let her go, but since he'd brought Gabrielle's name up, Santana had to come clean.

"She left me for good." "She left you? Why? What the hell happened?" Santana gave him a brief rundown of their last encounter. "Damn, Santana, I really liked you being with her. She's a good girl. A diamond in the rough. Maybe you're *not* ready to commit and nothing's wrong with that because you're still young. But I will tell you this and don't you ever forget it; you truly only get one love in a lifetime. And for you to accept being without her, then she can't be the one. So keep searching because that special one's still out there. But for *your* sake, I hope it isn't Gabrielle and she slips away."

Santana was experiencing dèjá vu as Kevin Kash said those exact words Monica sang as he made love to Gabrielle for the last time. He understood what his mentor was telling him, but he firmly believed that if you love something, let it go. And if it finds its way back to you then it was destined to be. If not, then there must be another who's considered to be that one like Monica was referring to. Even after receiving a few words of wisdom he decided to stick to his guns and leave the situation with Gabrielle as is. But that didn't stop him from buying her an entire wardrobe. Every time he shopped for himself, it was his natural instinct to do the same for her.

He'd made up his mind that that day would be his last time buying something for her. He'd mail the items he purchased in Vegas for her to her house so they wouldn't have to cross paths. And he'd continue putting money in her account and love her from a distance.

The first day of the Magic Show had come to an end on a good note. Kevin Kash was accurate with his projected earnings by taking in over two and half million dollars in orders. Afterwards they headed for the strip.

On their way to the casinos, Santana had witnessed hundreds of people passing out fliers with pictures and phone numbers of women looking for dates - legal prostitution without using the word soliciting would be a more precise way of describing the fliers. Kevin Kash said, "They've been passing out those type of fliers forever and a day."

Within seven hours' time, they'd been to three casinos. At the first two casinos, Kevin Kash had lost a pretty penny while Santana won. After they'd settled in at the third casino, the money that Kevin Kash had lost at the other two were only donations because he'd knocked fire from the *MGM Grand Casino* and so did Santana- with his hot streak. And as they were leaving for Kevin Kash's condo for the night, he said, "Aye, Santana, it looks like you never lose." "Actually, cuz…I don't."

The next day was the same as the first with an added incentive of more customers. They didn't stay at the Magic Show until closing because they wanted to go to *Circus Circus* for a bite to eat at their renowned buffet. Also, they wanted to hit up a few more casinos early so they could get freshened up for a party they were invited to by Jay-Z.

There were dozens of star-studded parties to choose from, but Jay-Z had some important business to discuss with Kevin Kash, so he invited him and Santana to his 40/40 Club. It would be the perfect time for the meeting because both men had hectic schedules which would prohibit them from having a sit down anytime in the near future.

Santana and Kevin Kash had another triumphant day at the tables and decided to pull the plug while they were ahead. Afterwards, they went to a shopping mall that was on the strip, then headed to the condo to shower and change their attire to have a blast for the night in Sin City.

While they were in the club, Santana enjoyed the atmosphere but his mind was preoccupied. His thoughts were keyed-in on the *Columbian Job*. Rubbing elbows with the stars was uncharted territories for him, so he lounged in the V.I.P. section and scanned the club as near-by Kevin Kash conversed with Jay-Z. They chopped it up for about a half an hour then Jay-Z moved on.

With his fatherly intuition, Kevin Kash knew Santana all too well to know when something was weighing heavily on his mind so he initiated a conversation with him.

"You good, Santana? You seem to have your head in the clouds." "Yeah, cuz, I'm Gucci." Kevin Kash knew that whatever it was that had Santana's attention, he wasn't about to share it with him.

"You *know* that you can talk to me about anything, right?" said Kevin Kash. "Yeah, cuz, I know that. It's really no big deal. I'm just sorting out some things in my head to make sure I'm always on point."

"That's the right attitude, Santana. You have any idea as to why I wanted you to come to Vegas with me?" "Yeah, to hit the casinos, shop and have a good time."

"That's part of it but the main reason is because I wanted you to see a small part of the business world and how you can still make millions *legally*."

Without Santana ever breathing a word about his illegal activities to him, Kevin Kash still knew what Santana was into in New Orleans because he'd kept his ears to the streets. He never wanted Santana to take that path so he advocated to him all the time about business.

"There are many opportunities that await you, Santana. There's been countless times where I've offered you a part of my empire but you refused because you want to get it on your own. That's why I love you so much because you remind me so much of myself. Now, here's some food for thought that should never part from you; out of all of the hustles in the entire world, there's really only two that exist- legal and illegal. And *true* hustlers can do either. Now, let *that* marinate."

All Santana could do was smile because Kevin Kash always gave him some sound advice. Santana loved him furthermore because in so many words he was telling Santana that he knew exactly what it was he was doing to make money, which meant that even though Kevin Kash went completely legit, keeping his ears to the streets was still embedded in his DNA.

On the third day of the Magic Show Santana floated around to pick up on a few more items to add to his collection. Meanwhile, since Kevin Kash had purchased enough merchandise for *Mo' Sicka Fashions*, he'd spent his idle time in each of his booths crunching numbers. Hours had passed before completing the task and he was more than satisfied with the prosperity of the event.

"Well, Santana, I can breathe easy now since my terrific staff has everything under control. Since I have other affairs that can be addressed a day in advance we can blow Vegas today." "I'm cool with that, cuz, because I for damn sure don't want those casinos to get their hands in my pockets after I hit'em for three-hundred grand."

# CHAPTER 12

WHILE SANTANA WAS STACKING CHIPS in Vegas, Korey Witha K and Get'em were busy boosting up their body count. Ever since the night they were at the Sports Bar, Get'em had been tied down with Michelle with every minute of his spare time while Korey Witha K had been enjoying his threesomes.

The brothers were known to breakdown a kilo of cocaine and sell all dime pieces, so they both had a fair share of product left that they'd gotten from Santana. Then a new customer had come along to make a big buy.

Jessica and Andrea - the Puerto Rican females who Korey Witha K met at the Sports Bar - were scheming from the very beginning. The night after Korey Witha K met them, Jessica requested Get'em's cell number to call and invite him to join the party because she wanted a taste of both of the brothers at the same time.

At the hotel room that night, Jessica overheard a conversation the brothers were having which confirmed they were moving weight. She then plotted to put two shysters on the lick to make an easy come-up. But Andrea didn't participate. Instead, she looked on as the brothers had their way with Jessica. And once they were done, Get'em found his way back to Michelle.

The next morning Jessica said that her cousin was looking to score three kilos and asked Korey Witha K if he knew of anyone who could fill the order. Korey Witha K figured they were some scandalous bitches which is why the conversation he had with Get'em occurred in front of them.

It was all done for the sake of bait-play and the hoes bit on it. And he was the right person to give them what the hell they were looking for.

So, Korey Witha K told Jessica to set up the buy for later that night then he left the hotel. As soon as he jumped in his car, he notified Get'em for his assistance when the transaction took place.

Almost two hours before the deal was scheduled to occur, Korey Witha K went back to the hotel to pick up Jessica and Andrea in his 745 BMW to grab some daiquiris. While they were gone Get'em got into the room using the key that he'd gotten from his brother then hid Korey Witha K's twin Micro Dracos under the pillow. Get'em knew that hiding in the bathroom was ancient, so he'd wait patiently until he saw them coming then hide under the bed.

While Korey Witha K was at the daiquiri shop ordering their drinks, he noticed Andrea walk outside alone to make a phone call. It didn't bother him one bit because he got a rush off of murder. And he knew if Jessica and Andrea were attempting to pull off a shady act, they wouldn't leave out of that hotel room alive.

Once he got the drinks he raced back to the room because he thought, *'it'll be a shame if these bad bitches gotta get knocked off tonight. I might as well get one last piece of action before all that good pussy goes to waste.'*

After arriving back at the hotel Korey Witha K had Jessica call her cousin meet them at the room in an hour. The time frame was only a little cushion for him to have his final fuck-fest with the Puerto Rican duo.

When they were finished with their *sexapade* Korey Witha K ordered them in the shower with him to cover his tracks by washing away any dna of his off their bodies. Just minutes after they finished there was a knock at the door.

Jessica's cousin, Zairo, accompanied by his unknown Puerto Rican accomplice, entered the room. Zairo walked over to give Jessica a hug and said, "Hey, Jessy-boo, it's kind of steamy in here. Did someone just get out the shower?" "Don't I smell like I just did? And quit call me Jessy-boo, you know how much I hate it when you call me that." "Okay, little cousin, you got that."

"It's not a problem if I use the bathroom, is it?" the unknown man asked Korey Witha K. "Is it a number one or a number two?" "Just a number one. I've been holding it for like twenty minutes." "All right, go handle your business and don't be long." "I won't. Just a few seconds is all I need."

"Is everything cool, player? Feeling like there's a little hostility in the air," said Zairo. "For *now*, everything is. I mean, with all due disrespect, what y'all came here for? to use the fucking bathroom and a family reunion or y'all came for business?"

"We came for business. No harm intended." Then Zairo tossed Korey Witha K the bag of money as his accomplice exited the bathroom.

Korey Witha K knew instantly that it was nowhere near the correct amount because he'd been counting money with Santana for a while, but still went along with their little game. He counted the money at the table in front of them to force their backs to be against the bed area where Get'em lay in hiding.

When he got to the last stack of money he said, "I don't know what type of games you playing, Zairo, but you don't have enough right here to cover the whole ticket, homeboy." "I'm afraid your calculations are wrong, *homeboy*. You see that gun in my friend's hand over there makes us have *exactly* what we need."

Korey Witha K looked over at Jessica and Andrea as they sat on the bed then asked, "So this is what our little fiesta was all about? I thought y'all bitches was really feelin' a nigga." Andrea had an apologetic look on her face and didn't respond, while Jessica started laughing and said, "You called me a bitch, huh, Korey? Well, that's a very nasty word. But don't take it personal because this is what I do, baby. And it's such a pity that you'll be dead in a little while because we won't be able to have fun anymore."

As all of the Puerto Ricans were laughing with the exception of Andrea, Get'em slid from under the bed undetected. With everyone's focus on Korey Witha K, Get'em eased up with his 45 equipped with a silencer then let off four muffled rounds into the unknown man with the gun pointed at his brother.

At the same time Korey Witha K tackled Zairo as he was reaching for his piece and knocked it to the floor. As Zairo scrambled for the loose gun Get'em shot him twice in the back causing him to collapse. Then Korey Witha K went for his guns underneath the pillows to point them at the screaming women.

"Bitches, shut the fuck up! A few minutes ago y'all hoes were laughing and shit. Now y'all wanna hit high notes in this bitch?" yelled Korey Witha K. "I never laughed at you, Korey," said Andrea.

Then Jessica began with her pleas, "Oh *please* don't kill us, Korey. I'm so sorry baby but my cousin, Zairo, forced me to do this."

"He did, huh?" Korey Witha K looked at Zairo as he squirmed on the floor and said, "You hear that, Zairo? Your own cousin says that you coerced them into setting me up. If that's the case Jessica, if you want to live, then you have to finish him off."

Korey Witha K handed Jessica one of his guns as he and Get'em had their weapons pointed at her. Jessica said, "Zairo, I'm so sorry I have to do this, but it's the only way I can save myself." She cried as she continued, "It looks like you're about to die anyway…Jessy-boo loves you, Zairo." Jessica closed her eyes as she shot Zairo seven times then dropped the gun.

"Damn, Jessica, you act a fool with that tool, huh, girl?" asked Get'em. Then Korey Witha K looked at Andrea whom he'd liked the most out of the two.

"Andrea, are you related to Jessica and Zairo?' "No, Korey, but I've known them for years." "All right then, I'm about to give you an ultimatum. If you wanna walk out here alive you gotta kill Jessica. But if you don't, you die."

As Korey Witha K passed Andrea the gun, Jessica began pleading for her life. At that point, Andrea knew they'd kill her anyway and had accepted her fate even though she wasn't in on the set-up.

She looked at Jessica with discontentment and said, "Jessica, there is nothing in this world that would ever make me kill my own blood…even if it meant I had to save myself." Andrea spit at Jessica's feet then continued, "But since I think of you as family, by no means will I take your life."

Andrea dropped the gun then looked at Korey Witha K and Get'em and said, "I am a peace with God and myself, so I am prepared to die." Korey Witha K said, "Damn, lil mama, you got heart. I guess it's true when they say, if want something done you gotta do it yourself." He then aimed both of his guns at Jessica, sending her on to the next life in a blaze of glory.

Korey Witha K was impressed with the way Andrea was taking her lick and the loyalty she had for family. He said, "for some strange reason, I'm *really* gonna hate doing this to you, Andrea, cause you're a real soldier."

While Korey Witha K was talking to Andrea, Get'em was checking a voicemail on his cell phone that he'd gotten earlier. When Get'em finished listening to the message, he said, "Big brother. Maybe you don't have to kill her after all." Korey Witha K looked confused. "Why not? After she just tried to get me hit?"

"It's because the message I just checked was Andrea calling me to tell me that you were being set up and for me to get to the hotel room as quick as possible. She even said she left a key under the door mat for me to get in."

Korey Witha K went outside to see if a key was indeed under the mat like she claimed. He found it then used it to see if the door would open and it did. He then walked back into the room and said, "Andrea, I don't know if you have a sixth sense to know that I was onto y'all or if you really were trying to save a nigga. You know I could've killed you before I did Jessica. Why didn't you say something?"

"Because I would've sounded like a lying ass scared little bitch and I'm not going out like that." "So, what made you wanna come to my rescue?" "Because I really like you, Korey, *duh*. When I first laid eyes on you at the Sports Bar I knew I wanted you. I hated having to share you with her but Jessica's freaky ass insisted we have a threesome. And since that was my girl, I went with it. I've never done anything like that before. That's why I never ate her pussy or let her touch me period because I don't rock like that."

"So when exactly did you call Get'em to leave him the message?" "When you brought us to the daiquiri shop." Korey Witha K recalled her going outside to make a call.

"How did you get his number?" "When you left us in the room earlier I stole it from out of Jessica's phone when she was in the shower once I knew what she was planning."

"And how did *she* get the number?" "She saved it when she got it from *you* when she wanted to call him and invite him to our private party. Jessica's the one who wanted Get'em from the beginning, but she sweated you even harder because she knew y'all were brothers. And Get'em was with that other girl, so she knew eventually she'd get her chance with him. And when she finally got him to come, I just sat there while y'all flipped the bitch. I'm not saying that you're not cute, Get'em, but I only had eyes for your brother."

Korey Witha K thought about the entire situation. He always went with his gut and it told him that she was being truthful. "All right, Andrea, where do we go from here?" "Hopefully to your house and put this all behind us so we can really get to know each other. I am single, you know."

Korey Witha K was at a loss for words so he asked, "What do you think, Get'em?" "I think my new sister-in-law's as real as they come."

With Get'em's approval, Korey Witha K determined she was worthy of a chance of proving herself.

"This is some bizarre shit, Andrea. I just hope I don't live to regret believing in you." "You won't, Korey. I promise you on everything I love. And for the record, Jessica better be the last bitch to ever come into a bed of ours." With that being said, they wiped down the room, grabbed all of the drugs and money, then doused the dead bodies with gasoline and set the room ablaze.

# CHAPTER 13

IN ANOTHER PART OF THE CITY, Levi had his own beef cooking. Since the first night he'd met Tiffany at the Sports Bar she'd been bombarding him with request to spend time with her.

He was flattered to have her in his company, but he lived by the motto: *Money Over Everything*. And since his running mate, Santana, hadn't made it back from Vegas, he chose to push his work aside for a night out with Tiffany.

They dined at the five star restaurant, *Dickie Brennan's Bourbon House* in the French Quarters. Hot beignets was next on the menu as they strolled through Jackson Square until they reached *Café du Monde*. Afterwards, they cruised down the Riverwalk holding hands as they watched the stars and moonlight reflect off of the Mississippi River. Since their night was headed in a good direction they concluded upon extending their outing by hitting *Harrah's Hotel and Casino*.

At the casino the couple had the tables sizzling. Tiffany was rolling the dice since she had the hot hands while Levi placed all of the bets. With her beginner's luck she hit seventeen straight points before crapping out, pulling in over seventy grand for Levi which wasn't bad for only thirty-five minutes of work.

In spite of her lucky streak ending, onlookers and people who'd bet in her favor were clapping and cheering for the good job she'd done. Most of the happy campers even tipped her with a few chips. During the cheers, there was a whisper in Tiffany's ear, "I knew I was picking a winner when I first met you," said Meatball. Tiffany was startled to turn and see him but held her temper since she had a man like Levi close by that would run him lost.

Tiffany had met Meatball a month prior while she was out shopping at the *Saks Fifth Ave* store inside of Canal Place. They exchanged numbers and days later went out on a date which was documented as the worst she'd ever had in history. Meatball's conversation was limited to three things: The amount of money he had; how much he could spend on her; and the criminal enterprise in which he was involved in. But Tiffany was no charity case and certainly not impressed with his big money talk. She was an established physician with an exceptional upbringing from a mother who was a heart surgeon and a father who was a U.S. District Court judge.

When she saw how the date was going, she prepared herself to initiate a bailout plan. She texted her girlfriend, Stacy, to let her know what time to call her cell phone so she could pretend there was an emergency at the hospital. That did just the trick and the next day, Tiffany changed her cell number and never contacted Meatball again.

Before Tiffany could respond to Meatball's unwelcomed intrusion, Levi stepped in, "What's up, Meatball? She related to you or something?" Levi asked through clinched teeth.

Levi was well aware of everyone in the casino knowing he and Tiffany were together because all eyes were on them from the moment they entered the building. And regardless of how much money Meatball had or the fact that he was Donavan's main man, Levi wouldn't give anyone a pass who tried to show disrespect towards him.

"Naw, Levi, we ain't related. But I *know* you not trying to check me behind an old friend." Meatball's comment had gotten under Tiffany's skin in the worst way. "Old *friend?* We went on *one* boring ass date and that was it. That doesn't even qualify for us to call each other *acquaintances.*"

Levi never sparred over women but since Meatball had violated him, he was ready to take it to whatever level Meatball wanted to take it to. Levi stepped in once more, "Damn, Meatball, you didn't catch that? Nigga, I *am* checkin' you since you think you can step on my toes when you already know she's with me."

"Levi, you better slow ya roll, pimpin'. You must've forgot who you're talking to like that, homie." "Naw, playboy, I know exactly who I'm talking to…a nigga that bleeds just like me." With the two now locked in a faceoff that told it all as to what was on the other's mind, Meatball retracted and informed him, "Watch yourself in them streets, Levi. It's dangerous out there." "Likewise." Having nothing further to say, Meatball departed.

"He got some nerve. That's got to be the lamest guy I've ever met. I can't believe you actually know that piece of work," said Tiffany.

"Yeah, I know him, but I never got any positive vibes from that cat and we're not about to spoil our good time by talking about him anymore, okay?" "All right, baby, I'm just happy he's gone."

"I *will* say just one last thing about him, though. All he really did was make me wanna knock some sparks from that pussy even more than I was planning to." Tiffany smiled and said, "Well, if that's how you're feeling, Levi, I can't wait to see the fireworks."

They both laughed as she and Levi cashed in his winnings then he said, "Tiff, if it weren't for you we wouldn't be walking out of here seventy thousand to the good." Then Levi handed her thirty-five grand as they headed out of the casino.

# CHAPTER 14

**New Orleans, Louisiana**
**9:27p.m., February 8, 2008**

WITH THE DESERT IN HIS REARVIEW Santana was home sweet home. Kevin Kash offered him a ride only to enjoy a few more moments with him. As he looked at Santana he had a flashback of the absolute worst incident recorded in his entire life which occurred two decades in retrospect.

At the age of four Santana's father, Rashad, and Kevin Kash's four year old son, K.J., were both murdered on a day the four of them were riding together as they did every weekend. Kevin Kash was driving while Rashad rode shotgun. Santana and K.J. were in their car seats positioned in opposite places behind their fathers so they both could have a good view of their dads.

After they'd purchased some crawfish from the seafood store they headed to the lakefront to play football and fly kites. Then all of a sudden, someone pulled up in another car along the passenger side of them and began shooting recklessly. It resulted In Rashad and K.J. being hit.

Kevin Kash swiftly sped off disregarding red lights and anything else in his path to get his wounded son and closest cousin to the hospital. K.J.'s gunshot wound didn't look so bad and he wasn't losing much blood but Rashad, on the other hand, was in pretty bad shape. He was coughing up blood all over the place.

And as he slipped in and out of a conscious state, he was able to relay the priceless information of who the shooter was to Kevin Kash. The sniper was the same person who Rashad had shot and left for dead in a botched robbery attempt months earlier.

During the ride to the hospital, Rashad caught his second wind and was able to harvest enough strength to fetch his son from his car seat to hold him tightly.

He turned to his cousin and said, "Take care of my son." Kevin Kash cried as he responded, "Don't talk like that, fam. You're gonna make it." "I'm not gonna pull through, cuz. Just look at me... I'm all fucked up. Promise me you'll look after Santana." "God forbid but if anything happens to you, I promise, you have my word that I'll raise him and love him as if he was my own."

Rashad felt liberated to know his son would be in good hands, so he kissed Santana, told him how much he loved him, how much he would miss him, and that Kevin Kash would always take care of him.

And just as Kevin Kash pulled in front of the emergency room an opened Rashad's door, he died holding Santana in his arms.

The paramedics came out and rushed K.J. to surgery along with Rashad. seeking to revive him. Amazingly, they brought forth a heartbeat. Kevin Kash and Santana were covered in blood as they clung to each other while their loved ones were in I.C.U. fighting for their lives.

Unfortunately, all of Kevin Kash's hopes of recovery were shattered as the head surgeons from both units came out concurrently with the look of defeat on their faces to pronounce Rashad Bailey and Kevin Kash Jr. deceased.

Kevin Kash twinged as he let out a thunderous roar then grabbed Santana and left out of Charity Hospital. Over the next twenty-four hours Kevin Kash had waged a one-man war on the entire city of New Orleans by turning it into a danger zone. No one was safe. The gung ho assailant had hell to pay and not even diplomatic immunity could save him. The floodgates were opened and death came rushing through. Kevin Kash killed the shooter's younger brother, his baby's mother, two of his cousins, one of his uncles, then held his mother at gunpoint until he was forced to come out of hiding. And when he did, Kevin Kash never missed him. He hit the shooter up with every bullet he had in the clip of his AR-15. Kevin Kash had spared the guy's mother and even gave her the money she'd needed to bury her younger son.

After his moment of redemption, Kevin Kash vowed to fulfill his word he'd given to his dying cousin and raise Santana as his own. He then looked at life from a different perspective and turned his back towards the lifestyle that he and Rashad once lived that ultimately caused him to have such a huge void in his own life.

Kevin Kash didn't like to sound as if he preached to Santana but he always dropped jewels on him because he knew Santana had the potential to exceed his success. Santana always knew he meant well but never expected to hear what Kevin Kash was about to tell him.

"What do you think of me, Santana?" "I think you're the best. I couldn't have been blessed to have a better father figure since I was robbed out of mine. You've always given me good advice on every aspect of life. Not to mention you've always had the *baddest* bitches and money. If I had to sum it all up for you, I'd say you're that *real* Boss nigga who always kept me motivated."

"Well, let me share something with you that you may not be aware of. *You* are my motivation, Santana. Sure, I've always had money because I've reached for the stars since I was a kid but a vow I made long ago is the reason I feel the way I do about you." "What vow, cuz? What are you talking about?"

"The night I lost my son and you lost your father, I held you in my arms and I knew we'd need each other. I believe that if I didn't have you in my life, I would've lost my sanity. But you gave me strength to press forward every time I've seen you from that moment till this day. And I vowed to change the pattern of my life after they died and to honor your father's dying wish." "*Dying wish*? What dying wish?" Santana asked as he fought back tears.

"To always take care of you and teach you all there is to know about becoming a man." Santana was taken aback. "So, after all these years you've been there for me, a major part of that was to honor your word to my father?"

"Yeah, Santana, after all these years. I found it to be rather easy, actually. They've had those times when you rebelled but what kid doesn't? Besides, I'm no saint either and I've always loved you from the moment you took your first breath." "And I've always loved you."

"If you haven't noticed yet, every conversation I've ever had with you somehow finds its way to the subject of business." "Yes, I have. And somehow, I knew it was coming. So, what's today's lesson?"

"Shit or get off the pot, which happens to be my favorite subject because I love *shittin'* on these niggas." Santana laughed as Kevin Kash boasted.

"But first, since I've opened up to you during this heart to heart like never before, I'm gonna put you up on something about my yesteryears."

Santana knew those rumors on the streets were likely to be true. He was overexcited to know he was finally about to hear confirmation from Kevin Kash, himself.

"I began my pursuit to riches as one of the biggest drug Bosses this side of the equator. I was blinded by the fast money without an exit strategy in sight. But when I lost my son and your father, the shells in my eyes like Paul in the bible fell from my face. Then the picture of my life became vivid. I was too deep in the game to just quit cold turkey, so I weaned my way out. It took some time, but I did it and never looked back.

"So in other words, Santana, there are millions of ways to succeed and I've experienced being the best in both worlds—the underworld and the so-called white man's world. I've learned that if I kept all of my dealings legit then I wouldn't have to live a life of having to look over my shoulders for those lurking in the shadows to steal me or my spot, nor do I have to worry about the long arms of the law. And my reward is living freely to enjoy the money I make."

Santana was stunned at how Kevin Kash was coming straight from the shoulders with his confessions. He knew Santana's occupation and the majority of the Bosses he dealt with, even in different states. His endeared time with Santana was almost over as he arrived at Santana's estate and wanted to give him one last piece of wisdom.

"It would just kill me, Santana, if I were to sit around and let you throw your life away. I've lost the closest two people to my heart already and I couldn't bear to lose you the same way. So take heed to all of the advice I've ever given you."

"I will, cuz, and you have my word on that." "What's with all these guys named Santana always talking about, '*give me your word, or you have my word*'?" They both laughed.

"But on a more serious note, I'm sure you know by now, Santana, that there's not much you do that I am not aware of." "I kinda figured that from the way you're talking to me today," Santana said as he silently admitted to his wrongdoings.

"Although you may not know it yet, Santana, you are in a class all by yourself." "What's class is that?"

"You are the *Ambassador of Bosses*. And the reason why is because an average person seeks things from the Boss, but the Boss seeks things from you. In return, that makes *you* just as important as *they* are."

Santana was blown away by the label he was given and cordially responded, "I never knew you thought of me in *that* way. I mean, you were always *my* inspiration." "And you were always mine.

What we do for each other is basically a formality of iron sharpening iron."

As Santana watched his mentor's Ferrari pull away, he thought of how blessed he was to have him in his corner. He reminisced about everything he'd learned from Kevin Kash and knew that if he ever wanted to elevate to a farther peak of accomplishments than him, he'd have to leave the drug game in the wind. Furthermore, he knew the game wasn't designed to last a lifetime. So one day he would have to separate himself from the lifestyle that dubbed him as the *Ambassador of Bosses*.

He thought about Jay-Z's *40/40* club in Vegas and how it might be a worthy investment to open an even nicer club in a different city. Miami, even. His mind was finally transforming into business mode and he'd owe every bit of success he'd acquire to the one and only person who constantly drilled it in his head: Kevin Kash.

# CHAPTER 15

OUT OF ALL THE SIT-DOWNS Santana's ever had with Kevin Kash, the last was by far the best. He suddenly realized that his father had been advising him all along. When Santana and the man who avenged his father's death, were victimized by the horrific tragedy that occurred, at that exact moment they gained from one another what they'd both just lost.

Finally, those powerful pointers that Kevin Kash had given him stuck to his ribs and were deserving enough for Santana to take a stab at it. But his departure from the *Pyrex* jar and kitchen stove would have to be put on the back burner until after his date with Javier Ochoa.

Santana had about one hundred and forty kilos stashed away that he'd accumulated over time from fees he'd charged when he prepared cocaine for his customers. He knew the men in his small circle were loyal to him so he decided to payoff everyone involved in the mission to have them out of the way. With forty-five kilos each going to Levi, Korey Witha K, and Get'em, he'd still have five kilos remaining.

Since he was still in the rear with Derrick and Ham for three-hundred grand each, he'd knock off a nice chunk of the payout by giving them one-hundred fifty thousand each from his winnings in Vegas. That meant that all he had left to kick out was another three-hundred thousand plus overhead, and the entire submarine would be his free and clear.

The flight to Miami was two weeks away and Santana had a backlog of Bosses that needed their packages prepared. It was more than enough time he'd need to square up with Derrick and Ham. Although he believed the mission would have a good outcome, Santana still understood that shit happens. So by him clearing his balance with everyone in advance, they'd have a jump start on whatever they had planned with their earnings since there were no guarantees that any of them would make it out of Columbia.

Santana checked his answering machine once he got inside to find a message he'd gotten from Derrick. He returned the call to discover Derrick was over at Ham's house. It was perfect timing for Santana since he'd be able to kill two birds with one stone by dropping off the money and addressing any issues they may have had.

With Santana's Porsche jeep still in Levi's possession, he chose other means transportation from his four-car garage. He felt like feeling the night air so he pulled out his 1300 Hayabusa motorcycle since he hadn't ridden it in a while and three-hundred thousand dollars could fit inside the seat hassle free.

At Ham's house the three of them had to go to his garage for the meeting. The space had recently been converted into a mancave which consisted of a bar/pool room. It was the only place in the house where Ham could have any privacy since he was married with five children. When Santana saw all of those kids running around, he thought, '*I most definitely have to give Ham a bonus with all of these kids.*' He understood why Ham chose the money over the drugs because he was a true family man.

"I like what you did to the room," said Santana. "I just completed it today thanks to *you* with that advance you gave me." "Which bring me to the reason I'm here tonight." Santana tossed them each one-hundred and fifty-thousand dollar stacks of money.

After Santana broke the balls on the pool table, Derrick said, "At our last meeting you mentioned if we have any helpful ideas to let you now. Well, Ham and I've been thinking and we both came to the conclusion that it would be an added incentive for you to bring in one more guy." "You got somebody in mind?" "Actually, we do." "So, who is he?" "His name is Tri Phan but we call him Chinky." "How can he be helpful to us?" "Chinky's an explosives expert."

"Oh really?" "Yeah." "Where do you know him from?" "He got out of the SEALs around the same time as us." "Is he good at what he does?" "Chinky's the best I've ever seen. I've seen him in action on numerous missions he went on with us. In fact, we even went on one in Columbia together. He has lots of resources there also."

Santana was impressed and liked the idea of adding Chinky to the roster so he asked, "You guys trust him?" "With my life. He's saved my ass a time or two," said Ham. "Has he been briefed him about the mission yet?" "No way. You know when you drafted us for the job that we were solid. So don't even go there, Santana," said Derrick.

Santana shared a laugh with his childhood friends. "All right, all right. I was just checking." "But he *has* heard of you before, Santana," said Ham. "He *has*? From who?" "From us through conversations about our childhood days. You'd be surprised by all of the things we talked about in the jungles when it was just us, the enemy, and big ass motherfucking killer mosquitos." They were all dying laughing.

"Okay, fellas, I trust your judgment. But I want to meet this Chinky guy so I can get a feel for him." "No problem," said Ham. "And I'll be the one who brings up the *Columbian Job* if I choose to bring him in," said Santana. "Sounds like a winner," Derrick concurred.

"Another thing about him, Santana, is that I believe he'd be content with only half of what you're giving us," said Ham. "Is that right?" asked Santana. Derrick respond, "Yeah, man, Chinky's nothing but a kid trapped inside an assassin's body who loves to blow up shit."

# CHAPTER 16

AFTER PARTING WAYS with Derrick and Ham, Santana hit the I-10 zooming towards Levi's home. Upon his arrival, he noticed a convertible BMW parked next to his Porsche jeep which suggested that Levi was not alone. As he walked inside, he saw that the car belonged to a familiar face…Tiffany.

"Good to see you, fam. I see you made it back from Vegas in one piece," Levi said as he embraced Santana. "Yes I did, and I see you've been put under restraints since we left the Sports Bar." Levi looked over at Tiffany and responded, "Yeah, something like that." They both started laughing. "I don't find anything funny. Don't have him thinking I've been holding you hostage, Levi," said Tiffany as she stood with one hand on her hip.

"We were only kidding around, Tiffany. No hard feelings," said Santana. "Oh, you remembered my name, huh?" "How could I forget? I told you at the Sports Bar not to let anything happen to my dude or It was going to be trouble in paradise." "Well, you can take me off your hit list now that you see him standing here in good health." "You got that. And you've done a great job looking after him." "Thank you."

"We'll be back, Tiff. Me and my man's going out back to the patio and chop it up for a minute," Levi said as he kissed her and tapped her on the behind.

While they were on the patio feeling the night breeze Levi fired up a cigarillo of Granddaddy Purp. "So, how's things been since I've been gone?" asked Santana. "Like clockwork. I still have a brick left from the last package I got from you." "That's good because tonight I'm paying you, Korey, and Get'em everything I'll owe y'all for the job since I already have it. I just need to get to my stash."

"I'm with that. I've been thinking about doing something big with *that* much paper. In the meantime, until I figure out what that something is, I'll just keep stacking money to the ceiling." "You can't go wrong with that philosophy. And it's funny you mentioned that because I've been thinking about making some type of money moves, myself."

"Oh yeah?" "Yeah, homie. I'm thinking on a level of an exclusive nightclub and a few other things." "That's wuzzam. Which part of the city are you thinking about putting it?" "Nowhere in the city… I'm talking M.I.A." "Miami? You're thinking about moving to Miami?"

"Yeah, Levi. It's been on my mind a lot lately. Ain't nothing here holding me back. I'm single, don't have any kids, my mom's been living in Cali, forever. Plus, I got my money right. And once we get back from Columbia my cheddar is gonna be stretched out like Durant's wingspan, Shaq's feet, and Chris Bosh's neck combined….the long way." They both were cracking up.

"But on the serious side, I'm moving to another level, my nigga. And it's time for a change. A change of scenery. A change to meet a different breed of bitches. Just a change of lifestyle in general. I've been living in New Orleans for my entire life. The world is a big place that's full of opportunities and I want to see what else it has to offer besides the streets of New Orleans."

"So you're leaving the game behind for good, also?" "Yeah, but not just yet. Once I push the last pack I get from the Columbia job, I'm out. Finito." "Damn, Santana, you just dropped some heavy ass shit on me, my nigga. I knew when you went on that trip to Vegas that you were coming back here on some other shit."

"You know me all too well, Levi." "My nigga, we've been running as thick as thieves for as far back as I can remember. And this entire game changer with you has two words written all over it: *Kevin Kash*. That nigga *stays* on some multimillionaire shit." They both laughed.

"We laughing and shit, Santana, but I'm serious about *that* nigga. I use to read a lot of urban novels and most of those stories sound like scripts taken right out of Kevin Kash's life and how he be on that big money shit. The only thing it seems like the authors did was change the character's names and put a nice twist to the stories."

"I agree, Levi. He *is* book-worthy and probably could have a fire ass movie made about his life. He always lacing me with that business talk. But this time around he was hittin' me with some hard shit and it finally registered."

"He *is* the right person to put you on that level." "There's no doubting that. But at this very moment, *you're* the right person to put me on that level." "What makes you think that?" "Because you have the power to pass me that motherfuckin' blunt you been handcuffin' for the last three minutes." They both laughed and choked involuntarily.

On their way to the stash, Santana said, "I just thought about something, Levi. After we snatch that shipment, the city's gonna have a drought. And if we fall back for about a week the whole city's gonna feel it. Then we could *really* put the squeeze game on 'em." "I feel that, my nigga. Tax season!"

"There's only a handful of Bosses who be copping a hundred kilos like Donavan and I fucks with all of them. So, I know just about how much work they holding and they all should be running low around the time we hit that lick. Donavan won't see a gram of that package. And Javier's gonna be skeptical about sending out any type of emergency shipments once he takes the blow we're gonna deliver."

"Speaking of Donavan, Santana, I forgot to lace you up about the run-in I had with Meatball at the casino." "What went down?"

Levi gave him a run-down of what had occurred.

"*Damn*, Tiffany shitted on that nigga, huh?" Like a *dawg*." "That's good for his ass. I know he was heated when you told him he bleeds just like you." "*Was* he?! That nigga had smoke coming from his nose *and* ears." They laughed tears from their eyes.

"I've never liked that dude anyway. He always had negative energy. I only dealt with him on the strength of Donavan." "I told Tiff the same thing about me not liking him." "So wassup, you ready to bring drama to that nigga's doorstep?" Santana asked in a serious tone.

"I *gotsta* hit him up. Even though we only passed a few words he should've never told me to watch myself. I already know he's a grimy nigga." "Yeah, you got'em right."

"You already know how I rock, Santana. I would've crept down on him the same night. But I wanted to clear it up with you first since you have dealings with Donavan." "Shiiit, that nigga could get it *too* if he wants to be head-first behind that ole duck ass nigga, Meatball. But as I'm thinking about it, we gotta be smart about this one, Levi. We really can't make a move on Meatball yet because he probably told Donavan what happened.

"If he did, Donavan's gonna holler at me and I'll play it like everything's cool just to buy us some time because if we flip Meatball's ass now, we might have to do the same thing to Donavan if he comes out there guns blazing behind his right hand man. And if Donavan 's dead, Javier won't be sending a package at all if there's no one to send it to."

"I see where you're coming from, Santana." "This shit might've just turned into two jobs because once we rape Javier for his shipment, we might as well knock off Donavan and Meatball as well and hit'em for all *they* got." "I'm with that."

"And to be honest, I'd probably be doing Donavan a favor by killing him." "Why you say that?" "Because if Javier suspects Donavan had anything to do with that act we're gonna pull off, his ass is curtains. I'd kill him quick and easy. But Javier, on the other hand, I saw the way he did one of his own men and let me tell ya, it was *not* a pretty sight. That nigga, Javier, is *ruthless*. So before I sign off on Donavan's head I want to see what his take is on the situation. And that's out of respect for Donavan never coming at me sideways.

"Although I don't trust Meatball, Donavan possibly can influence the nigga be easy and let the bullshit go. But if he says Meatball wants war then we'll put his ass in something tight. Who knows? Donavan may even say the nigga's too reckless and wash his hands with him. And if he does, then Meatball will be our only quarrel." "Well, that's cool. We can wait it out since Donavan's a cool nigga. So whichever way it turns out, I'm all for it."

Once Santana had given Levi his package and gifts from Vegas, he said, "After I drop you off, I'm going hit Korey Witha K and Get'em with their package and put them on alert about the Meatball dilemma." "The two live wires. I sure am happy those lil niggas is on *our* team." "Yeah, Levi, I am too."

# CHAPTER 17

GET'EM DROVE HIS CORVETTE up to his brother's residence just moments before Santana arrived. He spotted Santana's Porsche Jeep approaching and waited for him so they could walk inside together. "Hey, Get'em, come here and grab two of these duffle bags out of the jeep while I get the other two." "What's good wit'chu, big brudda? Vegas must've treated you swell if you came here bearing gifts."

"Yeah, I picked up on a few outfits for you and your brother while I was out there. You keep those two bags, Get'em. And, Korey, these are for you." "Good lookin' out, fam," said Korey Witha K.

"It was nothing. You know I always look out for my team." "True dat." "The clothes I bought for y'all haven't even hit the stores yet and won't until next season." Korey Witha K and Get'em were scampering through their bags like excited kids opening presents on Christmas day.

"As you can see, I've also brought y'all the remaining balance for the job." "I thought you were gonna pop us off after we hit the lick. I wasn't in a rush to get paid, my nigga," said Korey Witha K.

"I know that already. I just wanted to pay off everybody earlier since I already got it on tuck so y'all could start stacking now." "*Ooh woo*! We about to be SoccaBallin like a motherfucker, ya *heard* meh?!" Get'em said as he smiled so hard he revealed all thirty-two of his gold teeth.

As the three were entering Korey Witha K's arcade room Santana heard a noise coming from the bathroom. "Korey, I didn't know you had company." "Naw, my nigga, that ain't company. It looks like I've found the Bonnie to my Clyde."

"Not you, huh? So, who's the lucky lady?" "You remember Andrea from the Sports Bar the other night?" "The Puerto Rican broad?" "Yeah, that's her." "It looks like those ménage-a-trois finally got hooked and reeled in."

"Actually, I killed the pussy." "I would've killed the pussy too, if I had two bad broads runnin' around the crib in thongs all day." "Naw, Santana, I *really* killed the pussy." Santana looked deeper into Korey Witha K's eyes and knew that murderous glare from anywhere. "So, what went down?" asked Santana. Then Korey Witha K gave him an account of the events that transpired from beginning to end.

"Damn. I saw that shit on the news when I got back in town. I said to myself, '*they have some crazy* ass loose cannons *runnin' around here in New Orleans.*'" "Yeah, big homie. You know we had to flex on 'em ," said Get'em. "That's why I fucks with y'all as tough as I do because y'all never slippin' out there in them streets even when pussy's involved."

"Only weak niggas get blinded by them hoes. Fuckin' with them scandalous ass project bitches finally paid off because I read the whole play out the gate," said Korey Witha K. "It sounds like you've finally met your match with Andrea."

"Big dawg, you know how we be running through them hoes so you *know* I wasn't looking for a companion. But I can't deny it, even though it's only been a few days since we've known each other, she's the realest broad I've ever met. And everything's been all gravy between us and I really don't plan on letting her ass go nowhere."

"It sorta sounds like love at first sight." "Maybe I'm trippin', or it just might be." "*Might* be? *Shiiit*, nigga, the way y'all love birds been running around here, it would take nothing short of an act of Congress to make Andrea give you permission to let her go," said Get'em.

"Let *who* go?" Andrea barked as she walked in. "Nobody, baby, we were just talking," said Korey Witha K. "I didn't know you were having company, Korey. I could've cooked something." "You were in the shower when they popped up."

"Are you guy's hungry? I could whip up something real quick if y'all planning on being here for a minute,"Andrea offered.

"Why not. I wouldn't mind tasting some Puerto Rican food for a change," said Santana. "Yeah, sis, I'm kinda hungry anyway," said Get'em as he rubbed his stomach.

While Andrea was off to the kitchen, Santana filled in Korey Witha K and Get'em about the arising predicament concerning Meatball. "I can't wait until we get back from Columbia so we could smoke their whole click!" Get'em howled.

"It's like I said…Donavan *may* just toss his ass to the wolves." "You might be right, Santana. Once Meatball is out of the equation, Donavan would have less heat on him plus he'd stand to make a lot more money," said Korey Witha K as he offered his opinion. "That's a good point," Santana responded.

"That's nigga lucky he didn't get smashed *in* the casino because Levi don't play no games,"said Get'em. "You see that right there, Get'em, is a perfect example of why our team is so strong. We think before we react. And as long as we stay that way, we're gonna be out here for a minute, lil whoady."

AFTER THE BRIEF MEETING WITH THE METZ BROTHERS, Santana went home. He had a hard time dosing off because of the undisturbed scent that lingered on his silk *Polo* sheets from Gabrielle. He thought of how he'd soon relocate to Miami and make his exit from the world of crime. He tossed and turned with excitement because he knew that the lifestyle, he was about to embark upon was exactly what it would take to have a good life and win Gabrielle's hand in marriage.

But his high hopes were quickly blotted out for the sake of three reasons: He didn't want to seem selfish by uprooting her from the normalcy she had in her life surrounding her career; he refused to separate her from her family who were close knit; and he knew the thrill Miami would bring to the table and needed assurance that lust was completely out of his system.

As he arose from his sleep, it was business as usual. The Bosses from surrounding cities who needed their packages prepared were in a frenzy since he'd left for Vegas.

In total, Santana had one-hundred and twenty kilos awaiting his special touch. And to patronize all of his clientele he decided to do all of their packages, even if it required two days of almost nonstop work.

After completing the tiresome task he added twelve more kilos to his collection and was now seventeen kilos strong. He stretched the cocaine out to twenty kilos in order to cover the remainder of the payout for Derrick and Ham.

The next day Santana dedicated his entire itinerary to turning his payload into cold hard cash. He had a league of loyal retailers who'd be more than willing to purchase anything he had on the market. By nightfall Santana had sold every crumb he had and took in six hundred thousand dollars.

At that point he had enough to clear all of his debt plus get Chinky out of the way in case he decided to recruit him and still have fifty thousand in pocket change. He thought, '*I sure am gonna miss this fast money when I retire.*'

# CHAPTER 18

"NOW THAT YOU'VE TOLD ME how it all went down, I gotta give it to you straight. If *I* was Levi, I would've responded in the same lines of how he did, Meatball," said Donavan. "Damn, my nigga, whose side are you on?" asked Meatball.

"When you're talking about smashing Levi *especially* behind something so senseless, we'll be forced into an all-out war against Santana who just happens to be a viable asset to my business. Not to mention he has a unfearless squad that don't back down from nobody. You know that we won't back down either but if we're all busy at war, bodies'll start popping up, we'll be putting additional heat on us *and* the streets, and everyone involved from both sides will be disrupting their flow of money. And it'll all be behind you feeling belittled by Levi from shining on you for taking him lightly."

"Fuck that. *You* know how I get down, Donavan. I'm *Meatball* and niggas fear me in these streets." "Apparently, Levi's not one of them." "I won't give nobody a pass for talking to me like he did. I refuse to go out like dark-skinned Jermaine."

"Fuck it then, Meatball. If that's how you feel about it and you can't see things from my perspective, then by all means handle your business. Don't let your business handle you. And since you *are* my nigga, I gotta warn you that Levi is official with his murder game so don't sleep on 'em."

After the heated debate Meatball left without the backing of his partner. And in order to make his stance known about matter, Donavan made the call to have Santana and Levi meet him at a daiquiri shop. As the three men got their drinks and took their seats, Donavan took lead of the conversation.

"I arranged this sit-down, Santana, because of our business relationships and to bring you, Levi, up to speed with this frivolous feud with Meatball." "I'm listening," said Levi.

"I've spoken to Meatball about the situation and basically told him he was out of line. Unfortunately for him, he isn't the brightest bulb in the chandelier and is apparently fueled by his, quote-unquote, reputation.

"Apparently, he's taking the way you put him in his place, to heart. At any rate, since Meatball can't seem to fathom the idea of letting bygones be bygones, he does not have my blessings or backing with whatever actions he deems necessary."

"So, it's up there between Meatball and Levi, huh?" asked Santana. "Yes, it is. The gloves are officially off. And since I value our business relationship, Santana, and would like for it to continue, I called the both of you here tonight to show you that my hands are clean in this matter. And I will remain neutral, regardless of the outcome."

"You have my word, Donavan, that our business won't be interrupted," Santana told him. "I appreciate that. And to you, Levi, I know we really don't know each other but I've always held a sense of respect for you. I mean, who could actually hate a stand-up guy, anyway?"

"Thanks for the heads up, Donavan." "No problem. Although Meatball *is* my nigga and I have a lot of love for him, I won't condone his actions or go to war with a man that stood up to him when *he* was the one at fault. Unfortunately, his life may be the ultimate price he'd have to pay for his arrogant ways because at the end of the day I'm a business man with a beautiful family that I love going home to every night."

While Donavan and Levi were shaking hands to signify a mutual understanding, Santana asked, "So, where *is* Meatball?"

"Don't take it personally, fellas, but on the strength of Meatball being a friend of mine, I will not disclose his whereabouts. But out of respect for you, Santana, and you as well, Levi, I have made the playing field even. So be careful, Levi, and may the sharpest man win."

As they watched Donavan drive away in his Maserati, Levi said, "That was a good call you made about seeing what was Donavan's take on the situation."

"I agree. Although Donavan's a Boss, he's also a smart business man that knows when it's time to cut his losses, or in this case, get rid of his cancer. Besides…we have too much riding on this upcoming lick to be making any rash decisions." "Donavan earned my respect tonight for coming at us correct. He didn't cut any corners by putting Meatball's ass on blast."

"When we were in Columbia, Donavan had told me how Meatball was beginning to become a thorn in his side." "And as of tonight, Meatball became an even bigger problem for himself."

As Santana raised up from his seat to head to his Hummer H2, he said, "There's no need to prolong the inevitable, Levi. It's time for us to pay Mr. Meatball a visit." "Naw, Santana, I'm doing this one solo dolo."

Santana looked at Levi with a raised eyebrow and said, "I know you can pull your own weight but Meatball's as slick as fish grease and he might have a hit squad plotting with him." "He sure as hell's gonna need 'em. And they'll just be target practice. I already know you'll lay your life on the line for me and the feelings vice versa. But it's times like these that keeps me from getting rusty. That's why I need to hunt this shark down on my own."

"I feel you but if shit gets too hectic for you don't hesitate to hit me up ASAP because I'd never forgive you *or* myself if something were to happen to you." "There's no need for you to lose any sleep over this, Santana. I *gots* this."

# CHAPTER 19

WHILE SANTANA WAS HOGGING THE HIGHWAY in the opposite direction from Levi, he got a call from Derrick. "I'm happy you answered, Santana. Are you busy tonight?" "No, not really. I'm glad you called because I have something I wanted to give to you and Ham. Is he around?"

"Yeah, Chinky and I are over at his house now shooting pool." "That's right on schedule. I finally get the chance to meet Chinky." "That's the reason I called." "Well, hang tight for a few minutes, Derrick. I'll be there shortly."

When Santana walked into Ham's house, he was

amazed to see there were no children in sight. "Where are all the kids, Ham?" "The wifey put them to bed early tonight since they were acting up."

"Y'all are probably giving those kids too much sugar at night or something." "I don't know what their problem is but I *do* know they're too damn hype." They both laughed as Ham led the way to his sanctuary.

"Santana, this is our friend, Tri Phan, but we call him Chinky," said Ham. "Nice to meet you, Chinky." "Nice to meet you too, Santana. I've heard countless stories about you." "I hope it was all good things," Santana said as he shook Chinky's hand.

"So, who's kicking ass and taking names at this table?" Santana asked as he greeted Derrick. "Chinky's got the hot stick tonight," Derrick responded.

"Of course, you all know that every sport has it's legends and it's unknown legends. When it comes to shooting pool, I'm sure you've all heard of the legendary Minnesota Fats. Well, tonight I am proud to present to you the greatest unknown legend of all time known as New Orleans Slim," Santana said as he pulled out his handcrafted pool stick and screwed it into one piece.

As the guys shared a few laughs at Santana's expense, Derrick asked, "So, where *is* this New Orleans Slim guy, Santana?" "You're looking at 'em." "I never knew you had an alter ego," Ham joked. "New Orleans Slim only shows his face when it's time to put his cape on."

Since Chinky and everyone else was dead set on seeing this *New Orleans Slim* character in action, he let Santana break the balls which soon proved to be detrimental.

From the break, Santana sank three low balls. Afterwards, he hit a combination shot, dropping two more balls. And since he knew exactly what the end results would be, Santana said, "Aye Chinky, I really hate to be the bearer of bad news, but you're really holding that stick in vain because you won't be taking any shots *this* game." The entire room erupted into laughter as Chinky placed his stick aside.

Santana continued on as he hit a straight in shot, then hit a bank shot cross corner. At that point, he was down to the last ball to win the game. The eight ball. Chinky had all of his balls remaining on the table and still hadn't taken a shot. So when Santana A.K.A. *New Orleans Slim* prepared to take the game winning shot he chose to finish off Chinky with a shot that neither of his friends had ever seen before.

He aimed steadily at the cue ball by holding his pool stick in midair with one hand as if he was holding an ink pen, about a quarter's length away from the thick end of the pool stick, in the two o'clock position. "What in the hell kind of shot is that?" asked Ham.

"This is my trademark trick shot." "Well, it looks like you'll be getting your turn after all, Chinky, if he thinks he's gonna make *that* shot, said Derrick. "You got that right. There's no way that ball's going in," said Chinky as he reached for his stick.

Santana had tuned out his onlookers as he concentrated on the shot. He beamed in on the location of the eight ball that he needed to make contact with in order to obtain the victory. With no margin for error he knew that by attempting to cut the eight ball into the side pocket it would be extremely difficult to make with one hand. But being the risk taker that he was, he also knew that making the shot would silence his critics and solidify his title as the greatest unknown legend of all time.

"Eight ball, side pocket," Santana said as he zeroed in on the cue ball with his unflinching hand. The fellas murmured out of earshot of Santana to avoid breaking his concentration. Then suddenly, with an accelerated stroke, Santana fired off on the cue ball. And like a heat seeking missile that found its target, it struck the eight ball with precision and sent it rolling into the side pocket.

While Derrick and Ham were in shock with their jaws hanging to the floors, Chinky cringed at the sight of what they'd just witnessed. Santana jogged around the pool table with both fist in the air mimicking Muhammad Ali and yelling, "Who else wants some of Deebo?!"

"Man, now *that's* what I call an awesome shot, Santana," said Chinky. "Thanks, Chinky. I see you're not a sore loser." "No way, man. I don't have a jealous bone in my body. I've always congratulated a person deserving of it." "That's good to know."

"That was some classic *ESPN* shit right there, Santana. Where'd you learn how to do that shot?" asked Ham. "I taught myself. I started trying it one day when I was at the pool hall and I had a daiquiri in my hand. The drink was tasting so good, I didn't want to put it down. Ever since then, I've been nailing those shots."

"Well, you've earned the title as the greatest unknown legend in my book," said Derrick. "Thank you, thank you, and thank you. You are all far too kind. Your compliments were appreciated guys but I'm sorry to say that I won't be signing any autographs tonight." Everyone was rolling on the floor laughing.

Over an hour had passed and the guys were still taking turns attempting to make the trick shot that Santana did. They also reminisced about some of the times that Derrick and Ham had in their younger years with Santana and some of the missions they'd been on with Chinky.

Feeling adamant about his decision, Santana was ready to bring Chinky in as a hired hand for the *Columbian Job* since he'd made it through his comfort barrier. So Santana decided it was time to cut to the chase and break the ice.

Santana glanced at Derrick and Ham, giving them a wink as a hint of his approval of Chinky. Then he proceeded. "Hey Chinky." "What's up, Santana?" "The reason why I came here tonight was to meet you." "Meet *me*? What for?" "Because those two guys over there, that we share as friends, recommended me to."

"So, what's this about?" "There's a mission that we're going on at the end of the month in which your skills could be of assistance. And I am prepared to pay you a fee of a quarter million dollars in advance, tonight, if you'll join the team."

"Whoa, that's a lot of money, Santana. Since my buddies here thought enough of me to think I'd be helpful to the cause, then count me in," said Chinky as he shook hands with Santana.

Without any further delay, Santana scurried outside to his Hummer to retrieve his briefcase with the payoff money that was already divided into three parts.

# CHAPTER 20

ENGAGING IN THAT VERBAL SLUGFEST at the casino had upgraded to potential warfare so Levi conjured up the notion to keep tabs on Meatball. He knew he was contending with a lethal individual and had a slight advantage to know Meatball Achilles' heel…women. Whenever Levi needed to use a female as a pawn, he'd touch bases with Imani, who was the ring leader of the Cut Throat Cuties A.K.A. the C.T.Cs.

The makeup of the C.T.Cs consisted of a diverse team of eight women from different areas of New Orleans. They were evenly split with four of them from downtown and the other four from uptown. The downtown portion had three of the girls claiming the ninth ward section as their home.

Imani was from the Lower Ninth Ward which was known throughout the streets as the C.T.C., which is the abbreviation for Cross The Canal and Cut Throat City (where the name of her crew was derived). Sabrina, known as Nina, was from the Florida Project, and Keisha, known as Baby K, was from the Desire Project. The last of the downtown girls was Chasity who was from the seventh ward's St. Bernard Project.

The Uptown segment of the C.T.Cs had Yonnie from the Magnolia Project, and Laina from the Calliope Project, which were both in the third ward. Then there was Ronkeike from the Parkway, and Lydia from Hollygrove in the seventeenth ward.

The C.T.Cs specialized in a wide range of services stemming from setting up individuals, prostitution, smuggling contraband into penal facilities, pulling off heist and murder for hire. Each of them studied a book titled *The 44 Rules Of The O.G. Code by O.G. New New,* so they play the game exactly how it's suppose to go. So since it was Levi who'd reached out for their services Imani was forbidden to put a price tag on whatever it was that he needed handle.

Levi had a certified g-pass with the C.T.Cs because whoever was within Santana's immediate circle was patronized. Each member of the C.T.Cs allegiance lie with Santana because not only was he responsible for giving them their name, he strategically orchestrated the C.T.Cs by drafting each member and placed Imani at the helm.

At the meeting, Imani asked, "Do you have any background information on Meatball?" "Yeah, he's originally from the seventh ward and once he got in high school, he moved in the third ward, and he never moved back to the area he grew up in," said Levi.

Imani knew it was a sensitive situation because if a target was from a certain area in the city, she'd send in one of the girls from the opposite side of the city from where the individual originated.

By Meatball growing up downtown in the seventh ward then moving uptown in the third ward, he'd have an enhanced possibility of either knowing or hearing of the line of work the girls were into. They'd be putting themselves in a line of fire if Meatball smelled a set-up. Imani determined that since Chasity was the last installment of the C.T.Cs, moving to New Orleans six years prior from the Bronx, New York, she'd be the perfect candidate. After Imani gathered enough details about Meatball, she congregated with the rest of the C.T.Cs to get *Operation: Smoking Meatball* underway.

As Imani gave them a description of Meatball, Yonnie said, "I know that ole obnoxious ass rep hunter." All he does is run his mouth like he's King Ding-a-ling." The girls were hysterical. "That's a plus for us, Yonnie, since you know exactly who he is, you just saved us a lot of leg work. So, how can we lure him to Chasity by tonight?" asked Imani. "That's easy. All we have to do is throw a party at one of those clubs uptown and he'll surface," said Yonnie.

In spite of Imani not charging Levi he still hit her off with five thousand dollars being optimistic that she'd make contact with Meatball. So after her plan was conceived, Imani set the trap for Meatball to walk right into. The C.T.Cs had covered an exceptional amount of ground promoting the party in a matter of hours and had a moderately good turnout at the mid-city nightclub called The Chocolate Bar.

All of the C.T.Cs were at the festivities sticking to formality. One of their decrees were to keep the downtown C.T.Cs separated from the uptown C.T.Cs whenever they were in a crowded environment in New Orleans. Imani enforced that law because despite their discreet actions, the streets talked and she never left any windows open for anyone to have an opportunity to link any of their faces to the mysterious female extremists known as the C.T.Cs.

Just as they presumed, Meatball came waltzing in around eleven o'clock that night. Yonnie laid eyes on the man of the hour upon entrance while she was on the mic hyping up the party. So she took a break then grabbed Ronkeike and hustled to the ladies room to text Chasity specific details so she could pinpoint her mark.

After she receiving the text, she scanned the club until she located Meatball and discreetly revealed his identity to Imani, Nina, and Baby K. The trap hadn't taken ten minutes for Meatball to fall into once he'd made eye contact with the most gorgeous half Filipino and black Pocahontas look-a-like he'd ever seen. Chasity's features had him bedazzled. Meatball had found his prey for the night.

As he and his counterpart, Mitch, approached the girls, Nina and Baby K made way to the bar for another round of drinks. Meatball made a pass at Chasity while his sidekick attempted to strike up small talk with Imani. But she vindictively whisked off to the ladies'e room leaving Chasity behind to fend for herself.

Feeling like a flunky, Mitch digested the harsh reality of Imani not being delighted with his presence so he humbly moved around in the club to avoid looking like a third leg and left Meatball alone with Chasity.

At the commencement of their greeting, Chasity held a bleak expression on her face, coming off as the finicky type with Meatball. But his persistent course of action empowered his determination to prevail in her good grace. She eventually cut out the charade of cat and mouse and caved in, leading Meatball to believe his mouthpiece actually coaxed her into leaving The Chocolate Bar with him. After a few rounds of *Balboa* tequila, Meatball chunked the deuces at Mitch so he could crank it up a notch with Chasity.

As Meatball and Chasity pulled away from the Chocolate Bar in his Cadillac Escalade Ext, she reached over from the passenger seat to unfasten his *Torrey Tirrell* denim jeans and gave him a head job he won't soon forget. He got so overzealous he started driving erratic, nearly crashing twice. Somehow, he still managed to make it safe to his house undeterred by the skipped heartbeats he was encountering.

Once inside, Meatball insisted upon returning the gesture to Chasity for her stellar performance in the truck show. They were butt ass naked in no time and he was going berserk with his face buried in between her legs and she wrapped them around his head and had him in the *cobra clutch.*

However, he was bent on engaging in penetration but disappointment had set in for Meatball because an underlying condition in which he had had seized the moment. Meatball had an erectile dysfunction and he was fresh out of *The Hidden Vault's Strike* pills.

Chasity put on a facade like she was dissatisfied with the circumstances but she was really overwhelmed that he couldn't have sex with her. So in order to lighten the mood a bit she gave him a second round of action for a short period then they cuddled each other to sleep.

As part of his pitch to win Chasity over when they met at the Chocolate Bar, Meatball had promised to buy the mall up for her. On the following day he'd made good on his word by splurging nearly four thousand dollars on her. And since she didn't want Meatball to know where she laid her head at night, she had Nina scoop her up once she was finished with her outing with him. The C.T.Cs then reported to Levi and Chasity briefed him with an account of all of the info she'd gathered.

"Thanks a million, Chasity. That was fast. I thought it would've taken at least a week before tracking him." "Anything for the home team, Levi. You already know we gets that *bizness* in." "So, how'd your date turn out?" She kindly exposed Meatball's little secret. Levi responded, "I *knew* he wasn't a stand-up guy." They bawled over laughing.

"Hey, Chasity, if it's not too much of a problem I want you to keep him in your company for at least a few more days to learn his routines and duck off spots." "I got you, Levi. I can't say that I like hanging with his lame ass but it might as well be me who he's spending his money on." "Now that's the spirit. Dig up in that nigga's pockets, Cutie."

# CHAPTER 21

WHEN LEVI SEPARATED FROM SANTANA at the Daiquiri shop, he gave Chasity a call. She'd done as he requested by spending time with Meatball. Levi hadn't taken Donavan's warning lightly so he pressed the countdown button to the demise of the hot-headed Meatball.

"Hey, Chasity. It's me, Levi." "I am *so* glad you called. Man, that dude is borderline crazy. How much longer is this job supposed to last?" "It'll all be over tonight. I'll even give you a bonus for toughing it out for me."

"Thanks, Levi. I *have* been giving him the benefit of the doubt, only because you're in the family, but a bitch got a breaking point." Levi laughed. I'm serious, Levi. The nigga got that Dr. Jekyll and Mr. Hyde thing going on. One day, he can't have any sex because of his problem, then the next day, he's murkin' a bitch pussy."

Levi laughed harder. "That shit ain't funny. I swear I'm dealing with a nigga with split personalities." "When was the last time you talked to him?" "About an hour ago. He called and asked me to come over to his house for the night." "Good. Is that the same location you gave me the address to the other day?" "Yeah, that's the place."

"Well, I'll be paying y'all a visit tonight so be sure to put on an Oscar-winning performance." "All right, Levi. Be careful, okay?" "No doubt. You be easy, lil mama, and don't forget to leave the door unlocked."

Chasity huddled her belongings after refreshing up, then reported in with Imani to advise her about the near conclusion of *Operation: Smoking Meatball.*

When Levi made it home, he suited up with his war armor. He slapped on his baseball gloves, Teflon vest, and all black attire. Then grabbed his .40 caliber handgun and placed it in the small of his backpack and tossed a SKS assault rifle in a duffle bag. He got a hunting knife and hooked it on his side. And for his last line of defense, he strapped on an ankle holster then secured a .380 handgun and then headed for the door.

During the stakeout of Meatball's home, Levi observed a silhouette of two individuals moving about in the living room area. For at least a half hour he heard the sounds of R&B music blaring from within the place drowning out any possible conversation which may have been underway between the occupants.

Chasity must've sensed Levi's presence in the vicinity because she walked out onto the patio to smoke a cigarette while catching a view of the crescent moonlight. It was a calculated move on her behalf because she and Levi had orchestrated which signals she'd send when it was near showtime.

As she re-entered the living room she found no trace of Meatball anywhere in sight. But she did hear the sound of running water coming from his bedroom's bathroom. She tiptoed her way into the room to discover the bathroom door was ajar. So she peeped in to see if Meatball was indeed in the shower.

Once it was confirmed, she hightailed her way back into the living room to unlocked the door then flicked the porch lights twice to send the final indication of everything being a go on her end.

Afterwards, she hastily made her way back into the bedroom in an attempt to beat Meatball in there before he finished his shower. But as she was crossing the threshold to the room he was coming out of the bathroom wearing only a towel wrapped around his waist.

"I thought you crept out of here on a nigga since you didn't care to join me." "You already knew I was sleeping over so it could've waited." "Well, I left the water running for you in case you wanted to hop in." "Actually, I took one before I came here so, no thanks."

In an attempt to subside the tension Meatball unleashed his Casanova persona. "I hear that friction in your voice but there shouldn't be any reason for us to extinguish the flames on the candles I've lit for the rendezvous I have planned for us tonight."

"Well, *you're* the one who got all theatrical talking 'bout, '*since you didn't care to join me in the shower,*'" Chasity said as she mimicked Meatball's raspy voice tone. "Don't take that the wrong way. I was only hoping I'd get the chance to have some of that soapy sex, that's all."

With her lethal intentions at the brink of unfolding Chasity egged him on and decided she'd put on a show for the grand finale. "Aww, I think that's so sweet of you to want me almost as soon as I got here. I didn't know I turned you on so much." "As long as I've been looking for my own Pocahontas, turning me on is a huge understatement," Meatball cooed.

Since he already had a permanent stripper pole installed in his bedroom Chasity chose to send him out with a bang by giving him a strip tease. She set the tone by cranking up his Bose surround sound system with the tunes flowing from Lil Wayne's song called *Lollipop*.

She shot him a provocative look as she dimmed the lights then shed off her clothing piece by piece until only a bra, thongs, and stilettos remained. Her Nicki Minaj type of bodily structure had Meatball entranced as she strutted her way to the dance pole.

"Damn, Chasity, you *sure* know how to make a nigga rise to the occasion the way you stompin' like one of those Budweiser Clydesdales in this motherfucker." "The only two things you should be doing right now is sitting down and making it rain," Chasity said as she pointed Meatball in the direction of the *Lay-Z-Boy* recliner near the pole. And he did as she commanded while *The Hidden Vault's Strike* pill he popped before getting in the shower began taking effect.

# CHAPTER 22

CHASITY SWAYED HER VOLUPTUOUS HIPS from side to side to the rhythm of the beat like a seasoned vet. Then she dropped into a split while looking over her shoulder and giving Meatball a spellbinding look directly in his eyes as she sucked on her pointing finger with an in and out motion.

She exerted herself the way she bounced her eye candy up and down one ass cheek at a time. In her next sequel of the exhibition she climbed to the top of the pole and flipped upside down and began twerking as if she had a vendetta against every stripper and exotic dancer in the world and she could effortlessly show them that she was the best that ever done it.

Meatball was mesmerized by witnessing her in action. She slid downwards slowly then paused midways, gripped the pole with her legs to free one of her hands to pat her pussy then curled her finger towards Meatball inviting him to come over to the miniature stage.

She guided her *Chanel* thongs to the side to give him a close view of her clean shaven magnet for dead presidents. Once he pulled out a wad of cash Chasity smiled then scaled her finger down the crease of her womanhood to coat it with a nice glaze. Then held it out to give him a taste of her intoxicating love juices. He sucked off the wetness and it made him enthralled as he returned to his seat.

Chasity reached her vantage point when she twirled her body the remainder of the way down the pole without missing a beat as she made her ass do the thunder clap. Needless to say, she forced Meatball's hands to throw every dollar in his possession in the air to create a thunderstorm.

"*Bravo, Bravo,*" said Meatball as he gave her a warm round of applause. "Thanks for the tips, handsome," she responded as her Jimmy Choo heels landed back onto the stage. And she proudly swept up the few thousands of dollars she'd earned. In the process, she saw Levi creeping up stealth mode aiming an SKS at the recliner while circling around it until he was faced off with Meatball. Chasity let out a startled scream as wide-eyed Meatball asked, "What the *fuck* you doing in my house?!"

Levi slapped him across his face with the barrel of his assault rifle as he said, "Take that bass out of your voice ole bitch ass nigga. Since you wanted to act like Jada Pinkett-Smith and *Set it Off,* I came here to nullify that shit." "I *knew* Donavan turned sour on me and sold me out to y'all niggas. As many times as I went out there head-first behind his ass, I should've just offed him the minute he showed me he didn't have my back."

Then without warning, Chasity fainted at the sight of what slithered from out of the bathroom behind Levi. She crushed the glass end table with her head as she fell from the stage. Reluctantly, she gained Levi's focal point but his attention span towards her was short-lived once he felt the barrel of cold steel pressed against the back of his head and heard the clicking sound from a cocking hammer.

"Drop it like it's hot, nigga, or I'll push your brains so far forward I'll leave you forever wondering why you died frontin'," said the anonymous trigger man.

Levi knew he'd heard the sound of that familiar voice before. He took into consideration that he had to be hallucinating because he was having a hard time comprehending who the voice belonged to. As he put down his SKS and turned towards the bandit, his face turned pale and he nearly blacked out like Chasity did after verifying that his ears had not mislead him but his eyes most certainly had. Levi was eyeballing a man who was the spitting image of Meatball.

"Damn, Levi, you're acting like you saw a ghost. It's only my brother, Jermaine. Let me guess… you didn't know that I had a twin, *did* you?" asked Meatball. "I can't say that I did," said Levi. "No need to feel left out because nobody knows about him not even Donavan. Our parents divorced shortly after our third birthday. Then our moms moved out to Cali and she took Jermaine with her while I stayed behind with our dad. And my brother only dip in and out of New Orleans for times like this."

"I gotta give it to you, Meatball, you pulled off a Houdini move tonight but aye…I take my lick." "Speaking of taking your lick, it's about time for a little payback." Meatball politely picked up Levi's SKS and returned the gesture.

Levi responded, "That's all you got, Meatball? Nigga, you hit like a little bitch." The next blow that came from Meatball was with much more force than before and sent Levi hurling to the floor next to unconscious Chasity. Levi's .40 caliber expelled from his back then landed on the aft side of Chasity and out of view of the twins.

Meatball tossed the assault rifle aside as he walked over to Levi and kicked him in the stomach and said, "You talkin' all greasy to a nigga. You *must* be ready to die." "At all times, nigga. It is what it is."

"Let me scorch this ole slick talkin' ass nigga, Meatball," said Jermaine. "Naw, not yet. That's exactly what he wants us to do so he can get this over with but I won't let him entice me to let him get off that easy," said Meatball. "Aight then. So, wha'chu wanna do with him and that bitch?"

"I'll save her fine ass for last, but *him*…he has some valuable info that I want to extract." "Oh yeah?" "Yeah. He run with a group of niggas who got their money up. His closest potna's name is Santana and *that's* the nigga who's holdin'. And Levi's gonna lead us to the dough."

"Oprah'll go broke before I tell you anything about my nigga, Santana," Levi said boldly. "Yeah, that's what your mouth says. Jermaine, let's tie his hands behind his back around the pole on the stage."

After constraining Levi to the pole, Meatball said, "It ain't funny when the chicken got the grease, huh, nigga? You're gonna tell me where Santana keeps his cash and them bricks he be gettin' from all of those niggas he be cooking up cocaine for. And you can try holding back if you want to and act like you a diehard nigga but that's gonna be all on *you.* And your route to extinction's gonna be so excruciating with even the slightest hunch of some type of fuckery.

"But before we get into that conversation, let me hip you to how you got yourself in this pickle. First of all, what the *fuck* were you thinking when you sent a bitch at me? You shook me with *that* one, killer. I really gave you more credit than I should have.

"I realized she was on some other shit days ago but I didn't know who she was plotting with. The first night I met her she slept at my crib. That was her first mistake. As soon as she crashed I searched through her cell phone just like I do every other bitch since it's obvious you can't trust these hoes. And I saw a text she got from that bitch, Yonnie, that described everything I was wearing. That instantly raised my antennas.

"I heard about that click of females called the C.T.Cs and I always thought Yonnie was a part of that because of those letters tattooed on the webbed part between her fingers. So I checked Chasity's fingers to see if she had the same tat and she did. Then I started playing' her more closely and bought the freaky bitch all types of shit to keep her in my sights just to see who was scheming on me for. On the next day the picture was painted like Picasso did it.

"When her girlfriend, Nina, swooped her up from the mall I remembered seeing them together at the Chocolate Bar. So I shook Nina's hand then twisted it around like I was scoping those diamonds she was rockin' on her fingers and saw the same tattoo that Chasity and Yonnie had. Then I asked Chasity to use her cell phone to make an important call since my phone couldn't catch a good signal. I distanced myself from them like I needed privacy and scrolled through her contact list since I didn't do that the last time I went through it and you'll never guess what I stumbled on… *your* name and number, Levi. Ain't that a bitch?"

Meatball then glanced over at Chasity who was still in a state of suspended animation and said, "You see your little *jump-off*, or C.T.C. bitch or what*ever* the fuck she is to you, I only spared her ass so she could lure you into my hands. Plus the added incentive of bringing my brother in on the action to switch up on her like we always did them hoes." *'That explains the different sexual experience Chasity was talking about,'* Levi thought.

In addition to the awkward position he was in, Levi knew that time was of the essence. Being sharp-witted, he needed Meatball to hit him at least one more time to reposition himself in order to abate those precious inches between his hand and the knife. And since Meatball brought up the touchy subject of sex, Levi knew his next punch line would be sure to provoke Meatball's anger.

"*Always*? Aww, stop with the shenanigans. You don't have to puff yourself up on my account, Meatball. I've heard all about your little… *imperfection*," Levi said as he chuckled.

And just as he expected, his words infuriated Meatball to administer a walloping backhand slap to Levi's face. "Oh, you think that shit's funny, huh, nigga? Let's see if you're still laughing in a few minutes."

Levi was now able to retrieve his knife and began to cut the rope from around his wrist. Once his bound hands were freed he unsnapped his ankle holster from the outside of his jeans. His main focus was on Jermaine since he had him held under gunpoint.

But as he tried to slide his jeans up to attain his last line of defense, Meatball caught sight of the shiny chrome piece and quickly backpeddled away from him and said, "Whoa…wha'chu got in them Timbs, Levi? Aye, Jermaine, this slick ass nigga got a piece in his boots. If he even flinches I want you to knock fire from his ass."

Meatball circled around Levi to see that the rope had been cut. "How'd you cut that rope? You must have a knife, too." Levi knew now that he was in a no-win situation. Even if he attempted to take a stab at Meatball he'd be dead before he could swing the knife but he refused to go down without a fight. So to buy himself a little more time he chose to sacrifice by disarming himself then threw his hands in the air and said, "That's what happens when you tie a nigga up without frisking 'em. What the fuck would you do if you were in my shoes?"

All Meatball could do was smile and said, "I ain't even mad at you, Levi. I would've tried to pull off the same type of act as you did. But that's all over now, so raise up easy so I can get that knife and that piece off you."

Levi complied. After surrendering his hardware, Meatball forced him to his knees. "I'm done fuckin' around, Levi. Now tell me where Santana's holding his stash." Levi stayed silent.

Meatball pointed Levi's .380 at the center of his forehead, then cocked back the hammer and said, "It would be real fucked up to get smashed with your own gun, so it's up to you. You got five seconds to start talking before I get ta squeezin'."

Although Levi was ready to die, he was quick with his hands. So before Meatball would reach the count of one, he would go with the move by deflecting the gun. Then Meatball began the countdown.

"Five…four…Three…Two…" Levi stared Meatball in his eyes and said, "When Santana finds out about this, you better run for the hills, nigga, because you won't live to see the next sunset. I'll see you in hell shortly, motherfucka'." "Wrong answer, Levi…one."

Suddenly, three gunshots rang out. Both Levi and Meatball were stunned to see Jermaine hit the floor. The shots came by way of Chasity who'd regained her senses and felt Levi's .40 caliber behind her and fired upon the nearest enemy. Then Meatball took aim at Chasity and discharged two rounds in her direction.

He landed one shot in her upper shoulder as Levi rushed him to clutch his wrist and interfere with Meatball's course of direction. But Meatball was unmoved with Levi's wrestling assault. With a death grip on the murder weapon he was able to maintain the gun and quick to rebound to own the upper hand once again.

Murder and fury was in his eyes and tone as he pointed the gun at Levi once again and said, "Fuckin' with you, I let that bitch steal on my brother. I could give a fuck *less* about Santana's stash now, nigga. I'm bout to end this shit."

Meatball kept the .380 aimed at Levi until he picked up the SKS to make sure he sent Levi away in style. "Now this is more like it. You got any last words, nigga?" "Does it look like I got any worries, ole duck ass nigga? What the fucks wrong with you trigger finger, pussy ass lil boy?"

"*BWAOW!!*" was the sound as only one bullet was discharged. Blood and brain particles rained over Levi's frozen face and shirt as he watched Meatball collapse with blood oozing from his head. In the background stood Santana with his burning torch in hand. "One shot, one kill," said Santana.

"Where'n the hell did *you* come from?" Levi asked gratefully. "I'll explain later but for now we need to clear out of here. Grab all of the guns while I check on Chasity."

Santana scurried over to Chasity's side and turned her onto her back to evaluate her condition. With the amount of blood that seeped over her chest area Santana was inclined to accept the reality of the injury she'd obtained was fatal.

Then he checked her wrist for a pulse. It was still beating. Chasity hadn't given up at all and was fighting for her life. And Santana wouldn't give up on her either. He lifted her head until their faces were a foot apart and said, "I just know *my* Cut Throat Cutie ain't going out like *this*?!"

Chasity gravitated to the sound of Santana's voice and it gave her assurance that she could recover. Her eyelids must've seemed to weigh a ton but she managed to lift them enough to see his infectious smile which caused her to do the same.

"It hurts, Santana. And it burns like hell." "I know, I know. Just hang tight while I find something to stop the bleeding and clean you up." "Whatever you say, daddy," mumbled Chasity as he dashed out of the bedroom.

After Santana was finished patching and cleaning her, he said, "I heard what you called me as I was leaving out of here. Now, you *know* I've never seen you this close to being naked before. And that body's looking so tempting that you got a nigga wanting to sample that," Santana said in an attempt to keep her in good spirits. "Oh, you got jokes, huh, Dr. Bailey?" "Yeah, I'm just fuckin' with you."

After helping her put clothes on, Santana carried her to his Yukon. Levi was with him to put the bag of guns in the back seat of Santana's truck. "I'll meet up with y'all at the hospital after I finish house cleaning, Santana." "Bet that, my nigga. I'll be waiting for you in the E.R."

# CHAPTER 23

FIFTEEN MINUTES LATER Levi pulled into the parking lot by the emergency room's entrance. Santana spotted Levi's Audi then ended his call with Imani to walk outside and meet Levi.

"How's she doing?" asked Levi. "No word at the moment but that's one of my lil souljarettes so she'll come out smelling like roses. The doc said that if she pulls through it's because I plugged the wound and got her to the hospital when I did." "That sounds like good news."

"How about you, you good?" asked Santana. "Hell *yeah* I'm straight thanks to *you*! I just knew Meatball was about to use my SKS and tear my ass to *Reese's Pieces*!" They both had to laugh at his comment.

"Aight, Santana, that's enough about me, nigga. The billion dollar question of the night is how'd you find out what was going down?" "Because of a simple law I enforce called chain of command." "Chain of command? Now I'm *totally* baffled."

"Let me break it down for you. You already know the C.T.Cs are my personal female squad I put together and that Imani's my go-to girl. Well, I laid down the law from the beginning that if *any* of my niggas ever came to them for work, to let me know every detail. So Chasity reported to Imani with every step of her assignment then Imani reported to me and there you have it."

"Damn, you're too high-powered for *me*, my nigga. Your ass knew all along that I was fuckin' with Chasity and didn't say shit to me about it." "*You're* the reason why I held my trump card." "How?" "Because I respected your mind when your exact words to me about Meatball were, "*Naw, Santana, I'm doing this one solo dolo, and there's no need for you to lose any sleep over this, Santana. I gots this.*' Remember that?"

"Aight, aight. You tried to warn me but I *had* that nigga. I just never knew he had a twin." "Shiiit nigga, neither did I. Like I told you, the nigga was slick. You can't put *nothing* pass any nigga who's known for dressing up like a female to murk something."

"Well, I'm sure glad you stuck to your guns and checked up on me. I owe you my life." "That's enough of all of that mushy talk, nigga. What I want to hear is how Chasity wound up in a thong and bra. Her ass is fine as fuck." Levi recalled all of the particulars leaving no stones left unturned.

After Levi spoke of her performance he said, "Let's go in the waiting room to see if the house fire was reported on the news." "Torching the spot is your version of house cleaning?" "Aye, it was the least I could do after I snatched all of the nigga's cash, coke, and jewelry I saw." "You came up off that nigga, huh?"

"Naw, Santana, I'm giving all of that shit to you and Chasity to split. Y'all earned it." "You don't owe me nothin', my nigga. You already know I would've wigged out if anything happened to you.

But if you want to, just give it all to Chasity." "She'll be laughing all the way to the bank once I hit her off with *that* stimulus package."

While seated in the T.V. area, Levi got the validation he was looking for as a news flash took over the airwaves. Aerial coverage of Meatball's house was being shone as firefighters fought vigorously to extinguish the flames. "Damn, my nigga, you lit that bitch up like *Left Eye*," Santana whispered. "After a stunt like Meatball pulled off by unleashing his twin, I *had* to roast them niggas extra crispy."

During the broadcast the head surgeon Dr. Brittney Anderson came from out of the E.R. to give Santana an update on Chasity's condition.

"How's she doing, Doc?" asked Santana. "She's in stable condition. All of her vital signs are normal. She suffered a minor cut to her head and a gunshot wound to the left shoulder. However, there was no exit wound. But during surgery I was able to successfully remove the bullet and stitch her back together. Although she lost a small amount of blood and should be just fine, she still needs to take it easy."

"Thanks a lot, Doc. So, how soon tonight will it be before I can take her home?" "Oh, she won't be going anywhere tonight. We're gonna run a few more test on her and monitor her throughout the night and she should be good to go no later than tomorrow afternoon."

"Is it possible for me to cover the expenses and see her before I leave tonight?" "Sure. The billing office is down the hall to your right and she was transferred moments ago from out of surgery and into her private room which is in the same direction. And she's awake so you could see her now if you like." "I appreciate that, Dr.

Anderson. You're a lifesaver…literally." "No problem. I live for times like these."

After hearing Chasity was on her road to recovery, Santana said, "Levi, hang around in the waiting area for Imani and the rest of the girls to get here while I check on Chasity." "Aight, fam. I'll be right here."

Santana sprinted to the hospital's gift shop to grab two dozen roses, some balloons, assorted chocolate candy, a huge teddy bear and a get well soon card. When he made his way into her room he saw how jaded she was and how she had to force a smile.

"You're a charming sight for sore eyes. All of those goodies for me?" asked Chasity. "Of course they are. How you feeling?" "Like shit." "You *do* look like you've been in a dog fight." Chasity laughed freely. "No, I don't." "That's the smile I was looking for."

"Is it over?" "Yeah, you won't ever see Meatball again. You did good." "Man, I think I blacked out when I saw his twin." "You did and your head shattered that glass end table when you fell." "Is that why I have this bandage on my head?" "Yep, sure is." "Thanks for taking care of me, Santana. I'd probably be dead by now if it weren't for you."

"You know I always look out for my girls." "So when can I get outta here?" "Tomorrow sometime. Why? You got somewhere to go?" "I know it's against your rules and everything, but I was kinda hoping you'd spend a little time with me because I'd really like to show you my appreciation."

"You're doing that just by breathing right now. You don't owe me anything." "I know I don't but Santana, this is an emotional and mental moment for me. All I'm asking is that you to set aside your rule just this one time to fulfill my dreams of sexing me."

"At a time like this you're actually thinking about sex?" "Seems like my only chance." "If I did that I'd have my whole crew of C.T.Cs trying to kill me because I've denied them all. Besides, it'll just make your feelings get involved and I'd never think of hurting any of you."

"But all of the girls love you and as you can see we'll even kill for you. And if you ever decided to put a ring on any of our fingers, every bitch would jump to say *I do*, including me. Therefore, my feelings have always been involved so it's really all the same. And to make sure things stay cool between us, I'll bury that secret the same night you bury that bone in me…I promise."

"I don't know, Chasity. I think that medication got you trippin' right now." She frowned and said, "You think I'm trippin? If you can honestly tell me that this has never crossed your mind, then maybe you're right…I *am* trippin'." Chasity completely opened her hospital gown to expose her nudity.

"*Dammit*, Chasity. Close that gown *right* now!" "Nope! Not until you tell me you'll grant my wish." "Aight, aight. At least let me think about it." "Has it ever crossed your mind?" "Maybe a time or two. Now close that gown or I'm out." She finally covered up.

"Jesus, woman. You're something serious. I can't believe you actually have me in here negotiating a sex deal." "Is that a yes?" Santana sighed.

"Levi told me all about that show you put on at Meatball's house. He said your skills are nothing short of the work of a perfectionist. Where'd you learn how to do that shit?" "Boy, I've been pussy poppin' since I was in pampers."

The thought of seeing Chasity in action made him throw his rule completely out of the equation.

"So when can I get my private show?" Chasity's face lit up and she said, "As soon as I heal up, handsome. Trust me...you won't regret it." Santana kissed her on her forehead then headed back to the waiting area. All of the C.T.Cs had made it there and were waiting like they were standing on pins and needles.

He spoke to them all and second the motion from what they'd learned from Levi. And once Levi saw how Santana had put the girls at ease, he pulled him aside.

"Santana, you'll never believe what I just saw." Santana sensed the disturbance in Levi's voice and asked, "What happened?" "The news broadcast. *Look...* they're showing it again."

The news reporter began, '*Alicia Barfield, coming to you live again from the scene of that dangerous house fire we aired earlier in which the firefighters did an amazing job of extinguishing. Homicide detective, Trenton Sanders, has informed us that there was a fatality inside the home and it appears to be foul play, so the case is being treated as a homicide. I repeat...one person was found dead. The owner of the house, Jermott Briggs, is the assumed victim and right now the detectives are combing the area for any traces of forensics evidence. Investigators are asking if there is anyone who has information about the crime, to call crime stoppers. The only lead they have thus far is from a nearby neighbor who reported seeing a possible suspect fleeing on foot shortly before the fire but unfortunately a positive ID's not confirmed at this time so the police do not have any solid leads on the perpetrator. Remember a week ago, there was a triple murder at a hotel that ended in a fire and the police are unsure if there's a connection to this case...*'

Santana looked at Levi and said, "Damn, this shit seems like a carbon copy of the situation my father was in." "What happened?"

"My father shot a guy who he thought was dead without making sure of it. And my father's dead because the same guy came back for revenge."

# CHAPTER 24

SANTANA HAD TOO MUCH riding on the *Columbian Job* to shift his focus to the mystery man that survived the fire. So he and Levi went forward as planned and left for Miami. They got a penthouse suite at an exquisite hotel on Collins Ave.

Santana walked out onto the balcony with his military marine tactical binoculars to catch a panoramic view of the scenery and masses of individuals who appeared as ants from the heights he stood. The sun descended as droves of beach goers enjoyed the ocean breeze. So Santana and Levi chose to partake in the fun.

They trotted down the straightaway until finding a cozy looking lounge to knock down a few drinks. It was happy hour so they decided to stick around and mingle a bit with the multicultural crowd. Santana knew a few Bosses in Miami who could've shown him a few spots to dock the submarine but thought of it to be more conducive to meet a new face for a tour guide and remain incognito.

As he and Levi sat at the bar sipping their drinks a very sophisticated looking woman whose attire suggested she raided Erykah Badu's closet had made an advance at Santana.

"You guys sure stick out like sore thumbs. New here?" "Is it that obvious?" asked Santana. "Well, *yeah*." The woman responded.

"We're vacationing and somehow landed in here for a few drinks." "So, where are you from?" "Chicago." "Chicago, huh? Okay, Mr. Chiraq. Can you explain why you have such a strong New Orleans accent?"

Santana laughed. "Aight, you caught me." " We've only been acquainted for a few minutes and you're telling lies already. Just *like* a man." "I see you're all on my case, but where are you from with that accent?" The woman smiled and said, "Dominican Republic," then extended her hand, "Jasmine Diaz...nice to meet you." "Santana Bailey and the pleasure's all mine," Santana said as he kissed her hand. Levi distanced himself to accompany a female who was giving him the *fuck me* eyes while Santana and Jasmine walked over to a booth to get more acquainted.

"This place seems real laid back. It kinda has that homey feel to it. What usually goes down in here?" asked Santana. "Spoken word." "That's when the audience's version of clapping is snapping fingers, right?" Jasmine laughed and said, "That's right."

"I've got to admit, I never had a desire to watch a live show to actually appreciate the art form. But I do know that the artist are very conscious-minded individuals and their wordplay and metaphors are wicked." "They have some talented people who come through displaying their works."

"How often do you come here?" "Almost every day." "Almost every day?! So, are you like a spoken word junkie or something? "Jasmine smirked, "I see you're into standup comedy, Mr. Bailey. That type of club is a few blocks up the street. But to answer your question, no I'm not a *spoken word* junkie. I'm in here so much because I happen to own this establishment."

"Oh shit, you're the *owner*?" "Last time I checked, I was." "Thank God for giving us a sense of humor. I knew you had too much class to be sprung." "Don't try kissing up now, Mr. Bailey. If you plan on staying in for a little while, you'll get the chance to witness your very first spoken word performance."

"Since you're not kicking me out I'd love to watch the show, but under two conditions." "What are they?" "As long as you're keeping me company, and if you start calling me Santana." "How could I resist, Santana, when I can't stop smiling? By the way…my friends call me Jaz."

"Well, I have a strong feeling we're going to be exactly that. Okay then, Jaz, tell me something… I bet you harass all your patrons this way, don't you?" "I do *not*. To be perfectly honest, *you're* the first person I've ever approached in this manner. I haven't been in a relationship in nearly a year."

"Did he hurt you?" "I guess you can say that. But it was because he left me." "Why in the world would any sane man choose to part with a woman who is the pure essence of beauty? And judging from the impression I'm getting, even more beautiful on the inside."

"He said I never spent any time with him because I'm too wrapped up into my business." "I understand you have your independent thing going but I can't say I blame the man." "Oh no. Not you, *too*. What's wrong with that?"

Santana took her by the hand, "Stand up for me, if you will. Now, look in that mirror behind you and tell me what man wouldn't want to spend every waking second of the day making love to you and spoiling you rotten?"

"Now, you see how you got me blushing again? I swear y'all boys from New Orleans ain't nothing but some slick-talkers. And speaking of talking, I just love the way y'all say the word - *baby*. Can you say it for me one time?" "*Baby*." "Ooh that sounds so sexy."

"If you keep flirting with me like that and you might be hearing, *baby,* more often." "How is that possible when you live in a different state? I definitely don't do long distance relationships." "I came here in search for my own nightclub, actually. I could use a good tour guide to show me around. You know any?" "Are you kidding me? I'd *love* to show you the city. I happen to know mostly every club owner in town, clubs you may want to re-open, clubs on the brink of folding, and great locations for new construction."

"Looks like I came to the right place for a drink." "You *sure* did. Ooh *look*…the show's about to start. I see your drink's running low, I'll call the barmaid over for a refill." "That isn't necessary, Jaz. I can pay -" "Shh…listen."

The announcer came onto the stage, "Good evening, everyone. Welcome to The Red Room where the stage is always set for those who have been waiting to exhale and ready to let their soul bleed. Ms. Jasmine Diaz has put together another marvelous show for you guys tonight. So open up your minds and brace yourselves for some invigorating words.

Our first guest came here to showcase his talent all the way from Houston, Texas. So without further ado, lets all welcome this bright young brother with a warm round of applause. Ladies and gentlemen, give it up for *Rhyze*." "Good evening my brothers and sisters. You all are looking very beautiful out there tonight. The word I'm about to bring to you is entitled; "*No Justice - No Peace.* Y'all with me on that?" In unison, the crowd cheered.

*"Lady Liberty is blindfolded for a reason*

*Just look a little closer and you'd see*

*She must've blindfolded herself cause both of her hands are free...*

*Her motives are to see no evil and treat my people as though they*
*are not of equal...*

*Like we don't add up...*

*My black brothers need to man-up and stand up*

*because they want us to fall for anything.*

*We have to overcome the ratio and the level of being another*
*statistic...*

*Although a lot of us are the fruits of poisonous trees*

*We don't have to produce the exact same seeds...*

*We have to keep each other uplifted,*

*much higher than the ropes they hung us from because we are*
*gifted..."*

"Hey, Jaz, I'm kinda feeling this vibe. Dude's deep," Santana whispered. "That's good to know, but you'll have to stay quiet and pay attention to the message because there's a chance we might miss out on something." "My bad."

*"Lady Liberty's scale has always been uneven when it comes to us*

*Which causes a reaction for most to kick up dust.*

*But thus says the Lord that those who are first shall go last and*
*the last shall be first*

*And to make matters worst*

*They act like being black is a curse*

*What if my color was of the majority instead of the minority*

*Caucasians or maybe even Asians, just to name a few...*

*Would I have the same point of view?*

*Nine times out of ten, I would be on the outside looking in...*

*They want to keep us on the inside looking out to keep us question-ning*

*Why am I in the skin that I'm in*

*No Justice - No Peace"*

The audience responded to the conclusion with scores of snaps. "Enjoy yourself?" asked Jasmine. "Yeah, that was pretty good. I could see myself implementing this onto my pastime list." "Well, always remember you saw it with me first. So I'd better get first dibs at accompanying you anytime you decide to see a show. And that's only because you don't look like you're taken."

Santana thought of Gabrielle then realized he'd made the right decision by letting her go because Jasmine could prove to be a very lucrative asset in Miami. By having connections added to her resume, her exotic features made her Miami's number one prospect for Santana's frequent satisfaction.

"Since you've given me no say so in the matter as to who I bring on a date, it's obvious that you're psychic for you to assume correctly that I'm available. So have me as you wish." "Hmm… that sounds submissive." "I wouldn't exactly describe it in *those* terms, but I'd love to be your sex toy as long as you aren't anything like that *Fifty Shades of Grey* guy." "My God! I sound *desperate*?"

"No, not at all. You sound very intrigued just as I am." "I pinky swear I won't torture you." "Then, I'm all in." "Now back to you calling me a psychic; *you're* the one that's from the voodoo capital. I've heard all about the things you people from New Orleans do."

"I've lived in New Orleans my entire life and I've never met a person who does that voodoo shit. So, don't believe everything you've read in books or hear on TV I think it's all a hoax to attract tourist to the French Quarters. So, stay away from those type of people if you ever visit." Jasmine laughed.

"So, where are you staying while you're in town?" "Me and my dude are sharing a penthouse suite at the *1 Hotel* just a few blocks away." "Do you think your friend would mind if I steal you away for the night? You can sleepover at my house if you like."

"He'll be fine. I'll just let him know my whereabouts in case I get held for ransom or something." She punched Santana's arm and said, "Just for that, I can't wait until we get to my house. I got you. And just so you'd know, I live in a private area in Hallandale Beach and my backyard's the Atlantic Ocean."

'*Jackpot*,' Santana thought. Jasmine had the prime location to dock the submarine. He freed up a gang of time towards locating the perfect spot for a nightclub. And with her assistance he could see himself moving to Miami a lot sooner.

"Santana, forgive me for having to shorten our conversation but I need to check on my business." "By all means, Boss, do what you gotta do. I'll be okay." "I promise I won't be long. I just need to wrap things up, grab a few items, and get with my manager to let him know I'll be leaving soon so you and I can go play in the sand." "I can't wait."

As she was leaving, Levi was making his way over to Santana. "Shorty was all over you, huh, Santana?" "Yeah, homie. She's got everything I'm looking for." "Shorty's bad and all but I *know* she didn't hook you with love at first sight?"

"Naw, it's nothing like that." Santana enlightened Levi about Jasmine's attributes. "My nigga, you must have some type of magnetic genes for pulling the good ones while my jinx ass got chosen by the weirdest bitch in Miami. I'm trying to duck the shit out of her crazy ass." Santana chuckled.

"What in the hell did she say like *that*?" "Aight, first of all, the bitch starts claiming I'm the man she sees in her dreams and how she's really into this spoken word thing. The bitch *knows* this is my first time coming to some shit like this. Then tells me how she comes to these shows at least four days a week, and talking 'bout how it's mandatory I come with her as long as I'm in Miami. I don't like this shit like *that*!" Santana laughed.

"Yeah, I know the shit's funny but here goes the weird part…the bitch said since I'm the man from her dreams it's non-negotiable for me to carry out her wildest fantasy."

"I'm a little afraid to ask but what's that?" "She wants me to fuck her midair." "That's not as weird as I thought. It sounds like she's got all types of kinky shit at her crib that you can hang her from.""Naw, Santana. The bitch wants *both* of us in the air."

"What in the *hell* type of gadgets she got that can hold both of y'all in mid-air while y'all fuckin'?" "What part don't you understand, Santana. *Ain't* no fuckin' gadgets!" "*Now* it's starting to sound weird. What in the hell is supposed to hold y'all in the air while y'all fuckin'?"

"*Nothing*! The bitch wants to go skydiving and start fuckin' while we're on the plane and then - while I'm still inside of her - she wants us to just jump off the motherfucka'. She has this theory that says the thrill she'd get from the sex in the sky added to the danger of knowing possible death is below us should equal out to a record number of ten orgasms she'd have before we hit the ground." Santana spit out all of the drink he was sipping he was laughing so hard.

"That bitch is crazy *forreal*." "I told you that shit." "So when are y'all going skydiving?" "Tomorrow." They both were in an uproar.

"Nigga, you know I'm bullshittin'." "Yeah, I know you're not *that* fucked up in the head. What's her name?" "Maxine Montana." "She kin to Tony?" Santana joked. "That's just a movie. She isn't Cuban, she's Columbian."

"You're talkin' that crazy shit about her, but I'll bet you a bando you're smashin' her tonight." "Like a *dawg*. I figure for as long as I've been jammed up with her ass, I might as well get some compensation for my conversation."

"I feel you on that." "I can't complain, she may not be as thick as the broad you met but she's still sexy. Plus she sounds like she's a super freak."

"While you're busy getting freaked out by her, I'll be having sex on the beach and making sure the spot's in a good enough location to land the sub. So you'll have the penthouse all to yourself." "I'm not sure if that sounds like a good or a bad thing."

"Why you say that?" "Because the crazy bitch might try to push me over the balcony." "Sounds like you have yourself a handful." "Guess I'll find out soon enough." "You *sure* will because she's coming this way." "Aww, damn."

"Hey, Levi. I've been looking all over for you. I see you've reunited with your friend. I hope I'm not interrupting you guys," said Maxine. "Naw, Maxine, not at all. This guy here is my brother, Santana. Santana, meet Maxine."

"Nice to meet you, Maxine." "Same here, Santana. I saw how you had the owner's undivided attention. I've never seen her talk to anyone for a length of time besides her staff. She greets her customers and all, but that's about as far as it goes."

Santana chose not to entertain Maxine's comment about Jasmine and squirmed his way from out of their company by saying, "Hey, I'm sorry you guys but I really need to get to the men's room before I have an accident. So he's all yours, Maxine. Again, it was nice meeting you. And Levi, I'll catch up with you later."

Coming from out of the restroom Santana witnessed Jasmine exiting her office with her personal belongings as if she were retiring for the remainder of the evening. He looked on as she surveyed the club until her eyes found their target. Him. A smile instantly crept over her face as they drew nearer to each other.

"Looks like you're about to make a run for it. Going somewhere?" asked Santana. "Sure am and you're coming with me. You ready?"

"As I've ever been." "What about your friend? He knows you're leaving?" "Yeah, I told him. Looks like he's occupied for the night, anyway." "I saw him over there conversing with what's her face?...Maxine. She's...a little off her rocker."

"He already knows. He's just enjoying the city." "Well, let's get out of here so I can make sure you do the same." Santana smiled and said," After you."

# CHAPTER 25

JASMINE'S JAGUAR PURRED as she took Santana on the scenic route through the city. She showed him some spots she frequented, the neighborhood she grew up in, and a few places which might spark his interest for his nightclub.

"Wha'duya think about *that* building?" asked Jasmine. "It's a nice sized club. What's its history?" "The owners name is Brandon Jackson. He played in the league years ago for the Dolphins until he tore his ACL then got the boot. Business was booming for him up until recently."

"What happened?" "Last month the D.E.A. raided the club in search for Molly and Ecstacy pills. They got a tip that Brandon was distributing thousands of pills weekly from out of the club. They came up empty but almost fifty people went to jail for parole violations and outstanding warrants. It gave the club a black eye because ever since that night, Brandon hasn't been able to pack the house. He's mentioned to me that he wants out of the business. So, your timing couldn't have been better because all of his regulars have dispersed in search for another club to congregate and they'll fall right into your lap."

Santana knew she made a valid point. He could start out on a good note immediately. But being from New Orleans, Santana witnessed the outcome of a nightclub that left A bad taste in the mouths of the community. It was the most popular hangout called *Club Rumors* which was a good place to have a nice time but also a good place to get murdered. Once the city got fed up with all of the killings, the owners were forced to make a change. That change was renaming *Club Rumors* to *Club GQ21*. Things ran smooth for a while but then the murders started again and eventually, the city vetoed the building from ever becoming a nightclub again.

Then Santana recalled one of the jewels Kevin Kash dropped on him from one of their many sit-downs, '*If you build it, the people will come.*' He decided right then and there that that's what he'd do. Besides, he was a trendsetter and saw no need to save a ship that already sank.

"I understand where you're coming from with picking up the ball from where Brandon fumbled but, Jaz, you just helped me realize exactly what I want." "What do you have in mind?"

"Either a building that's never been a club before or built from the ground up." "New construction will be too costly. I'm not saying you don't have the funding but it'll take a while before you can open up for business. And you can get the same point across with an existing building after you refurbish it."

"You know what I think, Jaz?" "What?" "I think you'd make an excellent financial advisor." "I think you'd make an excellent club owner." "How would *you* know? You've only known me for two hours." "Trust me, I can spot class a galaxy away. I would've never approached you otherwise, and you have way more swagger than *any* of the club owners *I* know."

"Thanks for the compliment. So, do you know of any other locations worth looking at?" "I'm thinking now. What size and type of club are you looking for *exactly*?" "That's easy. I want the biggest and most exclusive nightclub in Miami Beach. Preferably in a location that's guaranteed to bring the millionaires out to play."

She scanned through the geographical map inside her mind then it hit her, "I know the perfect place." "Where is it?" "Right here in Miami Beach. It's about twenty minutes away from my house. You'll love it."

The building was a three level furniture store that went out of business with a sign on it that read: *For Sale By Owner 786-555-6562.*

"Now *this* is what I'm talking about. A wise man once told me that if I was ever going to do something, do it big. And it don't get any bigger than this," said Santana.

"That number looks familiar," Jasmine said as she retrieved her cell phone and started dialing the number." "I *know* you're not calling that number *this* late in the evening." "If the seller had certain hours they wanted potential buyers to call I'm pretty sure they would've specified that on the for sale sign. I doubt they care whatever time it is that phone rings if they're about to make a big payday."

"I guess you have a point, I mean, it's not *that* late anyhow." "Hold up, someone's answering. 'Hi, please excuse my timing but I'm really interested in the property you have for sale.'" "Which property, ma'am?" "The old furniture store, sir."

"Okay, as you may already know, it has three floors, approximately thirty thousand square feet on each level, it's in an upscale location, and zoned for basically any type of business. The building's been unoccupied for quite some time and needs lots of repairs so it's listed to sell for five point five million. So if you're *really* motivated then you may want to get on it sooner than later because I already have plenty of offers who are all waiting on financing."

"Are there any liens against the title or outstanding mortgages?" "No ma'am I own it free and clear. Excuse me for asking but *who* am I speaking with?" "My apologies, sir. My name is Jasmine. Jasmine Diaz." "Jasmine Diaz from the Red Room?"

"Yes, sir. Do you know me?" "Of *course* I do. I sold your father the building he bought for you. And I must say, I've heard lots of wonderful things about the Red Room."

"Mr. Pat Riley?! I *knew* I'd seen that number somewhere before." "So, are you looking to do something bigger?" "No, actually I'm calling on behalf of a dear friend of mine." "Which means they're a friend of your father which makes them a friend of mine. Shit! There goes my new Lamborghini and shopping spree in Milan."

"Wha'duya mean?" "It means I can't charge a dear friend of yours that amount. Your father would have my head delivered to my wife in a box."

"I'm sure he'd understand. It's your investment and this is a part of business." "I know, Jasmine, but I'm not strapped for cash so if I can pass the building on to someone you find favor in then a price reduction is in order. And I'm sure they'll do well with their new business."

"I can't argue with that, Mr. Riley." "So, what does your friend want to do with it?" "Turn it into a nightclub." "Wow! That'll be one big nightclub. The biggest in all of Florida, I believe." "He said that's what he wanted."

"So what's his name?" "Santana Bailey from out of New Orleans." "Never heard of 'em. But you tell him to come with four point seven five and the building is his."

Jasmine had the phone on speaker the entire time and the price reduction had Santana grinning from ear to ear. She hunched her shoulders for approval and Santana replied with a hand gesture of four point seven with a thumbs up.

"Okay, Mr. Riley, four point seven million and you have yourself a deal." "*Christ!* Can he hear me?" "Yeah, I've got you on speaker." "Mr. Bailey, sir, please excuse my french but you're busting my balls more than LeBron's agent. But all right, you got yourself a deal. And by the way, you owe me *big time*, Jasmine Diaz. Dinner's on you for me *and* my wife and Mr. Bailey gets his building."

"Thanks a million. Just give me a heads up for a day your schedule's clear, Mr. Riley, and I got you." "Good." "When is a good time for you to do a showing?" "Tomorrow around noonish."

"We'll be there...but before you go, Mr. Riley, I have a quick question. "Wha'chu got?" "What did you mean by LeBron's agent giving you a hard time?" "That kinda slipped when I said that. This goes no further than you so you can't tell a soul, okay?" "My lips are sealed." "I'm working a deal that'll bring Lebron to the Heat in a few years. Just wait and see."

"That would be wonderful because D. Wade definitely needs help if Miami ever wants win another championship." "Tell me about it."

"And one more thing…you got any floors seats on hand so I could show my friend a good time?" "I can do you one better than *that*. Anyone who's about to put four point seven million dollars in my pockets can use *my* skybox."

# CHAPTER 26

AS JASMINE NEGOTIATED the price, Santana saved the address in his cell phone. After she ended the call, Santana said, "Thanks for saving me a few jingles." "You don't owe me any thanks. I would expect the same from you if it were the other way around. Now you have extra money for renovations."

"Sounds like your father has clout in this city." "People like him around here. He was the number two guy at a Hedge fund firm called Hankton, Prince, and Hoover. The company's in the Fortune 500 and my dad actually had the privilege of gracing the cover of the Forbes magazine."

"That's impressive." "Yeah, their company had former Governor Jeb Bush as a client at one point. But when George W. won the seat by the deciding vote that was in the hands of Florida, my father severed ties with the firm and publicly spoke out against the way things were handled." "So he worked for the ex-Governor but didn't like him?"

"First of all, you don't have to like a person to work for them. But that wasn't the case with my father. It didn't matter to him if the scales tipped in Bush *or* Gore's favor. He's all about fairness and the people who shared the same views donned him as the number one *Advocate of Righteousness.* Since then, political figures, sports figures, entertainers, business owners, average Joes and everyone else in between have all treated my father like royalty."

"Sounds like a Cinderella story." "It does, doesn't it?" "And I take it you're the princess." "You got *that* right." "How'd he meet Pat Riley?" "My father's the commodore of a yacht club where Mr. Riley's a member."

"So, basically anything you wish for is at your disposal?" "Pretty much. Just mentioning my father's name and I get a discount." "I'd cash my name in if I could get the red carpet rolled out like *you* do." "Since you can afford that building, I think your name seems to be working just fine if you ask me."

"Your father sounds like a great man. I'd like to meet him one day." "I'm sure he'd be delighted as well." "I really appreciate the love price Mr. Riley gave me on the strength of your father. Just know that I never use people because of who they know. I got my own lane." "You've got to be the first guy I've met who could care less about my father's influence. Now, enough about him, let's get inside."

"When you said your house was in a private area, I see you really meant it." "I don't do neighbors. People are too nosey." "You have any children?" "No way. I enjoy my free time. How about you?" "None that I *know* of. But I'm thinking that this is one of those rare moments when I should try making a political baby. Then I'll be connected with you for life."

"Have you lost your *mind*?! I don't plan on having kids *anytime* soon." "I'm only kidding." "Oh, okay. You had me scared for a second." "So, what's a lonely girl like you need with all this space?" "I'd rather have too much space than not enough." "You seem to have an answer for everything, don't you?" "What woman doesn't?"

Santana trailed as she led him to the kitchen. "Make yourself at home. If you're hungry, I have some really good Jamaican jerk leftovers in the fridge." "Don't mind if I *do* eat. My damn ribs are touchin'."

"I don't know about you but I could use a drink." "Me too. Wha'chu got?" "I just restocked the wet bar, so what'll you have?" "Got any *Balboa*?" "Of course. *Balboa is* my favorite tequila. Double shot?" "That's cool." "On the rocks?" "One ice cube." "Coming up."

Santana was sitting in the living room admiring posters of Bob Marley and Jimi Hendrix, an Andy Warhol painting, and other of Jasmine's taste in decor when she came in with their drinks.

"Let's make a toast, Santana." "To what?" "A toast to a newfound friendship, a new beginning, and to a successful career in the nightclub industry. Cheers!" "Cheers!" **CLING!** "Bottoms up...*aah*, that'll loosen me up. You already know where the food is so feel free to help yourself while I go freshen up and slip into something a little more comfortable." "Yes, ma'am."

Twenty minutes later, she came out wearing a bra top and boy shorts. "How was the food?" "It was good as hell." "I knew you'd like it." "You gotta show me where the restaurant is where you got it from." "I cooked it myself." "Ohh...I see I have a little chef on my hands, ehh?" "I love to cook." "Well you're in for a treat young lady because I'm known for moving around in the kitchen, *too*."

"Oh really?" "You said that like I probably couldn't boil water. I see now that I gotta make you out of a believer." "You sure do." "One of these days, I'm gonna come in here and whip up a dish of that real old-fashioned New Orleans style seafood gumbo. It's nothing like that thrown together shit they be serving in the French Quarters." "Mmm, that sounds good. Now you got me hungry."

Jasmine hopped off the sofa and said, "You ready now?" Santana grinned and responded, "For what?" "To show you my backyard." "Oh. Yeah, I'm ready." "You thought I was talking about sex, didn't you?" "I'm busted." "They said y'all New Orleans boys are fast." "You got one more time to say something about my city." "Okay, no more comments. I swear. Now take off your shoes and let's go play in the sand."

"It feels like utopia every single time I come out here. Isn't it a gorgeous sight?" A sense of exaltation rushed over Santana from how he saw his plan formulating just as he'd envisioned. Not only was the location perfect, she also had a boathouse that would mask the submarine's view.

"Yeah, it's a beautiful sight." "You should see it out here when the sunsets." With the ocean breeze blowing through Santana's linen *Givenchy* short set, he said, "the weather's so refreshing." "Isn't it, though? I couldn't dream of living any place else."

"You love it here *that* much?" "Like it's the last place on *earth*. There are so many things here that I love to do." "Like what?" "Like, going to the beach, jet skiing, riding my speedboat over there, and the yacht parties…they're the *craziest*. But most of all is because of the diversity of our city's multiple cultures."

"Sounds like you're fascinated with anything associated with water." She smiled as she responded, "You're such a smart cookie, Santana. Now you've figured out why I picked this house."

As she guided him towards the speedboat his cell phone chimed. He'd been ignoring all of his calls since he arrived in Miami until he saw it was Korey Witha K.

"Wuzzam, Korey?" "Just coolin', big homie. How you livin'?" "Just runnin' my toes through the sand. What's up?" "I was just giving you a heads up that me and Get'em were in motion and we'll link up with y'all tomorrow afternoon sometime." "That's a bet. Just holla back when y'all touch down." Santana disconnected the call.

"Sorry about that, Jaz. I had to take that call." "No need for apologies. You're a business man. Wanna go for a ride?" "Sure, why not."

Jasmine cranked up her two-seater then they were skirting across the waters and into the night.

"You're a little speed demon, aren't you?" asked Santana. "I've been called a lot worse." "Just looking at the boat before we took off I would've never thought it moved this fast." "If you think this is fast, we haven't hit top speed yet." "Well, what are you waiting for? Push it to the limit."

"I can't right now because it's time for me to get the engine serviced." "How long before that happens?" "The mechanic's swinging by tomorrow to bring it to the shop and I should get it back in a week. So, tonight's the last night to take it for a ride until it returns."

Santana's mind was doing cartwheels and jumping for joy. The idea of the boathouse being cleared for when the submarine arrived was the icing on the cake. Then about fifteen minutes away from the shores of Florida, she killed the engine.

She pointed to the sky, "You see that arrangement of stars over there? They call that Orion's Belt. Those over there are the Little Dipper and that big baby over there is the Big Dipper." "Should I be adding astrologist to your resume now?"

"No, silly. I learned about that in grade school." "I believe I skipped class on the day *that* was taught." "If it was daytime, you could actually see the Bahamas from my telescope." "I didn't know it was *that* close to Miami."

As Santana stared towards the Bahamas, she leaned over to steal a kiss. Then piece by piece of their clothing fell and they had passionate sex under the moon in the middle of nowhere.

# CHAPTER 27

WHILE EATING THE INTERCONTINENTAL BREAKFAST Jasmine prepared, Santana received another important call. "What's poppin', Santana?" asked Derrick. "Out here in Miami Beach according to plan. Wha'chu got?" "Ham, Chinky, and I have everything we could think of that'll be of help. We're gonna get a head start and fly to South America today to track down a contact we have out there to pick up on a few more items."

"That's cool. Just make sure to keep in contact so we can link up when we get there." "We already have that covered. Ham met with Get'em and Korey before they headed your way and gave them four satellite radios and earpieces which are already set on the same frequency as ours."

"Good. So the next time I hear from you guys , it'll be over the radio, correct?" "Correct." "Then I'll see y'all in Columbia." "Aight, Santana."

On her phone as well, Jasmine went out onto the deck in the backyard to join Santana after seeing him end the call.

"*'Yeah, he's right here. I'll ask 'em'.* Santana…Mr. Riley wants to meet with us in the next hour. Are you ready to see the building?" "As ready as ever. Tell'em we'll be there."

Santana quickly reached for his cell. "Levi, you up yet?" "Am I up? That sex fiend didn't let me get any sleep!" "Wild night, huh?" "That's an accurate way to describe it. She's gone now, so what's up?" "I need you to grab my suitcase with the gold handle and meet up with me within the next hour. I'll text you the address and the specifics after we hang up." "Aight, bet."

Without a change of clothing, Santana was faced with viewing the building in yesterday's threads. "Jaz, I have these stains on my shorts we made last night and there won't enough time to rush to the hotel for a change clothes and then make it to the building within an hour's time. So is there a store nearby where I can grab something from real quick?" "Sure. I'll run you over to the *Balenciaga* store over on NE 40<sup>th</sup> street. The stores are just about to open so you'd be in and out."

A Rolls Royce Phantom was the only car in the parking lot when Santana and Jasmine pulled in. As they walked over to greet the car a tall slender Italian man wearing an Italian suit opened the suicide back door and out came Mr. Riley.

"Jasmine, my darling. How've you been?" asked Mr. Riley. "I've been fine. Sorry we're late." "*Nonsense.* I just got here a minute ago. And you are Mr. Santana Bailey, correct?"

"Yes, sir." "Pat Riley. Pleasure to meet you." "Likewise." The two shook hands. "Now that the meet and greet's over let's get down to business, shall we?"

Mr. Riley took his time walking them through every level of the building. Jasmine played the role of a natural born secretary the way she jotted down every detail of the changes Santana wanted to make. She even chipped in with her two cents by giving him some very good pointers.

In Santana's eyes, the building was exactly what he wanted and the change he would need to ease his way out of the ruthless drug world. And he was minutes away from making the first step towards following his mentor's advice.

After wrapping up the forty-five minute long tour they headed back outside. A third car was in the parking lot but neither of the three bothered to give the car a second look. "So, wha'duya think, Mr. Bailey?" asked Mr. Riley.

"I think I'll take it." "Great. Now, who do you bank with?" "Bailey Bank and Trust." "I've never heard of that branch before. Are they local?" Santana motioned a hand signal to the third car then Levi came out of it with a briefcase in hand walking towards them.

In the text Santana sent Levi it included the address along with instructions to take out eight hundred thousand of that five and a half million that was in the suitcase to make Mr. Riley's money exact. Levi handed the suitcase over to Santana then went back to his car.

"I guess you *can* say it's local. Here you go, Mr. Riley...four point seven million dollars to the penny." Mr. Riley smiled with a devilish grin and said, "I like your style, young man. Hey, Jasmine, where'd you find *him*? He's *my* kind of guy."

"I think it's safe to say we found each other." "Mr. Bailey, I've already alerted the title company that you were coming over so they're expecting you. They have the paperwork drawn up and I've already signed them. So, the sooner you get there the sooner you'll become the proud owner of your new property. And with that being said, congratulations are in order, Mr. Bailey. I wish you much success." The two men shook hands once again.

"Thank you, Mr. Riley. Nice doing business with you." "Anytime. And the agent also has those skybox passes for you so don't forget. And *you*, young lady, take care of yourself and have the old man give me a holler." "Will do, Mr. Riley. See you later."

Jasmine waited patiently in her car as Santana conversed with Levi. "Santana, was that Pat Riley?" "Yeah, that was him." "What was *he* doing here?" "Selling me my new club." "You're turning that big ass building into a club?" "And you know this...*man*."

"You outdid yourself this time, my nigga. This spot's gonna be something major. Got a name in mind?" Santana faced the building and thought hard for a second then turned to Levi and said, "the only thing that comes to mind when I look at that building to think of what it's going to be... and that's *The Million Dollar Spot*."

"So what's next on the agenda for the day?" "Why are you asking? What you got a skydiving appointment to get to or something?" "Fuck you, nigga." The two shared a laugh.

"Seriously though, I was about to ask if you brought that eight hundred grand with you." "Yeah, it's in the car." "We'll let me get that out 'cha so I can finish handling the rest of this business with the building and we'll link up back at the hotel once I'm done runnin' with Jasmine."

# CHAPTER 28

ONCE THE DEAL WAS ETCHED IN STONE at the title company, Santana said, "Hey, Jaz, I want to thank you for taking the time from your own schedule to assist me with everything. You've been terrific and here's a little token of my gratitude." Santana handed her fifty thousand dollars. "I can't accept *that*! Besides, I told you that I'd expect the same in return and I sure wouldn't be doling out *this* much money if all you did was show me a building and chauffeured me around."

"Either take it or this friendship is officially over." "Ooh…you are so stubborn. All right, I'll take it. But only because you're twisting my arm. I'm gonna get you back for this Santana…just mark my word."

"Don't think of it that way, Jaz. I consider that to be free money because if I would've consented to Mr. Riley's initial discount that fifty thousand dollars would be in his possession right now.

"But I thought of you when I asked him to drop it down to four point seven so I could squeeze something out of the deal for a broker's fee." "But I'm no broker."

"You might as well be one because without you Mr. Riley would still have a building for sale and I'd still be looking for one." "Since you put it that way, thanks a lot."

"Jasmine, do you remember the upgrades I was talking about during the walk-through?" "Of course I remember… I wrote it all down. So, what about it?" "For everything I want done to the building, can you give me a ballpark figure of about how much you think it would run me?"

"By me knowing a good contractor who's been sweet on me since like… *forever*, I'd say roughly in between the ranges of five and seven hundred thousand and that's with the bar fully stocked and open for business. Who knows, he may even do it for free if I ever decided to show him some interest. But then it would be more like you were pimping me out if I did that."

"I would ask you to do no such thing. But I *will* do this…take this money right here. It's three- quarters of a million. I want you to be my overseer for this project, Jaz. Just take care of everything we discussed and get it open for business as soon as possible. And anything under that budget is yours to keep. But if by chance you were to run short on funds, I'll get the money to you. Can you handle that for me?" "Sure, Santana. I'll jump on it right away."

As Jasmine parked at the hotel to drop off Santana, he said, "I've got other affairs out of town but I'll back in a few days. So if you don't make any money off the deal I'll put something in your pockets when I return."

"You've given me enough money already. I'm more than sure this will cover everything," Jasmine said as she lifted the bag full of money. "For the record, Jaz, I won't think any less of you if you decide to come up on a few extra grand by giving that contractor guy the plumbing job he's probably dying to give you. Then it wouldn't be considered as me pimping you." She sucked her teeth at Santana as she hissed, "You're absolutely right. Assuming the role of a high-priced hooker has a better ring to it, so don't even go there."

As Santana exited the car, she called out, "Santana." "Wassup, sexy?" "I've never done anything like I'm about to do ever *before*, so hear me out. It doesn't sit right with me to know you're staying at a hotel. So I want you to keep this so you can have a place to stay whenever you're in town." Jasmine tossed Santana a set of keys to her house. He looked down at the keys for a moment then back at her.

"You sure about this, Jaz?' "Of course I am. If you could trust me with *this* kind of money it's only natural that I trust you in return. Not to mention you've already sampled my goodies."

"But what if you have company and I pop up in the wee hours of the morning?" "Company?! Please. You're the only *company* that's ever seen my new house so consider yourself as lucky." "I do. Now keep me posted on everything involving the building." "I will, Santana. Talk to you soon."

"Levi! You in here?!" Santana yelled. "Yeah, I'm in the kitchen!" "Are we alone?" "Yeah, ole girl struck out this morning right before you called." "Nigga, you'll *never* guess what I came up on." "There's something besides that big ass building?"

"Hell yeah, my nigga…these keys right here." "What are they for?" "The spot I needed to dock the submarine." "Damn, you work fast. I thought we were gonna scope that out today. So, where's the spot?"

"Jasmine's house. And *these* are the keys to her crib." Santana dangled the keys in the air." "I remember you saying she lived by the ocean." "She *told* me her backyard was the Atlantic and she meant every word."

"That's wuzzam. Now we have a whole day ahead of us. So what's next?" "House hunting." "Damn, my nigga. You buying a house and all? Looks like New Orleans in the wind fa' sho *now*."

"I'm not getting a house yet. I want a condo in one of those high rises for the moment. But you're right, Levi… it's over for me living in New Orleans. At least full time, anyway. When I bought that building this morning that sealed the deal for me moving out here."

"You know I'm wit 'cha, my nigga. I'll just be back and forth cause Lord *knows* I can'thave them ole shade tree ass niggas in the city cooking my coke."

"That's another thing… I'm *still* gonna hook up the packages until whatever's on that submarine's all gone. And after that, I'm done with that life. If you, Korey, and Get'em decide to keep hustlin' afterwards, I'll just pass my skills onto whichever one of you still chooses that route.

"I don't know about Korey and Get'em but I won't need it. I'm leaving the game behind, too, since I'll be straight enough with my paper to make my own power move."

"That's exactly what I wanted to hear, Levi. All I have to do now is get Korey and Get'em on the same page so that my whole team will be legit. I doubt they're ready to quit cold turkey because they're still young. But at least I'll have that bug planted in their minds." "Speaking of those two, have you heard from them lately?"

"As a matter of fact, Korey hit me last night to let me know they were en route with the truck. They should be here in the next couple of hours. By that time I should have my condo and the four of us can hit the beach and fuck with the hoes."

# CHAPTER 29

**In the jungles of Medellin, Columbia
March 1, 2008, 6:15 p.m.**

"HEY THERE MY OLD FRIENDS. It's been a long time. So what brings you guys to theses parts of the world?" asked Antonio Gomez. "We're in need of some heavy duty hardware and we couldn't think of a better source than you," Chinky responded. "Well, you all have come to the right place, Amigos. Come with me so I can show you my selection."

Ham, Derrick, and Chinky followed Antonio into his bunker. "Okay, guys, this is my war chest. I don't know exactly what you're looking for but I am sure you will find some pieces of heavy duty artillery in here to suit your needs."

The trio's eyes grew wider and wider as Antonio opened up compartment after compartment. Antonio had weapons galore.

Everything imported. There was an assortment of assault rifles: M-16's, AR-15's, and AK-47's to name a few.

"Holy shit, Antonio. There's enough hardware in here to overthrow a goddamn third world *country*." said Chinky. "In my line of work, Tri, you have to stay ahead of the game."

"Is that a toy over there?" asked Ham. "I wouldn't leave that *nowhere* near a kid if *I* were you. It's one of my newest gadget that just hit the market. Pretty neat, actually. It's a helicopter drone that's equipped with a camera and night vision. That baby'll spit out more friggin' rounds than four AK-47's." "Just when I thought I was up on technology," said Chinky.

"How many of those you got in stock?" asked Derrick. "That one, my friend, is the only one in South America." "Box it up, Antonio. It's comin' with us." "Got any more disguisable weapons laying around?" asked Derrick. "That's about all I have at the moment. No wait…I almost forgot. There's these special necklaces I've been having for a while that I can't seem to sell."

"What kind of necklace is it?" asked Ham. "It's called the kamikaze pendant." "What can it do?" asked Chinky.

After Antonio explained all of the details of the necklace, Derrick began sweating profusely. "I *see* why you can't sell them motherfuckas'!" said Ham. "Hold up, guys. I really think we're overthinking those pendants. I believe they'll be a valuable asset to our cause," Chinky pleaded.

Derrick looked at Chinky as if he'd officially lost his mind and said, "You know something, Chinky, you are one insane motherfucka' but I'm riding with you on this one." "What about you, Ham?" asked Chinky. "Fuck it, they don't call me Ham for nothin'. We'll take seven of 'em, Antonio."

During the next half hour the trio stockpiled all of the weapons and ammunition they needed to get the job done. Afterwards, they sat around with Antonio trading war stories and reliving events from their last tour of duty together in Columbia. And as darkness reigned over the skies above the reunion came to a halt.

Derrick, Ham, and Chinky forged ahead on their excursion leaving behind, ex-delta force soldier, Antonio Gomez. They made it to an abandoned warehouse in which they'd passed along the way to locate Antonio and claimed it as their resting place and headquarters. A safe house by default - if you will.

They dedicated their spare time to setting up maps of the drop-off point, practicing tactics, and devising strategies for the sneak attack. And after hours of sharing thoughts and training, the trio ceased their actions and rested up until the arrival of Santana.

# CHAPTER 30



"I'M OUT MY *BODY* ouchea, big brudda. The whole beach gridlocked with bad bitches," said Get'em as he scanned the entire beach in search for every woman in a bikini. "This is all day action in M.I.A., Get'em. It goes down even harder on the weekends, summertime, and spring break," Santana responded.

"Fuckin' round with this city, a nigga'll have insomnia like a motherfucka', " Korey Witha K added. "Speaking of insomnia, I haven't had a lick of sleep since I got here," said Levi.

Being an instigator, Santana replayed the story of Levi's date. After everyone settled down from laughing so hard Korey Witha K said, "You better sleep with one eye open around that type of broad, Levi. Sounds like she's on some Lorena Bobbitt type of shit."

Then Get'em professed, "Y'all niggas talkin' that shit. Maxine sounds like *my* kinda girl. And if you don't want the bitch, Levi, let *me* have the hoe. I'm *tweakin'* to jump off a fuckin' plane!" They all were in stitches.

For hours they enjoyed themselves like they didn't have a care in the world. They went water skiing for a while. Then parasailing. And while they were jet skiing, they tried their best to knock each other in the water. And after maxing out the fun they had with watersports, they took their recreational time to the sand.

Santana and Korey Witha K chose to partake in a volleyball match against two hardbody divas who challenged them to a duel. Levi found pleasure in throwing a Frisbee with a female he met. And Get'em returned to his childhood days by attempting to build sand castles with a girl who was a freshman cheerleader at the University of Miami.

As Santana took in the splendid view of the sunset in which Jasmine spoke of, he knew it was time for a change of settings. They found themselves in the living room of Santana's extravagant condo admiring Miami's skyline from elevated heights.

"Damn, big brudda, you ain't been in Miami for nothing but a day and you already copped a club and a fly ass crib?! You be dropping' your nuts for everything," Get'em declared as he stepped foot inside Santana's new home for the first time.

"You only live once and self-made niggas do as they please. So it's imperative that I put on every chance I get." "To see you winning is inspirational to me, my nigga. You're on some George and Weezy shit. Yeah, *Dat Way*," Korey Witha K implied.

Santana stood in front of his ceiling to floor windows gazing out into the city as he came to grips with the admiration his young gunners had towards him. He had a premonition that post-Columbia, they'd all breathe, eat, sleep, and shit success. They were his team. Each of them had come from nothing but all roads would point upwards for them in the imminent future.

"In due time, guys, we'll all be calling shots in our own spots," Santana declared. "Speaking of calling, Derrick gave us these radios before my brother and I left New Orleans," Get'em recalled as he fetched the devices from a duffle bag.

"He alerted me earlier this morning about them. Let me see one of those things."

Santana turned on the radio then plugged in an earpiece, "Come in, Derrick. Can you hear me?" "Loud and clear, Santana. You're in Columbia, already?" "Negative." "I thought you were gonna call when you got here." "I was, but I wanted to test the strength of the signal."

"As you can see, they're working as if we're standing next to each other." "I see that. So, how are things coming along with locating that contact out there?" "We found 'em and we got more than we bargained for. The only things we're missing are the four of you and some mosquito repellant."

"Sounds great. I love it when a plan comes together. So, where are the others?" "Ham's right here and Chinky's outside playing with one of the toys we picked up on." "Are y'all situated yet?"

"We stumbled across a safe house about thirty miles east of ground zero and it's segregated from civilization." "Good job,

Derrick. You guys keep a low profile in the meantime and we'll see you all tomorrow."

Boredom began to take its course as they sat around in Santana plush condo. Santana thought about the possibility of someone in that very room not ensured to make it back from Columbia. Since their flight was scheduled for the next morning there still was enough time to paint the town with his closest friends and *SoccaBall* to the fullest as if it were their last time.

"Hey, fellas, since tonight's our last night in Miami until we return, the floor's open to suggestions as to where we're going for some last minute fun," Santana implied. "I don't know about y'all, but I wanna hit the strip club to see some ass and tits," Korey Witha K recommended. "That sounds like a plan. Any of you got one in mind?" asked Santana.

"I do. There's one called *King of Diamonds*. I heard they be having hundreds of top-of-the-line bitches in there whose on the same level as J-Lo and Halle Berry and shit," Levi pointed out.

Get'em responded, "I'mma cut up *bad* in that motherfucka'. Show 'em how a New Orleans nigga do it, ya *heard* meh?! So we might as well vote now on whose gonna be the designated driver because tonight I'm gettin' white boy wasted."

Gathered from the intelligence Levi received about *King of Diamonds*, he had a reliable source. Get'em made good on his word by downing drink after drink from the minute they hit the door. He spent the majority of his time entertaining every dancer to grace the stage by making it rain all one dollar bills. Ten thousand in total as if he were the sole heir of Jeff Bezos or Carlos Slim.

"Well if it isn't New Orleans' finest- himself, Santana Bailey. The man with the golden touch whose name is engraved in stone by all Bosses as Mr. America's Most Wanted. And most importantly, the *only* man I know who can show up in my city unannounced."

"My man, Hurricane El Jefe - the Boss of Miami. Last I heard you were still runnin' the city with an iron fist. Must be a wonderful feeling to always have the sun shining your way." "I've seen better days whenever *you're* in town, Santana. But other than that, I can't complain."

"You come here a lot to let off some steam?" "Steam? No. For business? Yes. And that's only to play the car switch game. As we speak a transaction is being made. There are two vehicles outside: one with money. The other with fifty kilos of cocaine."

"El Jefe, a man of your significance certainly shouldn't be getting his hands dirty anymore." "Right you are, Santana. I never touch a thing. My driver is in the restroom exchanging keys of the vehicles with the worker of another Boss who's down from Georgia. By the time the next dancer comes to the stage, my money'll be in transit to one of my stash houses and the drugs'll be on their way to Atlanta."

"Those traits should carry you very far, El Jefe." "So should yours, Santana." "What are you talking about?" "As of now, the rate of your services went up another five percent." "That isn't true. Who told you that?" "Your name has been resonating in various circuits amongst the Bosses throughout the states pertaining to something you unearthed about a month ago and we've all concurred that you are the best in your craft and indeed worthy of a raise."

Santana suddenly felt as if a spotlight that he couldn't see had been cast down upon him. He knew Hurricane El Jefe was referring to the incident in Columbia when he exposed Hector. The only witnesses were Donavan Mercadel and Javier Ochoa. Santana wasn't sure how Hurricane El Jefe got that information, but asked for clarification.

"What exactly is it that the Bosses *think* I discovered?" Hurricane El Jefe smiled at Santana. "It's not that many things which can be kept secret in a small world, Santana. Always remember that the Bosses are all affiliated in one form or another. It's a brotherhood creed that we have, comprende'? Now to terminate your curiosity, let me explain.

"My former connect, Hector, was brutally murdered in Columbia when you and Donavan were there and the new guy, Domingo, spoke good things about you as he told me and a few of the other Bosses what took place."

"I didn't know you knew Donavan." "I just told you we're affiliated. Every time Hector came to Miami to deliver a shipment Donavan and I always ran into each other. In fact I seen him about a month ago when we both got our last package."

"So the four hundred kilos were all for you?" "My ticket was supposed to be five hundred. But when the new guy, Domingo, arrived with the package, he said Javier ordered him to give an allotment of one hundred kilos to Donavan because of what Hector had done."

Santana was overcome by the extent of knowledge Hurricane El Jefe had on him and enlightened with certain specifics he was unaware of. He recalled being in Miami a month ago telling Donavan, others must be waiting also. It was Hurricane El Jefe.

He knew Donavan was too solid to speak on his name. Hurricane El Jefe was right about Domingo. It was Domingo who was in Javier's office that day to hear about Hector and was awarded his spot. Domingo who'd mentioned his name over the wire. And Domingo whose loose lips had caused the Bosses to congregate at some round table to discuss his finances.

Now that Santana knew that the Nariño cartel was Hurricane El Jefe's supplier, the *Columbian Job* would affect him as well as Donavan and other Bosses.

Santana figured now would be the perfect time to mention the building he purchased so it wouldn't arouse any suspicions as to why he was in Miami just days before the heist. Also, not to look like he came up on some type of fortune afterwards.

"Looks like you know people in high places, El Jefe. Everything you've said was on the mark. But I want you to pass on this message to the rest of the Bosses: I appreciate them coming together to offer me a generous raise for my art form but Santana Bailey's officially out of the business."

Hurricane El Jefe had a look on his face as if Santana dropped a nuke on him. "Out of the *business*?! Why on earth would you *do* such a thing?"

"Because I came here to Miami to open up a new club." "A *club*? But a club won't make you as nearly as much if you take on the jobs that the Bosses all have lined up for you." "Trust me, El Jefe, that is very well understood. But it's not about how much money I can make. It's about doing things differently with my life." "What made that change in your life find its way to Miami?"

"Since you're well versed about the details of my trip to Columbia it couldn't hurt to tell you why I made my decision. When Donavan and I flew here after we left Columbia, I went my own way just riding around Miami for hours. And during that time I thought about my present and my future.

"I've made millions with these hands and I really don't have anything to show for it besides money. All I know is drugs and you know as well as I do that very few in our field get to retire without seeing either prison or death in which neither is an option for me.

"So I figured no time was better than the now to get out while I'm still young with a hefty sized nest egg set up for myself. And before I flew back to New Orleans my mind was made up that soon Miami would be my new home. So I came here on yesterday and bought myself a building in which I'm transforming into a nightclub."

"You've got the building already?" "With renovations underway." "I must say, you move swiftly, Santana. You know, the other Bosses are gonna be a bit uneasy with your decision. But eh…what can we do? You're a freelancer and aren't bonded to any of us. And as a friend I'd say, what the hell, I don't blame you. You're doing the right thing.

"Maybe one day I'll build up the courage to say I'm done. Well, I guess that explains your presence here. Nevertheless, Santana, I welcome you to Miami with open arms and wish you all the success in your new venture and I'll cosign on your behalf to the other Bosses so we can all come together and give you the biggest farewell party ever seen."

"Mucho gracias, El Jefe." "So when is the club opening?" "As soon as the contractors are done. I give it a week at best." "What'll be the name of it?" "The Million Dollar Spot." "I like that, Santana. Has a nice ring to it. Soon I'll have a new place to pick up on some side chicks."

"This strip club has a gang of potential draft picks for side chicks." "I usually leave out of here with three or four of 'em whenever I come in this joint. But I've noticed how every dancer that came to the stage seems to be ignoring me and focusing more on the one guy over there that's throwing money at all of 'em like he's a mad man."

Santana looked over at the presumed mad man, "That guy you're referring to is my little brother, Get'em." They joined each other in laughter. "I should've known better. You New Orleans boys *sure* know how to become the center of attention. In any event, I'll let you resume doing as you were while I get back to Solomon, the Boss from Atlanta, and break the news of your retirement.

"By the way, don't forget to send me an invite for the grand opening for the Million Dollar Spot and I'll make sure that all of the Bosses are present for the celebration." "You'll be the first person I call, El Jefe. Take care."

During the intermission between performances, Levi, Korey Witha K, and Get'em all found their way back to Santana. "Glad to see you all made it back over here. I was beginning to think it was gonna take a presidential pardon to break y'all free from those girls," Santana said as he teased his friends.

"They got so many bad hoes in here, they can shoot a *"Trip Drill, Part 2"* video," said Levi. "I'm so turnt up, every bitch in Miami's gonna hear about me before we leave *this* motherfucka' tonight," said Get'em as he took another swig off his bottle of *Balboa* tequila.

"After all those one-on-one sessions I just had, I ran across the coldest bitch in here and I got my eyes set on her," Korey Witha K said. "Which one is that?" Santana asked. "The Brazilian broad over there who's entertaining that dude who you were just politicin' with," Korey Witha K mentioned in reference to Hurricane El Jefe.

"You're talking about the one who calls herself, Angel?" asked Get'em. "Yeah, that's her name." "Aww, *fuck* no! I know that hoes are supposed to be for everybody but you gone have to fall back off her, big brudda. I think I'm catchin' feelings in this bitch, ya *heard* meh?!" "They all were in tears from laughing so hard.

They parlayed a little while longer until they exhausted all of the fun out of their system. Then went back to Santana's condo and altered their mindset to a more severe matter…The *Columbian Job*.

# CHAPTER 31



"THIS ISN'T THE MOST STERILE environment I've had to lay my head for a night but under the circumstances the location's ideal," said Santana as he surveyed the safe house. "Considering our unofficial sojourn to Columbia, we weren't bias to the condition the building was in," said Chinky.

"These mosquitos is gangster than a motherfucka', ya *heard* meh?! Break out the repellant spray!" Get'em said as he swatted ferociously at the swarm of bugs.

Inside the building the foursome evaluated the conglomeration of apparatus that Derrick, Ham, and Chinky had chosen.

"Damn, fellas, y'all got enough shit in here to take on Al Qaeda," said Santana. "We didn't want to be out here half-cocked so we spared no expenses knowing our lives are all on the line," Derrick said.

"They say you can't go to war unless you have your money right, so I ain't mad at 'cha. I'm sure everything in here'll be of use." Santana responded. Get'em was first to select his desired hardware. An M-16 and a Sig Sauer. "This is all I need, ya *heard* meh?! I'mma put some niggas in the matrix with *these* two bitches."

"Y'all bought a damn toy helicopter, too?" asked Korey Witha K. Derrick took the initiative to explained how the rare piece of machinery operated. "We should be able to wipe out at least half of them niggas, if not all of 'em, with that," Levi reckoned.

"Antonio told us that it has the tendency to find it's mark ninety-five percent of the time. I've been practicing with that baby all night without missing anything I've aimed for," said Chinky. "Is Antonio the guy that you've known for a few years, Chinky?" asked Santana.

"Derrick, Ham, and I *all* knew him from a mission we went on out here when we were servicemen. Antonio was one of the natives who stood shoulder to shoulder with us in the jungles."

Adjacent to the helicopter were the Kamikaze pendants. "What the fuck are those funny looking necklaces for?" asked Korey Witha K. The inquiry caused Derrick, Ham, and Chinky to give each other uneasy looks. Derrick felt he'd have a better shot at selling the idea of getting everyone on board to wear them so he took the lead.

"Don't freak out when I tell you guys this. Those necklaces are called the Kamikaze pendants and they're solely designed for an extremely significant role for missions like ours...to protect us."

"The way y'all just looked at each other y'all actin' like that's a bad thing or something. But what I don't understand is how in the hell is that little pendant supposed to protect us?" asked Santana. Then each of the foursome grabbed a necklace to examine it closer.

"Theoretically speaking, if something were to happen to any of us tomorrow and that person or persons had to be left behind it would be impossible for the Columbians to find out who we are. So those who made it out would never have to worry about the Nariño cartel discovering our origin to be able to track us down."

"I hear you, Derrick, but you're not making any sense to me. What does a damn Kamikaze pendant have to do with any of this?" asked Santana. "Each of us will wear a necklace and whenever we disconnect the chain links we'll have a ten second window before any pendant that's still connected detonates with the strength of five grenades."

Get'em dropped the Kamikaze pendant back on the table as if it were as hot as the gun that killed Kennedy. "I ain't fuckin' with *that*! I know I'm tore up in the head, but y'all niggas is crazy *forreal forreal!*" "I'm wit 'cha on that, lil brudda. I ain't scared to die but I ain't with that suicide bomber shit," Korey Witha K asserted.

Santana pondered on the value of the necklaces then shared his insight with his crew. "Let me first say this… I feel the same way as you, Korey and Get'em. But Derrick and Ham, I've known you guys forever and the one thing I know for sure about you two is you've always looked at situations from a different perspective.

"You both are exceedingly tailored for war as well as potential repercussions thereafter. So I speak for myself as I say this; if I were the one who fell victim tomorrow and had to be left behind, I wouldn't want any of you who got away to have the Nariño cartel coming back to haunt you later on in life. And I hope you all feel the same. So with that being said, I'm all for the Kamikaze pendants."

Derrick responded, "Thanks for acknowledging our merit, Santana. I couldn't have put that any better." "You've made a good point, big homie. Besides, I know I'm certified with these right here, so I ain't got nothin' to worry about," said Korey Witha K as he reached for a German AK-47 assault rifle and, of course, a Draco.

"I guess it really wouldn't make any difference if one of us had to get blown to kingdom come because we'd already be dead and wouldn't feel a damn thing," said Levi as he measured the amount of sense Santana had made.

Then everyone in the room looked at Get'em for his reaction. "Y'all niggas got me fucked up if y'all think *I'mma* be the odd man out. I ain't never scared!" Now that everybody was on one accord they packed up all of the combat paraphernalia then went to the site of the battlefield.

Being conscience of their alien environment, they encompassed ground zero to confirm it was deserted. Once they found it to be free of the opposition they cautiously canvassed the area in its entirety within a quarter mile radius in search for hidden surveillance and possible booby traps. The region was clean.

They began staging setups. In specific locations they dug trenches large enough to lay comfortable in with their weapons of choice. They found hiding places up high in trees with clear views of the site. Even camouflaged hardware around the immediate area.

Then acted out a few drills that Derrick, Ham, and Chinky had practiced the night before.

Santana felt optimistic about the preparations and exercise they'd ran. So with less than a day until the grand larceny he abolished all actions for the remainder of the night so they could hurry back to the safe house to build up an adequate supply of stamina for the main event.

# CHAPTER 32

**Medellin, Columbia**
**Ground Zero**
**March 3, 2008, 6:15am**

TEAM SANTANA WAS DRAPED in army fatigues and war paint while holding their composure until the moment of truth. They were sectioned off in various locations, communicating in minimal tones through ear pieces. The time was approaching.

"I sure hope these motherfuckas' show. I got ants in this ditch biting me all up my ass," said Get'em. "They'll show, Get'em. Cartels operate on time schedules and Javier Ochoa's no exception to the rule. So don't get impatient on me, lil brother," said Santana. "I'm good, big brudda. As many hours as I've spent laying underneath niggas houses waiting for 'em to come home so I could knock their ass off, I'm built for this shit."

More small talk owned the frequency waves for entertainment purposes during their down time. The foursome ran yesterday's eps about their day at the beach to their night at the strip club, while the trio had yesteryears conversations from their times in the jungles of South America. Including the stories of Derrick and Ham's upbringing with Santana.

"Y'all took me all the way back with those memories, Ham and Derrick," said Santana. "This is the exact same way that Chinky heard about you, Santana. We were just killing time like we're doing now." Derrick responded.

Finally, they saw headlights coming their way.

"Here they come, guys. This is the moment we've been waiting for. We're at the point of no return so take no prisoners and show no mercy. Wait for my cue fellas and then let's get it," Santana stated with conviction.

The truck came to a rest. Doors opened and men with guns spurted out. "How many are there, Ham?" asked Santana. Looking through a pair of infrared binoculars, Ham responded, "Four came out of the cab and four from the back of the truck."

"That half a mill's about to be the easiest money I've ever made," said Derrick."

"Okay, guys. We're gonna do this just as we rehearsed. After they get the submarine off the truck, we go in for the kill. Roger that?" said Santana. Everyone agreed.

Within minutes the submarine was off the truck and ready to swim in the ocean.

"That sub's a little larger than the one I saw a month ago. I hope you Navy SEALs won't have a problem driving it," said Santana.

"Size doesn't matter. With that tutorial we gave everyone at the safe house, any of you should be able to drive it," said Derrick.

"Everyone all set?" asked Santana. Each member of Team Santana responded, "*ten-four.*" "Got that chopper ready to go, Chinky?" "Ten-four, Santana." "It's that time, fellas. Be safe. Now on the count of three, let's get this bitch poppin'. One…Two…Thr…" Santana was abruptly cut off by Ham. "Wait, Santana! Another truck's coming." "Everyone, hold your positions," Santana responded.

The men from truck number two acted in the same fashion as the men from the first truck. Four men came out of the cab with guns, on guard, as four more men removed something from the back of the truck. It was a second submarine.

"Damn, Santana. It's another submarine," said Levi. Santana felt exhilarated. "I was only expecting one. Depending on the quantity, you guys may be looking at a handsome bonus."

Santana had raised the bar. The craving Team Santana had to ensure the mission would have a triumphant ending had just been amplified.

"Don't quote me on this, but I believe this just might be the largest heist in underworld history," said Chinky. "We'll see. That's for sure," Derrick concurred. "How many guys are out there in total, Ham?" "Sixteen. Copy that, Santana?" "Roger that. See any more traffic coming?" "Negative."

A few minutes later the second submarine was side by side with the first. "Before anymore company comes our way let's get this show on the road. Chinky, get that bird in the air and when we start firing that'll be your cue to do the same. Roger that?" "Roger,

Santana." "All right, fellas, again on three, let's air these niggas out. One…Two…Three…"

Hardcore pistol poppin' reigned supreme as Team Santana picked off six of the Columbian militia. The remaining ten rebounded rather quickly. Some wild gun firing, others aiming in the direction of the incoming sparks. Domingo was the most aggressive.

"Hos estan attacando. Llamen mas soldados!" Domingo said to one of his mercenaries. Shell casing and more rounds precipitated from the heavens as the chopper guided by Chinky found two of its prey. Eight more to go.

"Did any of you understand what that guy just said?" asked Korey Witha K. "He just ordered one of his men to call for reinforcements so we don't have much time," said Santana. Domingo took heed to the aerial assault and demanded his men to seek refuge. "Ai un elicoptero en el aire disparand nos. Corran por cubierto!"

Team Santana took notice of how their adversaries shunned then moved to phase two of the attack - malicious combat in close quarters. Chinky grew agitated from being unable to get clear shots of his evasive targets. So he left his post from up high in a tree to join Team Santana in Operation: *POP IT OFF*.

They gained ground as they charged in from sporadic angles, boxing in the endangered eight. Bullets flew in Ham's path. Near misses. He was only inches way from being an ex-SEAL with no brains. Levi keyed in on the gunslinger and took him out with his vicious trigger squeezin'.

Seven remaining.

No longer outnumbered, the killing field was evenly matched.

Forbearance was obsolete for the lionhearted brothers, Korey Witha K and Get'em, as they took to the frontline like Desert Storm soldiers, like they practiced the night before. The methodical move was to their advantage because three of the guerillas came from out of concealment like they were ready for a Mexican standoff.

Their final standoff, to be exact, because waiting in the wings were Derrick and Ham to put down the three amigos before they could get off a single shot. Get'em and Korey Witha K also contributed to the massacre. The battle royale was in full form. Three more down. Four left.

The angle that Santana took lead him in the proximity of Domingo. They exchanged glares. Domingo was shell shocked to see Santana's face. "It's you! You'll die a thousand deaths over once Javier finds out what you've done."

"It'll never happen Domingo because you're about to die one horrible death from speaking my name to the Bosses in the States."

Then two of the mercenaries came to either side of Domingo, ready to fire upon Santana. But he was no stranger to danger and have had the keys to his life inserted into the locks of Death's front door on a number of occasions. The door never opened and it wouldn't today.

As they blasted at him he made a daring nosedive to the ground then mimicked the *death roll* like a cajun alligator. Fortunately, Santana was an expert at doing the murder dance because bullets were hitting blades of grass where his body rolled pass mere fractions of a second beforehand.

During his gutsy roll Santana spiraled by an area he had a grenade planted, nabbed it, then came to rest in one of the trenches they'd dug the day before. He pulled the pin then sent the grenade airborne. Luckily for Domingo, he'd seen what Santana had thrown then tried to warn his commandos, but his attempt was thwarted. ***BOOOMMM!!*** He was too late. Their bodies had been tossed in the air like beads from a float at a Mardi Gras parade.

Two remaining. Domingo and another.

Domingo was dazed and sluggish to recuperate. The impact from the blast caused him to drop his weapon and his only other alternative was to flee from the ambush.

During his run he picked up one of the guns that lay next to one of his dead soldiers. Like a feline, Domingo was on his ninth life and he wasn't planning on going down without scratching.

More headlights were approaching. *Beau coup* headlights were approaching and they were coming fast. Santana chased Domingo. Team Santana searched for Domingo's renegade - the second to last of a dying breed. Domingo *had* to die. If not, he would foil Santana's entire plot if he lived to share the news with Javier Ochoa.

Time was running out. Domingo turned around shooting recklessly trying to keep Santana off his ass. A safe distance away, the motorcade's truck doors were opening with a mob of unwanted visitors. Domingo tried to get to them. He was running towards them as if his life depended on it.

It did.

But Santana had switched into overdrive while Domingo was running on fumes. Santana had him in his scope. "Domingo!" Santana yelled. He turned around to see Santana. Domingo laughed. "It's all over now! The rest of my soldiers have arrived so surrender yourself now. Maybe Javier will go easier on you."

It was Santana's last chance to silence Domingo forever. His last chance to keep his identity anonymous. Santana's bullets had ran low but he had more extra clips than the former Mayor of New Orleans, *Ray Nagin,* had counts of conspiracy charges. For Domingo, only one would suffice.

He inserted the magazine. Fifty more attempts on Domingo's life. Santana took aim then unloaded every round at Domingo. Successfully, he plugged the potential leak and as for that particular part of the mission; it was finished. Santana had made Domingo famous. The print shops in Medellin, Columbia would finally be able to press up Domingo's Rest in Peace t-shirts. In New Orleans, there's a traditional celebration that usually takes place when someone dies called *second lines.* Some Columbians would soon be *second lining* for Domingo in the days to come.

It was time for Team Santana to retreat to the submarines. Domingo's backup was on foot. Eighty yards away. Runnin' and gunnin'.

"Mission complete, fellas. We have guest on the way. Let's move to the submarines, *now!*" yelled Santana.

From out of disproportionate areas of the thick forest, Team Santana made it to the sands. The first to the submarines were Derrick, Korey Witha K, and Get'em. Vessel number one was cranked and ready to swim with the sharks. Next was Levi who was closely followed by Santana and then Ham. Chinky was not that far behind.

Then the renegade from Domingo's first crew came from out of the forest bustin' sideways with his rod. He made contact with the closest man…Chinky. The vest Chinky had on would be of no use to him. He'd caught a head shot. More redness covered the sand than it did on the flag for the country of China.

"*Chinkkyyy*! screamed Ham. When everyone heard Ham scream through their earpieces, Santana ordered Levi to start submarine number two and the rest of Team Santana to stand down while he climbed back out of the vessel to help Ham and Chinky - his fallen soldier.

Levi started the engine but that was the only order he followed. In fact, none of the other members of Team Santana followed his order to stand down. One by one they all poured out of the vessels and were ready for whatever.

Ham ran towards the renegade suicidal style engaging in extreme pistol play. He'd gotten his retribution. Then he and Santana made it to Chinky's side. Unfortunately, a portion of Chinky's head was missing. Needless to say, he was dead and they'd have to leave him behind.

The rest of Team Santana saw the tragedy from afar. They also saw Domingo's backup army coming. They were ten yards from the sands. All fifty of them. The Columbian militia was coming up fast to claim what was rightfully theirs.

"Come on, Ham, Chinky's gone. And so will we if we don't hurry up and get the hell out of here," said Santana. They pulled themselves together then hurried back to the boat launch to leave behind an arena of bullet riddled bodies. Slugs began flying their way.

Then there was another blast **'BOOOMMMM!!!'** Three more of the Columbian militia were thrown to the air like popcorn kernels sitting in a hot skillet from tripping over and setting off a booby trap of explosives installed by Chinky.

The occupants of submarine number one each dropped into the vessels, making it to safety shortly before they heard rounds ricocheting off the outer shell. They sealed the door shut.

Levi and Santana dove in submarine number two, ducking the not-so-friendly fire. But as Ham was dropping down into the submarine he was hit. He fell hard on the floor board of the vessel and grunted a strong man's sound as Levi closed the hatch. And then both submarines disappeared in the depths of the ocean.

"I heard someone yell. Did someone get hit?" asked Derrick. "Yeah, Ham took a bullet as he was coming in," said Santana. "Is he okay?" "I'm taking off his shirt and vest right now to see how bad it is." "Where'd he get hit?" "Looks like the lower part of his back."

"The vest didn't stop it?" "Negative, he's leaking some blood." "Whatever you do, Santana, stop the bleeding. We've got a long ride ahead of us." "Roger that." "Does he still have his earpiece in?" "Yeah." "Ham, I know you can hear me, cuz."

"I hear you, Derrick." "Good. You know we were trained for this type of shit. So make sure Levi and Santana knows everything they need to do to make sure you pull through. Aight?" "Okay, Derrick. I think I'll manage. Santana and Levi's doing a great job of plugging the wound."

"Good. Now, what the fuck happened?" "I went back to try to help Chinky. I didn't want to leave him behind but when I saw he was already gone, I snapped. I'mma miss that dude." "I am too, cuz, but we all knew coming into this job we were also signing up as expendables."

"Speaking of Chinky and expendable, those Columbians are probably all over him by now trying to figure out who he is and where he's from," said Santana.

"The Kamikaze pendants!" said Ham.

"Guys, we have to hurry up and take these things off because If the Columbians take off Chinky's necklace while ours are still attached…need I say more?"said Santana.

Get'em jumped up, "I forgot all about these fuckin' chains! Let's take these bitches off ASAP!" "Aight, fellas. On three, remove the Kamikaze pendants. One…Two…Three," said Santana.

Every member of Team Santana took off their Kamikaze pendants with the exception of the late Tri *Chinky* Phan. A few seconds later, from the depths of the sea, they heard the sound and felt the vibrations from the Kamikaze pendant's astronomical explosion.

# CHAPTER 33



**Atlantic Ocean**
**March 4, 2008, 3:31 a.m.**

"JUST TWENTY MORE KNOTS to go till we reach U.S. soil, gentlemen, then we're home sweet home," said Santana. "You think she'll be at the house?" asked Levi. "Don't know. Don't care. Ham's gotta get to a hospital as quickly as possible and we need to clear out and dispose of these subs before day breaks."

"It's a good thing you got us to park the truck at her crib, big homie, cause if she's not home, we'll have a ride for Ham." Korey Witha K said. "Y'all parked the truck at her house?!" asked Derrick. "We did it yesterday before we left for Columbia," Santana responded.

"What did she have to say about the that ?" "I'd called her from the strip club and told her about my condo and that the moving company had driven my property to Miami a lot earlier than expected. So I asked her would it be safe for me to leave the truck parked behind my club until I return back in town. She insisted I park it at her house to keep it from getting burglarized."

"She actually thinks the truck's filled with furniture?" "I gave her no reason to suspect otherwise." "You always did think ahead, Santana," Ham said.

"Hey, fellas, I'm picking up something on the sonar. It's showing land just ahead of us. Going off of the latitude and longitude coordination we have for Jasmine's house, that area should be the shoreline to her backyard," said Derrick. "It's about time! All of this water got me so nauseated, I gotta shit *bad* as a motherfucka', ya *heard* meh?!" said Get'em.

They elevated the submarines to the top of the water then slowly advanced into Jasmine's boathouse. By having the speedboat taken to the repair shop, it left the pair of jet skis in there alone.

There was space for the submarines. Enough to fit them both perfectly aside one another. Team Santana docked the subs, killed the engines, and waited for Santana to give the word for them to exit the vessels after he got out alone to survey the scenery for anything that looked suspicious. Scanning inside Jasmine's residence for any activity, he only saw a single light shone from her bedroom. He assumed Jasmine was home.

With the earpiece still activated, he continued communicating with his team as he moved in closer to Jasmine's house. "It appears to be safe and sound out here guys and chances are she's home. She may become a little curious about my attire but it's nothing I can't handle. I'll be sure to have her out in a virtual we can get Ham to a hospital as quickly as possible. Now everyone exit the submarines and meet me with Ham by Jaz's car. And whoever has free hands, I want you to start offloading the product."

Walking into the house Santana heard soft music playing and saw steam coming from out of the bathroom as if Jasmine had just gotten out of the shower. "Hey, Jaz, it's Santana! Are you awake?!" She came from out of her bedroom tying her robe by her waist. "Oh, you startled me."

"This is one of those wee hours of the morning visits I was talking about. I didn't interrupt anything did I?" "You're fine. That's why I gave you a key. I told you I've never entertained any company here, remember?"

"Right." "Why are you dressed like that, with war paint and all? And is that *blood* stains?" "I went on an important mission abroad but there's an emergency. Something went wrong."

"What happened?!" "One of my guys was shot but my team and I managed to escape by hijacking two of the insurgent's submarines." "Oh my God!" "I wish I could go into further details with you, Jaz, but the assignment's classified. However, I do owe you an explanation for showing up at your home under these circumstances and that's because it was the nearest place I knew to come on the Atlantic coast. So, I hope I'm not imposing." "I'm okay with you showing up like this, Santana. And as far as confidentiality's concerned, I'm sure the less I know, the better."

"Thanks, Jaz. Now can you please hurry my friend to a hospital in Godspeed? He's really treading in dangerous waters." "Of course. Broward General Hospital's not far from here. Where's your friend?" "Out back and my guys are pulling him out of the submarine as we speak to meet us by your ca-" "*NOOOOOO!!!*" screamed Derrick as he found Ham to be unresponsive.

Santana didn't need an earpiece to hear the loud cry of anguish that was likely perceived from miles away. Unconsciously, Santana hightailed it back to his team while responding, "Derrick, what's happening out there?!" "It's Ham, Santana. He isn't breathing!" cried Derrick as he applied CPR to his cousin."

"Jasmine, call an ambulance *now*," Santana yelled out to her as she stood alarmed by the back door of the house staring at Ham's lifeless body from afar. "Get him to my car, Santana. We have a better shot at making it to Broward General hospital before an ambulance arrives here. Every minute counts." As if it were second nature for her, Jasmine was cranking up the Jaguar and was ready for it to sprint.

While Ham was being carried to the car, Santana handed down instructions, "For Ham to have taken a turn for the worst, more now than ever he needs someone by his side until hopefully he pulls through so Derrick and I will go to the hospital while the rest of you finish the task here. "

"Stay here with them, Santana. I'll go with Ham," Derrick offered as he climbed into the back seat with Ham. "You sure about that?" "Yeah I'm sure. In my heart I know it's too late to save him, but I'll continue with CPR until we get to the hospital. And our job here's not finished so you guys get to it and leave Ham for me to worry about."

"All right, Derrick. But before you guys leave, I need you, Jaz, to give me the keys to the jet skis so we can ditch those submarines because I'm not sure if they have tracking devices on them or not and I don't want you to have any foreign drama coming to your residence.

"Also make sure Ham's checked in before you leave and we should be finished here by the time you get back so the rest of us can go to the hospital. That's if you won't be too tired to take us."

"The keys are already in the ignition and I'm fully awake to bring you all back if need be. Oh, I almost forgot, sometime today I want to bring you up to speed concerning the status of your club." "I appreciate it. See you when you get back, Jaz," Santana said as he gave her a kiss then closed the driver door and watched her speed off.

"Get'em, come with me so I can show you where the bathroom's located before you have a major accident out here." "That's exactly what feels like is about to happen, big brudda, because my stomach is bubbling so much that if I even fart one more time, I'm *hit*."

As Get'em was on his way back outside, he noticed Santana backing up the truck as close to the boathouse as he possibly could. When the truck stopped, Get'em opened the back door, pulled the ramp out, then jumped inside to get the hand truck and roll it into the boathouse. As Santana and Get'em walked into the sheltered area, they saw that Levi and Korey Witha K had cleared out half of one of the vessels, with rows of kilos of cocaine stacked on the dock.

"Jasmine's gone with Ham and Derrick so we have about an hour or so until she gets back. And since its four of us, we should be able to turn up and get everything done within that timeframe."

As the process sped up, the foursome were working earnestly to deplete the vessels. The sun had begun to wink at Miami but they remained focus. And close to an hour after they started, they'd emptied both vessels, loaded the truck, and parked it back to its original position. Once they completed the most important part of their task, Santana decided to phone Jasmine for an update on Ham.

"Hey, Jaz. What's happening on *your* end? *Please* tell me they were able to save him." "I stuck around a little longer with hopes of having some uplifting news to share with you, Santana, but regrettably, your friend didn't make it. They said he was D.O.A. and that had we gotten him here a lot sooner and he hadn't lost as much blood as he did, they would've had a better chance at reviving him. I'm sorry for your loss."

"It'll be okay. So, how's Derrick holding up?" "A lot better than *I* am and I didn't even *know* your friend. Derrick seems to be accustomed to these sorts of situations. He's a really strong man." "He's been that way since we were kids. So, where is he *now*?" "Still at the hospital." "So I take it you left already." "I did a few minutes ago to get you guys back reunited with Derrick so I'll see you in a few." "Thanks for everything, Jaz. I really appreciate all that you do." "You're welcome." The call ended.

"Aight, fellas, Jasmine should be pulling up shortly so let's finish this. Levi, you drive a sub and I'll take the other one. Korey and Get'em, y'all crank up the jet skis. We're gonna take the subs at least ten knots offshore then climb out of the hatch and let 'em swim with the fishes. Then Levi and I'll hop on the back of the jet skis so we can hurry back to land. So everybody put your earpieces back in so we can communicate and not lose each other out there."

As he and Levi finally ditched the last of the evidence and then jumped on back of the jet skis, Santana thought of how he'd successfully engineered perhaps the largest heist in the history of the underworld just like Chinky had mentioned. With the use of falsified passports, not a living soul would ever know that he or his team had entered Columbia so the aggressors would forever remain faceless. Aside from the loss of Derrick and Chinky, they'd made a clean getaway. The sun had finally begun to smile at Santana Bailey and Santana Bailey was smiling back.

## Ground Zero
## Medellin, Columbia
## March 2, 2008, 9:01 p.m.

"It looks like Armageddon out here! Twenty-two of my finest soldiers are dead and you're telling me it only took the six men you saw to do the inconceivable task of taking my submarines and swindle me out of my fucking cocaine?! That sounds *prosperous!*" said Javier as he grilled his soldiers.

"Señor Javier, it was seven of them altogether. One of them was shot," said one of his underlings. "Well, where is the seventh man? Bring him to me at once!" "We can't, Señor Javier. As three of our men went to detain him, they saw that he was already dead. And as they searched his person in an attempt to identify him, his body exploded and killed all three men."

"Are you saying there are no traces left behind to hold someone accountable?" "I don't think so, Señor Javier. We scoured the entire area with a fine-tooth comb and the only things we found were freshly dug trenches, five hidden guns, and three grenades. Oh, and a toy helicopter. Actually, it's not a toy. Apparently, it's a drone that still has live rounds in it." Javier was fuming. As he speculated, he picked up an M-16 rifle that lay next to one of his dead soldiers and started pacing.

"No one knows of this location except a few of my soldiers. When I discovered that Hector was dealing fraudulently with Ivan from Baltimore I sent men there to take care of him. Maybe it was some of Ivan's affiliates who orchestrated this piracy as an act of retaliation. Or maybe one of the Bosses have been spying on my operation.

"Donavan was here. Maybe *he* has his fingerprints in on this. I should've never showed him this location when he was here. I'll send some men to New Orleans to see if he's flooded with work. I'll check on the other Bosses as well. I'll put men in every city to look for the new stamp that I put on my product for this shipment. And if *any* of the Bosses are caught with a kilo with the eagle wings insignia embedded in it, I'll annihilate *him* and his entire bloodline."

Javier held the gun in the air then began looking into the eyes of every soldier for any sign of deceitfulness. "Or maybe it was someone who's standing out here in my very presences. Maybe there's a traitor amongst us. "Maybe it was *you*," Javier said to one of his. "Oh no, Señor Javier. I…Iwould *never* betray you!" said the nervous underling. "Oh no? Okay then, tell me who you think did this." "I…I…don't have a clue, Señor Javier." "No clue, eh…?" Then Javier unleased his fury in the form of fire on his soldier.

"From this day forward whenever I ask any of you who stole my cocaine and you can't answer me correctly, you'll end up like him. Do I make myself clear?!" Javier stated as he pointed at the slain underling. "Sí, Señor Javier!" said every terrified soldier who heard his venomous words.

A few minutes later, Javier calmed down. "I'm going to turn over every stone, search every house, and look under every grain of sand in the world until I find out who it was that had the balls the size of coconuts to steal from the Nariño cartel. And I don't care if it takes me until the end of time."

# CHAPTER 34

**Broward General Hospital**
**Fort Lauderdale, Florida**
**March 4, 2008, 9:27 a.m.**

"I WILL NEVER BE ABLE TO fully compensate you or Ham's wife, Monica, for calling upon Ham to assist me on a mission which ultimately led to his death. "Life is all about making decisions, Santana. You didn't hold a gun up to any of our heads when we signed up for this so there's nothing you should feel guilty for.

"My cousin chose his destiny. And if he would've listened to you when you ordered everyone to stand down and stayed in the submarine, he wouldn't've gotten hit. And as sad as I am to know he's gone and ain't never coming back, death's something we all gotta face eventually and it was just his time," Derrick stressed to Santana as well as the rest of the team in order to remind them that he was tailored for situations like this.

"I understood casualties would be a possibility coming into this because it's a part of war. But still, my condolences go out to both, you, and Monica. Even for your loss of Chinky, " Santana said with heartfelt conviction.

"I appreciate that. Ham and I were probably the only people in the world who really knew him," Derrick explained. "What about his family?" "He had no family, no kids…nothing. When he was just a baby his father brought him to America and left whatever family they had behind in Vietnam. And when his father died, he retired from the Navy SEALs and have been on his own ever since."

"Well, remember when I said that you'd all be looking at a bonus depending on what was in the submarines?" Team Santana were all ears as he continued, "Just to inform you all of what the mission amounted to, the quantity of the contents on the subs totaled out to a whopping three thousand kilos of cocaine. Columbia's finest, I might add." "Whoa, Santana. You're a fuckin' mastermind!" said Derrick.

"I couldn't have done it without you guys. So when it's time to break bread, Levi, Korey, and Get'em, y'all are each gonna receive an additional one hundred and fifty kilos. Derrick, you get one and a half million dollars along with an added bonus of a half-million dollars."

"What's the additional bonus for?" asked Derrick. "Since Chinky has no next of kin, that leaves you as the co-beneficiaries of his million-dollar life insurance policy." "Insurance policy and co-beneficiary? So who gets the other half?" "Monica does. She will receive Ham's portion of Chinky's policy as well as a two-million dollar policy from Ham's own policy and each of their five kids will receive a million dollar trust fund in their names and it will all be paid out from a company called the Bailey Life Corporation." Team Santana went ballistic.

"You sure know how to keep it one-thousand with a nigga, big homie," said Korey Witha K. "Like a motherfucka'. My paper's about to be so major that I don't want none of y'all calling me Get'em no more. Address me as El Gwapo, ya *heard* meh?!"

"I *knew* you were gonna bless us with a lil somethin' extra but you're about to take us all into another tax bracket, Levi said. "My cousin's family will be financially secured and now I can finally tell those assholes at my job to fuck off. I ain't working for nobody else for the rest of my *life*," said Derrick.

"I'mma put it to y'all like this; on the strength of everyone's lives being put on the line for the sake of my strategy to hit this lick, I'm making it my business to see that *all* of my niggas SoccaBall. I wouldn't have it any other way. Besides, it would be far too lonely at the top all by myself." "What we got next on the agenda, Santana?" asked Levi.

"Now that we know Ham's fate and that Derrick can handle things from here, Korey and Get'em you two can hit the highway shortly and head back home. Then we'll all meet up again at the safe house in New Orleans to divvy up the product. Now if you guys will excuse me, I have a sexy ass Dominican broad expecting me in the waiting area."

Santana found Jasmine slumbering in a sofa chair. "Rise and shine, sleeping beauty." "Oh jeez, I must've dozed off," Jasmine said as she yawned. "I *told* you you should've left us here. I knew you were tired." "I'm fine, Santana. I wasn't going anywhere until I heard that Ham would be okay and we've discussed the business with your club."

"Well, Ham's doing great. You mentioned earlier that you needed to lace me up about the club. Wha'duya got?" "I've been speaking with the contractor, Michael Miles, since he took the job. He's got three different shifts working around the clock to finish the building. And judging from the progress they've made, Michael's prognosis for completion is a week away."

"Sounds like Michael was the right guy for the job." "He does excellent work and he's fast. Not to mention the price he gave me." "Did you need more money for the job?" "You gave me more than enough. Michael said my smile made him go easy on me."

"Aww…that's so sweet. You gave him some, didn't you?" "No I did not! Now could you please remove your mind from the gutter?" "Just kidding." "But I will admit that he asked me out on a date."

"Did you go?" "No. I stalled him." "Don't be so hard on the guy. At least take him to a game. Give him my spot in Pat Riley's skybox. I bet he'd love that." "I'll think about it. Now enough of talking about Michael for Christ's sake."

"All right. So, how soon will it be before I can open the doors?" "As soon as Michael's men come out. The license and permits and things of that nature have all been taken care of." "You're simply amazing, Jaz. That'll give me enough time to run back to New Orleans and say my farewells to a few people."

"I'll cover everything here while you're away. The radio advertisements, the posters, and I'll get a street team to start passing out flyers. Just everything you can think of as far as promotions are concerned. I might even pull a few strings to get Rick Ross to come and perform. I'm gonna pull out all the stops to make sure that the Million Dollar Spot nightclub lives up to its name."

"You know what I think, Jaz?" "No, tell me." "I think you'd make the perfect assistant. Would you do me the honor of coming to work for me? You'd make lots of money and would still be able to run The Red Room. So, wha'duya say?" "I'd really love to take you up on your offer, Santana, but I can't."

"Why not?" "Because its the club industry you're getting into. I know how the women target the owners and being as though we've had sexual relations I'd become too territorial behind you and you wouldn't want to see me when I'm angry. So, to nip it in the bud, I won't mix business with pleasure. Now, the ball's back in your court, Santana. How would you rather have me?"

It didn't take any time for Santana to make his decision. He knew how great of an asset Jasmine would be to his business and the thought of

choosing sex over that was asinine. *Money Over Everything* was the motto he'd learned years ago from Kevin Kash. And he'd live by those words today.

"So you're giving an ultimatum?" "You catch on fast." "I can't say that I'd rather do away with the sex. When I came into your house earlier this morning and saw you take off that robe I wanted to tear into you on sight.

"But for the little time we've come to know each other, I truly cherish our friendship more than the sex. Besides, I'm no good at relationships anyway. So keeping everything completely business with you, I'd have you as a friend for a lifetime."

"In other words, you want me to be your female version of a capo. Is that what you're saying?" "I'd never suspect you knew mafia terminology. But, yes. I do want you to be my *capo* but it comes with a stipulation." And what would that be?"

"Since we won't be having sex anymore I figured we'd go to the house and set it off in that motherfucka' for the last time." Jasmine shook her head with a disapproving notion, "You are so nasty, Santana Bailey, but very persuasive. That sounds like an offer I can't refuse. Let's get out of here."

Santana smiled, "Before we leave, I need to run and get Korey and Get'em so they can get to the truck to move my furniture into my condo. And after they're done and we've had our grand finale, I'll be headed back to New Orleans."

## Los Angeles, California
## March 4, 2008, 10:00 p.m.

He shot him in front of me, Tookie. And there was nothing I could do about it," said Meatball. "The only profile you got on this cat is his name's Santana and he's a federal - type of nigga from New Orleans?" asked Tookie. "Yeah, cuz, that's all I know." "Well, I'm originally from Louisiana. I lived there when I was a B.G. before moving to Cali where I became a co-founder in forming the Crips gang. So I'll drop a few calls to my people down there in New Orleans and see if they can locate that nigga."

"I'm glad I wore a vest because that bitch, Chasity, tried to send me. The shots hit me so hard they knocked me unconscious for a minute. And right after I regained my senses I saw Santana creep up from behind and dome check my brother.

"At that point, all I could do was lay there and play dead. Then they set my crib on fire and left us there to barbeque. I tried to pull Jermaine from the fire but the flames had gotten too hectic. So I saved myself and got out of there just in time."

"Sounds like he on some mob shit." "Yeah, cuz. The nigga and his crew be playin' for keeps." "Since Jermaine was a Crip, he was our brother just as well as he was yours. And when anybody spills the blood of one of us vengeance is an unwritten law."

"So, do I have the okay to send a few of your Crip brothers back to New Orleans with me?" "When you go to war you gotta have your money right. *Especially* when you're going up against a made nigga. It would be way too costly having to look for a needle in a haystack. So I won't approve of the trip as of yet. Let my people down south do the legwork of tracking him down. Just have patience, Meatball, because we *will* find Santana. And when we do, the Crips are gonna teach him the true meaning of showing *California Love.*"

# CHAPTER 35

New Orleans, Louisiana
March 5, 2008, 12:01 a.m.

"ONE FORTY EIGHT... ONE FORTY NINE... ONE FIFTY. There you go, Get'em. I gave you yours last since you're the youngest because that's exactly what I want you to do with all of that money you attain from it, make it last. Now that the three of you have been compensated for your services, I'd like to thank you gentlemen again for that ride or die spirit you've all shown me since day one. I wouldn't trade any of you for the world."

"I could never repay you for what you've done for me and my lil brother, Santana. But I will let them choppers pop until the casket drop for you, my nigga. Believe *dat*!" said Korey Witha K. "I'm slangin' them cutters for you *too*, big homie. How I'm feelin', even Obama's ass can get checkmated if you ever gave the word," Get'em added.

"To say you *showed love like Bub* would be an understatement compared to what you did for *me*, my nigga. You gave me the ammo I needed to shoot at those desires in my life that's on a larger scale. Now I'm in arm's reach of achieving those things. I'll forever be grateful for that," said Levi.

"Y'all are my brothers. Did y'all expect anything less of me...? Didn't think so. Now that we came out on top I need y'all to understand that we're not completely out of the water. Best believe that the Nariño cartel's gonna have their eyes and ears glued to the streets. Waiting for a foul up.

"One thing I took notice of is that whenever I whipped up some work for Donavan, every shipment he got came with a different logo on the bricks so every single one of these kilos has to be broken down because the insignia of the eagle wings are mostly definitely unique."

"Another thing...I suggest y'all maximize your profits because after the last gram is sold, none of you will be able to score a package on this level ever again without raising any suspicions. It's true that you can cop a few bricks here and there then build your way up to the status of dealing in large quantities but that could take some time. I stress that because the suppliers who has the echelon of the Nariño cartel is gonna do an extensive background check on y'all. Much more deeper than the F.B.I. would. And if they happen to have an alliance with Javier, we might as well buy every piece of hardware we can find because World War 3 would be in the making once they'd fit the pieces to the puzzle together.

"Now the last and most important thing I want to share with y'all, which Levi and I already spoke about, is my exit from the game." "Exit? With all of that fedi you be stacking?!" asked Get'em

"Yeah, lil brudda. This package right here's the last of the Mohicans for me. I'm kissing the game goodbye. Adios. Sayonara."

"So, what happens to all of that clientele you have when you know they don't want nobody else touchin' their product but you?" asked Korey Witha K. "Them niggas ain't got nothin' but two choices. Move around or lay down." "Damn, big brudda. I wish I knew how to twerk that *Pyrex* like you. I'd catch all of your slack fuckin' with them Bosses. Plus I'd be learning a skill that I could always fall back on in case of hard times," Get'em pleaded.

Santana could hear the enthusiasm in his young gunner's tone. Get'em wasn't prepared to retire at his early age. And Santana knew that Korey Witha K wouldn't let his younger brother take on such a harsh endeavor by his lonesome so they'd both still be living on the dark side. Santana decided he'd pass on his gift to Get'em and also give it one last push to eradicate Get'em's cravings for the pharmaceutical field.

"Although I'm opposed to the idea of you continuing in that manner any further than after your last pack is sold, I'm at liberty to implant my vocation in you because you're my brother. But always remember to keep in mind to never sleep on the severity of the ramifications when living that life. Like Yella Boy from UNLV said, *Don't cha be greedy*. The streets ain't got no love for a nigga...never did. Think of  longevity with the amount of loot you're about to make you could turn that into a lucrative business and be sittin' back for the rest of your life chillaxin' with financial freedom.

"So, don't make any decision on what you're gonna do just yet, you got time for that. But as I speak of the present, no time's better than now for me to have an apprentice. It could take weeks for me to cook up *this* much work." "I feel ya, big brudda. I'll give it some thought. I owe you *that* much." "That's all I'm asking."

"Now that we're back home, Santana, what do you think about that Meatball situation? I wouldn't know where to start looking for him or whichever twin it was who made it out of that inferno," said Levi. "Since we're not sure which one's alive, the only thing I could do is get at Donavan and see what he knows."

"I know Donavan's probably sick as a motherfucka' right now since he didn't get his package," said Korey Witha K. "He shouldn't be *too* upset. His package *did* make it to New Orleans. Only it's in our possession and not his," Santana joked. Everyone in the room laughed their hardest.

"A drought's about to hit. *Ooh woo*, I'm bout to kill the game! I'm breakin' my bricks down and servin' my shit zone for zone and I wish a nigga *would* complain. I'mma have that burner on me tellin' them niggas they better take that ounce and bounce, ya *heard* meh?!" said Get'em.

"Y'all know I need to hustle up that change for Ham and Derrick and I only have a week until my club opens. So I'll be on the grizzy as hard as fuck while I'm still here but once I leave for Miami, however many bricks I have left will only be for y'all to re up. And when they're gone, it's over with."

"Since I still have some work left over from the last package you gave me and you're about to teach Get'em the ropes, I'm taking these birds with me and just let Get'em hook'em up as I need'em. So I'mma leave y'all two to handle business while I get my ass up outta here and home to Andrea. She's been blowing my cell up ever since I left for Miami," said Korey Witha K.

"I *told* y'all that nigga was in love. Look at 'em. He couldn't stay away from that girl to save his life," Get'em teased. "Call it whatever you want, lil brudda. That's my fuckin' *baby*!"

"I'm bout to push out right along with Korey since Get'em's gonna be carrying the torch. I ain't saying I'm in love or no shit like that, but I know Tiffany's tweakin' to get her some *me* time," Levi added.

"You two lovebirds go right ahead and do y'all thang. Get'em and I gots this. But don't think we're gonna be in this motherfucka' all night. I've got a hot date lined up, myself. I'm sure Get'em's sittin' over there thinking about Michelle. So as soon as we whip enough bricks for me to take care of Ham and Derrick, I'm slapping on my flame retardant suit and going fight this fire that my lil *breezy* started with me."

# CHAPTER 36



"IT'S ABOUT TIME YOU CAME! After reading  I was beginning to think I made an ass of myself by coming at you like that," said Chasity. "I thought about you when I was at a strip club in Miami. And when I saw how those girls were tearin' it down I couldn't help but wonder if you had them beat," said Santana.

"Then I guess I'll have to show you some sports, huh?" "Only if you're willing and able. How's the shoulder?" "That's a small thing to a giant. Especially when this is the moment I've been visualizing for God knows *how* long."

"You kind of only answered half of my question. How's the injury?" "My stitches fell out yesterday. Does that answer your question?" "Take off your shirt so I can see for myself." Chasity ripped off her shirt as fast as Usain Bolt in a 100-meter dash. "You see? I told you I was good."

"I just wanna make sure you don't reinjure yourself on my account." "Satisfied with what you see?" "Hell *yeah*, I'm satisfied." "Not my body, Kinky man. I was talking about the wound."

"Oh…yeah, it looks fine." "Great. Now I'm gonna make sure this night is special in every way. I'm gonna start off by running myself some bathwater in my Jacuzzi. Care to join me?" "Don't mind if I do."

For a moment, they sat idle in the Jacuzzi and let the jet streams blow them into a state of relaxation. And for Chasity, the reality of having a naked Santana all to herself was a dream come true. With the level of anticipation she had for this moment, she knew he'd be ill-prepared. And just as expected her head game alone overwhelmed him before getting to the penetration phase.

For the first time in his life, he felt inferior to a female. To anyone, for that matter. Chasity was giving him her all and he knew it. But what he didn't know was which one of them were the wettest; his body from being in the Jacuzzi or her pussy from the multiple orgasms.

She rode Santana like a mechanical bull without letting up as if she wished she could have that moment for life. But exhaustion weighed heavily on him. Due to the heist, he really hadn't slept much. Only a few hours here and there in the past couple of days to be exact.

Chasity had the upper hand and she knew it. After seeing the drained look in his eyes, she decided to go lighter on him. He was too burned out. So she came from off top of him then took him into her mouth once again to assault his dick like she did to a blow pop for the bubble gum.

Getting weaker, Santana felt his body bracing for an explosive release. Then suddenly, he sent two-hundred fifty million potential offsprings gushing into her mouth that would never live to see the light of day.

"Damn, Chasity. Your ass really had it out for me, didn't you?" "That was only an appetizer. The real show's gonna go down in my bedroom." "If you call that an appetizer, I think I'll need to be rejuvenated for the main dish." "I can tell you were tired, so I'll tone it down for round two. But round three, I'm going platinum on that dick."

"Don't write me off just yet. Hopefully, I'll have enough energy by the time you're done with your audition…I mean, performance." "Audition?" "I meant, performance. Now, let's get to that pole in your room so you can show me what you're workin' with."

As Chasity put on the outfit she purchased specifically for her showdown with Santana, she said, "I hope you don't think that pole's in here for entertaining people." "If not, then what's it for?" "I had it installed the same day I came home from the hospital strictly for you." "That was real considerate. You must've prophesized this moment." "If only you knew."

After guiding him to her bed, Chasity docked her iPod to her sound system and let Beyoncé set the tone with the New Orleans bounce music version of the strip club anthem - *Dance for You*. She started off slow doing certain moves she knew Santana more than likely had seen before. Then gradually built her way into her eccentric style which left him captivated.

The measures she took to amuse him would make the dancers at *Magic City* and *Blue Flame* in Atlanta look like amateurs at the Apollo in New York. She continued to pull him deeper and deeper into her world as she illustrated the reason why she should be crowned as the Queen of Erotica.

At the conclusion of the song, Santana said, "If I could sum it all up in one word for what I should call your performance, it would be *epic*. You mean to tell me I've been having you as a secret weapon all this time and you never breathed a word to me about this?"

"I just love to dance. Never wanted to be a stripper." "Well, remember when I said audition?" "Yeah, that was a mistake, right?" "Not really. I was going to mention this sooner or later so I might as well tell you now." "Tell me what?" "I'm moving to Miami in a week and opening a nightclub out there."

"You're moving?! Have you told any of the other C.T.Cs?" "I haven't gotten a chance to tell'em yet." "What do you expect us to do without you?" "Y'all will always be my girls. So if any of you wanna tag along I'll put each one of you in your own house." "That's a relief. You had a bitch nervous for a second. We veered off the subject of audition. Audition for what?"

"I'm turning the entire second floor of the building into a strip club." "So, you want me to dance for you?" "Like a *motherfucka'*. Those mediocre dancers out there ain't got *nothin'* on you. So I'm taking you with me."

Chasity felt exuberated. "*Really*? Are you really taking me with you?" "Yep. Sure am. You're gonna be my main attraction. Sorta like being my bottom bitch so you can keep all the hoes in line." "When do I pack? Will I be living with you? Am I like…your girl now?"

"Slow down, Chasity! You're already my girl but not my woman. And yes, you'll live with me until I find you a house. So have your things together in a week." Chasity jumped all over

Santana. Kissing him, groping him and molesting him in the most obscene way. And he liked it. And before he knew it, round two was in progress. But it didn't last long. Only ten minutes from the sound of the bell, Santana began feeling dreary. So they called it quits for the moment and rested in a nestled position to stare at the backs of their eyelids and dreamt about white sands, terra cotta roofs, and palm trees.

Santana was awakened by the scent of a much-needed breakfast. Chasity had whipped up some grits with cheese, a few banana pancakes, a couple of slices of turkey bacon, sunny side eggs, and freshly squeezed orange juice.

"Thanks, lil mama. I needed that." "You can expect this type of treatment every day in Miami." "I'm looking forward to it." "Sorry I took advantage of you last night. I knew you were spent." "I've been on a three-day flight with only a few hours of sleep. But I hope you don't think I'm going out like *that*." **DING**. Round three got underway.

Fully recuperated, Santana was in his prime. Cutting no slack, he banged her lights out for at least forty-five straight minutes in all sorts of positions. Now she was the inferior but not for long. Staying true to her word, she took the lead and worked her pussy on Santana's dick until she reached platinum status. Refusing to let her get the best of him again, he had to up the ante to tilt the balance of power back in his favor.

Then her cell rang. It was Imani calling. Chasity ignored the call since she and Santana were so close to their apex. They went at it some more. The cell rang again, and once more, it was Imani. Still, she wouldn't let Imani spoil her happy ending and neither would Santana. He pumped her faster and harder, hitting her from the back with aggression and seconds later they made it to their sticky destination.

Chasity was able to catch the call before it went to voicemail. "Hello?" "Wassup, bitch? I've been calling your phone back to back. You all right in there?" asked Imani. "I was taking a shit, but I'm good. Wha'chu up to?" "Me and the girls are on our way over there to check on you."

Chasity didn't want the C.T.Cs to catch Santana at her house so she tried to think of something to deter them from coming over. "Y'all don't have to come way over here to see about me, I'm feeling fine." "A bitch ain't trying to hear that shit! We'll be there in fifteen minutes." "All right then, I'll see y'all bitches when you get here."

Once the call ended Chasity jumped up, "Santana! The C.T.Cs will be here in fifteen minutes. You gotta get out of here!" "So, you're kicking me out now?" "Naw, I'd never do that. I just don't want them to think something happened between us, that's all. Them thirsty bitches just love some tea and I don't want to give them no type of ammunition."

"Well, I ain't goin' nowhere till I'm good and ready." "But how will I explain you being here?" "I'll handle them. You just need to put on some clothes." "Whatever you say, but it still smells like sex in here." "Ain't nothing a little *Febreeze* can't handle." "The stripper pole also needs to come down and stored away." "I'll take care of that as well."

They got dressed and had the house back in order as if Santana hadn't been there but a few minutes. "Chasity, before they pull up I wanted to tell you that you really went platinum on a nigga." "And you went diamond on this pussy. The diamond dick. That's just want the fuck you got between them legs."

"You took me on one helluva ride. And I'm more than thankful for the way you've shown me your appreciation." "Believe it or not, I even shocked myself by some of the things I was doing. I had to go hard since I knew I only had this one shot with you, so I made the best of it."

"The way you just put that pussy on me, I think you've earned as many shots as you'd like." "Don't play with me, Santana. You mean it?" "Did I st..st..stutter?" "Then I don't care if you never make me your woman. At least I can still have you how I want. I love you already, anyway. So this pussy's officially yours. Even if you were to ever get married."

"I like the sound of that. But you gotta promise me to never get jealous or do anything to tarnish our bond." "I promise, now can you promise me something?" "Depends on what it is, you know you be having some outlandish ass requests." "Okay, here it goes… You know I'm a single lady without any kids and all, and I'm not getting any younger. So…can you promise to give me a child one day? It doesn't have to be soon, just whenever you're ready."

Santana was thunderstruck, "God damn, Chasity! You're really going in on a nigga. That's some hard shit right there." "I know but I'll never tell anyone who the father is. It could be our little secret. Besides, you're my dream man and not another nigga for the rest of my life's gonna have the courtesy to even peek at this pussy ever again. I hope you can understand that I only want a piece of you that I can call my own forever. No strings attached."

Santana looked at Chasity in a way he'd never done before. He knew he'd fucked up. Going against his own grain to ever have sex with a C.T.C. just to please a wounded Chasity at her vulnerable time, may have corrupted the chances of her ever finding love to be able to have herself a child with another man.

"You *are* bad as a motherfucka'. We'd probably make a fire ass mixed baby, huh?" "I *know* we would, Santana." "I tell you what Chasity, I won't give you my word as of this minute but I'll think about it. How does *that* sound?" "At least you'll think it over so I'm cool with that. I mean…just the other day at the hospital, you said you'd think about sexing me and it happened. So hopefully I'll come out on top two for two."

There was a knock at the door. "It's them, Santana. Let's go in the living room." The C.T.Cs all marched in one at a time. "I *told* y'all that was Santana's Hummer," said Nina. "Hey, Santana. *Wha'chu* doing over here?" asked Baby K.

"The same thing I'd be doing had any of y'all been shot. I'm making sure my girl's okay. Why? Did something change to where I'm not welcome by you all anymore?" "You sure know how to hit us with a hot track. But it's not like that, Santana. You already know how these bitches get jealous whenever you seem to show another one of us more attention than the others," said Imani.

"Look at that hoe, Chasity. I bet she's lovin' every minute of this shit," said Lydia. "Fuck all y'all bitches. A bitch gets shot and y'all in here holdin' y'all titties on a bitch," Chasity growled. "Don't take it to heart, sis, you know we all love you girl," Ronkeike reminded her.

"What the fuck does holdin' ya titties mean?" asked Santana. "The same thing it means when a dude say holdin' ya nuts on a nigga," Yonnie responded. "Female slangs. Y'all *know* y'all be swagger jacking'." The mood shifted and the women finally shared a good laugh.

When Santana felt his true motive for being there was unbeknownst to the C.T.Cs, he said, "I'm glad you all came because there's something I needed to share with you." Santana went onto explain his move to Miami, the club, and how he was taking Chasity with him. Their reaction was equivalent to throwing gas on a fire. The women exploded.

"That damn bullet was like a four-leaf clover for her lucky ass," said Baby K. "Fuck that shit. Let me see your gun Nina so I can shoot myself in the leg or *some* fuckin' where. Then maybe I can get some *act-right*," said Laina. "See what I'm talkin' bout, Santana? A bunch of jealous ass bitches," said Imani.

"Ladies, y'all don't have to act that way. You're all welcome to come to Miami."

"Do we get to move in with you, too?" asked Yonnie. "I only have a two-bedroom condo but what I'll do is move each of you out there in steps. Once I find Chasity her own house, I'll move another one of you in with me. And I'll repeat that process until I've bought all of you your own place. Fair enough?"

The women had mixed emotions. Some smiled, some frowned. "I guess that's fair," said Ronkeike. Santana was perceptive of their feelings, then said, "I just don't get it. What in the hell is it with you women? I just acknowledged the fact that I would buy each of you a house and I still see condemnation in some of your faces. Let me guess, would it be better if I were to make any of you my woman? Or better yet, if I were to pop a baby off in that ass? Would that make y'all happy?"

Everyone of them said yes while at the same time they gave cold stares to one another as if the other women should've kept their mouths shut. Santana sighed then decided to have a little fun with the women who loved him. "I tell y'all what I'm gonna do. Since y'all are gonna continue to act like that and be that way with each other, I ain't bringing none of y'all asses to Miami with me. Now how does *that* sound?"

Neither of the girls were trying to hear that so Imani quickly responded, "Okay, Santana you win. I'm sure the rest of the girls will agree to do things your way."

"Thank you. I don't understand why y'all are so crazy about *me*. Y'all are like sisters and wanna slick side beef with one another over *my* dog ass. As many broads as I deal with, I can't see how any of you could even look at me in that kinda way."

"Speaking for myself, Santana, that only makes you more attractive," said Ronkeike. "You're the hottest nigga I've ever seen in New Orleans. To be perfectly honest, you're the hottest I know from anywhere," said Nina.

"Well, in order to keep the peace between y'all, get it in your heads that I'm off limits. That's the last time I'm gonna say that, *capiche*? Now get your butts over here and give me a group hug."

Santana hugged them all, kissed them on their foreheads and cheeks - saving Chasity for last. "And *you*, lil mama, if your things aren't packed in a week from now, don't strain yourself. Doctor's orders. And I'll just take you shopping to get the things you need when we get to Miami. You're okay with that?" Santana said as he lifted her chin and stared into her eyes while awaiting an answer from her.

Chasity knew all eyes were on her so she decided to give her friend's one last dose of something to envy her for. "My shoulder is still a little sore so I think I'd much rather leave this shit behind and let you take care of the small stuff."

The C.T.Cs didn't show any signs of vexation but Chasity could tell she'd gotten under their skin from the way their noses were flaring.

"Okay, girls, y'all know I've only got a limited amount of time left in New Orleans so I have people to see and beau coup corners to turn. Now that we've gotten some understanding with one another, I'll leave y'all to pamper Chasity. And y'all better not try to kill her."

## March 5, 2008, 1:02 p.m.

"Having that guns and roses attitude like he was Mafioso or some shit is what got him where he's at today. I tried to tell 'em to leave that bullshit alone," said Donavan. "I gotta put you up on somethin', Donavan. It wasn't Levi who did that to Meatball," said Santana. "I thought fa' sho that was Levi's work." "He's partially involved but *I'm* the one who hit *'em up*. At least I think I did."

"Wha'duya mean you *think* you did?" "Levi had 'em on the ropes for a minute but Meatball's slick ass had a cake baking. He put my nigga, Levi, in a cold blooded wichita. It's a good thing I showed up when I did because Levi was seconds away from gettin' his issue." "What type of smoke screen Meatball put up?"

"The nigga had a twin brother." "A *twin*?! Come on, Santana. I would've known about that. Don't you think?" "Yeah, that's what I thought. But Meatball told Levi nobody knew about him. Not even you."

"*Damn*! That's some crazy shit. I can't believe that after all of the years I've been runnin' with that nigga, he kept me in the blind from something like that. I went to his funeral but how will I ever know if it was him or his brother who was in that casket?"

"The only way to tell is if you had any knowledge of where he was shot at." "I'm positive it was one shot to the back of his head." "How are you sure?" "I paid for his funeral expenses and dealt with the mortician personally."

"Then that was Meatball. His brother, Jermaine, was hit in the chest but must've worn a vest in order to make it outta there. Meatball also told Levi that you sold him out and he was gonna deal with you. So, if you ever run across his look-a-like I suggest you get off on him first and ask questions last because he'll probably wanna make his pistols sing the redemption song in honor of the remark Meatball made about you."

"What do you know about Jermaine?" "Levi told me he's from Cali. We think he's a member of the Crips gang." "What makes y'all think *that*?" "Because he had on a Seattle Mariners snap back with a blue bandana tied around his wrist. Plus he was throwing up gang signs and yelling at Levi saying, '*I'm Rolling 60's, cuz!*'" "I think that's the gang Tookie started."

"Well, if Jermaine's got a lick of sense or loves his life, he'd better had taken his ass back to Cali because if I were to ever see that nigga again it's gonna be a misunderstanding." "That's good lookin' out, Santana. I'll be waiting to flame that nigga up."

"The last thing I needed to holler at you about will affect you to a degree and that's my retirement." "Retirement?" "Yeah, Donavan. I told you in Miami this day was coming. I just didn't know how soon." "It would be selfish of me not to tell you I'm happy to see you changing your life. So what caused you to throw in the towel?"

"Remember me saying that if I liked what I saw in Miami I'd make it my home?" "I can recall that." "Well, I was out there a few days ago and everything fell in place for me when I bought this building I'd seen." "What type of business are you opening?" "A nightclub." "You're about to jump ship with the amount of loot you be making, all for a *nightclub*?"

"You know as well as I do that the dope game ain't guaranteed. Today or tomorrow I could lose it all. I got years invested in that shit and I'm still out here with nothing to show for it. And now that I got my paper where it needs to be in order to make this type of move, *fuck* throwing rocks at the penitentiary."

"I feel you on that, Santana. Especially when you said it wasn't guaranteed because even if you were still in the game, I wouldn't be in need of your services, right now." "Why? Business slow?" "Hell *naw*! Right now I'd much rather have slow business than *no* business."

Santana knew exactly what Donavan was aiming at but continued in his naïve state of mind. "*No* business? What happened?" "You'll never believe that some niggas jacked the Nariño cartel for their submarines and made off with all of Javier's work. So my package didn't come through for me this month."

"Get the fuck outta here. I *know* you bullshittin'!" "More serious than Jordan in the Finals. All of the Bosses have been talking about it. The bad thing is Javier doesn't have the slightest idea of who hit 'em up."

"Damn. That had to be some ill ass niggas who went with the move on Javier." "Whoever they were, they pulled off a bold stunt. And they'd better keep it on the hush because Javier's got soldiers in every city lurking." "He told you that?" "He didn't have to. I already know how them Columbian motherfuckas' comin'.'"

"Looks like I'm pulling out at a good time." "I guess so but if you have anymore work stashed, which I *know* you do, you might as well flood the city with all you've got because the streets dry. The niggas who still holdin' is taxin' like a *motherfucka'* but I'd rather see you wit it. So get 'cha money up like my rap homie Sess 4-5 said it. It's most definitely out there to be made."

"I feel you on that note but the amount of work you be scoring shouldn't cause the whole city to fall into a drought." "It wasn't just my issue on them submarines, Santana. Javier also had a few more niggas in New Orleans who were waiting for their birds to land."

"You got me dead to the right to know I always keep a lil somethin' tucked away for a rainy day. And I'll do just that. Bleed the block for seven days strong and then I'm strikin' out. My club's grand opening is in a week so come swing through and holla if you feel like getting away for a hot second."

"I ain't got shit else poppin' off so I'll book a flight later on today sometime." "Bet that." "So, what's the name of it?" "The Million Dollar Spot." "That's wuzzam. Well, Santana, I wanna thank you once again for the heads up about Jermaine and also for the superb services you've given me over the years. You're damn sure are gonna be missed."

"It was a gratifying phase in my life, Donavan. I had one helluva run. And I've always appreciated your business in return. In the meantime, be easy out there in them streets, homie. And I'll see you in Miami."

# CHAPTER 37



"THIS *CAN'T* BE THE SAME BUILDING I BOUGHT," Santana said with astonishment. "Is that you're way of saying you like what you see?" asked Jasmine. "Hell yeah! Now *this* is what I call a club." "Michael's crew did an exceptional job." "I agree. I'd like to thank him one day." "He's here so you'll get your chance."

The Million Dollar Spot nightclub was in a class of its own. The former furniture store building had been converted into the crème de la crème of nightclubs in all of Florida - maybe in America.

The first floor of the three-level edifice, known as the Gold Club, was the actual nightclub. It contained a huge elevated stage. Four bars, a small restaurant in its posterior, lavish décor - the works.

Level two, known as the Platinum Club, was transformed into a strip club. It had a sound proof glass wall with sliding double doors which led to a wraparound balcony for viewing the stage in the Gold Club for performances. Another elaborate feature was the revolving floor.

The top floor, called the Diamond Vault, was the casino. Exclusively reserved for the Big Wigs, Heavy Hitters, and Black Card holders. It had two entrances. The one for the middle-class patrons gained access through a door near Santana's office with an admittance fee of ten thousand dollars. The other entry point was for supreme clientele who entered into the casino through the rooftop's door which could only be reached by way of helicopter.

The red carpet was rolled out on the outside of the club like Santana had ordered. Camera crews filming. Spotlights positioned on the *Balboa* tequila sponsored backdrops for picture taking. From the looks of the capacity filled parking lot, Santana knew Jasmine fit the bill perfectly as his assistance. She really had the know-how to pack a house.

"What a wonderful job you've done, Jaz. Tonight's gonna be a good night. It looks like the entire city is in here," said Santana. "Thanks, Boss. I knew you'd be pleased."

"Enough with the silly antics. Don't call me Boss." "Well, that's what you are, aren't you?" "Of course I am, but not to you. So continue calling me Santana before we have some problems up in here."

"I knew that would ruffle your feathers." "I've met the detail cops I handpicked and the rest of the staff you've hired. They all seem to be very devoted people. Full of life." "Can't dispute that. I've been in the business for so long I've mastered the art of picking the good ones. Besides, a new business brings on a certain level of excitement and energy."

"I have a few people to greet so I'll catch up with you later but before I go, I just wanted to tell you how sexy you look tonight." "Can it, Santana. We have a hands-off policy, remember?" "I was only giving you a compliment but since you won't let me do that can I at least give my capo a kiss?" "Then that'll lead to sex in your office and that's a big no-no. Just to let you know, my vajay-jay's still sore from the last time a week ago." They both laughed.

"It was worth a shot." "Yeah, a shot you missed by a mile. Now let's get back to work." "Get'em's coming this way. I guess I'll make my rounds with him so call me over the walkie talkie if you need me."

Stepping in his *Salvatore Ferragamo* shoes and *Alexander McQueen* suit, Santana stirred his way through the club with Get'em. He saw lots of familiar faces scattered throughout who'd came to support his big night. Apollo Walker- the Boss from Chicago; Poppy Mendez - the Boss from New York City; Charlie Phillips - the Boss from Detroit; Romalis Rankins - the Boss from Philadelphia; Carlos Vazquez - the Boss from Puerto Rico; Brad Lucas - the Boss from Houston; Stephen Banks - the Boss from Memphis; Harry Heat- the Boss from Atlanta; Cup Hanks and Donavan Mercadel - the Bosses from New Orleans.

"Wuzzam, baby? Glad you could make it," said Santana as he greeted Donavan. "You got yourself somethin' *here,* Santana. I didn't imagine your spot being nothin' like this. You *did* the damn thang," said Donavan.

"Have you had the chance to hit every floor yet?" "Naw. I'm still stuck on this level. Wha'duya call it, The Gold Club?" "Yeah, that's it." "You a motherfucka', Santana. I can't wait to get back to the city to tell 'em how you're out here shittin' on these niggas."

"For me to leave the game behind it had to be for something big." "You got *me* thinking about doing the same thang." "Just like the rest of the Bosses: Got *all* of that money, but no imagination. That's a clear indication of a recipe for a disaster. But that's on them because if the *Alphabet Boys* were to ever pull any of their numbers they for damn sure got a place for 'em." "I guess you're right. Fuck it. I'll just find a nigga with a damn imagination and pay his ass for it."

"Ain't shit wrong with that because what's the use of having all of those millions when you gotta live out of a fuckin' box? Can't even enjoy it. My freedom is priceless." "I feel you, Santana."

"Well, finish relishing the moment, Donavan. I'm sure you didn't fly to Miami just for me to be sitting all up in your face." "You know I would've felt shitted on if you didn't come holla at 'cha boy." "No doubt. Just be sure to get at me before you leave."

Santana and Get'em took the elevator up to the Platinum Club. As the doors slid open, they saw Chasity walking onto the platform. "Damn, big brudda, Chasity's thicker than a Snicker, ya *heard* meh?!" said Get'em.

"Who *you* tellin'? Some of these niggas bout to go for broke by the time she leaves the stage." "You ain't lying, cause I'mma be one of 'em. What's her stage name?" "I named her Dreamgirl." "It damn sure fits her."

"Have you seen Levi and Korey?" "Yeah. They're sittin' in the booth on the other side of the stage." "I was wondering where they were." "You already know that if some half-naked bitches running around, them niggas is *some*where in the vicinity."

As they were chatting, Get'em realized something was happening that he hadn't known beforehand. "Damn, big brudda.

This bitch is live as *fuck*. I just noticed how you got that World Trade Center shit going on in here." "What are you talkin' bout?" "The floor. It's spinning like the floor in that club that's at the top of the World Trade Center in New Orleans be doing."

"Oh yeah, that's where I got the idea from." "Ooh woo! Chasity's ass is over there cuttin' up! Sorry, big brudda, but I got some money to throw. I'mma get back wit'cha in a minute, ya *heard* meh?!" "Go have fun, Get'em. I'm going make a lap in Gold."

As Santana came into the Diamond Vault, he was astounded to see it had big things poppin'. He looked around to see the call girls he had flown in from Vegas were crawling all over the big spenders. None in which Santana was acquainted with, but one. Sitting at the poker table puffing on a Cuban cigar. It was the Boss of Miami - Hurricane El Jefe.

"El Jefe, thanks for coming." "Santana! How do you do, my friend?" "Just enjoying the first night." "So am I. You really put this place together. I'm definitely making it my new hangout."

"You're welcome anytime. I see you've spread the word to the other Bosses. I've spoken with all of them." "When you extended your courtesy of inviting me I phoned them like I said I would. And they were anxious to come out and partake in the celebration of your opening night and retirement."

"So far everything seems to be running smoothly. Got an incredible staff." "Wish I could say the same." "Don't tell me you're losing a lot of money. Would you like me to switch dealers for you?" "No need, Santana. It's much bigger than that. I'm winning at the tables but losing bigtime in the streets." "I have a listening ear if you care to speak on it. If not, I can understand that as well."

"Although you're out of the business, you know the people involved so it wouldn't hurt to tell you. The Nariño cartel was robbed out of their entire shipment." "That sounds farfetched. Better yet, *impossible*." "Well it happened. Right now, I don't have any product and Javier's got me in limbo." "I wish there was something I could do to help." "It'll be okay. I've been in this business long enough to know shit happens. And breaks here and there have proven to be healthy."

"Yeah, I've experienced them as well." "But I know one thing, Javier's offering a king's ransom for any info on the mobsters. All hell's gonna break loose if he ever finds out who burned him." "I can imagine." "Right now, everyone's a suspect. He doesn't trust anybody. Not even me." "How do you know?"

"My gut tells me. So I'll stay out of his way until things boil over. Eventually, he'll see who's loyal or not. Some of the Bosses have already been probing for another connect. Not me though. Financially, I'm good so I'll tough it out with Javier until he decides crank up again."

"At least you're being a good sport about it." "Anger'll get me nowhere so, what the heck." "All right, El Jefe, I'll leave you to your winning spree and see you when my retirement party cranks up in the Platinum Club. Good luck at the tables."

As Santana neared the exit someone caught his attention at the roulette table. It was a woman. A woman wearing a *Fendi* cat suit, oversized *Fendi* shades and *Monolo Blahnik* heels. She wore her glasses raised up to hold her hair in place.

But it wasn't her attire that drew Santana to her. It was that aura of royalty. Her eyes. She had those mysterious eyes that told him she harbored more secrets than Area 51.

Santana approached. "Excuse me ma'am. I couldn't help but to come over and introduce myself. But before I do, I would like to thank you for granting me the honors of being in the presence of your unsurpassable and breathtaking beauty. I'm Santana Bailey and it's a pleasure to meet you - is it señora or señorita?"

Santana extended his hand but the woman declined. Instead, she shot him an unreadable glare and responded, "It's señorita, but sir, I don't speak to strangers nor do I recall giving you permission to do anything. So, what makes you think you're even worthy of knowing my name?"

"The absolute last thing I wanted to do was rub you the wrong way. Forgive me for being an opportunist, in which I know that in some cases it could be considered an act of selfishness. But I live by the motto: *You Only Live Once.* Reason being is because some occurrences are rare and it would be really eat at me if I'd never approached you not knowing if I'd ever see you again."

The woman pulled her glasses down to cover her eyes, "You're forgiven, Santana Bailey. But I live by this motto: *Two mountains will never meet each other but two people eventually will.* So if by chance we were to ever cross each other's path again, maybe *then* I'll let you know who I am."

The woman reached for her Birkin bag and casino chips then left Santana where he stood. Santana couldn't believe it. He couldn't remember the last time a woman's heart didn't melt at the sight of him literally throwing themselves at his feet.

But not the woman in the *Fendi* cat suit. She was cut from a different cloth. Even though he was known to move mountains as he saw fit, he decided he wouldn't push the issue any further.

Another lesson he'd learned from the *School of Hard Knocks* was to never chase a bitch. So he got back to the business and headed for his office because he figured if it were meant to see her again it would happen.

"Wassup, Jaz? I thought you'd be runnin' around in Gold or Platinum," said Santana. "I just left both floors pulling the draw from the cash registers and guess what?" "Lay it on me." "You said you wanted to clear a million dollars each week all three clubs are open and we've reached twenty-five percent of that mark already!"

"You gotta be kidding me." "I don't play when it comes to business. In Gold and Platinum. I only collected eighty grand so far. But Diamond's raking in the big numbers."

"You're a fucking genius, Jasmine! Will you marry me?" "Cut the crap, Santana. We gotta hurry and get to Gold because Rick Ross is about to take the stage.""He's here already?" "For a half an hour, he's been. Are you going on stage with him to introduce yourself to the club?"

"Naw, I don't need the attention. I'll just watch the show from the balcony in Platinum with my homies. So have security clear out a spot for us, okay?" "Ten four, Boss. Oops…that one slipped."

"There you go with that again. The next time it *slips*, I'm gonna pull you in this office and slip this meat pistol clean in that ass." "Okay, naughty by nature, won't happen again."

# CHAPTER 38

**South Beach, Florida**
**May 1, 2008, 7:36 p.m.**

THE MILLION DOLLAR SPOT was the talk of the town. It's been receiving rave reviews from Miami's leading radio stations and newspapers since opening day. Santana was flying high and another big night was taking place in a major way.

Ever since the day after the grand opening, Korey Witha K, Levi, and Get'em had all been back in New Orleans moving packs. But on this particular night they'd flown back to Miami to join the fireworks that Santana had in store.

He orchestrated a night full of events which were divided into three segments beginning with an old-school car contest taking place in the parking lot. Afterwards, the show would move to the Gold Club where an A-list of mainstream performers were set to rock the mic: Pit Bull, Jennifer Lopez, The Migos, and Drake. For the closing segment, Santana was gonna bring the house down with a foam party in the Platinum Club.

"Damn, big brudda, you got this club industry shit in a choke hold,"said Get'em. "I gotta be innovative to stay alive in this game, Get'em. If not, it'll take me under," said Santana. "That's wuzzam, fam. Keep your foot on these niggas necks," said Levi. "The way it's lookin' in here it seems like you *killin'* the competition," said Korey Witha K.

"Just last week, this guy's club went belly up. My spot took all of his most profitable nights away from him." "That's on *his* fuckin' body, ya *heard* meh?! A New Orleans nigga runnin' this bitch now and got the whole *city* under siege," said Get'em.

"I've been seeing a lot of new faces every night since day one. But I've noticed a few regulars like those guys over there in V.I.P. who's just sitting there looking at us." "Them Haitian niggas?" asked Korey Witha K. "Yeah, all six of 'em." "You think they're plotting on some shit?" asked Levi.

"Be there in a minute," said Santana. "Wha'chu talkin' bout, big brudda?" asked Get'em. "Oh my bad fellas. That was Jasmine talking to me through my earpiece. Hope y'all don't think I was talking to myself." "For a second, I thought you went loco," said Levi.

"Naw. Something just came up and I need to run to the office real quick." "We won't be hard to find. You can catch us lurkin' somewhere in the Platinum Club," said Korey Witha K.

"Now run that by me again," said Santana. "Just got off the phone with Drake's manager. He said their flight out of Minnesota's grounded due to bad weather. Said that he might need a rain check. It's kinda late to shoot for an add on. So, wha'duya wanna do?" asked Jasmine.

"I don't think it's too late. I know a few big-name people that's in town so leave it up to me." "All right, Bo…Santana." "You almost got yourself in trouble, Missy. We're already in the office." "I'm getting better at it but it's kinda hard not calling you Boss when that's what you are."

"I've been noticing how Michael's been in here a lot lately. What's up with that?" "Do we have to talk about this now?" Santana looked sternly at Jasmine. "Is there something you're not telling me?" "Oh all right, you'll find out sooner or later. Michael and I've been out on a date."

"I can't believe it. You finally gave 'em a shot." "Yeah, I did. I got to thinking when you said I should. I mean…he *is* a nice guy and all. So I followed your advice and took him to a Heat's game."

"No wonder you've been glowing around here lately. You don't even have to fess up for me to know that he hit the skins. It's written all over your face." "I see *you're* very opinionated tonight." "You can't fault me for being clairvoyant."

"Well, I plead the fif on that topic but I *will* tell you that Mr. Riley came up to the skybox for a minute. He sends his regards since he only came to see you and you weren't there. Said to tell you that with all of the gossip he's been hearing about the club, he might have to drop in to pay you a visit to see if he could talk you into selling him the building back."

Santana laughed. "Not on his life." "I'm sure you know he was only bantering." "I'm sure he was. So is there anything else we needed to discuss besides the cancellation?" "Nope. That's it for now." "All right, Jaz, it's time for me to get back to the money."

Walking into the Platinum Club, Santana saw one of his newest dancers, Angel, on stage. She and two dozen dancers had left *King of Diamonds* to become part of the movement formed by the Million Dollar Spot.

With a minor dilemma on his hands, not even Angel's enthralling moves could capture Santana's focus. Since he'd started gaining favor with the music industry, he figured it wouldn't be too high of a hurdle for him to jump to nab another hot artist. So he reached for his cell in an attempt to fill Drake's void.

The Master of Ceremony, D.J. Khaled, cranked up the concert shortly after the car contest ended. Santana tracked down his team in the reserved booth. Each of them had their dancer of choice in their laps. So he joined his crew escorted by Dreamgirl.

First up was the Miami native, Pit Bull. From the minute he grabbed the mic he had the party goers amped up. He had them chanting the lyrics to his songs word for word. J.Lo was up next. The moment she hit the stage in a provocative figure revealing dress, wearing it in a way that only she could, Get'em nearly lost his mind.

"Ooh woo! big brudda! You *gotsta* introduce me to her. I'll wife her fine ass on the spot. I *mean* that, ya *heard* meh?!" "But, Get'em, I think she's old enough to be your mother," said Santana. "That's exactly what I wanna call her; Mami and I'd be lovin' every second of incest." Everyone in the booth was laughing as hard as they possibly could. "Aight, Get'em, I'll put 'chu in the car with her so you can shoot your stick." "That's all I'm asking, big brudda, that's *all* I'm asking."

Towards the end of her performance Santana and his team made their way to the Platinum Club. Jasmine was already in route to the stage to inform the crowd of the no-show artist. She was unaware that Santana was a few yards behind her with a cordless mic in his possession.

Jasmine called for the attention of the crowd, "Are you guys enjoying the show?" The crowd whistled and applauded. "The staff here at the Million Dollar Spot has been working phenomenally hard to please you guys. I know y'all are expecting to see Drake., but his plane had to be grounded in Minnesota for extreme weather conditions."

The crowd roared, "WE WANT *DRAKE*! WE WANT *DRAKE*!..." Jasmine tried calming down the angry mob of clubbers. "We apologize for the inconvenience, but..." Santana stepped on the stage and stopped Jasmine in mid-sentence. "But we have another treat for you guys. And I'm sure you've all heard of him. Everybody show some love for *NBA YoungBoy*!" The crowd went bananas. Santana motioned for *NBA YoungBoy* to come on-stage and then walked off with Jasmine.

"The crowd was on the verge of bum rushing me! How'd you pull *that* one off?" asked Jasmine. "I found out he was in town so I phoned the person I needed to in order to bring him in." "I was thinking you didn't have a sure replacement."

"Never doubt the maestro." "That you are." "I think we make an unstoppable team, Jaz." "So do I, Santana. I'm so happy to have ever met you."

The foam party kicked off in the Platinum Club after the concert ended. But as the foursome was headed for the elevator, Santana stopped dead in his tracks. He saw a woman. A woman who was standing in V.I.P. surveying him. Her eyes were piercing through him like an x-ray machine. It was the woman from a month ago he once saw in the Diamond Vault. The lioness who wore the cat suit. She'd finally returned. A slight grin flashed across Santana's face as he moved in her direction.

'*She must've felt my swag*,' Santana thought. He tried to get to her. But with a crowd so thick he had to bob and weave through traffic. She waited for Santana. His moved towards her with sheer confidence in his stride. His hitters with him step for step guarding him like he was the President of the United States and they were the Secret Service.

He was only a few yards away from her when Santana's pathway was obstructed by six Haitian men. The same men who Santana had been taking heed to since opening day.

"'Cuse me. Dem say chu da man dat run dis ting," said one of the Haitian men. "Is there a reason why you would assume that?" asked Santana. "Me no assume. Me no!" responded the Haitian with cockiness in his voice.

Santana perceived the hostility in the Haitian's tone as well as the rest of Team Santana. "You've assumed correctly. Now if there's something you need to get off your chest then I suggest you let it rip or move the fuck around."

"Watch ya bum ba clot mouf. Me no take up too much of ya time. Me got message from me Boss. Him say you not from here, you pay graft."

Without even looking at his team, Levi, Korey Witha K, and Get'em all raised their shirts and clutched their straps. The six Haitians tensed up. So did Team Santana. Tight security hindered the Haitians from bringing any weapons in the club which had them at a disadvantage. They assumed it would only take their presence and a few words to tip Santana but they were dead wrong.

"Well, I have a message for your Boss. Who*ever* he is, he got me misconstrued, playboy. The only thing that *he, you,* and *any*body that comes behind y'all are gonna be receiving from *this* club are some drinks that you *will* pay for or some motherfuckin' bullets. Compliments of Santana Bailey. Now run and tell your Boss I said to pick his poison," Santana growled with his venomous million dollar mean mug. "Santana, let me flip these lil boys and put 'em in body bags," Get'em howled as he reached for his toolie. "Not in here, Get'em. *Way* too many witnesses."

While the Haitians were arguing amongst themselves in their heavy dialect another man came in between the confrontation. It was Hurricane El Jefe. "Good evening, Santana." "Nice seeing you again, El Jefe." "And Wesley, I see you've met my good friend, Santana," Hurricane El Jefe said to the Haitian.

"El Jefe, me not no him ya friend." "Of course you didn't. But, now you do. So what seems to be the problem here?" "Me got no problem, El Jefe. Me Boss make big mistake." Santana cut in, "Everything's understood *here*, El Jefe. They're just a couple of panhandlers who went about begging the wrong way. Nothin' I can't handle."

El Jefe looked back at the Haitian, "Well, you run and tell Daz I said Santana and his guys don't take kindly to threats so back off now before he finds himself in a war he won't win." "Kay, El Jefe, we go now."

Team Santana unclutched their hardware then let their shirts back down. "I didn't know you were here tonight, El Jefe. You certainly didn't have to intervene. My guys and I had everything under control."

"I'm sure you did, Santana. I've been in the casino for a few hours before I went down to the Platinum floor to look at the ladies. Then I saw the commotion from the balcony. I know those guys and how they're into extortion, so I rushed down here to diffuse the situation. You're in your establishment, Santana. That kind of ruckus could've given your club a bad name. And now that you're a businessman, try not to let petty hustlers like that cause you to react off instincts."

"You're right, El Jefe. This club thing is still new to me. Gotta learn to leave my street frame of mind in the streets." "*Now* you're learning. And now that *that's* over, I have a few babes waiting on me who's full of bubbles." "Enjoy, El Jefe."

After Hurricane El Jefe disappeared Santana remembered the reason he came to that area of the club. The woman in V.I.P. He couldn't see her anymore from where he was standing so he went to the spot where she was when he last saw her. She was gone.

He searched high and low for the mystery lady only to come up empty. The lioness who wore the *Fendi* cat suit was nowhere to be found. She'd left the premises.

Moving day was underway at Santana's condo for Chasity. Weeks of house hunting had finally paid off. "Thanks for everything, Santana, said Chasity. "Don't mention it. You know I got you, baby girl." "Guess this is the end of our little fling, huh?"

"You're acting like it's the end of the world. Forgot I know where your house is?" "No, I didn't forget. It's just that I'd gotten adjusted to being here with you. Cooking and cleaning and the sex. Lord knows I'm gonna miss those things."

"All good things come to an end *someday*, Chasity. Don't think I'm not gonna miss you being here, either. But the longer we stay with each other the harder it'll be on you for when it's time to move on. And I don't want to put you in that type of predicament."

"I understand." Chasity eyes began to water. "Don't do that, baby girl. Come here." Santana held her for a moment. "I knew you'd get like this. That's why I never wanted to cross that line with you or any of my C.T.Cs." "But I can't help it, Santana. I never knew how you truly looked at me but you think of me as just another freak bitch. I can feel it." "That came from outta left field. What made you tap into that subject?"

"Because I feel like I'm not good enough to be called yours. You know I fucked Meatball but it was only because I'd do whatever it takes to prove my loyalty to the C.T.Cs which are *your* girls. Before him, I'd been sex-free for a minute. I've been satisfying myself with my little silver bullet and other toys and don't have any problem doing that."

"Sorry to inform you that you've never been further from the truth. I've never looked at you or any of my C.T.Cs as freaky bitches.

I'll still be slidin' in your house every now and then but the minute you've had enough, we'll kill the sex. You *did* say that you'd still be getting what you wanted. Or do you want to stop it now?" "*Hell* no! Keep it going, of course. A bitch emotional but I ain't *that* crazy." They laughed together.

"All right, Chasity, you know we gotta get you on your way so you can get settled in. Then I can move the next girl out here. They're all killing me by calling every day to see if you moved to your own place yet."

"I love 'em, Santana, but them some hatin' ass bitches. And if they try to fuck you, which I *know* they will, you'd better leave my dick in your pants and I mean that." "Don't worry, baby girl, you're the only C.T.C. who'll ever have that privilege."

# CHAPTER 39



FOR THE PAST FEW YEARS AND RUNNING, the Million Dollar Spot owned the night. Santana was labeled as the King of Clubs in Miami from how he trailblazed his competitors. Leaving them no choice but to kneel down and kiss the ring.

With his ingenious act of conspiracy against the Nariño cartel remaining unsolved, Santana chose to widen his avenues of revenue.So he tapped into the real estate market and also started the *Amazin Kajin's* fast food franchise. His team even created their own businesses. Levi went into the construction field, building houses. Korey Witha K opened a car dealership, while Get'em had his own custom body and rim shop. They'd all went legit, with the exception of Get'em for whenever he felt the need to whip up a new *Rolex*.

The C.T.Cs each got their own homes as Santana promised. And his steamy affair with Chasity was still confidential.

Miami's climate was some of the best Santana ever encountered. Today's weather was no different from most days. With the urge to feel the zephyr he took his new convertible Ferrari for a spin. So he left Chasity's house and then dipped into traffic. NE 41st street in the Miami Design District was his destination to drop a few jingles on some designer threads and frames therefore making the Gucci store his one stop shop for the day.

Santana entered the store. Browsing, looking for nothing in particular. Just something more suitable for that moment in time.

Satisfied with his selections, he headed for the cashier. Only one other customer was in front of him. It was a woman. A woman wearing a three-thousand dollar pair of *Bottega Veneta* pumps with a vintage *Chanel* mini dress that clung to her body that was to die for. The purse to match.

Santana had to lift his *Bvlgari* shades for a clear view of the woman who was stunning from behind. He didn't have a full glance of her face. He waited patiently. Watched as she unzipped her purse. She reached inside her Chanel tote bag as the cashier said, "Cash or credit, ma'am?"

The woman turned her head to answer the cashier at an angle where Santana could see her face. Instantaneously, his heart began to flutter. It was that gorgeous face of hers. The face that could grace the cover and centerfold of any leading magazine. The same face that had been in his dreams gnawing at him for the past few years. It was the face of the woman from years ago who was in the Diamond Vault wearing the *Fendi* cat suit, and again in the V.I.P.

section of the Gold Club before the conflict with the Haitians. Santana had finally seen her again.

The woman came out of her purse with a wad of cash but Santana answered the cashier, "That'll be credit, ma'am." Then handed the cashier his black card. The woman turned to see who was the generous Samaritan. Santana stood behind her apparently feeling rather photogenic with his undeniable smile.

But the woman's posture was cryptic. Difficult for him to decipher. His smile depreciated. Feeling as if the woman could care less. He had an epiphany of this moment. And it was going nothing like he'd imagined. Nevertheless, he held his composure.

"I've heard people say the third times a charm. But I believe *your* choice of words are much better when you said, '*If it was meant to be*'."

The woman responded, "Excuse me, sir. I'm sure you must know I can cover my own bill since I came to this store alone. Second of all, do you even know me to be buying me things?" Santana saw which direction the conversation was going so he laid down his cards.

"So, you're gonna act like you don't remember me, huh?" "I never said I didn't." "Well, let me be the first to tell you that seizing the moment's a part of my repertoire and I do it without fear or hesitation. Now, during my analysis of what I consider to be sacred moments around you I conjured up the notion that you're very intellectual. So please correct me if I'm wrong when I say this: As we stand here today staring into the windows of each other's souls, I am convinced that you know you're in the presence of the finest. Now wuzzam wit'chu, baby?" The woman smiled. Santana finally made her smile.

"Thank you for the gift, Santana Bailey. But, being in the presence of the finest remains to be seen. That was a very bold statement, and I find it very attractive to know you're that sure of yourself." "You remembered my name?!" Santana asked excitedly.

"It's written on your credit card. Isn't it?" Santana's ice cold smile melted away A.S.A.P. "Oh…yeah, right," Santana said coyly. "But to be honest with you, Santana, I didn't get it from your card. I remembered it."

His ice grill returned with a vengeance. "I *knew* you were frontin' on me." The woman extended her hand, "Xiomara Vazquez." Santana accepted her soft hand, "Xiomara? Is that your name?" "Sí." "Your name's almost as beautiful as *you* are. So, what does it mean?" "It means *battle ready*." "Well, now that we've officially met, Xiomara - the warrior princess, have I ever told you how beautiful you are?" Santana kissed her hand as she smiled again.

"Yeah, you did. Twice, I believe. About five seconds ago, and once before, when we first met." Well, get used to it because I'll be reminding you of that every single day I'm blessed with a chance of seeing you or hearing your sexy voice." "Are you trying to flatter me, Santana Bailey?" "I'm trying to do whatever it takes, mamacita, to make you mine."

For the next couple of months Santana had been putting in overtime working tirelessly to win Xiomara over. Dining in five star restaurants. Walks on the beach. Picnics in the park. A two day get away to Atlantic City for some casino fun. A party Santana had been invited to in the Hamptons. Courting Xiomara like a royal heiress deserved to be.

In return, Xiomara adored that free hearted spirit Santana possessed. Continuously denying her the prerogative to pay for anything. But not this time. She'd heard about a five-day cruise to Jamaica for singles only and covered all the expenses.

By Santana being the captain of his soul and master of his fate he could take a leave of absence from his business whenever he deemed necessary. And anything concerning Xiomara was a good enough reason.

## Caribbean Cruise
## Atlantic Ocean
## June 2, 2011, 6:15 p.m.

"As many things as I've done in my life, being on a cruise isn't one of 'em," said Santana. "Neither have I. So I guess I can mark it in my diary as a monumental experience we obtained together," said Xiomara.

"Did I tell you how beautiful you are today?" "Si, Santana. That was the third time." "Just checking." "You know we don't have much time until the *mingle with the singles* party kicks off on the main deck."

"Guess I'll go and get myself together." "Why are you pouting, Santana?" "Wasn't aware that I was. But it's probably got a lot to do with you getting us separate rooms." "It's a singles cruise, Santana. We're not a couple yet. But it's not like we won't see each other. Our rooms are a few doors apart."

"Well, I'd better not see another man anywhere near yours because I swear it's gonna be a *man overboard* and I ain't talkin' about me." "You think I'd bring you with me while I go around meeting other men?"

"Actually, I don't. But this *is* a singles cruise, Xiomara and niggas gonna be shootin' for you the minute we're apart. To be honest, though, I know my value. So it really wouldn't bother me because I leave competing to the peons since I'm victorious when it comes to anything I go after…even if it's by any means necessary."

"You should know firsthand that I don't have any problem with shutting a person down." "Ouch! That one stung." "I didn't mean it like that. You were a special case." "Special?" "Yeah, I liked you from the minute we finished our very first conversation. But since I believe in destiny, I stopped it short."

"The second time I saw you, you'd came back to my club. So how is that destiny? Sounds more like pressing the issue." "For starters, I didn't know it was your club until you brought *NBA YoungBoy* on stage. Secondly, I been hoping I'd run into you again which really irked my nerves because I commenced to going out in public places a lot more than usual and what do I find? No Santana Bailey. Talk about frustrating."

"I know you saw me coming towards you. Why didn't you wait?" "Because I didn't want to get into the middle of a gun fight. I saw the way you handled those Haitians. I thought things were about to get ugly in there, so I left."

"That's understandable. But why you never came back?" "For you to get so close to me when suddenly that incident short-stopped you, I realized I was forcing the situation instead of letting destiny occur on its own like it did in the *Gucci* store." Santana hugged

Xiomara, "It took a while but at least it still happened and it was worth the wait." "I think so, too."

For every event that the cruise offered Santana and Xiomara were willing participants. Getting their money's worth. At least Xiomara was because the entire idea of choosing a singles cruise was her method of scrutinizing Santana's mental state.

Getting to know him more. Hearing his beliefs. Understanding his core values. Allowing him the time he needed to paint her a graphic description of his future, with and without her in it. He intrigued her in every way. Check.

She tested his yielding capability towards the abstinence of intercourse. Going no further in intimacy than kissing, hugging, and holding hands. Seeing if he'd vex her for sex. He didn't. Check.

In fact, the conception never formulated in Santana's mind. Every other woman he'd conquered always submitted themselves to him freely without procrastinations or complexity, excluding Gabrielle. Santana was her first and as far as he knew, her only.

Xiomara's last quiz for Santana was to explore his traits of trustworthiness. Leaving him alone in an area of the cruise liner that was filled with single women while she pretended to use the ladies' room. He flirted with none. Even turned two of them down before Xiomara could get back to him, so he thought. She'd been spying on him. Watching his every move. Xiomara saw that all he really wanted was her. Check.

She smiled at the thought. Santana had passed her examination with flying colors. He'd unknowingly graduated from the class of friendship to the second phase of Xiomara's five-layer heart. Companionship. By the time the cruise ended they were a certified couple.

Neither could've been any happier. Xiomara even molded herself a permanent dance partner out of Santana by turning him into a show stealing salsa pro. And they salsa danced their way off the cruise liner until their feet were back on solid ground.

# CHAPTER 40



"HURRY UP, SANTANA, we don't have all night," said Xiomara. "Aight, baby, I'm coming. I don't know what's with all the rushing. The club's awfully busy tonight and I know Jasmine needs me here to help out."

"You know I wouldn't pull you away from your business on a holiday night without covering all of my bases. I've already braced Jasmine for this moment days ago. I just spoke with her in the Diamond Vault to make sure she has everything under control, and she said she is holding down the fort and for us to get out of here."

"Ohh…y'all two collaborated on a nigga, huh?" "If that's what you wanna call it." "I can't wait to see what the big surprise is that you have for me." "Neither can I."

As Santana and Xiomara exited his office, he walked towards the elevator, but she stopped him. "Where are you going mister?" "If I'm not mistaken it appears to me that we're leaving now. And the best way to do that is to catch the elevator downstairs, walk outside to the parking lot, and then get in my car to drive off."

"I swear that flip little mouth of yours is gonna land you in hot water one day. But since you *think* you know everything, I'm sorry to burst your bubble, smart guy, but you're going the wrong way."

"Ah *ha*! My surprise must be up here somewhere since we're not leaving in my car. Gotsta be in the casino. See that, Xiomara…I catch on fast!" "Jeez, Santana. You're a horrible guesser. Our ride is waiting for us on the roof top. So can we go now?!" "Oh, forgot about the chopper. Aight, mami, let's get going."

Xiomara had Santana wear a blindfold for the short commute. After landing, she carefully guided him out of the helicopter then walked him over to a flight of stairs. Once they reached the top, they hung a hard right. Then Santana heard a door seal shut behind him. He felt air pressure like Xiomara had him in some type of confined space. His claustrophobic senses kicked in and he began sweating a little at his palms.

She sat him down in what felt to him like an Italian leathered executive chair. Then he felt movement. Whatever he was in was moving fast. Curiosity was getting the best of him. But before he could utter a word Xiomara kissed him then removed his blindfold. Then Santana looked around to see that she had taken him on a Gulfstream IV private jet.

## Charles De Gualle Airport
## Paris, France
## July 5, 2011, 2:13 p.m. EST

"YOU FLEW ME ALL THE WAY TO *PARIS*, Xiomara?! Let me find out you're trying to steal my heart," said Santana. "I've been dreaming of visiting this place for as long as I can remember. Not to sound like I'm making some sort of demands or anything, but I waited to come here until I felt I had a man in my life that was worthy enough to marry one day."

"You believe I'm the one?" "Well, *are* you?" "That ain't fair, Xiomara. How are you gonna answer a question *with* a question?"

"It's not unheard of, Santana. People do it all the time. So, *are* you the one that's deserving of me giving my all to?" "Hell *yeah* I'm him. You could always put 'cha money on me, I ain't gon' let 'chu down." They smiled at each other as they kissed then went out hand in hand into the *City of Love*.

In the limousine Xiomara reserved, they cruised through the historic metropolis with famous landmarks every which way they turned. She pleaded with Santana for them to stop and take photos of all they'd seen. But jet lag got the best of him. And for the time being, rest outranked sightseeing.

Seeing that they were at odds with each other they came into concession that if Xiomara stopped her impulsive quest for souvenirs for the evening, she'd be the designated escort in France for the duration of their stay. So she ordered the chauffer to bypass the scenic route and deliver them to their reserved rooms at the

Shangri-La Hotel on Avenue d'léna which ran her a cool $1,100 per room, per night.

When they arrived Santana soon learned that once again Xiomara had gotten them separate rooms. Knowing they'd never slept together he didn't have the energy to debate the separation. So, he accepted his room key, kissed Xiomara goodnight, then dragged himself to his chambers.

Xiomara noticed the uneasiness in his stride as he walked away. As he opened the door to his room, she said, "Santana, I know you were probably expecting we'd share the same room, but I hope you can understand that I'm not quite ready for us to inaugurate that level of our relationship."

"No pressure comin' from me. I do acknowledge the fact that you chose me to accompany you on such a special trip that you've always wanted to take to this country. The thought in itself is enough to know I've reached another milestone in our relationship. So everything's all gravy with me, Xiomara... Just as long as I'm here with you."

At the crack of dawn, she was beating down Santana's door. Abruptly awaken from his deep sleep, Santana answered wearing only a pair of Ralph Lauren Polo boxer briefs. The initial sight of his ripped physique had her tongue in knots.

"M..morning ssleepy head. Uhmm…, we have a full day ahead of us." "It seems kinda early, Xiomara. What time is it?" "Three a.m. Miami time. Eight a.m. Paris."

"Aight, mami, I'll be ready in a minute." "I never knew your body was so toned. You must do a lot of push-ups." "Naw, no push-ups, Xiomara. I do push downs." "Push downs? I've never heard of *that* before. Are they something like doing burpies."

"Not even close. It's an exercise I became accustomed to from making money." "What in the world does making money have to do with exercising?"

"For every thousand-dollar stack I collect, I push them down deep in my pockets like this...one-one thousand, two-one thousand, three-one thousand and so on." Santana made a gesture of motioning his hand in and out of his pocket after every thousandth count.

Xiomara laughed, "All right, funny man, now that was a good one." "I only said that to get that heartwarming smile out of you. It always makes my day." "Now you have my cheeks turning red."

"Just being honest. And by the way, you are so beautiful when you wake up." "Thank you, Santana. You're pretty handsome yourself but if you keep complimenting me all morning we'll never go anywhere."

"All right, I'll go and get ready now." "Good. And be sure to pack a to-go bag with some beach shorts or better yet, a pair of briefs like those'll do just fine."

First location on their agenda to visit which was walking distance from their hotel was none other than the iconic Eiffel Tower - the most popular landmark in Paris. Santana and Xiomara were so into each other like never before. As well as every other couple who were in the vicinity.

"Love is most certainly in the air, I see," said Xiomara. "It sure is. Maybe there's some type of spell hovering in the clouds because I'm definitely feeling the vibe," Santana said as they began to ascend inside the elevator of the world-renowned structure. Once they reached the peak of the tower and were able to get a visual of Paris in panoramic fashion, Xiomara was rendered speechless. "Oh my! The landscape of this city's so breathtaking!"

"I concur, mami, but it's a far cry from what I have *my* sights set on at the moment." He gently reached out for her chin then turned her face towards his and planted the most passionate French kiss on her France had ever witnessed.

For the remainder of the day, he played the back seat as promised while Xiomara took the lead. She had a things-to-do list that was quite extensive and well-prepared. She even had a few appointments and reservations made months in advance. They went from a pit-stop at the *Boulangerie Julien* bakery on Rue Notre Dame des Champs to shopping at *DOUCHERON Paris Faubourg Saint-Honoré* store for watches, sunglasses, and pricey jewelry. They also stopped in the *Le Bon Marché* department store on Rue de Sèvres for a high-end shopping experience. And after working up big appetites they treated themselves to five-star dining at a the *Pur'- Jean-Francois Rouquette* restaurant on Rue de la Paix.

Then there was the Louvres Museum - the largest art museum in the world. Being in unfamiliar territories it took no time for the street savvy Santana to comprehend that in the field of art he was way out of his league. But every step of the way Xiomara was there to educate him.

Overall, he was very intrigued with her touring selections but even more with her. To Santana, it was ever so clear that all aspects of her character carried the traits of a *Boss Bitch* and he felt fortunate to be her significant other.

With the moonlight fast approaching, Xiomara had to get them to their last engagement for the night. Per itinerary they chartered a helicopter for an hour-long flight to Xiomara's idea of the most romantic setting which was a temporary dining area partitioned on the Deauville Beach in Normandy.

She wanted the dinner she had in store for Santana to be a last-minute surprise. Her method of keeping it concealed was parking near a section of the beach which would be a brief journey by foot to their dining destination.

In the Bath House located on the beachfront, they slipped into something more appropriate while inside a cabin-whose name was in honor of Keanu Reeves then consolidated their items into one bag and began their hike on the boardwalk. Small talk brought forth thoughts they shared involving the gradual surge of closeness in their companionship. And neither could be happier with the way things were progressing.

With a feeling of tranquility expelling from the English Channel they continued on course towards Xiomara's feast. Approaching the midpoint along the way, Santana observed a group of people congregated on a make-shift stage.

"This spot is the perfect getaway from a big city like Paris. And just look at that crowd down there. I wonder what they're doing *this* late in the evening?" Holding steadfast with a poker face, she responded, "Who knows? Maybe it's something entertaining.

Wanna crash the party?” “You actually felt the need to ask? You should already *know* I’m wit’ it.”

As they drew nearer Santana realized the people he thought were partygoers were musicians and caterers instead. Xiomara had hired all 119 members of the *Orchestre de Paris* symphony orchestra in addition to the top-rated *Emperor Norton's* catering service of Paris.

“I think we’ve drawn the wrong conclusion coming over here, Xiomara.” “Are you eating your words now, Mr. *'you know I’m wit' It'*?”

“Normally, I’m down for whatever but that table set up for two tells me it’s a private function. And a certain couple with extravagant taste has yet to reap the benefits of this romantic display. I just don’t want to intrude and make asses out of ourselves, baby…that’s all. “I guess you’re partially correct. What if I were to say that this is *our* private function?”

The sly smile that crept across Xiomara’s face helped Santana to understand that her question was more of a statement and he was astonished by her initiative.

“You put all of this together?” “Sí, Santana. Are you pleased with my surprise?” “By all means. I’ve *never* had a woman go to this extremity to serenade me. And frankly, I find it quite enchanting and refreshingly original on your part.”

“You’ve never held any punches nor spare any expenses when it comes to making *me* feel special. And I wanted you to see how far I’m willing to go to show my gratitude and interest in you.” “I can assure you that the gesture’s been duly noted and etched into my memory forever.”

With that being said, they took their places to indulge in a taste of France under the sounds of crashing waves mixed with elegant music.

Afterwards they took to the sands to have a more in-depth conversation. They even had a little fun in the water along the way back to their awaiting limo. In that moment they declared to have just had their most romantic encounter to date. And with a bond that was clearly soaring to newer heights Xiomara had a confession to make.

"There's something I need to share with you, Santana." "Shoot for it, beautiful. I'm all ears." "For this feeling I have, I believe you have reached a place in my heart that has never before been penetrated."

"Would you believe me if I were to say I feel the same?" "Judging from the way you treat me and make me feel, I would have to say, I do." "And that would be an accurate assessment." There was a brief pause in their stride for a much-needed heartfelt moment. "What I'm trying to say is...I'm in love with you, Santana Bailey." "Just when I thought you were made of steel." They chuckled as she lightly tapped Santana's arm. "I was only kidding, sweetheart. But seriously though, if you only knew how soothing it is to my soul to hear those words escape from your lips. As for me, I've been in love with you from the very first moment I saw your beautiful eyes."

They found themselves back at the hotel after proclaiming their true feelings to one another and Santana was finally smiling at the thought of how he slid into the third notch of Xiomara's heart.

Love.

# CHAPTER 41

New Orleans, LA
July 4, 2011, 10:35p.m.

"HEADS UP, MITCH, he's coming our way." "Is that a Pug he has?" "Yeah, he named him Rocky and he's been walking him faithfully every night at 10:30 since Rocky was a puppy. For as long as I've been gone, I would've thought his predictable ass switched his routine," said the ski masked man as he did surveillance on his target.

"I can't wait to see the expression on his face when he sees you. The nigga might shit a brick," Mitch said as he prepared to move into position. "He's a few yards away, Mitch. Stick to the script." "I gots this, my nigga. Don't trip."

Mitch walked over to the supposedly disabled vehicle with a gallon of antifreeze to fill the radiator as if the vehicle overheated.

As he poured the fluid the target passed by and commented on his supposed misfortune.

"She ran hot on you, huh?" "Yeah, I think it's low on antifreeze." "Good luck with that." Being cautious, the target kept it moving. He was acquainted with all of his neighbors and knew this guy was an alien on a mission.

With the target's back now facing him, Mitch reached for his piece and slid one in the chamber. However, the still of the night was not in his favor because the sound alerted the target who just so happen to never left home without his banger  even if it was the smallest task of taking out the garbage or walking his dog. The target's first instinct was to keep walking and call for back up but cancelled the idea was upon the realization of his cell being left at home.

And since he would bust his guns in a heartbeat which would complement his sweet aim he decided to address the issue like the true soulja he was. In efforts of creating a safe distance between himself and the neighborhood intruder he and Rocky returned home on the opposite side of the street.

Mitch eyed him approaching and readied himself to apprehend the target. Then Rocky passed followed by his master. Mitch began keeping pace. The target heard footsteps drawing nearer to him. Mitch raised his Glock .30 with a smile at the thought of how easy this job would be considering the caliber of man his target was. Then came the unexpected.

The target fell to the ground after stumbling over an uneven section of the sidewalk. At first Mitch found humor in seeing the clumsiness of the guy. But when the target quickly recovered with a reversed roll Mitch found himself on the receiving end of a gun.

That smile he had was washed away with a look of horror. And with the target having a *shoot first, ask questions last* mentality, the three shots he got off left Mitch's corpse dead before it hit the ground.

As he reclaimed his footing and began retreating to the house, more shots rang out taking him down once again. But this time he was on the receiving end of an assault rifle held by a masked man.

"Go right ahead and aim that motherfuckin' piece at me if you ready to die. If not, then I suggest you toss it out of your reach," said the masked man as he watched the intended target choose the second option.

"What's the reason for the mask? I know that voice from anywhere?" "You do, huh?" said the man as he removed his mask. "And who the *fuck* do you think I am?"

"You're Meatball's twin brother. Invading my comfort zone. And for what? Vengeance for his death which had nothing to do with me?" The man removed his mask. "You never *did* have an imagination did you, Donavan? You're just assuming shit that ain't true."

"What *other* reason would bring you here?" "To show you the repercussions of betrayal." "Betrayal? Nigga, I told Meatball to leave that petty ass bullshit alone with Santana's people. I *never* betrayed your brother!"

"That's the first thing you were on point with all night." Donavan was confused. "What the fuck is that supposed to mean?" The man gave Donavan a piercing glare, "It means you didn't betray a brother by giving Santana and his crew the green light. Nigga, you betrayed *me*!"

Donavan tightened his gaze to look deeper into the man's eyes then realized who he was. "Meatball?" "You finally guessed it. I'm back from the dead, nigga, and I ain't going nowhere until I run down your business associate, Santana, for killing my brother. He's been off the scene for a minute. And I've run out of patience looking for his elusive ass, so I decided to use you to flush him out."

"Santana don't live in New Orleans anymore. So how do you expect that to happen?" "You'll find out soon enough. But then again…maybe you won't. Now crawl your ass over to that car and get in."

## Paris, France
## July 6, 2011, 1:25a.m.

Stepping out of the shower, Santana heard a knock at the door of his suite. He knew Xiomara should be sound asleep in the connecting room next door after such an exhausting day so it couldn't be her knocking. He wrapped a towel around his dripping wet frame to address whoever it was petitioning his presence at this time of the night. He glanced through the peephole but saw no one. Then, opened the door to find a deserted hallway. *'That's strange,'* he thought.

He closed the door with a rare moment of second guessing himself as if maybe the knock was at someone else's door. Or just maybe he was hearing things and there was no knock at all.

As he slid into his *Givenchy* boxer briefs there was another knock. But this time he knew it wasn't coming from the front door. The knock came from the door that connects his suite to Xiomara's.

He opened it to find her standing there looking as sexy as ever in her erotic negligée. "I *knew* I heard someone knocking. I figured you'd be sleep by now, beautiful. Is everything okay?" "Yes, Santana. It's just that I find it harder to rest now that we've shared our true feelings."

"I understand. Is there anything I can do to assure you a good night's sleep?" "In fact, there is….if you don't mind, I would prefer not to see another sunrise without waking up in your arms." "I would *love* that."

With no other words needed to be spoken they were intertwined by the lips and back pedaling to her bed while caressing one another in the gentlest yet intense way. Xiomara preset the mood with lit candles, rose petals in a huge heart shape on the bed topped off with soothing sounds flowing from Adele's album titled *21*.

She slowly began undressing down to her silk Burberry panties. Not in a seductive way, but innocent. Santana laid her down on the bed then paused to take in his first look the most gorgeous body and skin tone combination he'd ever laid eyes on.

Again, he kissed her. Entangled his tongue with hers only for a short period. Then he licked the inner crease of her ears and nibbled on her lobes.

He palmed the back of her head to massage her scalp as he worked his way down to her neck. She lifted her chin to give him ample space. As he sucked all over her neck, he grinded on her pussy. She welcomed the motion by opening her legs wider to let him dig until he found what he was looking for.

Her chest heaved at the feeling of Santana's warm dick in which she observed through his Polo briefs. Then he went a degree lower. Taking a second to adore her perfect set of *double D* breast. He fondled the right breast while devouring her succulent left. Alternating special attention to both through the course of her soft moans with no rebuttal.

Being satisfied with bringing her nipples to an erection, he continued his southern expedition. Licking every inch of her skin in route to her treasure island.

Then he made landfall. Her fortress was still protected by a guard wearing plaid who went by the name Burberry. He noticed a breach of wetness on the silk shield caused by her aroused pussy. He licked the spot and found *her* berry to be as sweet as any berry he'd ever tasted. Then curtly, Xiomara halted him.

*"She stopped me. Here it is, my first chance granted at sleeping with her and my horny ass just had to try and go all the way."* He thought to himself as he began to wish he could regress back to the knock at the door. He raised up.

"Xiomara, baby I apologize for trying to rush into this. It just that I read the situation differently thinking you were ready." Xiomara shook her head in protest then reached out to kiss him.

"You have never pressed me, Santana. And your feelings are not misplaced. I am ready but first there is something I must share with you before we proceed, my love." "That's a relief. Speak your heart, baby…I'm listening."

"For all my life up until my father suddenly moved me to Miami for reasons unknown to me, he kept a watchful eye over me. I was guarded at all times." "So he kept you safe from the dangers of this world like any father's obligated to."

"That may be true, but he smothered me all those years by doing so. In return, I was deprived of finding my own way." "Now that you're on your own you have that opportunity." "I guess you're right…now, can I tell you a story from my past?" "Sure baby…you can talk to me about anything."

"When I was sixteen, I had a boyfriend who my father gave me permission to date. I was young and naïve at the time, thinking I was in love. Well, he talked me into letting him break my virginity.

"We were at my house the day we attempted to go through with it and as soon as it was about to happen my father burst in my room. He snatched my boyfriend by the shirt and slammed him to the floor then placed his foot on the poor boy's neck. I had never seen my father so furious.

"My father said, *"I gave you my blessings to court my daughter under two conditions, Carlito. And that was that she be the only girl you were interested in and that you would never attempt to have sex with her until you marry her. And you have failed at both."*

"I asked Carlito if what my father had said was true. Was there someone else that had his attention. Carlito couldn't even look at me. Then my father had his men drag Carlito out of my room and I had never heard from nor saw him ever again."

"Damn! Did he have Carlito killed?" "I believe so, although my father would never talk about it. After Carlito left my room my father sat next to me and told me how he'd been keeping tabs on Carlito.

"He knew Carlito was seeing another girl who went to the same school as me. I asked my father why didn't he tell me beforehand and he said he didn't want to be the deliverer of any news that would devastate his daughter. And he hoped that one day I would see through Carlito deceit and leave him alone on my own terms.

I asked my father *why say something now?* He said because he refuses to let that little snake steal something so sacred away from his little girl. And that was Carlito final straw. "But how could he have known what you and Carlito were about to do?" "I asked my father and he said, *'Don't get angry with me when I say this Xiomara…I had a hidden camera installed in your room.'*

"Although he asked me not to get angry, I couldn't help myself. I said, *"Father, how could you?! You don't trust me, Papa?"* And he responded, *"I trust you my darling. It was Carlito who I didn't trust. And if it's one thing I despise more than anything it's a snake.'*

"I've heard someone say that before," said Santana as he tried to recall where he heard the phrase. "I felt so ashamed as I lay naked underneath my comforter. I asked my father how long had he been spying on me. He said, *'Since the day I found out about Carlito's other girlfriend I wanted to be sure my daughter wasn't being taken advantage of or played for a fool. The camera was only powered on when he came to visit. And now that everything is in the open, I apologize, my darling. And I will take the camera out immediately. That is…after you get dressed.'*

"My father smiled at me, gave me a hug and kissed my forehead like he always does, then he left." "He sounds like a wonderful father. I would like to meet him one day. And I sure as hell wouldn't want to end up like Carlito." Xiomara smiled. "I'm sure you'll be fine and I believe my father would approve."

"Good. So, is that all you wanted to share with me?" "Not quite, Santana. The moral to my story is…I'm still a virgin."

Santana couldn't believe how fortunate he was. For the second time in his life he'd encountered a virgin.

"That's gotta be the best kept secret you've revealed to me thus far." "You mean you're not disappointed?" "No sweetheart, not at all. But I was wondering since you're ready to take this step…why do this now and with me since we're not married?"

"Because I asked you if you were worthy of me giving my all to and you said, *"Hell to the yeah, I'm him!"* Xiomara said in her best impression of Santana's voice. They laughed at her attempt, then she continued, "I believe you when you said it, Santana. And also because I've been preparing for this moment and I know the timing is right."

"Preparing how?" "I hope you don't find humor in what I'm about to tell you." "I won't…I promise." "Since I'm not experienced with having sex and wouldn't want to disappoint you, I've been watching porn videos for the past few weeks to learn different ways to please you." Santana smiled at her initiative. "Are you ready to show me what you've ascertained?" "Yes, my love."

They began relieving each other of the garments clinging to their bodies. In the process of tugging at his briefs she grazed his dick and almost instantly saw a bulge. Santana was rocked up to her first touch.

"Is this the time where I open my legs to let you lick my pussy?" Or do I suck on your dick first?" she asked candidly. "There's no particular format for sex so however you'd like to proceed is fine with me. And doing each other at the same time is an option also."

"That sounds like fun. Maybe we can try it in the near future. As for now I've been fantasizing about this moment and I'm anxious to go first." She reached for his dick to stroke it then looked at him to continue, "but bear with me, Santana, because I am a bit intimated by the size of this thing. It's a lot bigger than the ones I've seen on the videos. And please don't hesitate to stop me if I'm not doing it correctly, okay?" "Baby, whatever amount of effort you put forth I'm sure to love it."

Xiomara was wholly vested in catering to Santana's enjoyment and ready to receive rave reviews from him in the aftermath of her first experience. She began her seduction with a kiss to the apex of Santana's prized possession.

Then spiraled her tongue on the smooth head of it for a brief taste test before taking it into her mouth. Next, she ran the backside of her wet tongue down the length of his shaft until reaching his genitals to get familiarized with the area. Then back to sucking as much of his dick her mouth could take.

"Ooh Baby... *Damn*, that feels good!" Inwardly, Santana was enthralled to realize how hellacious Xiomara's head game was. Without coaxing her, he felt her creating her own rhythm. Inciting maximum hardness to his rod with her hand movement and the beautiful music she made with the sounds from her slurping and moaning.

The compliment for her efforts gave her a spurt of motivation as she began twisting his dick in a massaging manner while doing tongue tricks. Her intensity level heightened, nearing the point of Santana's release. But before he let loose his load he beckoned for his shot at tasting her so she halted her actions to entertain his desires. Then it was Santana's turn.

All of those months of being patient and just going with his heart had finally granted him access to the sacred grounds of Xiomara's Holy Grail. And he was as ready as ever to bless her game.

With ease he glided his tongue all over the immediate area of her clean shaven pussy. Leaving behind a trail of faint marks of passion for ownership purposes. Then gripped her ass cheeks as he licked between her kitty lips to massage her pearly trinket.

She extended her legs wider to offer him abundant accessibility. Using his fingers to part her lips, nothing was in the way of him whipping his tongue like a flagitious whirlwind. Showing her the true definition of a tongue lashing, which caused Xiomara to unleash a series of oohs and aahs. And he continued to do so until she creamed for the very first time.

"Holy Virgin Mary, Mother of Jesus, Santana. That felt sooo good!" "I'm glad you enjoyed it." "Enjoyed it? I *loved* it! I've never experienced such a feeling. Can you make me do that often?" "As much as you'd like to."

She went into the bathroom to wipe herself clean. Then retrieved different types of lubricants and a large disposable pad with plastic backing and brought the items back into the bedroom. "I see you came equipped."

"Sí, Santana. During my research about having sex I discovered that a lot of women agree that it is not as painful when lubrication is applied. So I brought a few to choose from as well as this pad to catch the bleeding."

She laid the pad across the bed and handed over the lubricants to Santana.

"So, which would you rather, Xiomara? *The Hidden Vault's* lubrication or KY jelly?" She surveyed her options for a short spell and then came to her conclusion by reaching back for the items. "At first, the thought of the pain I would endure made me timid…but as I look into your eyes I see a man who I am willing to go through *any* amount of pain for. And I've decided against using any of it." "By this being your first time I'm sure it's gonna hurt a bit. But I promise to go light on you and soon the pleasure will outweigh the pain." His words gave her assurance.

After tossing the lubricants aside she laid across the pad positioning herself on her back then opened her legs. "Thank you for making this easy for me. Now take me as you wish, Santana Bailey, my King. I'm all yours."

For a moment he admired the sight of her beautiful body as it glistened. Then slowly he crawled on top of her to get reacquainted with her breast and neck area as he sucked his way back to her mouth. Their kissing and breathing deepened.

During the heated moment Xiomara caressed his love pipe to exert it back to adamant standings. Upon attaining the stiffness in his rod she'd felt earlier, she ran the tip of it up and down the entirety of her pussy. But when she rubbed against the spot where Santana had concentrated on so heavily when he was licking her and gave her that bursting sensation, she zeroed in on the area.

Suddenly, she felt the friction creating natural lubricants. And they were grinding one another like tomorrow would never come. She then positioned Santana's piece at the gates of her juicy fortress and braced herself for a desired intrusion. He pushed with gentle force. She flinched. Still in rhythm, he propelled a bit more. She panted against each of his lunges. Even more, he advanced on her. Eventually he felt himself piercing through her fleshy obstruction. She arched her back as she bit her bottom lip in silent agony. Fighting through the pain like she said she would. He revered her bravery.

Began kissing her again in an attempt to divert her mind from the imminent pressure below. To help cease her distress he gave her one powerful thrust. Xiomara clamored from the impact causing her to bury her fingernails into his back. Then the pain subsided.

Santana stroked deeper and deeper as he penetrated her walls. She hankered for more. As the music switched to 'The *Weeknd's* song *Often*, he pumped her to the beat. Doing precisely as the song said, '*making that pussy rain.*

Her legs quivered uncontrollably. "Aye, papi…you made me do it again." "I told you I could," he whispered.

Eager to put her skills to the test, she flipped Santana over to straddle him. The excessive wetness gave her all the leeway she needed to prove her worth.

She slithered her way onto his python. Scaling slowly down every centimeter. Gradually, she picked up the pace while swerving her hips like a belly dancer. To confirm her attempts to please him were gratifying, Santana was now the one responding with oohs and aahs.

An aggressive side of Xiomara was ignited in which she hadn't known existed beforehand. She began whipping her pussy on Santana like a tactician at war. And he was loving every minute of it but wasn't ready for it to end just yet.

Hurling her over on all fours, he entered her from behind. She offered no objection as she spread her legs wide and tooted her ass up north. With his left hand he gripped her by her waist while palming her ass with the right.

"Yes, papi, give it to me just like that."

He banged her with finesse. She threw that ass back at him. He rammed her harder and faster. She advocated for more. He replied with action. Smacking her sweaty ass cheeks one at a time. "Whose pussy is this for?" "Ooh…It's for *you*, papi. ***SMACK***!!! "All mine?" "Sí, papi! For you and only you!"

***SMACK***!!!

Their heartbeats accelerated the longer they continued in the same mannerism.

Then he flipped her over to give her *tha bizness* missionary style. As her legs went into the air her flexibility allowed her to grasp her heels to spread her pussy open as wide as it could. They went at it once more. His rod grew thicker the faster he drilled.

"Aye, papi, I love you." "I love you too, Xiomara."

Then he kissed her long and hard as he stroked her and stroked her until finally, their explosions collided. Bringing her first time to a close. He raised up to look at her. Her face was wet, but not from sweat alone. It was also watered by tears of joy. He wiped her face.

"You okay, Xiomara?" "Sí, Santana. I'm just so elated to have fulfilled this process of my life with a man I truly love... I pray we never part."

"We won't. One day I'm gonna make you mine forever. And *that's* a promise." They smiled at each other. "All right, Santana. I'm gonna hold you to that. So you'd better not eat your words."

In his heart he knew he wanted no other woman but her. And from that day forward he'd work towards making good on his word.

"So tell me, Santana, and be honest with me. How was I?" "Baby, you gave a monumental performance. Showing no traits of a novice." "Muchos gracias. I really gave you my all."

As Xiomara left to discard the padded proof of her virginity Santana heard his cell ringing in his suite. Only a selected few had that particular number so he knew the call had to be urgent at that time of night. So he rushed to answer the call. It was Levi.

"Yo, Levi. What's good wit'cha? Shit straight out there?" "I'm not sure. That's why I called." "What happened?" "Somebody just killed Donavan." "Damn! So you're thinking the Columbians may have offed him?" "I don't know. I'm just putting you up on game just in case they're coming for us, too."

"That's wuzzam. I'm outta pocket out in Paris right now but I'm jumping on the first plane smoking to get there and get to the bottom of this. So round up my team and I'll see y'all in a minute."

Santana knew he'd engineered a retaliation proof conspiracy with the *Columbian Job*, but needed to investigate Donavan's murder for assurance. And if it was indeed the works of the Nariño cartel, Team Santana were about to get locked and loaded to prepare for a war they may never win against the most powerful drug lord the world has seen since Pablo Escobar.

# CHAPTER 42



"NIGGAS IN THE STREETS IS SHOOK after what happened to the homie, Donavan. Got these niggas out here fallin' back from pushin' their product until it's determined who killed him," Levi informed Santana as he, Korey Witha K and Get'em convened in the conference room of Santana's home.

"He ain't bullshittin', my nigga. They got a hit out for a hunnid bandos on anybody who had something to do with it. Yeah, *DatWay*," Korey Witha K added.

"For a ticket *that* big, I'm gunnin' for them niggas like the *Bounty-gate* Saints, ya *heard* meh?!" Get'em indicated as he patted the Glock .40 he had tucked in his waistline.

Santana paced as he countered, "the bounty should be the least of our concerns. We're here to discern whether or not if we have a war coming our way. Because more importantly it's still a mystery as to who took him out." "You're right, big brudda. You know I be looking for any reason to smoosh a nigga."

"Yeah, I know, Get'em. But you gotta reserve that mindset for the right moment. Now back to what I was saying…As I flew in from Paris I theoretically assessed Donavan's untimely demise. And three set of people came to mind on who's responsible: the jack boys, the cartel, or either it was someone he pissed off.

"Then I began my process of elimination after I paid a visit to his wife, Nikki. In regards to the conversation we had, nothing was taken from him nor did anyone contact her demanding a ransom. I also factored in the amount of respect that Donavan 's name carried in the streets. And the jackers wouldn't dare go that route in fear of repercussions so I believe it's safe to rule out robbery." "Maybe it *was* the Columbians," Levi suggested.

"I'm not sold on that assumption either. For starters, Donavan and I both saw firsthand the steps Javier Ochoa takes to eradicate those who cross him. And Donavan's having an open casket funeral without any missing body parts.

"Secondly, Donavan demonstrated his loyalty to Javier when he weathered the storm without jumping ship in search for another supplier after we ripped Javier for his submarines. I'm sure he commended Donavan for that. So my gut tells me his death was not the cartel's doing."

"The last option is enemies. You *seriously* think he had any?"inquired Korey Witha K.

"I honestly can't see that either because he packed fair when it came to business. But it's the only alternative that makes any sense. And I'm leaning in that direction because of an unsolved clue

Donavan left behind. Nikki mentioned Donavan being kidnapped from in front of their home while he was out walking their dog. Only a chosen few had the privilege of knowing the whereabouts of his residence. That tells me either someone had been keeping tabs on him or knew him very well." "In that case, Nikki should at least have a hunch about who did it," Levi offered.

"I would've thought the same thing but she can't seem to connect the dots. The night Donavan went missing, multiple gunshots rang out on their block. When the neighbors went outside, they saw a car speeding off, discovered a dead body person lying on the sidewalk, and found a gun in someone's lawn that was registered in Donavan 's name.

"And after a ballistics test was performed on the gun, law officials confirmed it was the weapon used to murder the person they found on the scene." "Damn, Donavan was really livin' like that huh? He went out like a soulja by takin' a nigga wit'em," Get'em professed as he openly saluted Donavan's gangster." "That's real talk, Get'em. He was really *bout that life*," Santana told him.

"So, who was the nigga Donavan laid down?" asked Korey Witha K. "His name was Mitchell DeSilva. And Nikki's never seen him before nor does she recall Donavan ever mentioning his name. That's what has her perplexed. And even though there's a slim chance of this being our war, I promised her I'd do everything in my power to figure this out so she and her children could have tranquility and move on with their lives." "Now I see why she can't piece it together," Levi reckoned. Santana lowered his head and closed his eyes as he contemplated. Then, as if he had a premonition, he lifted his head and reopened his eyes.

"She probably can't, Levi, but maybe I can…and if I had to bet my bottom dollar, I'd say somebody's sending a crystal clear message."

To further his investigation, Santana filled Imani in and advised her to relay the message to the rest of the C.T.Cs.

In the meantime, he made it his business to dip in and out of a few spots throughout the city. He had to admit that he kinda missed his hometown. And from the way he boasted on New Orleans during the flight there from Paris, Xiomara had to see things for herself so she tagged along.

The two-door convertible Rolls Royce Wraith was the vessel he chose to sail the streets since he had yet to drive it since it was purchased. Another reason he opted for the topless machine was to give the vultures an eyeshot of the tastiest arm candy to ever hit the Big Easy—Xiomara the Columbian princess.

Before showing her around he stopped at *Shonotchos* for some of the best nachos in town. Then went on to Cajun's Seafood to grab a few pounds of boiled crawfish, snow crabs, pig feet, turkey necks, sausage, corn on the cob, and potatoes. The works!

Since he was introducing her to a taste of New Orleans he knew they'd need something to cool down the spicy feast as they consumed it. So he treated himself and her to daiquiris from a shop located in the Gentilly Woods area of the city.

His drink of choice was named in honor of the slain rapper Soulja Slim - the most beloved rap artist from New Orleans that was gunned down in front of his mother's home which was roughly one mile away from the daiquiri shop. Santana reflected back to that November night for he was one out of nearly two hundred grieving spectators who were present at the atrocious murder scene of the fallen legend.

The tour officially kicked off in the largest component of NewOrleans - The Ninth Ward. To the underground world the area was also known as *The Mighty 9* and also a catch phrase, *I'm out dat 9 and I don't mind dying*, which was often uttered by the souljas, gangsters, b.gs and thugs who were born and raised there.

He cruised down Poland Avenue pass one of the largest housing projects in the United States, the Desire Project: childhood home of the NFL Hall of Fame running back, Marshall Faulk.

Next, he swung by *Musician's Village*, a revived neighborhood that was spearheaded by the famous singer and television talk show host, Harry Connick Jr. Then he headed to the Florida Avenue bridge to crossover the industrial canal and into the lower Ninth Ward, also known as the C.T.C. which is the abbreviation for Cut Throat City.

Upon crossing he hung a right turn at the first accessible street, Jourdan Avenue, which ran alongside of the levee. He floored the coupe until he reached the point of the levee that was breached by Hurricane Katrina.

There was a sign posted near the street that he stopped to let Xiomara read which noted the breach was marked as a failure for the Army Corp of Engineers for the first time in American history. *Since 'that's the case, some government officials ought to be held accountable for genocide,'* Santana thought.

Moving right along, he enlightened her about the houses in the exact proximity of the breached levee being constructed by the former power couple, Brad Pitt and Angelina Jolie.

Pressing on, he went a few blocks away to Caffin Avenue to show her the original home of the Blues pioneer, Fats Domino. And less than three minutes later he was pulling into a driveway of an abandoned house. A house out of a few in the lower Ninth Ward that endured the devastation of the historical Hurricane Katrina.

Santana got out of the car with the bags of seafood and daiquiris and then sat on the porch while Xiomara followed suit.

"So what famous person lived here?" Xiomara asked as Santana schooled her how to eat crawfish. "In all actuality, this is the porch I jumped off of as a youngin'." "Really? Is this your familia casa?" "It *was* up until the hurricane hit. I guess it belongs to the city now." "Does this house mean anything to you?"

Santana looked back at the house and thought of all of the memories it captured. Then responded, "More than any other house in the world." "Then it's settled…I'll buy it for you so it can stay in your family forever."

Never before had he thought to save his family's house. And Xiomara's gestures made him fall a few degrees deeper in love with her.

"That's a wonderful idea, Xiomara. It means the most that you'd do something so special for me. But it would mean so much more if I did it myself." "I understand, perfectly. As long as you save this house that's all that matters to me." They kissed on the subject then continued to eat.

"Who that is over there with that pretty car and sittin' on that porch in *my* block? Do I know y'all?" asked the lady who lived across the street as she made her way over to Santana and Xiomara.

"Is that *you*, Ms. Margie?" Santana asked once he recognized he woman he knew as the *neighborhood watch* when he was a kid.

"Yeah, I'm Margie. The Mayor of this street. Who *you* is?" "Look at my face real good, Ms. Margie. You don't remember me?"

She studied him closer then realized, "Is that my lil boyfriend, Tana-man?" "Yep. Lil Santana, just a few inches taller." "You sure are…and still handsome. And you some pretty, young lady. You his girlfriend?"

"Muchos gracias, Ms. Margie. Sí, I am his girlfriend." "Oh, okay. Well, what's your name?" "Xiomara, nice to meet you." "Same here, baby, You got a pretty name. So, Tana-man, how's your grandma and 'nem?" "Everybody's doing fine." "That's good. So what brings y'all here?" "I wanted to pick us a good spot for us to bust up these crawfish. Want some?" "Sure do! Don't have to ask *me* twice. That's why I came outside. I smelt 'em'."They all laughed and ate as *Ms. Margie the Mayor* carried on with the chronicles of Tana-man.

"You know what I hate, Tana-man?" "What, Ms. Margie?" "I hate having to come outside every day and the first thing I see is this ole ugly house looking right back at me. I wish the city come tear it down because it's been in the same condition for all these years after Katrina."

"It's funny you mentioned that, Ms. Margie. As of today, the city won't have a chance to do that because I've decided to go to City Hall after we leave here and buy the house." Ms. Margie's face lit up.

"Now that would be so nice of you, Tana-man. I can't *wait* to tell Mrs. Jackie, Cheryl and Patricia and the rest of the neighbors.

They'll be happy to know somebody who grew up in the house is the one fixing it up."

After they were done eating and washing their hands inside Ms. Margie's house they prepared to leave.

"Can you keep an eye on the house for me, Ms. Margie?" "Can I? Lemme to tell you something, Tana-man…when I told you I was the Mayor of this street, I meant that. And don't *nothin'* go down in this block without *me* knowing." "That's the Ms. Margie I remember. It was real nice seeing you again." "Same here. But before you go, Tana-man, I wanna ask you if I can borrow twenty dollars until the first of the month. I'm tryna get a lil somethin' to burn my hair."

Santana always admired her for being brutally honest. He knew she was actually referring to her wanting to get a buzz. So he went in his pocket and peeled off fifteen hundred dollars for her. "Here you go, Ms. Margie. Try not to spend it all in one place."

In route to City Hall he had to cross over the Claiborne bridge towards the upper Ninth Ward in order to reach his destination. Just before getting off the bridge he pointed to his right at another notable structure.

"Do you see the building with Villalobos written on it?" "Sí, what is that place?" "That's the home base for the T.V. series *Pitbulls and Parolees*." "To say you've only shown me parts of the *Mighty 9*, as you call it, I find your town to have a very fascinating history." "If you think *that* was something to see, just wait'll ya get a load of the French Quarters."

# CHAPTER 43

New Orleans, LA
July 10, 2011

THE CHURCH WAS FILLED TO its limits with droves of loved ones, onlookers, and fellow Bosses who'd all came out to pay homage to Donavan Mercadel - one of the *best that ever did it* from New Orleans. Immediately following the funeral his casket would be transported by a horse and carriage out to the seventh ward's *Hunter's Field* for a *second line* in his honor before bringing him to his final resting place.

Santana brought Xiomara to the affair to let her experience the true essence of how New Orleans natives celebrate one's life after they've passed on. With a brass band providing the music for the Indians and everyone else who attend *second lines* - where the people dance with unorthodox movements that comes from the depths of their souls - the tradition would surely leave a lasting impression on her.

Nearing the end of the service Santana's cell vibrated due to a call from Imani. But the pastor was officiating at the time so he sent her to voicemail. As the funeral came to a close the director called for the congregation by rows to view the body and pay their final respects to Nikki and the rest of the Mercadel family.

The audience spilled out into the street in front of the church and blended in with the awaiting crowd until the moment the pall bearers placed Donavan's casket in the horse's carriage. Then the *second line* began.

As the carriage set in motion to stroll through Donavan's old stomping grounds in the Seventh Ward, the *Hot 8* brass band furnished the music along the walk to the place where everything goes down at *Hunter's Field*. The multitude of second liners hadn't migrated a block away from the church when Santana's cell vibrated. It was Imani calling again. With everything going on with the funeral he hadn't gotten around to returning her call. He answered without a chance to get a word in.

"Thank God you finally answered, Santana! The girls and I rushed out here to the *second line* and we're scrambling trying to find you. Where is your exact location?" The desperation in her voice stopped him dead in his tracks.

"I just left from by my Porsche jeep near the corner of the church. Why? Something's going down I need to know about?" "I'm not so sure but you know how I keep my antennas up at all times and the signals I'm getting is giving me bad vibes." "What makes you feel that way?" "I just got the low on dude who ran with that cat, Mitchell DeSilva." "That sounds like *good* news, Imani. So, who's the guy?" Imani faltered as she replied, "It was…Meatball…"

For Santana, the warning came a bit too late. A hit squad formed by three gun toters emerged from the crowd aiming in his direction, with Meatball acting as the spokesman in the middle. "It's been a long time comin', Santana."

With zero margin for error Santana pulled his strap and yelled, "*Xiomara! Get down!*" Sparks started flying from the firearms of Meatball and company. The reaction from the *second line* participants equated to a favorable distraction for Santana to hustle Xiomara and himself to a safer spot as the panic stricken people scampered in every which way.

It wasn't an easy task for him seeking shelter. He had to duck, dive, and roll to outmaneuver at least fifteen bullets. Once he'd regained his footing, "**BLOOKA, BLOOKA, BLOOKA!**" was Santana's response as he fired back at the trio.

He managed to land a kill shot in the forehead of the opposition to the right of Meatball. But that wasn't enough to deter the remaining two men who were on a mission to attain their objective.

To add gasoline to the firestorm Santana was up against Twin had a second wave of shooters that surfaced to assist in the hit. Seven in total.

Seeing that he was at a major disadvantage Santana dove for cover behind a parked car, inadvertently landing on Xiomara in the process. Meatball and company continued their assault. After a short spell, the shooting ceased so Meatball could taunt Santana.

"Are you gonna come from behind that car and get ya issue like a man, Santana? Or do I have to come around there and give it to ya?" "It's your life. Lose it however *you* want to. I'll be waiting for you right here with these bullets with your name written on 'em." "We'll see about that. Playtime's over, Santana. Fellas! Let's finish him off." More bullets pierced the afternoon skies. But they weren't the works of the opposition. Eight women walking side by side gripping Dracos were dumping on Meatball and his goons. It was the C.T.Cs who'd come to even the odds.

After witnessing all of his helpers fall, Meatball scampered for cover in the vicinity of Santana. With all of the shooting going on, Santana didn't want to take a chance on moving to slip out of the jam he was in, nor risk Xiomara getting hit. So he used himself as a shield to protect her but was unaware of Meatball's close presence.

"I once heard somebody say, *Always look a man in the eyes before you kill 'em'*. Now turn your ass over and take your lick." In order to protect Xiomara's life, Santana had to face the music. He gave her one last kiss, told her he loved her and began to turn over. As he was doing so, a single shot was let loose. But Santana wasn't the recipient of the bullet. It was Meatball who had been shot in his left eye.

With his focus now lost, literally, he covered his eye as he ran around screaming. Then a white van pulled up to the corner with the sliding door opened with guys in it yelling out, " Meatball! We gotta move, *now*! Let's *roll*!"

Although the C.T.Cs were now spraying up the van, Meatball still managed to dive in and flee the scene. After the enemy retreated they rushed over to Santana. "He's gone, Santana. Greasy bastard done slipped through the cracks," Imani said as she and the girls helped Santana and Xiomara up on their feet.

"Thanks to *you* girls he's gone. I don't know which one of y'all shot his ass but I sure as hell appreciate it." "None of us were shooting at the time that shot went off," Nina explained.

"If not, then who *was* my guardian angel that came to my rescue?"

Xiomara was waving her custommade derringer in the air that Santana had gotten her just days ago. "It came from me, Santana. I wasn't about to let him lay a *finger* on *my* man."

Briefly, everyone was in laughter until seconds later they noticed blood on Xiomara's dress. "Were you *shot*, Xiomara?! There's blood on your dress!" Imani asked. Xiomara felt the area in question. "No, I'm fine. I don't know where it could've came from."

Then there was a loud thud. Santana had collapsed to the ground as he fainted. "Oh, my God! Santana's been hit!" Nina yelled in an urgent tone in her voice. Lydia ripped open his shirt to find the blood was indeed seeping from him. "We gotta get him to the hospital *ASAP!*" Chasity yelled as Xiomara fetched his car keys then handed them over to Imani.

With his adrenaline working double time from dodging death, he wasn't aware of being hit by enemy fire. And the C.T.Cs were hell bent on saving Santana how they pulled into the emergency room at University Hospital in under five minutes.

The paramedics whisked him out of the Porsche jeep then high tailed him into surgery. And the last image his eyes captured before he ultimately blacked out was a glimpse of that beautiful face of Xiomara's.

With a bullet lodged fractions of an inch away from his heart, Santana was fortunate enough to narrowly escape death. The surgeon had successfully removed the bullet, stopped the hemorrhaging and had him back to normal after hours of hard work. Having Team Santana along with the C.T.Cs standing guard, Santana had a heavy rotation of visitors around the clock. Even his mother, Cynthia, flew in from California to show the kind of support that can only come from a concerned mother.

On the fourth and final day of his hospital sojourn, as every other day, he awoke to see a smiling Xiomara at his side accompanied by a face he hadn't seen in a while. His mentor and favorite cousin - Kevin Kash.

First, he greeted Xiomara with a kiss. "*Mornin'* beautiful!" "Buenos diaz to you *too*, handsome. How are you feeling today?" "Like new money and bout ready to blow this spot." "You'll get your wish soon because the doctor said you'll be released in an hour or so." "That's great news."

He then gave acknowledgment to Kevin Kash. "I don't have to ask what caused you to cut into your hectic schedule to be here. So, thanks for coming to check on me, cuz." "Where *else* would I be at a time like this? I'm happy you pulled through."

"So am I." "I could've sworn I'd asked you to stay away from here. You're doing good for yourself in Miami." "Yeah, I remember what you told me. But don't grill me behind this because I only came here for a funeral."

"From now on let the dead bury themselves, Santana. New Orleans is nothing more than a modern day Sodom and Gomorrah. And when God purged this city with Hurricane Katrina you should've taken that as a sign to never look back. Unless you wanna turn into a pillar of salt, which almost came to pass."

Santana knew that some form of speech would come so he responded in a way that would get his cousin off his back.

"Can't argue with that, cuz. I've learned my lesson now." "I hope so. At least stay away from here until this problem is handled, which brings me to my next topic. Who is this guy, Meatball, that tried to kill you? We need to track his ass because I refuse to sit around and let history repeat itself after what happened to your father."

"Meatball died some time ago and I personally made sure of it. I don't know the guy's name but I *do* know he's Meatball's twin brother." "Both Imani and Chasity said the opposite."

Santana found that puzzling then looked to Xiomara as if she had the perfect explanation.

"How in the world could that be possible?" "On the day of the shooting some guys pulled up in a van and the girls heard them yelling for Meatball, by name, to get in."

Thinking back to the night he thought it was Meatball who he'd killed, now he knew the reverse role Meatball played even had *him* fooled. Santana just shook his head at the reality of Meatball's evasive nature.

"If that was indeed Meatball, it all makes since why Donavan was killed. Meatball was trying to bring *me* out after what I did to his brother. And since that's the case we've got our work cut out trying to pinpoint *that* slimeball."

Cynthia came into the room flaunting a gift bag containing an object that was ordered by Santana. "Good morning everyone. I got here as quickly as possible, Son. Here you go. It's exactly what you wanted," she said as she handed him the bag.

"Thanks, mom. Your timing was perfect. And the reason why is because of the very people who are present to witness the most pivotal step I'm about to take thus far in my life."

Without further delay, Santana tore through the bag to reveal his surprise. It was a gift wrapped box that easily fit in the palm of his hand. Before opening it his focus turned to Xiomara.

"Baby, this is for you. Chosen by me and approved by my mother. And since my father's deceased he's not able to give his consent. But my cousin, who's standing here with us, has filled that void and I'm sure to get *his* endorsement…

"From our very first encounter I knew you were special. And you've proven that to me with all of the love you've shown. Standing by my side through any and every obstacle. And most of all, now I know you'd go as far as knocking somebody's head off their shoulders from messin' with me." The room erupted in laughter. Then he continued as he got out of the bed.

"Seriously though, I will never be able to fully compensate you for saving my life." Xiomara's eyes began to water as Santana got down on bended knee to open the box that was harboring an engagement ring then continued, "But I can offer myself as a start. Upon awaiting a favorable outcome concerning the blessings from your family, I ask…Xiomara, would you do me the honor of becoming my wife?"

Without reluctance she responded, "sí, Santana! I would *love* to. But there's one request." "You name it, you got it." "I would like the wedding day to be on December 21st of 2013." "That's a little far out from now but I guess I'm okay with it. So, what's so special about *that* particular date?"

"It marks the 25th wedding anniversary for my parents, the 50th for my grandparents, and the 75th for my great-grandparents. And I want to perpetuate our family's quarter-century tradition."

"That would make our wedding the hundredth year mark. I can't wait until that day comes so we can make a leap in history together." Santana placed the ring on her finger to seal the deal as Kevin Kash and Tahiry cheered on the newly engaged couple.

During the celebration there was a woman wearing sunshades watching them attentively through the glass portion of the door. With a feeling of someone gazing at him, Santana looked towards the door. And the only thing he was able to see was a side view of the woman's face as she walked away.

# CHAPTER 44



"I RECALL YOU SPECIFYING that you've been here once before but not since you've known me. So let me take this opportunity to welcome you to my beautiful country," Xiomara said as she and Santana walked off the private jet and into the limo.

"Mucho gracias. I just pray this *pop-up* visit doesn't ensure us a negative response from your father and we leave here without his approval." "Don't worry yourself, Santana. At first, my father will be extremely inquisitive of you because he's never met you before or even knows you exist. But once he gets to know you he'll loosen up and I'm sure you'll win him over."

"You mean you've never even mentioned my *name* to him?" "No, Santana. My father's very overprotective when it comes to me. And I know him well enough to determine that I didn't want him probing you before we really got to know each other. So please trust me. This is the best way."

"I do, Xiomara. I can't front like this isn't an awkward situation I'm going into…but I've overcome a lot worse."

For the remainder of the ride to her family's estate Xiomara put Santana's mind at ease with tales that illustrated how only she could infiltrate her father's soft side. And she chose a joyous day to go to Columbia that she knew would solidify her father's favor. It was his birthday. And he always gave the biggest birthday bash in South America.

To keep their arrival as a surprise to her father until the very last second Xiomara ordered the driver to enter the compound using a dirt road which lead to the North West access point. By using that entrance Santana hadn't seen that side of the massive mansion during his prior visit. Therefore, he was clueless as to who owned it. He did however, ponder about the endless supply of cash flow Xiomara seemed to have. And from the looks of the back part of the mansion, he could see where it all came from.

After Xiomara punched in a pass code into the keypad they gained entrance into the uninhabited west wing. As they trotted down the hallway they heard sounds from the festivities growing louder and louder the nearer they drew to the great room. Crossing the threshold into the large area, they were now standing only a few yards behind her father.

However, he was encompassed by a mob of family, friends, yes-men and ass kissers who were all chanting a birthday song as he sat at the head of a table preparing to blow out the candles on his birthday cake. So Santana remained idle while Xiomara weaved through the masses to reach her father.

"Happy Birthday, Papa!" Xiomara's voice alone influenced the biggest Kool-aid smile of all time by her father as he turned to face her. "Xiomara, my darling! What a wonderful treat. Why didn't you tell me you were coming?"

"I wanted to surprise you, Papa." "You certainly accomplished *that*. So, how long will be staying?" "A few days." "Good. We have some catching up to do. And you have time to tell me all about your new life in Miami."

"Well, we can start now because I brought a new addition to my life along with me." "I can't wait to see it." "It's not an *it*, Papa…it's a *Him*. And he's standing to the back of the crowd that's behind us."

Her father's mannerism became more stern.


"For you to invite a man into our home could only mean you truly love this person." "Sí, Papa…I love him very much." "Then I would like to meet this man at once."

Taking her father's hand, she led him through the sea of party goers in search for Santana. But he'd strayed away from the pack. During a quick scan of the room she distinguished him from the other people seated at the bar, then walked his way.

She alerted Santana for his attention with a tap to the shoulder. And as he turned to face her she said, "Here he is, Papa. I am so delighted to finally introduce you to…"

The instant the two men's eyes locked on one another's a state of shock washed over their faces then her father interceded.

"*Santana*?!" "Javier?! Xiomara, *Javier* is your father?!"

For a flash Santana's mind raced from thinking of how Javier had deciphered the mystery of who'd robbed him, to considering Xiomara was indeed planted in his life only to lure him all the way to Columbia right into the lion's den. Then Javier had her use a different entrance so Santana wouldn't recognize the mansion. To make matters worse the only weapon he had to defend himself was a Corona bottle.

But he snapped out of his trance when Xiomara responded, "Sí, this *is* my father. I can't believe I'm actually witnessing something as bizarre as this…How on God's green earth could you two have known each other?" "But I thought your last name was Vazquez?" "It's my mother's maiden name. And my father had me use it when I abruptly moved to Miami."

Judging from her reaction, Santana found it plausible that the entire ordeal was purely coincidental. Then Javier shook Santana's hand while looking him in the eyes as he explained, "It's been quite some time ago when I had the pleasure of meeting this fine young man through a former associate of ours. And I must tell you, he's already proven to me that he's special."

As they moved the conversation outdoors Xiomara picked up where Javier left off. "I am so happy you approve of him, Papa, because words cannot describe how much he means to me."

"And *you*, Santana. How do you feel about my daughter?" "I love her so much, Javier, that I came here to ask for her hand in marriage."

Just like any other father Javier envisioned the day when another man would petition him to give his daughter away. Without Santana's knowledge he'd kept an eye on him for months after the heist. He knew of Santana's move to Miami and acquisition of the nightclub.

Initially, that raised suspicions. But Javier quickly dismissed the notion after learning Santana had purchased the building and had it under construction *before* the heist. Moreover, he was informed about the former occupation of the highly sought after individual and assumed Santana's funding to already have been in place and could have easily afforded a renovation project of that magnitude.

Knowing Santana's hobby would have been grounds for Javier to negate a relationship with his daughter. Mainly because he knows the dangers that come with the territory and would not want Xiomara in harm's way.

But according to a discussion Javier had with Hurricane El Jefe, Santana had withdrawn himself from illegal dealings and now had a clean slate. And as far as he was concerned Santana would make an excellent choice for a son-in-law. Javier looked to his daughter.

"Is this what your heart desires, Xiomara? Are you truly ready to take this giant leap?" "Sí, Papa. With all of my heart I believe that God has placed in my path my perfect match." Javier reached out for both of their hands.

"Very well then…you kids have my blessings but under two conditions, Santana." "Whatever you require." "Treat my princess in a manner you would insist a man treat your *own* daughter and never do *anything* to break her heart." "On my life, Javier, you have my word."

**Miami, Florida**
**September 7, 2011**

After the week long trip abroad and landing Javier's endorsement for marriage, the couple was back in M.I.A. Santana was eager to get back to work because it would be his first time stepping a foot inside the club since he left for Paris.

Upon walking into the club he was greeted by his entire staff. "Glad you made it back, Boss. We missed you!" Jasmine said as she spoke for all of his employees. "Feels good to be back and I missed you guys also. And if I can help it I'll never stay away for quite as long ever again." The staff returned to their respective duties, leaving Santana and his second-in-command, Jasmine, to themselves.

"Looks like you 've recuperated rather nicely. How's the wound, soldier?" "Like it never even happened. I can't thank you enough for holding the fort down for me in my absence. I love you, girl."

"Of course you know I love you in return, Santana. When I agreed to hop on board I told you I had your back, didn't I?" "Yeah, you did say that."

"All right then. Now it's time to get back to work, mister. Gotta bring you up to speed with the books'n all so you can see how well business has been." "Touché, Boss lady…let's get to it."

After hours of sifting through paperwork Santana was pleased with the outcome of Jasmine's performance. She saw to it that the Million Dollar Spot lived up to its name by averaging at least a million dollars per week since opening day.

To revel in his success Santana went online to order an Audi A8 that Jasmine had mentioned she wanted to get one day and had it delivered to the club to surprise her as a token of his appreciation. He also gave each of his employees a thousand dollar bonus.

When Jasmine left the office to resume her normal tasks it allowed Santana to have some time to himself. He had been out of contact with his Team since he left for Columbia and was ready to give an overdue call to Levi.

"Levi, what the lick read, my nigga?" "Ain't nothin'. Same ole shit. Wuzzam wit'chu? I haven't heard from you in over a week." "I'm finally back on my grizzy at the club I was calling to tell you Xiomara and I are officially getting married." "Congrats, my nigga. You told me you had to get consent from her family first. I guess they approved of you, huh?"

"With flying colors. And while we were in Columbia I was hit with the most inconceivable revelation. I'm talkin' bout me having a Powerball's chance of winning for determining what I did." "What was *that*?" "You'll *never* guess who Xiomara's father is…"

# CHAPTER 45



HAVING ACCUMULATED YEARS OF HARD WORK and generating a permanent pattern of lucrative nights, Santana had finally taken his first step towards turning his Million Dollar Spot brand into a franchise.

L.A. was the city of choice for the second location and Cynthia insisted he chose her to oversee the elaborate west coast operation. So he had Jasmine fly in town before opening night to be Cynthia's personal play-by-play coach to teach her all of the ends and outs of running the business efficiently.

And since the process could take up to a couple of weeks, Santana would have to leave Jasmine behind while he returned to the Miami location. The arrangement suited Jasmine just fine because she hadn't blown it out in the City of Angels in ages.

Considering Santana was a newcomer to L.A.'s Mega Market he held his ground like an old school veteran. Surprisingly, the club's grand opening was just as phenomenal as it was in Miami. Without a tally being taken one could argue that the amount of superstars to grace the red carpet trumped the number of those who attended the Grammys.

The event was trending on social media before, during, and even after the premiere including Kendrick Lamar's performance which was so lit it went viral. On the day after the Million Dollar Spot's debut, Santana had seized the headlines in the L.A. Times. The city had stamped him as *a star in the making* and welcomed him with open arms for creating an exclusive playground for the elite of the city.

After reading the article Santana mulled over his past. He prided himself on how he'd came from being nothing more than a two-bit drug cooking hustler to becoming a highly respected businessman. And he thought of how one day, just maybe, he would see the name *Santana Bailey* engraved in one of those stars on the *Hollywood Walk of Fame.*

## Medellin, Columbia
## June 16, 2013

"Is there any truth in what Luis explained to you, Manny? Is it indeed a replica of what I've been searching for years ago?" Javier inquired attentively. "Yes, Señor Javier. The way Luis described it to me it has all the same features. So I believe it's worth investigating, Boss." A malignant expression overcame Javier's appearance. "Very well then. Go and get Luis so he can lead me to the guy that has it. Today might be my lucky day."

Javier Ochoa's convoy escorted him in a lawless fashion. On his command they broke any laws mandated in order to cut an hour long trip in half. After reaching their destination they had to hike through a dense area of woodlands for another thirty minutes. Then Javier and a few members of the cartel arrived at a small building that appeared to be blighted.

"This is the place, Señor Javier," Luis told him.

At the brink of losing his marbles, Javier asked, "Is this your idea of some sort of prank, Luis? Surely this place is abandoned. And if you've made me optimistic for no reason I promised you'll live to regret it." "No, Señor Javier, this is not a joke. I told the guy that my Boss would possibly want to meet with him today and do big business. So he's definitely in there. I'll go get him now."

Before Luis could summons the man they'd came for he emerged from a bunker door on the side of the building. "Good evening, gentlemen. How may I assist you today?"

"I was just about to come knocking for you. I'm so happy you didn't decide to go anywhere. Like I told you earlier, my Boss would be interested in surveying your inventory. And here he is… Señor Javier Ochoa," Luis said as he introduced his superior. Then Javier took over.

"And you are?" "Antonio, pleasure to meet you, Señor." "According to Luis, you have some unique items in your catalog." "Yes, Señor, I have plenty to choose from." "Good! I would like to see all you have." "Okay, Señor. Follow me if you will."

Antonio led Javier into his bunker then began opening all of his compartments to exhibit the most advanced pieces of hardware he had available. But Javier was unimpressed with his selection. He was there for a specific item. And by the end of Antonio's presentation Javier still hadn't seen what he had come to see.

"Is this *all* you have for sale, Antonio? Is there anything you have not shown me?"

There was a box that was ready for shipping in his office which contained the only item Javier hadn't seen so he retrieved the package.

"I do have *this* gadget, but I was on my way to send it to a customer that already purchased it." "Open the box, Antonio. And if I like it I will triple your asking price."

The offer was too good for Antonio to pass up. He opened the package and revealed exactly what Javier hungered to see. It was a helicopter drone with the capability of shooting bullets that are used in AK-47's.

"This is it, Antonio! I've spent *years* searching for this." "That's ironic, it's been years since I've had one of these. They're extremely hard to come by. Apparently you've seen one before. Do you mind me asking where?"

"No, I don't mind. But first I would like you to answer some questions that I have." "No problem, Señor. What would you like to know?" "You said it's been years since you had one. Correct?" "Yes, Señor." "How many have you sold?" "Like I've mentioned before, these things are a rare commodity. This is only my second one." "How long exactly has it been since you sold the other one?" "Mmm, let me think for a sec…Oh! I have a ledger in my office with records that I keep with all of my transactions." "Then go get it,

Antonio." "Please excuse me for saying but this is an unusual way for me to conduct business, Señor Javier. I have never had anyone ask a question where I had to refer to my personal records." "That information is imperative to me. Now find out that date and *then* I will explain!"

Antonio saw how frustrated the drug lord had become. He knew of Javier's reputation and how matters would only grow worse if he didn't comply so he got the ledger. "I have it right here, Señor Javier…I sold it in the beginning of March in 2008." Inwardly, Javier was beyond overjoyed. Antonio had sold the helicopter during the time frame of the heist.

"Surely you must remember the buyer since you've only sold one of them prior." "Yes, I remember. It was three guys I remembered from the past. An Asian guy called, Chinky. And two African-American guys who were cousins named Derrick and Ham."

Javier recalled the man whose body exploded appearing to be of Asian descent according to one of the soldiers was a safe distance from the blast. Javier knew he was on the right path so he probed further.

"Two Americanos, eh? How did you meet them?" "When I was a serviceman they were Navy SEALs who'd joined forces with us to help out with a mission here in Columbia. And I worked very closely with them."

"None of those names ring a bell. Where exactly in America are they from?" "I'm not sure." "For them to make contact with you, you must be able to reach them."

"Chinky is the one who kept in touch over the years and it wasn't often he did. I even reached out to him after he and his buddies came to buy all of those weapons because he wanted me to keep him updated on all of my newest gadgets." Knowing that the Asian guy was dead and Antonio never talked to him again, Javier still needed to pry.

"So, what happened when you called him?" "Nothing. I've made several attempts but to no avail. I don't know if the guy went and got himself killed or what happened to him." "Tell me more about the American cousins." "It's not much I can tell you. I vaguely remember them." "When you worked together can you think of any conversations that stood out?"

Antonio seemed to be searching the files in his memory bank. Then he found something. "I remember some nights when we were at war, we were scattered out but wore earpieces to communicate. And to pass time during those moments the cousins use to tell childhood stories." "What kind of stories?" "The majority of them were about a lot of mischievous things they'd done with one of their friends who was the ring leader. They would talk about *that* guy for hours." "Do you remember his name?" "Let me think…I know it wasn't the kind of name you hear every day."

Antonio started whispering different names to himself but loud enough for Javier to hear, "Stanley…No, Santos…that's not it either…uhmm…shit. This is very hard for me. I would know the name if I were to hear it again."

A feeling comparable to a lightning rod bolted through Javier's veins. The names Antonio were stumbling over were extremely close to one he was very familiar with.

"Is the name, Santana?" "*Yes*! That is his name without a shadow of a doubt ""Are you sure?" "Yes, Señor Javier. I am one hundred percent positive." "Thank you, Antonio. You've been of great assistance."

As Javier began to leave Antonio said, "Señor Javier, I thought you were going to explain why you were asking those questions. I really would like to know, if you don't mind."

Javier certainly was a man of his word, but after discovering Santana masterminded the heist it slipped his mind to fill Antonio in. Unfortunately for Antonio, Javier was already fuming when he made the comment.

He responded, "My apologies, Antonio. Now, to make good on my word…" Javier pulled out a gun then shot Antonio in one of his knee caps. "*BWOW*!" "*ARGHH*!! Why would you shoot me when I just helped you, Señor Javier?!"

"Count your blessings, Antonio. I spared your life because you're nothing more than a naïve businessman whose only motive is money. And my visit here educated me to the fact that you the armed men who successfully plotted to hijack my multimillion dollar shipment and killed 19 of my finest soldiers in the process so you ought to be counting your blessings."

Javier pulled out a wad of cash and tossed it at Antonio's feet. "That should take care of your troubles, Antonio. Have yourself a nice day."

During the ride home Javier began formulating a plan to force Santana to come to him without alerting Xiomara. He couldn't believe he actually misread Santana. And more than anything, he gave him his blessings to marry his only child. For the first time in his life he felt like an idiot by letting Santana's conniving ass outfox him.

He thought aloud, "Finally, Santana. Retribution is on its way. And this time *you'll* be the one who's at a disadvantage. Although it will hurt me to break my daughter's heart it will only hurt temporarily. But *you*, Santana, are going to pay dearly."

It was the calm before the storm. The sleeping dragon was finally awakened. And in Javier's case that meant the person on the receiving end of his retaliation would be greeted with an unprecedented amount of fire and fury. With the cards now in the hands of the leader of the Nariño cartel, Javier was about to put on his poker face and show Santana which shark truly held *Smokin' Aces*.

# CHAPTER 46

UPON COMPLETION OF A DAY OF STRATEGIZING Javier was ready to set his two-part scheme into motion. He deployed eight men into the States to wait for his command to strike. Luis was assigned to lead a crew of four men for his part of the mission while Manny would only require two because his job was more simple. But Luis had some investigating to do.

In the days leading up to the *go ahead* from Javier, Luis had orders to stake out the Million Dollar Spot in Miami. He needed to study the movements of the police officers on the outside and the security guards on the inside.

On the same day Luis arrived in Miami, Santana had come back from L.A. He was beginning a five-day concert series to jumpstart a special account for a third installment of his franchised nightclub that he wanted to open in New York City. That would allow Luis an ample amount of time to do his research and by the third day Luis pretty much figured he had Santana on his radar and the routines of the officers and security guards down to a science.

During the morning of day four, Luis called Javier for an update.

"Good job, Luis. You asked me for this opportunity to earn a higher position in my organization and I find your work ethic very pleasing. And if you see this task to the outcome I'm looking for, you will have proven yourself."

"Gracias, Señor Javier! Is there anything else you require of me until you give the word?"

"No, Luis. I've already spoken to Manny and he is ordered to initiate part one of the plan tomorrow morning and you will enact part two tomorrow night. So rest until that time, Luis, because you're gonna need every ounce of energy you can muster when dealing with Santana Bailey."

## Minutes after Midnight
## June 23, 2013

"It's time, guys. The Boss just handed down the order. He confirmed Xiomara's somewhere in there so be sure not to shoot in her direction. The four of you know the plan so let's stick to it and get this job done." Luis told his men after ending the call with Javier.

The first order of business was to take down the two officers detailing outdoors quietly and unnoticed. As if on cue the officers separated by one of them checking the perimeter while the other walked the parking lot.

Luis's squad separated with two of his men snatching the officer that was coming around the building while the other two men assisted him in subduing the officer in the parking lot. With both officers being completely caught off guard they found themselves bound with their handcuffs, gagged with duct tape, then stuffed in the trunk of their cruiser within minutes.

Luis chunked the officers' car keys some twenty feet away then moved to phase two of Javier's plan: enter the club then start shooting as soon as they caught sight of Santana.

Not even a minute upon entering they did just that. They spotted him coming from behind the bar supposedly drawing money down from the cash register at his scheduled time. Then Luis gave his men the signal to get the shooting underway.

Clubbers were yelling, screaming, ducking, and diving to get out of Luis and his men's way. Still, their primary focus was only on Santana. Luis had to admit Santana was quick on his feet and equally elusive.

Meanwhile, Luis thought he heard return fire that was not coming from Santana's direction alone. And his thoughts were accurately assessed moments later as one of his men received fatal shots that sent his body coasting past Luis.

Immediately Luis knew Santana had help that wasn't coming from any security guards they had studied during the past few days. His help was coming from somewhere in the crowd. But the loss didn't faze Luis. He still had shooters on his side that would deal with Santana's savior.

Seconds later, another one of his men was taken out. This time the shot came from a different direction and was in close range. The graphic memory would stain Luis for life as he witnessed his man's brains sprinkle the faces of his remaining two shooters.

At that point he realized Santana had more than one person helping him. He questioned if there were more men on Santana's team that would overwhelm the three of them. He second guessed the research he'd done. And ignored the fact that Javier had warned him about Santana being a handful.

But he still had a job to fulfill. And after all of this was behind him he would be high up in the rankings in the Nariño cartel. As he thought of that, more tragedy struck on his end. His remaining two men were taken out at the same time by one man. It was a gold tooth having, dreadlocks swinging man that he witnessed firing two Mini Draco's at the same damn time. That goes without saying, Luis' mission was a failure.

He'd misjudged the opponent in Santana. And being the only man left he sought to retreat since he wanted to save himself. He saw now that Javier had sent him on a suicide mission against bravehearted sharp shooters. And no longer did he wish for a position in Javier's organization.

As he turned to run, he was startled to see the man who he had come for standing in arm's reach. But before he could react Santana had shot him in the hand which caused him to drop his weapon. Then he was taken into the kitchen. Being a hired assassin turned captive, Luis knew that he was still alive only to be grilled for information before they killed him. He planned on giving Santana nothing. And as he was being tied to a chair, he decided then that he was going to die like a man...or so he thought.

In a normal situation Santana would clash with conflict. But this was different. His heart was involved. After learning his cover was blown, he knew he would have to confer with Xiomara about his skeletons. And by doing so his honesty could possibly serve two purposes: Clearing his conscience and hopefully, finding common ground with Javier.

He left the kitchen in search for Xiomara. Apparently, she was seeking him also because after she saw the last patron off who was in the casino, they met in the center of the club while on her way to the kitchen.

He grabbed her tightly by the hand and told her, "Xiomara, there's something you need to know." Then her cell rang. "Let me catch this call first, Santana. Then afterwards, we can talk. *Hola? Sí, Papa. He's right here.* It's my father, Santana. He wants to speak to you."

He took the cell then walked out of earshot of Xiomara. "You wanna talk now after you sent those rookies in here?" Santana scolded. "I only wanted to get your attention, Santana. And now that I have it, I want you to know that you're living on borrowed time."

"I doubt that. I would ask you how you found out about me but that's irrelevant now. And just to let you know, I was planning for the right time to confess my wrong doings and repay you every dime *with* interest because you're my fiancé's father." "Do you really think your confession and restitution would have changed my stance?"

"Maybe. Maybe not. I'm an opportunist, Javier. Just like you. I saw a weak spot in your operation, plotted against it, then went with my move. You showed me too much. Simple as that. I can't take back what I did, Javier, but I am truly sorry for my actions and want to make things right between us."

"At one point I profoundly respected you, Santana. But that is no longer. For you to think that we could ever get pass what you've done it is apparent that I must reiterate something I shared with you years ago…If there's one thing I despise more than anything, it's a snake. Remember that?"

"Yeah, I remember." "*Good*! So you should understand I'm saying in other words, the only form of payback that equates your actions is to have your head on a platter." "For the voice of reason I gave it my all to make amends with you, Javier. But since you're clearly against a truce let the pieces fall where they may. So bring everything you got, old man. I won't go down easy."

Javier released a slight chuckle. "You strike me as a thinking man, Santana. One who plays the game of chess extremely well." "Haven't I proven that to you already?"

"Yes, you have. But the motive to the game is to checkmate your opponent." "So, what exactly are you?" "I'm saying those five men I sent after you were pawns. Expendables. But the move I made you *didn't* see coming is the one that will force you to deliver yourself to me."

"Are you serious?! There is no move you can make that will *ever* cause me to voluntarily walk into my death." "Oh, I doubt that. I have another one of my men who is standing here with me. His name is Manny Martinez."

"Don't know 'em. But what does he have to do with me?" "Since my connections are far reaching, Manny was able to follow through with the most significant step of my business concerning you. Are you a loving family man as I am, Santana?" "Of course, I am." "Well, the next voice you hear should make you see things my way." Javier placed the phone to the person's ear.

"Let him do what*ever* he wants to me, baby…I've lived my life already." Santana's heart skipped a couple of beats.

"*Mama*?! I'm so sorry I got you into this. Whatever I have to do to save you I'm gonna do it. Did they hurt you?" "No, son. I'm okay. You just make sure he pays for what he did if anything happens to me. I love you, Santana." "I love you too, mama." Javier removed the phone from her ear. "Do I have your attention *now*, Santana?"

At the highest level of anger in his life, Santana began yelling, "You're a fuckin' *maggot*, Javier! I swear to God that if you lay a finger on my mother I'm going into beast mode on your motherfuckin' ass!" "I am not as crazy as you may think. You have my daughter. And I know you love her enough to never harm her. So you have my word that your mother is safe. Love requires sacrifice, Santana. It's her life that comes with a price tag of your life. You have twenty-four hours. And Santana…come alone."

The call ended. Xiomara overheard him yelling and knew Javier kidnapped his mother. She was worried sick. "Santana, what is going on between you and my father?"

Before the call from Javier, Santana was going to share his darkest secret with her. But knowing now that his mother had been taken he felt no need to speak on the subject. Javier had crossed the line.

"Please forgive me but I don't want to talk about it…I love you, Xiomara, but I have to go."

He passed her cell back, gave her a kiss, then hurried into the kitchen to inform his team of his intentions. Until that moment she had never seen Santana so upset and she immediately called her father.

"Papa! I overheard Santana saying you kidnapped his mother as he was arguing with you. Is that true, papa?!" "Xiomara, my darling, Santana is not the man you *think* he is. He's the reason I had to send you to Miami from the beginning in fear of your life being in jeopardy. And it's like I pushed you directly into the hands of my greatest enemy."

"Papa, why would you kidnap that sweet lady and then send those guys in here to kill Santana?" "Because he stole from me, Xiomara!" "Stole what? Your narcos, papa?" "Sí."

"Then good for him! I've always hated what you did to make money. Ever since my uncle Hugo passed away you've never been the same. You act like a tyrant, papa. And I swear to you on my mother's grave that if *anything* happens to Santana *or* Ms. Cynthia, I promise you will lose me forever!"

For the first time in her life Xiomara hung up on her father. He knew she would go against his decision but Santana had sealed his own fate. He figured that one day she would forgive him but as for now his mind was made up.

Once Santana was finished with dropping the news about what happened to his mother and how he was going to Columbia alone, Team Santana exploded.

"Fuck that, big homie! I'mma ride or die and let them bullets fly, ya *heard* meh?! 'Who gon' pop us?" Get'em pleaded.

"He's right, my nigga. We fuckin' wit dat! You know we can't let you go out there by yourself. That'll be like we're letting you sign your death certificate," Korey Witha K reasoned.

"You're our brother, Santana, and we all made a vow to *ball till we fall.* So if this is our time, then we rockin' wit'chu to the end," Levi told him.

"Trust me, fellas, I know how you feel. But kidnapping my mother was a game changer. I couldn't fathom the idea of something happening to her if Javier found out y'all tagged along for a rescue mission. I really hate I have to leave y'all behind but it's the only way and non-negotiable."

Santana gave each of his brothers a strong hug and said, "I love y'all niggas to death! I gotta go now and I'm leaving my cell behind so nobody can track me down or contact me."

For the first time, Santana witnessed a couple of tears falling from all three of their faces from knowing this would be their last time seeing him alive. To give them one last boost of comfort he told them, "the last thing y'all should be doing is sheddin' tears. Whenever y'all think of me think of all the good times. I lived the *good life* to the fullest, my niggas. So smile at the thought of knowing the world will *never* produce another nigga as ill as Santana Bailey." Then he was gone.

As the three of them sat around trying to draft a plan to help Santana they found themselves leading back to the same conclusion: respecting Santana's wishes. Therefore, they were totally out of options.

But Levi continued to brainstorm. And while he was fiddling with Santana's cell, Xiomara walked in to find out Santana had already left. Suddenly, Levi thought of an idea. It was a longshot but worth a try.

# CHAPTER 47



THE ONE THING Javier failed to mention to Santana was that he appeared unarmed. In Santana's eyes, the chess match was ongoing since no one had yet to be checkmated. Unbeknownst to Javier, Santana had one helluva trump card and was about to put it to use.

Shortly after landing, Santana went to ground zero where the heist occurred. There was an emergency stash of weapons he'd left behind and was hoping recover. It took nearly an hour of wandering around the war ravaged terrain before he found the location. Then another fifteen minutes longer to dig up the earth hitting gold.

To face the deadliest cartel in South America all by his lonesome, Santana was now prepared as much as he could have been. Along his quest to dance with the devil, in order to save his mother, he made peace with God. He prayed for forgiveness for all of the wrong he'd ever done and was about to do before facing his destiny.

There was no greater gift that one could give to their mother other than life, itself. *A life for a life*, he thought. Sure he'd heard of those type of situations in movies but never would've imagined that a statement which carried so much substance would pertain to him.

Nevertheless, he was born in Charity Hospital in New Orleans which was also known as the *City Zoo*. And the doctors diagnosed him with having a heart of a lion. And his courage had never wavered before and it wouldn't on this day.

With a *ready to die* state of mind, he approached Javier's fortress. Using a set of infrared binoculars, he spotted an additional number of soldiers guarding the front entrance waiting for him.

Javier was well prepared for an attack on the home front which is precisely what Santana had hoped because he was about to hit him from the blindside. It was time to use that trump card.

What Javier didn't know was the way Santana and Xiomara had gotten into the mansion for his birthday party. He was so distracted by the celebration that he never bothered to ask how they had entered. And Santana remembered the passcode to the Northwest wing's access point. It was Xiomara's birthdate. How could he'd forgotten it?

As he closed in on the access point he noticed a soldier guarding the area. And in order to have a fighting chance at saving Cynthia the guard would have to be eliminated. Subsequently, that sparked the inauguration of part two of his Columbian killing spree.

Speaking in his native tongue the soldier was on his cell allegedly arguing with the person on the other line. As he neglected his post Santana utilized the opportunity to pounce on him from behind before he could have a chance to react.

In a swift motion Santana ran a cord around his neck then squeezed as tightly as possible. The soldier dropped his cell to put up a struggle. But his attempt was no match for Santana's strength. After almost a minute without any oxygen intake the soldier was finished. The verbal dispute he was having with whoever was still on the other end of the cell arguing would be his last.

As he stood in front of the access point he upped a Desert Eagle then screwed a silencer in place. Then punched in zero-four-one-five into the keypad. Luckily, a green light started blinking. With a twist of the door handle the door opened and he slipped inside. The long hallway seemed unoccupied as it was the last time he was there. With only two rooms in that section of the house, he checked the first one for his mother but found it empty. Then went into the second room to find the same results.

On the way out of the room he heard talking. The noise was drew closer his way. He assumed they were looking for him. Quietly, he dipped back into the room and closed the door. With his gun aimed at the door, he waited for it to open but the voices bypassed the room.

He cracked the door open by a hair and saw only two soldiers. This would be an easy kill. He eased into the hallway, crept up behind the men, then issued each of them fatal shots to the back of their heads. After dragging both bodies into a room he was on the move to another wing of the house.

In the section he started to go into he heard a multitude of voices. He peeped to see how many he was up against. There were at least seven more of Javier's soldiers. Santana could have wiped them out with the toss of a couple of grenades but didn't want to rouse any attention to his presence.

Instead, he opted for searching an area which may have had less adversity at the time: The second level of the megamansion.

Upstairs had a different echelon of employee's in Javier's workforce. People who weren't dressed in fatigues nor were they carrying any weapons. They were innocent house servants. Three women going to and fro cleaning the place. And Santana knew he wouldn't bring his wrath upon them. In a different light, one of the women could possibly serve a greater cause by telling him where Cynthia was being held captive.

He waited until they separated into different areas then went after the one who went into a room he was near to. Thinking it was one of her co-workers the woman never looked back to see who had entered.

He swooped in on her from behind to cover her mouth as he held her at gunpoint. Then whispered as he asked if she spoke English.

She shook her head no. That would not be an issue for Santana because he spoke Spanish fluently. He needed to let her know he would not harm her and for her not to scream after removing his hand from her mouth. And most importantly, he needed to see if she knew where Javier was holding Cynthia.

"Yo no estoy aqui para lastimarte, no grites cuando yo quite mi mano de tu boca. Yo solamente necesito que me digas en donde Javier tiene a la mujer afroamericana que mantiene cautiva." The woman shook her head yes she wouldn't scream then told him, "Yo se exactamente donde ella esta, Señor. Solamente por favor no me mates. Yo tengo familia." "No lo haria, tienes mi palabra."

That was great news for Santana. She knew exactly where Cynthia was being held. She also pleaded with him not to kill her because she had family and Santana gave her his word that he wouldn't. "Okay. Ella esta abajo en la primer recamara que esta a la izquierda de poes que pases el area de entretenimento."

She informed him about his mother being in a room downstairs to the left as he passes the entertainment quarters. That was bad news. He would have to go through the room full of guys he just avoided. If he had to make a big commotion with an all out massacre of the group of soldiers in order to get to Cynthia he'd do whatever it took. But before he decided to go that route he asked the woman if she knew of a different path.

She responded, "Sí. Hay otras escaleras al final del pasillo que te llevan al otra lado del area de entretenimiento. Y la recamara va a estar a tu derecha. Pero te advierto que hay un guardia en la puerta."

She advised him of an alternate route which would place him on the opposite side of the entertainment quarters. She also gave him a heads up about the soldiers guarding the door to the room where his mother was held.

"Gracias, mujer. Tu has sido de mucha ayuda. Ahora por favor perdoname, pero tengo que amarrarte para estar seguro que no te vas a ir a avisarle a alguien lo cual impediria que yo rescate a mi madre." "Ese no es ninguno problema, Señor. Prefiero eso a que me mates."

After thanking the woman for her help he asked her to forgive him for having to tie her up to make sure she didn't alert anyone and prevent him from saving his mother. The woman didn't mind. She said she'd much rather that than dying.

He hustled back downstairs. Jumping two steps at a time to get to the bottom floor. Coming into the hallway, he saw the soldier that the house servant was referring to. Santana was only thirty yards away from rescuing Cynthia. Since the mob of soldiers were nearby the one guarding the door Santana needed to take him down swift and soundless.

He pulled out another weapon. It was a dart which contained toxins strong enough to floor an elephant upon contact. Inching his way alongside the wall in the shadows he remained undetected for a long as he could. As if the soldier's sixth sense kicked in he turned to see Santana approaching fast.

He also saw the dart that was thrown as well. But not in time to dodge it from striking him in the neck. The poisonous fluids flowed into his bloodstream and dropped him like a sack of potatoes in nanoseconds.

His mother was in arm's reach.

He opened the door to find Cynthia constricted by her hands and ankles to a chair. She also was gagged and blindfolded. But still alive. He removed the bandannas from her eyes and mouth. Then pulled out a blade and freed her from bondage.

"For some strange reason, I *knew* you'd come!" "Shhh...we're not out of the woods yet." "You got an extra gun to spare so I can help out? I *have* pulled a trigger or two in my younger days., Cynthia whispered. "No, Momma. I won't put your life in anymore danger than I already have. So cover your ears after I leave out of this room because bombs about to be bursting in air like The Star Spangled Banner."

He went back into the hallway, ready to cause mayhem in the mega mansion. Once he reached the end of the corridor, he glimpsed into the entertainment quarters. The soldiers were still there. All seven of them: Three huddled up in the far right corner; Two by the bar; and two over by the pool table that was fifteen feet away from where Santana was standing. He'd deal with the pool sharks first.

He ran down on the closest one and snapped his neck. The former soldier's opponent at the pool table went for his weapon as Santana went for his…a hunting knife. Those precious seconds the soldier took by putting down the pool stick, reaching for his gun, and having to click it off safety mode cost him dearly. Santana hurled the knife at the soldier and buried it in his forehead. Had him looking like a unicorn.

Now Santana had the attention of all the others soldiers. Their reflexes were a lot faster than all of the others he had taken out. He heard them relaying messages of an intruder in their earpieces. The clock was officially ticking for Santana.

He had to annihilate the remaining five soldiers in a hurry in order to safely get Cynthia to the northwest wing for a daring escape.

But the soldiers weren't making it easy. They were shooting at him. Forcing him to dive behind the pool table for cover. Chunks of wood and felt from the pool table were flying right pass Santana. He pulled the pin from one of the grenades then reached for the Desert Eagle.

From the floor he could see the legs of the two by the bar. He aimed for their ankles. After seven attempts he dropped them both to their knees, giving Santana a clear view of their upper body. He shot three more times in each of their directions to put them down for good. Without a second to waste he threw the grenade near the last three soldiers.

"***BOOOMMM*****!!"**

Finally, the shooting stopped. Every minute was critical. He had to get Cynthia. He raced to the room. She was still there covering her ears as she hid under a table. "Hurry, Momma…we gotta get out of here *now!*"

They dashed back into the entertainment quarters. Santana could see one of the soldiers still moving that must've survived the blast. Santana plugged him one time in the head for good measure. Then he heard more of Javier's men coming his way. He and Cynthia were on the move. Gunning for the exit door of the north west wing. Once they got there Cynthia opened the door while Santana shot at those who gave chase, using an AR-15 he picked up from one of the soldiers he killed in the entertainment quarters.

Cynthia made it outside. And after Santana cleared the hallway, he followed suit. Then he closed the door shut and turned to see the worse; Javier Ochoa holding a gun to Cynthia's head.

Santana had failed. The chess match was over. He'd been checkmated. He had done all he could to save his mother's life as well as his own.

He kept his head held high because he was from out *dat 9 where they don't mind dying*, especially for the sake of his mother's life. So he wasn't afraid. He just had to show Javier that he wasn't going down without a fight. And since he accomplished that, he wasn't going to do anything further to provoke Javier to squeeze the trigger and end Cynthia's life.

# CHAPTER 48

"OKAY, JAVIER...YOU WIN. Just let my mother go as you promised." Santana surrendered every weapon he had at his disposal and tossed them at Javier's feet. "Do you really expect me to spare your mother after all you've done here today? You reneged on your word, Santana."

"I *kept* my end of the deal, Javier. Your only requirement what that I come alone. You never said I couldn't attempt to save my mother. Tell me, what man in their right mind that loved someone so gravely would not have done the same as I have?"

For a moment Javier thought of his choice of words during their conversation. Santana was right about doing what Javier told him to do. But it never crossed Javier's mind that Santana would have the balls to come waging a one-man war. Then again, he underestimated Santana for a second time. He was the same man that had the heart to rob him. So he put himself in Santana's shoes. And if the tables were turned, he would have done the exact same to save his mother.

"I commend you for your bravery, Santana. And for that I will honor my word. I will send your mother back home after I am done with you. I can't wait to show you how I deal with your kind."

"Do as you please, Javier. A soulja can only die once."

Javier had his men rough up Santana for a bit before bringing him to the torture chamber. To no avail, Cynthia bit, scratched, kicked, and screamed as she tried to break free from the soldiers' grasp as they beat Santana and carried him off.

Inside a room on the first level of the mansion, Santana was fully strapped to a chair with his sights set on the tools that would be used for his demise. There was an assortment of apparatus: scalpels, corkscrew, electrical cables, and a bucket of acid. But before Javier got the session under way, he wanted a final conversation with the young man he once admired.

"This situation with you has put me at odds with my daughter, Santana. That has never happened before. The sad thing is, I see a younger version of myself in you. A man who I believe was perfect for my Xiomara."

"If you know how much she loves me what would possess you to break your own daughter's heart? What possible satisfaction will you obtain by killing me and hurting her in the process? I told you I will reimburse all of what I have taken plus any added amount you deem fit."

Javier grew furious. He landed a hard punch in Santana's gut.

"At first you kill twenty-two of my finest soldiers then come in here and kill nearly the same amount! Not to mention you tied up my Aunt Rosa. Your money will *never* make things right between us. I have-…" Santana cut him off, "A level of respect to uphold? Then uphold it, Javier! Since I was a kid, I've been torn between two worlds. I've always wanted to live because of the love I have for my mother and wanted to die because of my strong desire to reunite with my deceased father. So in other words, Javier, I'll remain humble in victory or defeat. And I'm about ready for this to end. So do us both a favor and don't talk me to death. Let's just get this over with." "As you wish."

A little shock treatment would be Javier's first choice of administering pain. He attached the electrical cables to Santana's body, grabbed the switch to amplify the voltage, then clicked it on.

The currents rattled Santana, nearly causing him to go into convulsions for the duration of the five seconds it was on before Javier shut it down. Santana grunted throughout the process in an attempt to contest the powerful surge.

Not exactly what he was expecting to go through. This was torture at its finest. And the bad part was, it was only the beginning.

Javier taunted Santana. "Enjoying yourself?"

But Santana wasn't going to speak another word. The reward for saving his mother's life was far greater than any amount of pain he would have to endure before taking his final breath. So his presence was enough said.

"Don't want to talk anymore, Santana? That's fine. I'll just inform you of how the rest of our session is going to play out. After a few more times of my *shocking experience*, as I like to call it, I'll pour acid over your hands until they are completely melted since you like to touch things that don't belong to you.

"Next, I will use the corkscrews to pluck out your eye balls and drive into your nostrils.

"Next, I will use the scalpels to carve your chest open until your heart is exposed. And lastly, I'm gonna bury you alive in an upright position with only your head above ground and then dump a pile of ants on top of you so they can slowly eat at you piece by piece until nothing's left but your skull. And that will be the finishing touch on your life."

*'Javier is a real piece of work. The producers of 'Fear Factor' could definitely use a few pointers from him,'* Santana thought.

As Javier readied himself to continue tormenting Santana, there was a knock at the door. It was Raul, the man who has been the General of the Nariño cartel since Javier was in grade school. And he was the only soldier who simply addressed the Boss as Javier.

Javier let him in.

"I need to speak to you, Javier, before you go any further." "Can it wait, Raul? I *am* kind of busy at the moment."

"I'm afraid not. You have a visitor who we haven't seen in a while that needs to see you." "Very well then, Raul. Where is this person?" "Out back by the pool area." "Sit tight, Santana. I'll be back to pick up where we left off."

After making it outside Javier saw the back of the person who came to see him. To get his attention, Javier said, "For Raul to bring you this far into mi casa means you are not a stranger. Now face me so I can see who it is that came to pay me a visit."

Once the person veered their body around Javier's face produced the biggest smile it had in decades.

"Well if it isn't my dearest friend of all-time that I am forever indebted to…Kevin Kash. To what honor do you pay me this visit today?"

"I've told you countless times that you don't owe me anything, Javier. And the reason I'm here is because I'm seeking the favor of a lifetime. And if you insist on feeling like you can never repay me for what I've done in the past then grant me this *one* favor and it will make us even."

"You name it, you got it." "You have in your possession something very dear to me, Javier, that I pray you'll give back…a young man by the name of Santana Bailey." "That is certainly a petition of a lifetime, Kevin. But I have to ask, why does my business with him concern you? In what capacity are you connected to him?"

"Santana is my family, Javier. When my son and cousin - which was his father - were killed, he was with me and I've raised him like my own ever since. Only hours ago I've learned of what he did to wrong you.

"I'm sure you know I didn't plant those seeds in him nor condone what he's done. And you and I both know there's no dollar amount that will suffice his actions so all I have is my plea for his and his mother's life. So wha'duya say, old friend? Let me bear his sins and allow those kids to get married and unite our families."

The *Mother of all Bombs* had just been dropped on Javier. The only person in the world who he owed his existence to had requested the ultimate. To turn the other cheek for the only man to ever make a mockery of the Nariño cartel.

However, no matter how Javier felt beforehand he knew he could not refuse anything Kevin Kash asked of him because if it were not for him, the Nariño cartel would no longer exist. They would have been totally annihilated by the rogue cartel; Los Pepes.

Over two decades ago a gruesome war occurred when Los Pepes, who were once affiliated with the up and coming Boss, El Chapo, attempted to overthrow the Nariño cartel from their throne. Los Pepes received intelligence on the precise location of the Nariño cartel's inventory warehouse.

They stormed the building, killing most of the soldiers and workers as they seized all of the product. In the process of searching the warehouse they gained an added incentive when they stumbled upon a secret room that contained tens of millions of dollars and a stockpile of artillery.

The blow was crippling to the Nariño cartel. But Los Pepes didn't stop there. They lived by the code of cutting off the head and the tail will fall, so they persisted with the war for another three days and then the unimaginable occurred.

They assassinated Javier's older brother, Hugo Ochoa, who at the time was the leader of the Nariño cartel.

As the old saying goes, *it takes money to go to war*. And with the Nariño cartel taking a hit as hard as they did, money would be a major issue.

At that point in history Javier wasn't too much involved with the business. He was caring for his ailing wife while she was on her deathbed and raising his daughter, Xiomara. And even though he wanted vengeance for his brother's death, financially he was incapable.

A week later Javier got a visit from a man he never knew existed. The man was a business associated of Hugo's. He came bearing a gift that neither Javier or anybody in the Nariño cartel knew to look for except the deceased leader.

It was a gift that would certainly turn things around for the incapacitated Nariño cartel and that gift was $100,000,000 U.S. dollars, half of which was owed to Hugo and the other half was to assist Javier in restoring the cartel's power. And the man who delivered that gift was Kevin Kash.

The money enabled Javier to fully eradicate Los Pepes and recover nearly 80% of everything they had lost. And as for Kevin Kash, Javier now had a friend for life.

"How could I deny your request, Kevin? As angry as I am with Santana, I must admit, I truly admire the young man. And my daughter has gone against me for him. And Lord knows how long *that* little girl can hold a grudge. So I guess I have no choice but to forgive him. Then everyone will be happy." "Thank you, Javier. Now let's go get him so I can take him and his mother home."

# FINAL CHAPTER

**New Orleans, LA**
**December 21, 2013**

WITHOUT DIVINE INTERVENTION this day would not have been possible. It was a day of Santana's wedding. Not long ago he thought he would die in Columbia. But thanks to his best man, Levi, he had a different outcome.

The night Santana left for Columbia Levi conjured up the thought of shuffling through Santana's cell until he found Kevin Kash's number. In a cry for help Levi called to explain the situation and after asking him a few questions Kevin Kash told Levi he'd take it from there.

Santana knew only the watered-down version that Kevin Kash shared with him about his reign as one of the biggest drug Bosses of all time. But during their flight back to the states Kevin Kash went into further details about his involvements in the business.

He enlightened Santana of how the Nariño cartel was his supplier ever since Hugo was leader. And also, how he assisted Javier in reestablishing control of the cartel. And lastly, how they became partners until he ultimately retired.

He was highly disappointed with Santana for pulling off the *Columbian Job* because that wasn't something he had to do. He would give Santana anything he desired, but Santana chose to follow his own path. And despite the fact Santana's violation of Javier is something Kevin Kash would never accept from anyone. He'd much rather die before letting anything happen to him.

He knew Santana was exceedingly clever but never would have imagined him pulling off a feat so intricate and dangerous against an opponent as deadly as the Nariño cartel. But deep inside Kevin Kash knew exactly where Santana had gotten his traits of being so savvy and fierce. And to find the source, all he had to do was look in any mirror.

As much as Santana may have preferred a more private ceremony Xiomara would not allow it. Her wedding was the pinnacle of moments in which she'd dreamed of. She knew there was an immense number of people who either loved or respected Santana as well as her family and friends in Columbia that would want to partake in their celebration. So she advertised the details of the event on social media in order to reach the masses.

The results of the turnout were staggering. Of course Kevin Kash and Javier Ochoa were present. Just as were the C.T.Cs - even though each of them wish it were them who was about to be known as Mrs. Bailey.

Entertainers, actors, actresses, and professional athletes who knew Santana from the club were in the building. Even the Bosses who once upon a time ago did business with Santana came out to give their praises. Each of them with their own set of bodyguards.

There wasn't an empty seat in the church so a great deal of people would have to wait outside to catch a glimpse of N.O.'s finest and his new bride on their way out. However, amongst the outside spectators anxiously waiting inside an SUV was Meatball along with an army of Crips. Five cars deep. Meatball had caught wind of the wedding specifics via *Instagram* and he was fully prepared to finish Santana off once and for all.

In the dressing room with his groomsmen, Santana prepared himself to exchange the most sacred vows of his life. Wearing a half million-dollar *Christophe Claret* Soprano edition time piece, ten carat diamond studs in each ear, twenty-two hundred-dollar *Christian Louboutin* loafers encrusted with rhinestones and an all-white custom-made *Kiton* suit, he was draped in all of his splendor.

"Looks like you're all set groom", The best man, Levi, told him as he dusted off Santana's shoulders.

"Pretty much, and I owe this day to all of you. Lord *knows* I wouldn't be here if it weren't for your help." "Kevin Kash deserves all of the credit for mediating the situation…not me."

"But it trickles down to you since you thought to call him." "All right, Santana. If it'll make you feel as if you paid your dues from me making that call, pop me off a milli and then we'll be even." Knowing Levi was only being sarcastic, they all had a good laugh.

"You already know how we rockin'. We here for you, my nigga," Korey Witha K told him. "Straight like that, big brudda. We got you back, even in this church. Levi can hold that ring for you but I gots that glizzy with the dick on deck, ya *heard* meh?!" Get'em said as he opened his jacket to expose the Glock .40 he had tucked away in his waist line.

"For some reason I already knew you were strapped," Santana responded. Then someone knocked on the door and began calling out from the hallway, "Santana, it's me, Imani. You dressed yet?"

"Yeah. Come on in." She walked in and was surprised to see how nicely dressed they all were. "*Damn*! Are y'all gangsters or runway models? Looks like you belong on the cover of GQ Magazine, Santana."

After looking into a full body mirror and straightening his tie, he asserted. "I couldn't agree more, baby girl. You always *did* have an eye for fashion." His cocky response had them all laughing.

"So what's good, Imani? Is everything all good with my bride?" "She's as ready as *you* are and is slaying the hell out of that dress. I rushed in here because I know the wedding's about to start and I need your presence before it does. Or somebody's gonna miss the whole ceremony." "Who is it?" "It's Chasity. She ran to the restroom and when I checked on her, she locked herself in the stall."

"What's wrong with her?" "I don't know, but I told her she needed to hurry before things kicked off and she misses everything. She told me she'll probably just leave and catch up with us later." "All right. I'll go check on her."

He barged into the restroom unannounced, "Chasity, you still in here?" "Yeah, Santana. What are you doing in here? Aren't you about to get married?" Her attitude frustrated him.

"You already know that! You're acting jealous on me *now*?" "Santana…please just go. I'll be okay." "Not until you come out to face me." "I can't let you see me like this" "Why not?" "Because my makeup and dress is ruined." "I don't care about all of that. Now, come out of there."

When she came out Santana saw she was being truthful but she was crying. "Don't stress yourself over something so small. I'm sure there'sa gang of women out there that has a *Crayon Case* makeup kit you could borrow and you could easily wipe down your dress real good and blow dry it. What did you spill on it?" "I vomited."

"You must've eaten something your stomach didn't agree with." "That ain't the case, Santana." "If not, then what is?" "I wanted to wait for a better time to tell you, but…I'm two months pregnant, Santana. I found out a week ago."

Surprisingly, Santana had a warm reception to the news. "You're standing here crying a river when that's grounds for a celebration." "You mean you're not mad at me?"

"How *could* I be? You told me years ago that you wanted to have my child one day so you can have a piece of me forever. You're a strong woman, Chasity, whose been loyal to me since day one. And for you to respect the fact that I'm about to be a married man and you still love me the way you do, I'm honored that you're having my child. It *is* mine, isn't it?"

Santana always knew how to turn a frown into a smile. "Boy, don't play with me! Of course, it's yours. You ought to know that you'll always be the only man to get *these* goodies."

"I know that. I was only kidding. Just trying to cheer you up." "I'm okay now, Santana. Now get outta here…your bride is waiting." As he turned to leave she said, "And Santana…I'm still gonna keep this between us." "To be honest, Chasity, don't think I want to keep my baby a secret. I'll just have to break the news to Xiomara. I know she'll probably be a little pissed, even a little jealous until she has a child, but I think she'll be okay. She loves kids." "What about the rest of the C.T.Cs? Will you tell them also?" "They're gonna erupt but I'll tell them too." "Oh, thank you, Santana! Now I'm very excited about the baby."

As Santana stood at the alter exchanging vows there was someone standing midways down the aisle. It was a woman. She had on *Blvgari* shades and was holding something behind her back. It was the same woman who was watching Santana as he proposed to Xiomara at the hospital.

After the couple finished exchanging vows, Bishop T.D. Jakes addressed the congregation, "If anyone here finds reason why this man and this woman should not be united, speak now or forever hold your peace." The audience was silent as the Bishop paused for a few seconds then he continued, "I now pronounced you husband and wi-…" "Wait!" screamed the woman in the aisle. Now that she had everyone's undivided attention, her heartbeat accelerated as she took the floor.

"I am not a wedding crasher and have never done anything like this before. And sincerely apologize for interrupting this service. I've been in love with you, Santana, for most of my life. I have no idea who this woman is that has the honor to stand beside you on this occasion when I can't imagine it being anyone other than me. So Ms., please forgive me for intruding on your special day. But this is my last shot to fight for the only man I'll ever love…"

Then she removed her sun shades. "And if you can look me in my eyes and say that I don't own the place in your heart as your *true* soulmate, then I will walk right back out of this church wishing your marriage all the best."

After revealing the object she was holding behind her back, she continued, "But never forget that I, Gabrielle Celestine, fought for you to come back to me and complete our family. And this little boy right here is our son. Santana Bailey Jr.…age 5."

For the second time in his life, Santana blacked out.

To be continued…

# COMING SOON FROM PINNAKLE PUBLICATIONS

Dr. Julien Ulbrich is a prestigious anesthesiologist, a skilled and aggressive investor, and the sole proprietor of the Serenity Pain Management Clinic. His successful medical career and savvy investment strategies allowed him to amass an exhaustive financial portfolio. His pretentious lifestyle includes dating a multitude of women without making concessions for a commitment. In addition, he is notorious for exploiting them sexually, emotionally, and oftentimes – financially. And the second he appraises them as being insignificant, he unceremoniously moves on to the next date while callously leaving them behind to restore their dissected hearts.

When Dr. Ulbrich meets Susan Xavier – a US District Court Judge, he is smitten by her beauty and intellect. Eventually they begin dating and he finds her to be the foremost intriguing of all the women he has ever encountered. In fact, Susan holds his regard to the extent where she transcends his ceiling for entanglements.

Albeit they inaugurated a revered relationship, their chemistry decimates as Julien longs for his former lifestyle and abruptly returns to his promiscuous antics. Unfortunately, love is an emotion that is foreign Dr. Ulbrich. And once Susan determine her heart was broken unjustly, she vows to seek revenge by making the ill-prepared Dr. Julien Ulbrich feel a pain no one would ever suspect.

# MY ACKNOWLEDGEMENTS

**WARNING!!!** To the readers who don't know me, this section is a bit long for acknowledgements since I know many and this is my first book ever. So this section is strictly for them.

(I know it shocked the hell out of y'all to find out my good hustlin' ass wrote a book!) In efforts of avoiding a book filled with dedications, in which I truly dedicate it to everyone I'm about to mention, I chose to place you in this section so you'd know you are loved and most certainly thought of.

First and foremost, thanks go to the matriarch of my maternal family, Mrs. Rosie Lee Hagans; my beautiful grandmother who I've always called, Meme. I'll never forget all of the times we shared watching Wheel of Fortune. It was just me and you battling it out to see who'd guess the puzzle. Those are treasured moments I'll ever forget. I love you sexy! (She likes it when I call her that).

(Unfortunately, my last living grandmother passed away two weeks prior to the release of this novel). I thank God for blessing me to be a part of your life's journey.  You have your wings now, my

Angel, so rest easy. You fought a good fight and will forever reside in my heart. I love you, Meme.

To my children: Kedrick, congratulations on graduating from high school and going to college. It means the world to me the way you value my advice. You've grown into a fine young man and I'm proud to call you my son. Congratulations on creating your first child (my very first Grandchild)! I wish you all the success at fatherhood. I love you, Keddy.

To my beautiful first daughter, Kihree, who I call *Mook-a-Mook*. When the older folks say that a daughter latches to their father, I've learned from experience how true that statement is. I love our relationship. It's crazy how you inherited my boiled crawfish addiction. You are a very smart young lady. You've shared your desires with me, Mook-a-Mook, and my advice to you is to chase after your dreams with an unprecedented amount of passion and persistence, prioritizing them above all things in your life. Commit to that and watch how God blesses you. I love you, Mook-a-Mook.

To my youngest son, Kevin, who I call Champ. You are my blessing from God. (All of my children are blessings from God. I'll explain what I mean). You, Champ, are special because of the timing of your birth. My life wasn't going in the direction as I imagined. I was still mentally unstable from losing K.J. and to top it off, I was struggling on deciding what was more important to get for the house your mother and I lived in since we lost all of our belongings due to *Hurricane Katrina*. And then, you came. God already knew of my sufferings that never seems to diminish and the challenges of getting my life on track and difficulties of holding my marriage together. So he blessed your mother and I with you. And

I thanked God the day you were born for giving Keddy and Mook-a-Mook another brother, and for me- another son to love. I love you, Champ.

To my baby girl, Kaymin, who I call Mini-Pooh. My little twin. You are special because you're the baby. None of your siblings can have *that* title. Although you're my one child who spent less time around me than your siblings, we still managed to create a bond. It truly melts my heart every time I tell you I love you and you always respond, "*I love you more!*" I love how you're always anxious to help me cook. And how you always request the beignets I make from scratch. And when I cut them into heart shapes just for you, how your pretty little face lights up. I love you, Mini-Pooh.

To my unborn grandchild, I love you already and have never laid eyes on you. Just know that the things I do is to benefit generations to come so that includes *you.* Whether you're a boy or girl, I wish you health, happiness, and all of your heart's desires.

Back to Kedrick and Kihree, the both of you are special in your own unique way. The night I loss K.J., I didn't know how I would proceed thereafter. But when I made it home to the both of you, I saw your innocent little faces and knew I had to pull together fast because y'all deserved to have a father with a sound mind. Lord knows I was on the verge of losing my mind. Thank you both for giving me a reason to live.

To Imani, thanks for hanging in there with me through these tough times. I'll always love you for that, Phat. To Buster and Jabari, Mr. Alfred, Mrs. Claudette, and Imani's grand-parents.

To my lil brother, Korey, who I call my oldest son. Thank you for holding down the fort in my absence. And sticking to your dreams of becoming an actor. I'm too proud of you. I'm your #1 fan who's rooting for you to blow up on Instagram and everywhere else. You'll never know how much it means to me to have you and Momma there for me without wavering since I've been gone. You continue to stand tall and ASAP whatever I need handled. And for that reason, you are by far my #1 Ryda. Love you Bro.

I gotta shout out Odell Beckham Jr. for flying you to New York to catch the game vs our Saints and welcoming you into his home. Hope you make a full recovery from tearing your ACL. To the readers, you can follow my brother on InstaGram @Koreywitha__K. Check him out and share his videos. They are funny as hell. He and his partner Rob Kazi blazing the Gram with those videos. Hold it down for New Orleans, lil bruh-bruhs. I wish you both all the success. I love you, lil Bro.

To those who creating opportunities on Instagram and showing this world your capabilities, I tilt my hat to all of y'all. Especially the ones who support my brother's movement like Rob Kazi, Supa Cent, Bodiedbybrooke, 2realmacdatfee, Tokyovanity, OG NewNew, Sess 45, Laugh4laDerrick, Maeganrachel, and Ptown Moe....Much Love!!!

To my father Carl Michael Williams. You are a great father with a beautiful heart. Although we've had our ups and downs, I've never stopped loving you and I wouldn't trade you for the world. I love you Daddy.

Shout out to all your children/my siblings. To my sisters: Jevon, Yonica, Deyonica, Beyonica, Jolinda, Keisha, Jariele, and Makiyah. Thank you for loving me unconditionally and never turning your backs on me for the mistakes I've made. I love y'all and all of my nieces and nephews more than you can imagine. Shout out to my family in St. Bernard Parish. The Baileys and Williams, I love y'all.

I gotta give special thanks to my Denver connects. My cousin Kenneth Jones and your heaven-sent wife, Roshelle. I remember the day I met you, Roshelle. You and Kenneth had flown in town to come to my cousin (Kenneth's brother) Earl's anniversary party. I told Kenneth (Back on subject). At the party, I had this exact book, handwritten with me and told you I needed someone to type it who I can trust. And you, Roshelle, who didn't even know me before that night, volunteered your services. My heart told me you were genuine, and I wasn't misled with my feelings. Thank you for every second you spent on my project. Also, thank you for your criticism. I took it all into consideration during my editing process. Without the love and support from you and my Big Cuz, Lord knows how long this book would've been delayed. Again, I appreciate the time and effort you put into this book, in the midst of your everyday life. You mean the world to me.

To my cousin/big brother Darrick Singleton. You've had my back for my entire life. Until Korey was born, you were my only brother. Nobody can take your place. And to your fiancé—correction—*MY* fiancé, Tiffany, luv you Big Sis. Big ole ups to Mr. Earl Mackie. What up, Pops? More than anyone else, I owe you the world for always being there for my mother. I'll always love you for that.

To my brother, Sess 4-5. One out of three of my partners with our *SoccaBallin* clothing line. You get one of the biggest shout-outs of all-time for getting the right guy to create that fire ass cover for this book. "It's Lit!" I asked my mother what she thought of it and she said, "boy, you look like the God Father!"(LOL) I want you to let the guy who did the work I said, thanks for such a professional job. He the illest. And again, thank you, my nigga for any amount of time you had to push your busy agenda aside on my behalf. Love you, my brother.

To L.O.G and Dumo, my brothers from another mother. And also my other two partners with SoccaBallin. My heart goes out to y'all for losing your mother, Mrs. Judy "Juju" Green, who was my official second mother. To Wade "Alroc Kapezee", Dawn, and Jamel DeSilva.

To my cousin/sister, Christina Holly and your husband, Rob, in Houston, TX. Big ups to you for proving your faith in me. You were a few steps away from walking away from you career in the medical field to run with me to open N.O.L.A Daiquiris shop, out there in H-Town. Had the building and everything. But those unforeseen circumstances in my life abruptly halted that from proceeding further. Just like I was showing you, God knew I was all in. I just hate that I built up the energy and excitement of having our own business only to shift my money to my new construction project. At that moment, stability trumped everything else. The race against freedom's enough to send anybody into a different mindset. Nevertheless, I owe you, Big Shirley (Christina hates it when I call her that). And if the opportunity ever presents itself again, we're going to pop off something major. Love you, cuz.

Big thanks to one of the truest friends Jamond *Doodie Wop* Bourgeois.

To my nigga-nigga out in Atlanta, Harry *Heat* Rainey and your wife (who I call *Mama*). I love y'all to death. You're another one of my *real* Brothers. You're another person I can depend on. I remember we linked up in Virginia. Another time, we went to New York together. And the time you threw a birthday party in Atlanta and you and Mama both wanted me to come. And what do I do?

Tell my girl who I was with at the time to pack a bag, load up the BMW, and we shot straight to the "A". That's what love'll do. You're one of a selected few who I would drop everything in an instant to do something like that for. I hope y'all stay out there for years to come because eventually I'll be making it my home as well. I love y'all for a lifetime. Also A shout out to your brother Corey Jules out there in VA

To my Minnesota day-one, Gerald 'Loochie' Edwards and wife Toni (Black) and your mom's Betty West( my other official second mother). And Troy, Wolfie, Darlene, Big Roland, Kent, Flo, Wesi, and Toe Joe.. I MISS Y'ALL!!! Y'all have been trying to get me there for years and I always complained about how it's too cold out there. I guess it'll happen one day.

To my Dallas family. Alicia and Ariggo Barfield, and Michele Lewis and Byron; my favorites! I love y'all, the kids, and grandkids with all of my heart. Especially my Goddaughter Aniya. To my cousins Glen and your wife, Marie. Special thanks to Marie for keeping me on point with the taxes on my crib. To Carol Veal, Tu, Tay and Pat. To Damita and Hendrix. To  Natasha in San Antonio, Denise, and Jeremiah. And my cousin/sister, Tahnika, Curtis and them boys. We don't get to spend much time together, but I know how you feel about me. Can't wait to come see the boys of yours.

Shout out to my lil cousin, Keyoka Scott. You're another person who's always showed me love. Thank you for all you've done for me. And let Graylon read this so he'd know I thought of him.

To my Aunt Dorothy (who passed away a few months ago) and the rest of my Sacramento family. I love y'all! Especially you, Aunt Dorothy. From the times I spent out there in Cali, to the times she came to New Orleans, I cherished every second with you. You had the sweetest heart, one of the strongest people I've ever met, and I can't wait to see again. To your son and my favorite Cali cuz, Mike. Although you're from Cali, cuz, you sure as hell be rockin' with my Saints! I had fun meeting up in the Superdome to catch a game. Then hooked up with a few of your Cali potnas to show y'all a great time in the French Quarters, and then got y'all to wild out at the famous strip club in New Orleans East called *She-She's*. I can't wait until we do it again.

To my God brother/cousin Kevin Hammler in Austin your wife and all your kids. To my wonderful Aunts: My favorite of all-time is my Aunt Sharon Lewis, may you rest in peace. If only the world could've witnessed her reactions when I'd playfully but seriously say, "Auntie Sharon! Watch out for that roach!" Sometimes I thought I'd give her a heart attack. Those were the funniest moments. Like everyone else in my family, she called me by my middle name and would say, "Tirrell! Stop scaring me like that, boy!" I'd be so weak from laughing so hard. I miss you Aunt T-Sharon. I hope I haven't offended the rest of my aunts because you all are special to me. My Aunt Paula, Aunt Dorothy, Aunt Wanda, Aunt Francine, Aunt Betty, Aunt Matt, Aunt Faye, Aunt Linda, Aunt Nanette, Aunt Arlene "Pooh", Aunt Loran, Aunt Wanda Faye, Aunt Delores Jones, Aunt Leslie, Aunt Eloise Rose, Aunt Audrey, Aunt Melba, Aunt Avis, and my Aunt Sharon Brock. I didn't realize I had so many aunts until now. I love you all.

To my Uncle Charles Hagans, you are more of my father figure than any man I've ever known. You were always there for me as if I was your own son.

To my Godfather, my Uncle Kevin Hagans, who my mother named me after, thank you for bringing something you noticed about me into words. You said, "You, Tirrell, know the recipe to be successful. You know the purpose of the dollar. For the ones who don't they spend their money just as fast as it comes and they end up spending their whole lives living from paycheck to paycheck. But you use money as a tool by spending it on the things that turns into more money." And that's exactly what I'm programmed to do. I hate spending money on things that won't give me a return on my money. Not everything, but most. Thanks for noticing that, Unc. You have proven your love for me and the feeling 's reciprocated.

To my Uncles Joe and Peter Smiles, Brad and Curtis Williams. To my uncle Sam in Vidalia. My cousin Beady Lee, and my favorite cousin from St. Bernard Parish, Stanley *Sugar Billy* Bailey. To all my Mays family in Ferriday, especially, my cousin Wilford. The way you run my kids from Baton Rouge to Ferriday in a heartbeat.) Love you, cuz.

To my Mays family in Houston. I love you all. Leo, Glen, Sue, Margie, and Lionel. You all have loved me as if I was part of the immediate family. Thanks to Margie and Lionel for letting my mother put me on the airplane, since I was 9 or 10 years old, by myself to fly to Houston to spend my summers. I gained a lot of brothers and sisters because of that. Duck, Chris, Warren, Don, Lamont, Darrell, Kali- who won the election just days ago to become a Judge (CONGRATS), Stephanie, and my big sis/cuz, Karmen Green. Can't forget about cousin Deedee, she'd probably kill me. And to all of your children. I love y'all. To cuz Doris, Phaedra, and Juan. To Toshiba "Peaches" Moffett now living in Seattle. To Victoria "Pumpkin" Curry in Ferriday (she's my lil sister from Ferriday whose been trying to steal my Mother away from me and Korey. Lol). To my God sister Tamara Branch from Jonesville. To my other lil sister Anjerica Leonard from Ferriday.

To my cuz Lil Keith (Houston's Nightlife Architect), we haven't hollered in a minute but I see you still holding it down doing big things. Keep up the good work, cuz, and I'll see ya when I touch down. My Big sis Courtnetely Barber in Houston and Ebony. To Aunt Matt and uncle Sam son Ron. To Yolanda Kissam now living in Katy, Texas. To Gwendolyn "Ma Ma" Smith for looking out for me while I've been down. Love you, Teedie.

To Tony Stewart, my big brother Edwin Walters, my lil cuz E.P., To my 7th ward rounds - Geezy from back of town and Money Mike Stephens, Jessie Cage, Big Mike from Houma, Blue from Ocala, Florida, and Zairo Ramos from Puerto Rico, King Pooh – part owner of Streetking Motorsport . To Toya Pollard, Kristy Dorsey, and Denisha Dorsey. To my families in New Orleans. The Fergusons (Andrea, Big Melvin, Shaun (Congrats on becoming the Chief of Police of New Orleans), Monica, Angela, Terry, Lil Raymond, Kyle, Melvin, and Shayla), the Hendersons, the Henrys, the Scotts (Noel, Tige, Aubrey, Daphne, and Torrey), the Sams (my step-father, Donald, Thank you for being a good father to me when I was a kid. Although your relationship my mother didn't last, you are a good man and I'll always love you like a father). And to Danielle Sam (my sister from you).

To my lil cousin Charles Wallace Tanner and wife *Wakiki*. Byron *B-Love* Tanner and my Aunt JoAnn Sam.

To Joseph "Kid" Sam all the rest of the Sams, I love y'all. To my brother for life, Derrick Lucas, out there in Houston working on your hair supplies empire is motivation like a motha'. I love the way you stay super focused on following your dreams. You made me understand the rewards of cutting out the middle-man. There is nothing I wouldn't do for you and I wish I was out there with you now during this coronavirus pandemic making all that money off of that hand sanitizer you make! I ain't mad at ya my nigga. Get that money up continue building them houses in New Orleans. I pray you shoot to the stars with the Real Estate business. And shout out to your wife Toya. Houston Bridges, wuzzam, homie! You one of the few I know with a beautiful mind. Keep it movin'. To my nigga Big Jay out there in Baytown. To my people uptown around the Calliope Project. My Big cuz Torrey Scott. You taught me some valuable lessons. When I came home from doing my bid, all you gave me was one hundred dollars. I really wanted to pitch it back to you, but I opted to accept it as a blessing. Months later we had a conversation and you said, When I came home from the Feds, ain't nobody gave me nothing. I worked hard for every dime I got. So what I saying to *you* lil cuz is this, don't accept hand-outs. Work for everything you get, because when you do get it, you'll appreciate it much more. And that attitude will keep you from being broke." Nice words of wisdom, cuz, which your stingy ass! (L.O.L) I love you, nigga.

To my girl, Trinell Miller from Gretna, Buddy from South Acres, Brandon "L. Boogie" Jackson, My nigga, Jackie "PNut" Washington, Chris Turner from Ferriday. My Teedie, Mary, Sidney, and Keyunti Landor. To Lamecca "Lilgirl" Hewing, Lanita Smith, and Jennifer Bertlesen.

"Shout out to the homie Meek Mill for taking a stance against America's unjust criminal justice system. I just happen to go through exactly what you did. But since I didn't have powerful people backing me, I did 6 years in prison for a violation.

To my girl Ronkeike from off the Parkway. To Bass, Tontoe, Lil Ron, and Herman from off Dorgenois. Thanks Herman for the trip to Vegas. We had fun, huh?! We met all of those famous people out there in the Magic Show in the Las Vegas Convention Center. I can never thank you enough for the experience. To my homie, Curren$y, thanks for supporting me before you went Nation. To Mr. Marcelo and Big Freedia. To Shaneka "Nikki" Stubbs and Yolanda "Lonnie" Stubbs. To two of my homies outta Press Park-the New Orleans Legend Fila Phil, and the homie Big Twine for letting me finish editing this book by using his jack (cell phone) while we were fed-bound along with Dorian Doe Givens and my homie Rell from Independence, La. Good looking out. Can't forget about my dawg Glenn "Shorty" Green. #Free Kristopher "Dody Wody" Holly, #Free Terrance "Toe-Toe" Williams, #Free Ken "Snoop" Jones, #Free Gary " Toe" Hagan, #Free Oliver Howard, #Free James Swift/ Charlie Hansen" Farlough, #Free Mckinley "Mac The Camouflaged Assassin" Phipps,# Free Christopher "B.G." Dorsey and #Free Corey " C- Murder" Miller. And most of all, ***#FREE KEVIN KA$H!!!***

Big ole shout out to Quiniata "Missy" Johnson, I wish you all the success with the New Orleans Mardi Gras Kitchen in Denver. Check out her Organic Seasoning MGK!. To the C.T.C (Cut Throat City/Cross Tha Canal) and the rest of the 9th ward. I do this for all of y'all to show the world that a person from a hood that is so-called bad as mine has creativity. And there are many others So I encourage you all to discover your talent and show the world what you workin' wit. That's coming from a person who ran in those crazy streets and never imagined I'd write a book.

To my entire city of New Orleans. If I'm not mistaken, I believe this is the first novel coming from an ex-Dough Boy from New Orleans. And I'm trying to put us on the map in a whole new light. That's why I made the main character, Santana, born and raised out of my hood. Just in case a movie was made off of my idea. I love my city and the people in it. And if I had a choice to be born and raised anywhere in the world, I would still choose New Orleans. The swag we were born with is like no other on Earth. It's in our attitude, our slang, how we dress, the way we talk, the way we cook…the list can go on. Keep leading, my people, and let the rest continue to follow. Never let that uniqueness die, my City. I love y'all to the grave.

My final shout out goes to Stephen Banks. We had a bunch of fun times way back when. You're my brother, forever…

To the purchaser of my book, thank you for supporting my very first writing endeavor. I know the dedications and acknowledgements were long as hell, but when it's a person's first novel, I would hope they wouldn't leave anyone out, even though I probably still did anyway. And to those folks, just know that my heart was in the right place and you are still loved, so please forgive me for that.

P.S. For all of the people I've mentioned, this book **BETTER** go platinum! (For those who want to be technical- It BETTER be a #1 Bestseller!)

# SPIRITUAL DEDICATION

I dedicate this book to my belated son, K.J. For you are the cardinal reason I aspire to write. December 1ˢᵗ of 2020 marked 18 years it's been since God chose you to depart from this life. Somehow, it still feels as though it happened yesterday. If only you knew how razor-close I was that night to making a suicidal thought turn into a reality.

In the beginning stages of my perpetual grieving process I was encouraged to see a psychiatrist. Upon the conclusion of my visits to his office, I was amazed to determine how the world seems to believe those doctors (who haven't personally experienced the loss of a child) have insight of an antidote for individuals, such as I, who's had a piece of their soul literally ripped from out of them without notice. The medication that the doctor prescribed was done in vain because I refused to take any drug he suggests that would not give me my K.J. back. But if a discovery were ever made in medicine that *would* bring him back to me, I will freely check myself into a rehabilitation center for overdosing.

What the doctor *did* recommend I do was write down my feelings to release some of my contained sorrow. It took me years later, but I eventually followed up on his advice. I started writing about my life. All sorts of things I'd been through. And the therapy grew on me. Then I got an idea for a novel. I had no title in mind. I didn't even know how to go about creating a book in its proper form. But I knew I wanted it to start off with action. And I couldn't think of a better way to come straight out the gate other than, *RUUUUNNNN*!!! That's exactly how this novel began.

I can honestly say that since you've been gone my life has never been the same. Being torn between life and death is no easy task. Nevertheless, I live. Longing for the day I see you again. Until that time arrives, I live for your 4 siblings: Kedrick and Kihree (who were the only two born at the time and blessed with the chance to know you), Kevin (who I named in honor of you), and Kaymin (your baby sister who's the spitting image of you).

For they are my desire to breathe. With that being said, you all give me life. And for that, I am forever indebted to each of you. So the one thing I can offer to you and your siblings besides all of my heart, is my strength that was reciprocated from *you*, K.J. I'll never forget the way you were laughing and smiling as you were clinging from my neck as I hugged you tightly while spinning in circles till we both were dizzy.

I was bringing you back to your mother that night so she could take you back home with her in Texas. It always saddened me to see you go. I cried each and every time. I just never would've imagined in a million years that moment in time would be our last we'd see each other. But that Golden little 4-year-old heart of yours empowered you to leave me something behind to hold onto. After

I finally finished spinning, I gave you the biggest farewell kiss as I buckled you safely into the car seat in your mother's car and you said to me, "*I love you, Daddy!*" Your very last words to me. I couldn't have prayed for a more perfect ending. If I could have read between the lines, that look on your handsome face said it all. It's as if you had premonition of that tragic accident occurring on your way home.

That was so special of you to bless me with that everlasting and most cherishing memory. It gave me the foundation I so desperately needed to build strength as I continue to do daily and beyond. And I can feel it deep in my soul that you are still here. That is why every time I recite my prayers, I always end them by saying, "Please God, send me an Angel and let it be K.J., Amen." So for *you*, my Guardian Angel, I will forever keep my Gucci shades on, like I'm wearing on the cover of this book, because whenever I look to the heavens and see the sun, I know it's you shining my way.

I love you for an eternity, K.J., and I miss you indescribably…

Until we meet again,

Love Daddy

# PHYSICAL DEDICATION

I dedicate this book to my beautiful mother, Ms. Cynthia Marie Sam. My #1 *ride or die* chick. Lord knows I'm no angel, but NONE of my wrongdoings were ever that severe to the point where you would turn your back on me. You've shown me the true meaning of a parent's love. I see who I get it from… (smile, Baby). Something else I inherited from you, Mama, is your hustling skills. Nothing illegal. That's the lane I chose. Besides, you're too scary for that life (L.O.L.).

But seriously, you gave birth to me while you were still in high school and didn't let that stop you from graduating…congrats on that accomplishment! Then you got your first apartment for the both of us on North Rampart in the lower Ninth Ward. You worked at Charity Hospital for years to assure we kept a roof over our heads and food on the table. I even remember you taking me to work with you on numerous occasions. I'm not sure if you didn't have a sitter to look after me during those times or what the case may have been. What I *do* know is, at the end of the day, you always made sure we were straight. And you've done that consistently till this very day.

"If that's not a hustler, wha'chu call that?" That's a quote from a Jay-Z song, Mama…it fits you perfectly.

When I was in school, I was considered small for my age. The brand-name clothes in my size were a little cheaper so you kept me fresh to death. Then a time came while I was in high school when Bally shoes became the most popular trend. I wanted a pair of Bally Mirage's that cost $212.55. In the early 90's that must've sounded like I was asking for a pair of thousand-dollar shoes. You kindly told me "Tirrell, if you want the type of things that cost *that* much money, you'll have to pay for them yourself."

And that's when the hustler in me emerged. So all glory goes to you for making me into the hustler and the man that I am today, because after that little life lesson, getting' money was brought to the forefront of my thoughts to attain whatever my heart desires.

Till this day, you still go out of your way to prove your love for me. As I'm up late night writing this dedication to you, it is less than an hour away from my birthday. I mentioned that because you drove through the rain for hours, picked up my children from Baton Rouge to come and give me a much-needed surprise visit on yesterday. That was the ultimate present for me. I hadn't seen you nor my children in a long time. I can't deny it, being caged in behind these walls gave me a bittersweet feeling after visitation was over. It's hard not to think of how I let y'all down when you need me the most. Putting y'all in the same situation once again. But I shook that bad spirit off and counted my blessings because everyone of you know how much I love you.

When I was doing the things that landed me here, I hated it. Mainly because I had broken my vow to God to never place myself in a situation that would lead me back to prison. I pray it doesn't cost me my soul. But since I still have life, I still have a chance to get things right with God, which I feel I have. The reason why is because my heart was in the right place as I was doing dirt. And God knows how my wrongdoings ate at my soul. The God of my life is a forgiving God. And I'm his son, so my soul should not be in jeopardy.

Although I'm behind these walls, Mama, I'm still reaching out to do all I can for you and my children. This book is the proof. I pray it turns into a best-seller and gives you more than enough money to live comfortable. What's mine is yours and vice versa. It's always been that way between us. We have a wonderful relationship. We always eat boiled crabs together. Drink together. I clean up the kitchen after you cook. Peel and eat shrimp together. I even go to the club with you when I visit you in the country. In your generation, you're everyone's favorite cousin. In my generation, I'm everyone's favorite. So you see, Mama, when you created me, you made a male version of yourself.

Sometimes I wonder how did I get so lucky to have a mother like you. To have a love that never waivers through, thick and thin or the good and the bad, I believe you are the world's greatest mother and grandmother that God has ever created next to Mother Earth. That's the reason I give you roses whenever I'm able to. You deserve so much more than money can buy. And I pray you never leave me. I already have the hardest time dealing with my loss of K.J. That pain never seems to diminish. And I couldn't imagine me being in a world without you in it.

I love you, Mama.

Your favorite son,

Tirrell

To the readers, Tirrell is my middle name and what my mother has always addressed me as. And I call myself her favorite son because I know it'll make my little brother, Korey, jealous! So kick rocks, Korey, you'll *NEVER* have my spot! (L.O.L.)

P.S. And Mama, I think Korey got another tattoo…don't tell him I told you that! (That ought to land him in hot water).

# ABOUT THE AUTHOR

**Kevin Tirrell Kashmir** (formerly known as Kevin Sam) was born and raised in New Orleans, Louisiana. He is the proud father of 4 living children and 1 deceased child. After Hurricane Katrina, he evacuated to Baton Rouge, Louisiana where he would stay for a year before moving to Houston, Texas. A few years later he was incarcerated for over 5 years for a probation violation. (Absconding.) When he came home, he struggled to find stability and turned to the quickest way he knew how to raise a substantial amount of money to make a power move; selling drugs in large quantities. Eventually, the Feds were alerted to his activities and the ending result landed him back in prison where he currently is in Yazoo City Low. Upon his return, he will be living back in his own home in New Orleans while getting back to the money (the legal way) and spend as much time possible with his children and family.